Station 12:

The Lantern Society

Station 12:

The Lantern Society

d.l.noyes

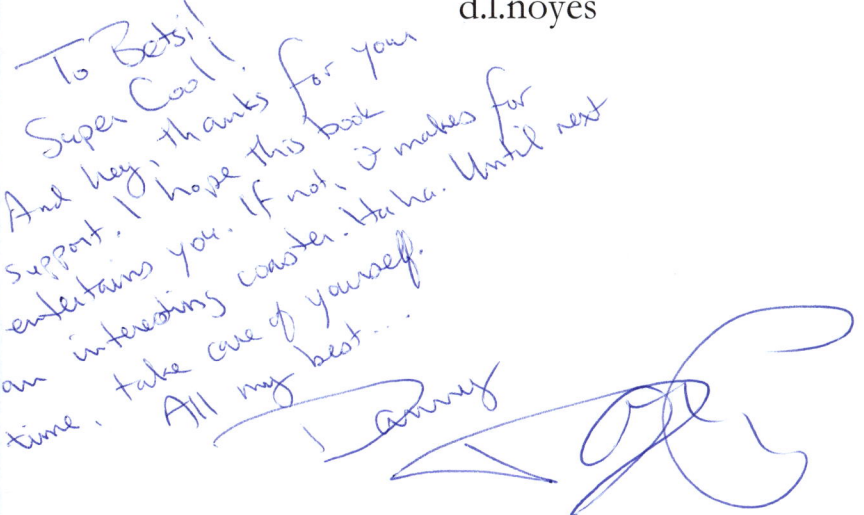

Infinite City Studio
New York MMXV

Copyright © 2015 by Daniel L. Noyes

All rights reserved. This book or any portion thereof may not be reproduced or used in any manner whatsoever without the express written permission of the publisher except for the use of brief quotations in a book review.

First Printing, 2015

ISBN 0-692-49355-7

For news go to www.facebook.com/station12universe

To Jaime, who waited a long time to see me finish…anything. I dedicate this effort to you, my love. Of the multitude of life choices that have been put before you, I'm glad you chose me.

To Edwin & Libby who dabbled in this new universe for a time.

To my great friend, Tony, who believed in the project like no one else and put on Strivelli's boots to prove it.

And thanks to my FB cover crew: Amanda M, Barbara G, Cindy D, Dan V, Jean F, Ken N, Laura M, Leigh K, Mary D, Paula G, Peter I, Richard V, Ron M, Tami F, & Tony D

And to the creators that came before me, for seeing me safely through the *Crisis on Infinite Earths*. I was *Lost* before your guiding pens led me safely through *Myst* to the *Dark City* and beyond to *The Dark Tower*. When I finally slept, I dreamt of *Electric Sheep* and came to the conclusion that truly *It's a Wonderful Life*. Thank you one and all for the many worlds you have shared and the universe you inspired.

Table of Contents

Prologue: The Interview   1
Chapter One: The Professor   15
Chapter Two: The Investigation   25
Chapter Three: Global Armour   39
Chapter Four: The Turncoat   59
Chapter Five: The Sounding Tunnel   78
Chapter Six: The Mercenary   92
Chapter Seven: End of Day   111
Chapter Eight: The Computer   129
Chapter Nine: The White   144
Chapter Ten: An Alliance   148
Chapter Eleven: A Wanted Man   170
Chapter Twelve: The Truth Squad   189
Chapter Thirteen: A Brief Debriefing   209
Chapter Fourteen: The Lantern Society   216
Chapter Fifteen: The Devlin You Don't Know   238
Chapter Sixteen: The Oculacrum   257
Chapter Seventeen: Reality Displacement 276
Chapter Eighteen: The New Reality   297
Chapter Nineteen: The Professor Recalled   309
Epilogue: The New Truth Squad   319

Prologue: The Interview

"All we're asking for is an honest account."

Professor Daniel Askew greeted both Sienna Bennett and her daughter, Patty, with an enigmatic smile and an apology as their eyes adjusted to the light. The blindfolds, he said, were a matter of confidentiality, suggesting it was somehow the Bennetts they were protecting and not the powerful investment firm that had brought them there. A tall man in a yellow sweater led the tentative Bennett family into a sun-filled room. On the way, he stopped and whispered into Askew's ear, and the professor scratched nonchalantly at the roots of his silver goatee. He then nodded toward a big mirror and followed the group into the center of the room.

Contrary to what mysterious destinations they may have conjured up during the drive, mother and daughter found themselves in a perfectly inviting tea room. It was a welcome end to a nerve-wracking ride. Patty kept her back to her mother as she took in her new surroundings. She was surprised at how beautiful it all was. Though still unsettled by recent events, her need to feel good about something far outweighed her caution and she began to think of the room as a sanctuary. She had found no solace at home, or among the many doctors they'd called upon. Sanctuary, yes, but it remained to be seen if she was going to place her fate in the hands of strangers.

"I'm sorry for the cloak and dagger," Askew went on to say, "but this impromptu gathering is in the best interests of you both, believe me. You must be Patty," he said, turning his attention to the blond, green-eyed teen.

He took Patty's hand in both of his, intentionally keeping Sienna from his line of sight. If she deemed the gesture inappropriate she didn't say, and he didn't want to read it in her eyes.

Askew sensed something familiar about the young girl. He didn't understand it, but he was drawn to her. It was powerful, like meeting a daughter he never knew he had. Something made her stand out from past

Witnesses and he hoped the interview would shed some light.

"I promise you," he said, "we'll get you right as rain in no time." He winked at her and guided her by the shoulder toward the center of the room. For a second, Patty shrank from his touch, but a reassuring squeeze from Askew helped her relax and remain on the path he set for her. "I'm sure you both have questions. However, I must ask you to set them aside. The sooner we get to the heart of the matter, the sooner we can put an end to it. Ladies, allow me to introduce you to Alan Griffin. He'll be conducting today's interview."

Dressed in a dark suit, crisp, white shirt, and a narrow, dark blue tie held in place by a simple, gold tie clip, Griffin bowed his head in acknowledgement. The only thing missing from his portrait, Sienna thought, was a glass of scotch and possibly a fedora pulled over his short, neatly combed hair. And though his smile appeared genuine, it wasn't enough to put Sienna at ease.

"How do you do?" Griffin asked, but Askew pressed for a start to the interview.

"We understand you're having trouble sleeping, is that right, Miss Bennett?" Askew took a seat at the center table and looked up at the girl, holding her arms as if to support her. Sienna understood he was trying to comfort her troubled daughter, but the hands-on approach was making her uncomfortable. His lack of eye contact didn't help. A reassuring glance would have gone a long way. Still, Sienna held her tongue.

Askew continued to probe. "Maybe headaches, confusion?"

Patty said nothing. Askew nodded sympathetically and pressed on.

"It's frustrating, I know," he said. "There's no one to talk to about it, no one who understands, and these dreams…" Askew's mind drifted as his own nearly forgotten encounter approached the gate of his memory. In a sudden fit of fatigue, his hands no longer seemed to support Patty, but rather the reverse. Patty stared down at Askew and watched his over-sized eyes behind thick lenses straining to remember. She was shocked when she recognized in him a kindred spirit. She felt an impulse to lay hands upon his shaved head, but held back as a conciliatory gesture, to avoid compounding her mother's grief.

Snapping back to the moment at hand, Askew continued with his former verve.

"I assure you, you're not alone. We do understand and we're going to make you feel better." He stood up, offering his seat. "Would you care for some tea, something to eat? Mrs. Bennett, why don't you have a seat as well?"

The tall man in the yellow sweater led Sienna to a wingback chair in a sunny corner of the room. She continued to remain silent, relieved at the thought of her daughter being someone else's problem for the moment. This was immediately followed by a stabbing pang of guilt. Griffin took a seat with Patty at the white, whicker table. Askew sat in the diagonally opposing corner from Sienna and placed an unlit pipe between his tea-stained teeth. He then rested his hand on an open leather-bound journal, an accompanying steel-barreled pen at the ready. Sienna tried to read him from across the room but his features were diminished by shade.

Like sea glass on a beach, sunlight sparkled off the glass table tops and polished silver of the tea room. Rattan ceiling fans turned silently and lace curtains billowed softly on a gentle current of air. There was a tension in the atmosphere, however, that belied the room's comforts. As far as Sienna was concerned, that tension skirted the border of menace. A dark cloud hung over her, a miasma of grief and guilt; grief over her daughter's weakened state, Patty had had very little sleep in the past six weeks, along with a disturbing lack of appetite; and guilt over the anger she was feeling toward Patty for bringing them to this time and place.

What began as a simple sleepover for Patty and a friend had morphed overnight into a nightmare of lost memory, insomnia, and a recurring dream; a dream that spoke of madness. A bevy of doctors had been called, but no explanations or diagnoses had been proffered. A part of Sienna couldn't help but wonder if her daughter was making it up. This only added to her mounting guilt. *Why? Why would she make up such a story*, she wondered? *She wouldn't. Not my daughter.* When she looked into Patty's face, into those diminished eyes that sought only rest, she knew it couldn't be true, and if there was a chance these people could help her as they claimed, it was the right thing to have come. *God, I hope we've done the right thing.*

"Are you nervous, Patty?" Griffin began as he poured her a cup of Earl Grey. Patty accepted it with both hands, nodding as she blew on the hot, steaming brew. "Well, trust me, there's no call for it. You're in good hands. Just tell us what happened the night of the sleepover and then we'll all go home."

"I don't know what happened," she said glumly. "I can't remember anything."

"You remember the dream?"

Patty nodded yes.

Griffin paused a moment, drawing his eyebrows together. "You're among friends here, Patty. Do you understand that you're not in any kind of trouble? We're not here to judge you."

Sienna felt another anxious wave of guilt.

"I guess," Patty said shrugging.

Griffin uncrossed his legs and leaned in. "Then why don't you show me a smile?" He pushed a small plate across the table. "Have a cake. I made it myself." Patty allowed herself to smirk. "What, you don't believe me?"

Despite her unease, she let out a small laugh and shook her head. The sound surprised Sienna who hadn't seen her daughter so much as crack a smile since the ordeal began.

Griffin's demeanor helped to lessen the girl's worry. "You're a smart girl, Patty. I'm a lot of things but I'm no baker." Griffin spoke into a table mike and recorded the date, time, and other pertinent data as he prepared to kick off the interview officially.

Sienna dabbed at her damp face with a cloth napkin and looked out the window in a subconscious effort to distance herself from the proceeding. She tried to guess at their locale, wondering if they were still in Connecticut. From her vantage point, she could see a flower garden just past the sill. A bluestone path snaked through the beds to a short gate on a white, picket fence. Beyond that stood a vast stretch of recently mowed lawn. Further still was an old, Victorian home complete with Widow's Walk. To the left she could see a slow moving river flanked by tall reeds and pussy willows.

Sienna closed her eyes and inhaled deeply through her nose, inviting the smells of cut grass and late spring blooms, and frowned when she found no such reward. Looking out to the far side of the lawn, she saw several children playing on a tire swing beneath the boughs of a large oak. She envied them their fun for her daughter's sake.

Griffin pushed a bowl of sugar cubes toward Patty. "This dream is keeping you awake at night."

Patty nodded.

"And it's the same dream every night."

Again, she only nodded.

"Well, that seems as good a place to start as any." Griffin pushed the microphone an inch closer. "Why don't you tell us the story of your dream?"

#

The time is midnight in the dream. It's always midnight. Patty's excited because she's never hosted a sleepover before. There's also an underlying sense of dread. Despite knowing that she and her best friend are having fun; despite seeing with her own eyes the contentment on Candy's face; and despite that wonderful feeling of intimacy that comes with time spent with a best friend, sharing the late night hours together in hushed whispers and stifled giggles, Patty is uneasy.

The bedroom is dark except for her favorite nightlight. It was made to look like the sun, bearing a wide smile and eyes of indefatigable good cheer. It was the same nightlight that had kept the monsters at bay when she was a little girl.

There's a hiccup in the dream and Patty, the dreamer, experiences a moment of precognitive clarity and now understands what's bothering her. It's her sister, Amy. She's outside the bedroom door warning the girls to keep quiet, but Candy is laughing, and even the nightlight is laughing. Patty is not, though the vanity mirror says otherwise. It makes her sad because she wants to share in the fun. Worse, she knows the feeling of dread comes not from the warning itself but from the messenger, and she wishes her sister would go away before ruining what was left of the night. She turns to the nightlight hoping it will chase away just one more ghost, but finds the light of that small sun has dimmed.

The hallway outside the bedroom is dark and it's longer than it should be, with more doors than Patty can account for. There's only one door that concerns her, though, the door at the top of the stairs. She makes her way toward it, silent footsteps on plush carpet. Candy is breathing heavily through her braces in Patty's ear, hands clasped to her friend's shoulders, fit to bursting from holding in her giggles. Every step closer to Amy's door tightens the knot in Patty's stomach, but still she doesn't understand the feeling of foreboding attached to her sister. Sibling differences aside, she loves Amy and she knows Amy loves her. Regardless, the door looms ominously ahead of her and she grows weak in the knees.

Suddenly the feeling of dread is gone. They're safe now, Amy's door has remained closed and the long hallway has been replaced by a cozy basement rec room, submerged in the pink glow of a neon crab behind the bar. The girls are simpatico, exuberant, and they rush to the high bar stools with tubs of ice cream they've pilfered from the kitchen. Stories are told and secrets shared. There's talk of boys and the upcoming summer vacation. There are moments of introspection, and an unspoken awareness of their mutual affection, culminating in warm embraces. Patty remembers in the dream a desire to freeze the moment in time. She's never been happier in her life, and worries that she never will be again. It's at that moment that the bells begin to chime.

#

Griffin appeared relaxed, but listened intently as Patty shared the dream that had barred her from her rest for so long. In the shadowed corner, Askew took copious notes using a custom form of short hand, abbreviations and acronyms for words and phrases that came up often during Witness accounts. He'd heard many variations of the story over time and this version offered nothing unique on the surface. Both Askew and Griffin made note of the dream's participants. Askew scrutinized Patty's face, measuring her honesty and grief. He watched Sienna's reactions as the tale unfolded; determining if any specific parts of the narrative struck a nerve. Sure enough, a pattern quickly emerged and he knew how the story would end.

Griffin inquired about the bells and watched as Patty added lumps of sugar to her tea. Three in all, and he was satisfied. She informed him that her home was only a few blocks from a railroad crossing and that the bells in her dream reminded her of them.

"Do you get a lot of railroad traffic in your neighborhood?" he asked.

"Yeah, well, not a lot. I don't know." She tasted her sweetened tea and decided it was just right. "I've lived there my whole life so I guess I don't notice anymore."

Even though Sienna understood her daughter to be relating a dream, she remembered the night of the sleepover quite differently and she didn't like what she was hearing. And Patty hadn't yet gotten to the craziest parts. A part of Sienna wanted to leave, to step outside and put her feet in the river.

What is wrong with me, she asked herself. *Patty hasn't done anything wrong. So, why do I keep blaming her?* Sienna had trouble processing the incident, and its aftermath, in particular. Unfortunately, she had nowhere to direct her frustration except toward the person she loved most in the world.

She turned her attention back to the picturesque scene out the window. The cool breeze carried the sound of children laughing and it dawned on her that Patty's laughter had been a tonic in her own hectic life. She missed it terribly. She tried focusing on that ethereal laughter in an attempt to distract herself from the sounds of the interview. Her eyes roamed through the garden and watched as the bees made their rounds in a buzzing flurry of transparent wings. One fat, black bumblebee caught Sienna's eye as it drank of the flowering azaleas. She studied the bouncing bee as it moved in her direction until it suddenly dropped six inches and vanished into thin air. Sienna blinked and furrowed her brow, unsure what it was she just saw. Another bumblebee appeared a short time later, looking quite like the previous one. It followed an identical course along the bushes until it, too, dropped six inches and disappeared. It occurred to her at that moment that this was not typical insect behavior.

If Sienna had started to relax at all by then, the feeling vanished along with the bees. Something was definitely wrong, though she tried her best not to let it show on her face. She turned her head slowly back to the room and began to inspect every nook and cranny for anything out of the ordinary. The tea room itself was odd. Though it had ample seating capacity, it was neither a standalone restaurant, nor did it appear to be part of a hotel or inn. Everything else seemed right, the furnishings, the artwork on the walls, and the flowers on the tables; everything was perfect. Maybe the over-sized mirror stood out a bit. Then she noticed that the curtains were blowing inward on both sides of the room. *That doesn't seem right.*

A tear trickled down her cheek as she stared at the back of her daughter. *What have you gotten us into, Patty?* She wanted to turn back to the window but was afraid. The bees. Movement caught the corner of her eye. They…it…was still there, dancing among the flowers, until it dropped and vanished from existence. She started to sweat profusely and she was sure her agitation was clearly visible to everyone in the room.

Station 12: The Lantern Society

She closed her eyes for a moment, both to compose herself, and to work up the courage for what came next. Keeping her head perfectly still, she looked back into the room to make sure no one was watching. Then, acting purely on instinct, she took a deep breath and held it as she slowly moved her hand past the window sill. Her hand continued to stretch slowly outward and still she hadn't exhaled. She knew she would be caught at any moment, only she hoped it wasn't... quite... yet.

#

It sounds like music in Patty's ears, new age chimes, as the wine glasses in the overhead rack tap each other delicately, heralding the arrival of the dream's mysterious denizens. Patty, well into her recurring nightmare, recognizes the road ahead like the commuter recognizes the well-worn path to the office. There's a tremor, accompanied by the sound of something mechanical, something large, heading their way. Anticipating its arrival does nothing to assuage her fear.

The rec room starts to shudder. The girls jump off the high bar stools and run into the center of the room where they're less likely to be struck by falling debris. One of the ice cream spoons falls from the bar to clatter silently on the linoleum floor, the sound swallowed up by the growing cacophony. Candy is talking to Patty, pointing to the ceiling, gesturing perhaps that they should leave, but Patty can hear none of it.

Suddenly the adjoining laundry room is filled with bright light. The girls instinctively shade their eyes but continue to peer through the spaces between their fingers, hoping to catch a glimpse of the light's origin. Then the light turns and the girls are left blinking in its wake. Patty, the dreamed, wants to investigate the laundry room, but Patty, the dreamer, remembers what's coming and shouts a warning. Patty, the dreamed, fumbles for the light switch on the other side of the doorway. Candy is at her back again, talking a blue streak, but continues to be drowned out by the mechanical roar. Patty's hand slaps at the wall while peering into the dark, searching for the washer dryer, the furnace, anything from the life she's known. She can't see the floor in front of her. Not even the glow of the neon crab penetrates the boundary of the door frame.

From an unlikely distance, the light returns. More of the dream loads into Patty's memory and she remembers what's coming and backs up. She bumps into Candy who's staring back at her with a curious expression. Patty, the dreamed, has no answers for her. And Patty, the dreamer, has only memories. Memories of the relentless dream that accosts her nightly, forcing her eyes to gaze upon a ceiling festooned with the lurking shadows of the trees outside, and only a small, smiling nightlight to protect her.

The girls link arm in arm and watch. The approaching rumble takes the form of a gleaming, bullet-nosed train painted blood red and bold, mustard yellow. It slows to a stop, the din already winding down, a bass engine sound followed closely by the decelerating whine of electric turbines. The engine passes the girls and they're left staring up at the enormous plane of a passenger car, lit here and there by amber signal lights.

Patty and Candy look to each other. They see in each other's eyes that neither of them has lost their minds. This is happening, the eyes say. Together, the girls step through the doorway into what was once the Bennett family laundry room, but is now something quite different.

Patty's feeling of dread returns. It frustrates her because its cause continues to elude her, and the teasers have once again ceased. Her head is spinning, and that hovering dread tugs at her heart.

The girls look to their right at the engine three cars down. A single headlight shines out to infinity. An unnatural silence is shattered by the sound of metal on metal and the scalding hiss of pressurized steam suddenly released. Both girls utter a single scream, covering each other's mouths in the hope of avoiding unwanted attention.

A bright work light snaps on at the back of the engine, casting a beam toward the rear to reveal in silhouette a slowly unfolding staircase on the first passenger car. The outline of a very tall, extremely thin person steps out onto the steps, all detail lost in the garish light, although the girls can make out that it's wearing a conductor's cap. Its great height suggests it's a male. They watch as he reaches to manipulate something unseen above the door before stepping back into the train. Then someone, or something, takes the conductor's place. Even from a distance, it appears to be a giant of extraordinary proportions.

It makes its way down the stairs and stands motionless on the invisible landing. Its head is huge on a body standing slightly hunched, with arms long enough to touch the ground, like an over-sized gorilla, but fully dressed and wearing a tiny hat. It starts walking in the girls' direction, arms limp, and its large hands brushing the ground on either side. With hearts racing, the girls dash back into the rec room and wait for the giant to make its entrance. The silence stretches out interminably.

The knot tightens in Patty's stomach. She looks up toward the stairs and sees in a rush of imagery how the rest of the dream will play out. She wants to shout a warning but she can't take the chance, not with the giant just outside the door.

Patty's sister barks an order from the top of the stairs and Candy's eyes grow wide. She looks to her friend for guidance but Patty is crouching ineffectively behind a plastic chair, shaking her head, her hands pressed to her ears. Patty is hoping Amy will go away, but she knows it's not going to play out like that. She peeks into the inky blackness of the former laundry room. Still no sign of the giant.

Amy stomps down the stairs in fuzzy slippers and an over-sized t-shirt and looks down at the girls. She can see they're looking past her, mouths agape. As she turns to see what it is that has captured the girls' attention, the giant's huge hand comes down on her neck and one shoulder. A long arm follows slowly as he pushes her gently into the room. The creature squeezes through the door frame, ducking dramatically under the archway. In the pale, pink light, it looks like a human male.

Here the dream's pace crawls in direct contrast to Patty's increasingly fast heart rate. The man stands about eight feet in height. Or he would have if not for the seven foot ceiling. He's wearing a charcoal gray suit, tailored to fit his disproportionately short legs and unnaturally long arms. Red piping lines his lapels, one of which showcases a cloisonné pin depicting a stylized locomotive. The giant's head is massive and rough-looking. His five o'clock shadow looks like heavy grain sand paper while a very pronounced brow hangs over deeply inset and beady eyes. His lips are substantial, as is his jaw, in direct proportion to his prominent and pugnacious nose. On the top of that massive head sits a laughingly small, red pillbox hat. The elastic strap is wrapped so snuggly around his cleft chin, it pushes out his beefy, elephantine ears. To Patty he looks a lot like the gangsters she'd seen on old Bugs Bunny cartoons.

Once completely through the door, the giant turns Amy to face him. Fear causes her breath to stutter in her throat. The giant, anticipating a scream, puts his forefinger in front of her mouth, a finger that covers most of her face.

"Shhhhhhh."

It sounds like an echoing, subterranean wind in Patty's ears.

Amy stares into the giant's eyes and begins to smile, then relaxes completely, all traces of fear leaving her body. The giant releases his grip on her then digs into an inside jacket pocket. He removes an envelope, bringing it close to his face to read the imprint. Satisfied he's found his passenger, he squats on his haunches with a grunt. Resting his forearms across his knees, he cocks his head and takes on an almost sad expression. Sighing deeply, the giant in the tiny, red cap hands Amy the envelope, which she accepts absently. He again raises his forefinger, this time touching her forehead, and Amy's face goes blank. The giant rises, avoiding the ceiling as best he can, and steps away from the doorway. Like a gentleman, he extends his long arm graciously, and Amy walks as if hypnotized through the door and into the darkness.

Patty, the dreamer, and Patty, the dreamed, whisper with one voice, "Amy?" No further attempt to stop her beyond that single utterance is offered. She knows there's no turning back for her or her sister. The dream only ends, always ends, one way. Amy Bennett vanishes into the blackness, never to be seen or thought of again.

The giant turns, looking at the girls with a smile that is barely able to lift his stony face. Shuffling his feet, he resumes his former squat and gestures to them with both hands to come to him. The giant waits patiently, absently scratching. His fingernails make crunchy cereal sounds against his rough stubble. The girls make their way tentatively toward the giant, stopping simultaneously five feet from him. He sighs once more and looks them over. They feel his warm breath.

"Booooooard!" The enthusiastic voice of the conductor captures the attention of the giant, and he acknowledges the call with a slight nod of his head.

Raising his forefinger one more time, he touches Candy's forehead. "Sleep," his powerful bass voice resonates. Then, he moves his hand to Patty and repeats the process, only this time he says, "Forget."

#

In the tea room, Sienna made contact with something cool and invisible. It felt like a wall of glass. The beautiful spring day in the country was turning out to be---.

A baritone voice whispered in Sienna's ear. "Would you like a cookie, Mrs. Bennett?"

Sienna swallowed a scream in the vain hope of avoiding notice. Clutching her chest, she looked up at the tall man in the yellow sweater and said in a strained whisper, "Jesus, you scared the shit out of me!"

"I am so sorry," he replied as he moved the plate closer. "Have a cookie."

That was it! She'd had enough! She was ready to put a stop to the whole thing. They had obviously been brought to some fabricated location and made to break bread with these crazy people under the pretense of helping her daughter. What they were getting out of it, she couldn't figure. She told herself to stand up and demand that they be returned to their home. She would remind them that kidnapping was a crime and unless they brought them home immediately, she would call the police.

Instead, she took the cookie.

Griffin looked toward the sunny corner of the room. "Is everything alright over there, Mr. Amsterdam?"

"Perfectly fine, Mr. Griffin," he said, refilling Sienna's tea cup. "Apologies for the interruption." Amsterdam smiled at Sienna as he reached past her to close the window.

Griffin turned his attention back to Patty whose eyes had glazed over as she recounted her story.

"My mother woke us up the next morning," Patty said, wrapping her story up. "We were sleeping on the basement floor. The laundry room looked like it always did."

Griffin sat for a moment, letting the story sink in. "Isn't that just like a laundry room?" he finally said, folding his arms.

"Ha! Yeah." She couldn't look him in the eye. "It's just a crazy dream."

"And neither one of you remembered anything when you woke up?"

"It was just a dream, wasn't it?"

Askew got up and made his way to the center table. "When did it start, Patty?"

She shrugged. "After the sleepover. At first it was just little bits. Each night there was a little more to it. After a while, the whole thing was like a movie in my head. The same movie, over and over. I couldn't sleep. I can't sleep. And I've been wondering ever since, what happened to my sister?"

A tea cup shattered on the floor. All heads turned. Sienna was standing in the corner of the room with fear and confusion washing over her face.

"You don't have a sister. You never had a sister! I keep telling her but she won't listen. She's an only child but she keeps talking about a sister. There is no sister! Why does she keep asking---?"

To avert outright panic, Amsterdam offered a calming hand. She didn't like that and yanked her arm from his gentle grip.

"Candy's mother said you people could help."

"It's a dream, Mrs. Bennett," said the bald man. "Haven't you ever had a strange dream?"

"Don't patronize me."

"Did you take everything you dreamed as fact?"

"Of course not!"

"Then why do you keep treating Patty's dream as such?"

"I'm not, but she talks as if---."

"She just wants to understand."

"I want to understand!"

Behind his Coke bottle lenses, it was difficult to discern Askew's reaction. "You don't have to understand, Mrs. Bennett. It didn't happen to you, it happened to your daughter. Trust me when I say you'll never understand what she's been through. You mustn't try to assess her state of mind based on criteria derived from your own experiences, it cannot be done. Empathy and understanding is what your daughter needs. If you want to help Patty through this ordeal, just be there for her."

Amsterdam eased Sienna back into her chair. Askew wrapped an elastic band around his journal and tucked it into one of his many pockets. He bent to whisper in Patty's ear then patted her on the shoulder and cheek before exiting through a hidden door. Patty seemed satisfied with what Askew had to say and even managed a weak smile.

Alan Griffin stood up. "This concludes the interview. Subject 1014 is hereby released. Verity Corp will follow up with the family in two weeks," he said, nodding slightly toward the over-sized mirror. He smiled and looked at Patty who already looked much relieved after having told her story. The sleepless nights had aged her beyond her teenage years, but now she looked younger, more suited to her age. Her green eyes recovered some of the sparkle of her youth and dampened hope had been reignited.

Griffin walked over to Sienna. "Mrs. Bennett? It's time to go. We want to thank you for allowing us to speak with your daughter."

Sienna looked up at Griffin with red-rimmed eyes. "That's it? She's cured?"

"She'll sleep like a baby tonight, I guarantee it. She'll start feeling more like herself as time goes on."

Patty shouldered her way past the big men to stand in front of her mother. They shared the same expression, as if reuniting after a years-long estrangement rather than the six weeks that had actually passed. Patty was too tired to cry, but Sienna's eyes filled with tears. That was all Patty needed to see. She rushed into her mother's arms and Sienna pressed her hot, tear-soaked face into her only daughter's.

"Mom?" asked Patty, her eyes already closing, thanks to the drug-laced sugar cubes she had dropped into her tea. "Can we go home now? I'm tired."

Sienna looked around as if waking from a dream of her own. "What is this place? Who are you people? Why did you really want to see my daughter?"

"Mr. Amsterdam, would you escort the ladies home? Mrs. Bennett, we'll speak again and address your questions at that time. For now, it's time for you to take your daughter home."

He reached into his pocket and took out two blindfolds.

Chapter One: The Professor

From his hotel window, Daniel Askew gazed into the night sky, trying his best to envision the end of all things. He liked to think his imagination stood just behind his intellect, but when it came to visualizing the death throes of an entire universe, his inability to do so vexed him almost as much as the possibility. So he stared out the window, hands clasped behind the small of his back, paralyzed by a running stream of imagined cataclysmic scenarios as he only half-listened to his unexpected and uninvited guest.

Askew wasn't an emotional man by nature. He was simply too busy to acknowledge feelings that played no part in the work at hand. On this day, though, removed from his element, the end of all reality staring squarely into his broken eyes, he recognized the presence of melancholia. Try as he might to limit his thoughts to the concrete, a persistent and intangible sadness threatened to overturn his sense of logic.

The professor had had a busy day and there was much to mull over. First, there was the disturbing dream he'd had that morning on his train ride to Hartford. A dream in which a glass man spoke to him with the delicate voice of a flute, a voice that had fallen on tone deaf ears, leaving Askew none the wiser for the encounter. Then there was the discovery that he was under the watchful eye of a mysterious private security firm; a company no one back at the office could account for, yet the organization in question seemed all too aware of Verity Corp's hidden agenda. For all Askew knew, Global Armour was in league with the Lantern Society. If those issues weren't enough to account for his preoccupation, there was the recent Rewrite that had taken place to remind him why he did what he did for Verity Corp.

And, of course, there was still Armageddon to consider.

"I'm not sure I'm getting through to you, Professor," said a male voice. "You should be back in your lab, working on the problem."

Askew turned from the window and fell into the couch with a great exhalation. He knew he should be offended by the uninvited guest's tone, perhaps take him to task for the slight. After all, they weren't friends, and their so-called alliance was never clearly defined. In the end, though, he was simply too tired.

"What do you know about the Lantern Society?" he asked, pursuing his own line of thought.

"Time is of the essence, Professor."

Time was indeed of the essence, but Askew didn't think it held the same meaning for his guest.

Looking up at the ceiling, Askew ruminated, "Reality is a construct made up of choices."

"Doc, please, I'm not one of your students. I think I know a little something about the nature of reality."

"Every decision every person makes impacts the future and puts it on a new course. Sadly, over time, we've willingly and voluntarily shaped our universe into this..."

He searched for just the right words to describe the state of the world, but only managed to issue a weary sigh.

"Professor?"

"Unfortunately, things will never change, because the people who inhabit this universe believe they are simply its passengers rather than its drivers. They are going with the flow of history, doing what they have to do to get by in each of their inherited realities. But it's a lie. We have always had a choice and this is the world we've chosen to make. This is the reality we've constructed."

"Professor?"

"I wonder, Orwell, what happens when our ability to choose is taken from us. What then? How will we perceive the world then?"

"Your concern is premature."

"I'm not talking about your railroad or even the abductions," Askew said. He shook his head, surprised by Orwell's one-dimensional take on his musing. "I'm talking about something else entirely."

#

The week prior, an elevator came to a stop twelve stories below ground. Askew stepped off and into what at first glance looked to be little more than a cold, damp cavern fit with stadium lights. A short walk down a cement path, however, revealed the gated entrance to Verity Corp's massive Central Laboratory. He waved to the guard stationed in the security hut, then passed through a full body metal detector without slowing. Over an intercom, the young man asked to Askew's health to which the professor responded by waving a stack of papers in the air and grumbling incoherently.

A magnificent iron door set into the rock stood between Askew and the lab proper. Locks clicked and clacked after he placed his hand down on the print reader and the door snapped open with a hiss of released atmosphere. Cavernous in scope only, the laboratory was a finished edifice deep below the streets of New York City. Its walls and floors were painted uniformly white and lit in clever ways to prevent hot spots. The ceiling was overlaid with a projected image of the sky that mirrored the days, nights, and weather patterns high over the Verity tower above. In this way, employees stuck underground for extended shifts could maintain a sense of time and place.

Askew walked into Section 1, a 'room' about half the size of a football field, and known affectionately among the scientists and staff as the Drone Room. A crew of one hundred sat at long tables, dividing their time between Verity's IT Help Desk and acting as the first line of inquiry for Recruitment Services. There they chatted with potential initiates over state of the art headsets and monitored input and output on large viewing screens above their heads. Recruitment was always on the lookout for new Witnesses to grow Verity's underground workforce. It was the Drone Room's job to weed out the crackpots and pass the viable candidates onto their supervisor, Alan Griffin, who perched overhead in a mezzanine office overlooking the staff.

As Askew continued past the Drone Room and into Section 2, Rachel Henderson, his hand-picked second in Verity Corp's science division, drove in from Section 3. After spotting Askew, she hurried to park her electric cart. The section designated Administrative Support was equal in size to Recruitment Services, but rather than two rows of fifty employees each, the admins were set up in round quads. Each of four employees sat at a workspace that faced their coordinator. The coordinators sat in the center and utilized a three hundred and sixty degree workspace. There were twenty-five such quads in the space leaving plenty of room for delivery carts to wend the circuitous mail route, whizzing back and forth for pick-ups and drop-offs of interoffice communications.

Administrative Support was also the hub of Verity's extensive pneumatic delivery system.

"Professor!" a frazzled Henderson shouted across the enormous space. "I need to speak with you!" A few heads turned, but only for a moment. They were used to seeing the two scientists excited over one thing or another.

Askew held papers up like he was leading a tour. "Rachel! Come with me."

The two wore long, white, lab coats, though Askew's was blousy and gave him the appearance of someone who had shrunk. Henderson, in contrast, made the coat look fashionable with navy blue pencil skirt and matching walking shoes. Her chestnut hair was pulled up in a bun and dark-rimmed reading glasses hung suspended from an antique chain. Stockings finished the ensemble, not something she generally wore, but they kept her warm in the chilly lab. Though barely out of her twenties, she possessed the stiff demeanor of a scientist from a 1950s newsreel. This had earned her the nickname, Dr. Duckandcover.

She ran to catch up and said, slightly out of breath, "We missed you at the Tunnel test."

"Couldn't be helped. How did it go?"

She informed him it had gone flawlessly, although she thought that the new man, Dmitri Gusarov, should have sat out the test until he was better prepared. Askew didn't seem to register much of what she said. He took her by the elbow and steered her toward a section of conference rooms that divided Sections 2 and 3. He entered Conference Room 9, the Galileo Room, and dimmed the overhead lights to half their strength before taking a seat. On the table, he manipulated the built-in computer interface to log into his profile.

"I received an email this morning," he said as he double-clicked a message and displayed it on the wall screen. "It came from InfoFile@VerityCorp. Who is that?"

Henderson, clearly distracted with burning news of her own, waited patiently for her turn.

"Don't know. I'll check with Ellen. 'Verity Corp has a problem'," she read aloud from the body of the email. "It's a little broad. What's it supposed to mean?"

Askew opened the attachment, revealing a scanned image of a flier.

It looked like an inexpensive, letter-sized piece of paper, like advertising for a flea market or a low budget rock show. The faded background image depicted the tripod UFO from 'War of the Worlds.'

Henderson gave it a quick once-over. "That's not helping."

"Did you read it through?" Askew asked, folding his arms. "All of it? It may as well have been composed in this very lab."

"What? Prof, really, that's a huge leap."

"Read it again and tell me you don't see a problem."

He got up and grabbed the wand to the vertical blinds, yanking them roughly aside to reveal Section 3, the area designated Command Central. He stared out at the room's focal point, at what appeared to be a large, floating sphere, referred to as the Egg. The manned control center was actually suspended by a single, slender, steel column, and could only be accessed by a retractable bridge.

Askew stared out at the beating heart of his lab, the product of his genius, and like a parent watching their child heading off to school, he felt anxious and fearful of exposing a loved one to danger.

Henderson asked, "Have you ever heard of this Lantern Society?"

"No, I haven't." He placed his hand gently on the window.

"I admit there's an interesting turn of phrase or two..."

Turning quickly back in her direction, he said, "If you substitute the Trans-Dimensional Railroad for the flier's UFOs, and Verity Corp for this nameless government they refer to, the flier takes on a whole new meaning."

Henderson, doing her best to deflate Askew's concerns, said, "Of course it would. But it doesn't say those things."

Askew rejoined her at the table. "It mentions abductions!"

"A staple of UFO conspiracy theorists! You can't..."

Something dawned on her and she suddenly felt very heavy. It was as if someone was pressing her down into her seat.

"To me," Askew said, taking no notice of Henderson's change in demeanor, "this flier reads as if what Verity knows is no longer exclusive to our organization."

Blood drained from Henderson's face. "Jesus."

Unused to seeing Henderson flustered about anything, Askew raised an eyebrow. "Rachel?"

"It's why I was in such a hurry to see you." Henderson forced herself up and started pacing the room with lead feet. "Mind you, we're still in the early stages of our investigation."

Askew clamped down on his pipe stem and pulled at the end of his waxed mustache as he asked her to elaborate.

"Ellen was deep-cleaning one of our primary servers, reviewing files, databases, purging in prep for archiving."

"Yes, yes," Askew said.

"She found some unusual code, non-sanctioned code, deeply nested at the root of the file tree."

"What kind of code?"

Henderson hesitated. She and Askew had become close over the years, like family. Rachel, the dutiful daughter to Askew's father figure, she took great joy in making him proud while minimizing failures. To the rest of Verity Corp she was a tough, no-nonsense leader of Verity's science division, but she was ever vulnerable to Askew's opinions.

"She referred to it as a leech," Henderson said. "Its sole function appeared to be copying any and all available data and routing it to a location we've yet to determine. Offsite would be difficult, if not impossible, but we're not ruling it out."

Askew inhaled deeply and shifted his pipe from one side of his mouth to the other. He didn't like how the day was playing out at all. When he asked Henderson what she thought they were looking for she referred to her notes.

"Nothing of immediate use that we can determine. It's a small array dedicated to the Sounding Tunnel. There's also a medley of project and resource files that have been brought over from other servers to make space."

Askew's brilliant mind played a scene out in his head and the result struck him like a hammer, almost knocking the wind out of him.

"There's no need to raise an alarm," Henderson continued, "unless their intent is to sell the plans to someone who actually has the economic and technological resources to follow through. That is, of course, they have any idea what they're looking at, and I find that highly unlikely."

"Access to Null Space…" Askew said as he continued to imagine the worst case.

"The odds of achieving any measure of success are astronomically against them. In addition to the Tunnel plans, they would have to have the tech to read the TDRR's energy signature in order to piggy-back. The idea is ridiculous."

"Access to Null Space is the least of our worries, Rachel." Askew stood up again, pushing his back into the nearest corner.

"I find that hard to believe," said Henderson.

"We created a failsafe called the Outsource Protocol. The plans are incomplete."

"I don't understand," said Rachel frowning, "I assembled that data myself."

Askew stared back at her and she slowly nodded in comprehension, pretending she wasn't hurt to learn that Askew had excluded her from his confidence. She thought she'd earned her stripes a long time ago. "So, if anyone tried to build it, it wouldn't work."

"The end result would not satisfy the intent." Askew leaned into the corner for support, his lab coat practically swallowing him up, and tried his best to share the earnestness of his dread. "However, if they did construct it, based upon those plans, and they activated it," he chewed on his pipe as he searched for the right words, "there could be a disaster of incalculable proportions."

He couldn't believe he said it out loud. The statement left Henderson speechless and Askew gave her a moment to process it. She was doing her best to keep her growing anger at bay.

"In what way a disaster?" she finally asked.

"It's very possible displacement could occur."

By far, it was not the answer she expected. Anything she imagined in those few seconds paled in comparison to his actual response. It was the one event for which there was no contingency. Henderson ground her teeth, trying to maintain a neutral expression, certain it wouldn't last.

"Without the proper frequencies," Askew continued, "there would be no phasing process. In all our simulations using conventional, well, incorrect frequencies always caused…"

Henderson couldn't tell if Askew was searching for just the right words or trying to avoid them.

"The arrival of the Trans-Dimensional Railroad could force the displacement of an equivalent portion of our reality."

Henderson asked where the equivalent portion of reality went. Askew practically shrugged.

In a tone betraying her stifled anger, Henderson said, "And that could cause a chain reaction." It was as if the picture of disaster being painted was a personal affront.

"It would be quite likely," Askew said sheepishly.

"Confined to---?" Askew stopped her with a small but firm shake of his head. Henderson was stunned. "Do you know what you're saying?" She began walking circles around the table. "You're talking about the erasure of known existence!"

Askew looked down at his hands and shook his head. "In favor of its new matrix..." he mumbled.

"Are you quoting Star Trek III?!" Henderson realized that an uncontrollable urge to laugh was brewing inside of her. "Why wasn't I made aware of this possibility?"

"The likelihood was so infinitesimally small. I guess I got sidetracked. Rachel, you said it yourself! What were the chances someone could accomplish all those things you listed? The funding, the power---."

"Unacceptable! That is unacceptable! There is no acceptable level of risk for a disaster of this magnitude."

"Potential disaster."

Henderson almost slapped Askew without thinking, but held fast to her emotions. Her imagination drifted to her family farm in Idaho. She could see her mother and her twin brothers standing in the dusty driveway, watching as a wall of white overtook her father in the field. They saw him turn toward them with a devastating look of confusion and loss. His arms outstretched, reaching out for them, his fingers pleading for rescue, until the wall of white swallowed him up. The Henderson twins looked to their mother with tears in their eyes. She clutched them tightly as she stared into the blank abyss.

"Do you know what this means?" Rachel asked as she shivered the thought away. "The reaction won't stop with this planet. It won't stop with this solar system. Everything gone. Everyone---."

With a reverberating slap of his hand on the table, Askew shouted, "I know, God damn it! I understand! What began with a bang would go out in a whimper of self-destructive foolishness."

Henderson, breathing hard, stared at Askew for a moment, deliberating with herself whether there was any value in pushing the subject further, the mad laughter still bouncing around in her head, keen on an exit. She went back into business mode and changed the subject.

"We've done a very thorough review of our existing security measures and we've ruled out the possibility of outside criminal activity."

"The mainframe cannot be compromised from outside Verity Corp?"

They took seats, exhausted by their heated exchange, which was unproductive and contrary to the nature of their relationship.

Henderson nodded. "Correct. It's not possible according to the tests we've run. However, there is some vulnerability from within."

"Obviously. There's obvious vulnerability."

A conspiracy played out in Askew's mind whereby an outside agency had gotten hold of a disgruntled employee and used him or her to assist in their nefarious plans. To what end, he couldn't guess. *Even if they did gain access to Null Space, what would be the point?* And the thought of a disgruntled employee, knowing Verity Corp's mission and what it meant to the world, was an even bigger mystery. And a big problem. He could think of only one person who might have fit the label, 'disgruntled employee,' but he'd disappeared on a mission over a year ago. And Hugo Jascowitz wasn't so much a disgruntled employee at Verity Corp as he was dissatisfied with its procedures.

Zooming in on the flier, he reread the section that stated, *'The Lantern Society will shine a light on the truth. No one government, no one corporation, and no one man can keep us in the dark.'* He had a terrible feeling he knew to which man the flier was referring.

"Do you think this is a coincidence?" ask Henderson.

"No, I don't," was Askew's response. "Who did you say you have working on this?"

"Ellen Cheever."

"Good." Askew stood up. "Keep this between the two of you. I don't want to publicize our weaknesses and I certainly don't want to start a panic where potential Armageddon is concerned. I'll meet with Bellows and fill him in. Let's see where we go from here. Try to find out how much of a head start they might have gotten. I'll forward this email to you so you have the flier and the address that sent it. There's a website mentioned on it. See what you can learn from it."

As they met at the door, Askew grasped Henderson's arm. "I'm sorry, Rachel. This is a lot to take in."

Station 12: The Lantern Society

With layered looks, Henderson looked into her mentor's eyes. She had regained the cool, analytical disposition of a scientist, but Askew saw beneath that, saw the fear and disbelief.

"It's impossible," he said. "But we'll find whoever's responsible and we'll make them---."

"If we don't stop them, everything Verity has accomplished will have been for nothing. We won't have saved anyone in the long run."

Askew nodded. "We must move quickly."

Chapter Two: The Investigation

A week later, Askew found himself heading to Hartford, Connecticut in search of answers, leaving Henderson and Cheever to comb through the Lantern Society website in search of clues. Although the site was of little use in determining the Society's physical location, they were able to extract from the site source code an address they believed belonged to the domain host. With little else to go on, and not wanting to widen the circle of the informed, Askew decided to visit Connecticut's capitol personally and uncover what he could about Verity's mysterious adversary.

With two hours before his train's scheduled departure, Askew walked briskly along busy Canal Street, puffing on his pipe, smoke billowing behind him in thick knots. The sky was turning dark with the threat of inclement weather so he decided to buy an umbrella at one of the many kiosks in the Chinatown market. He shook his head in disappointment as he handed the vendor three dollars, knowing that the very same umbrella cost three times as much at the nearby drug store. *Is this really the reality we've chosen?* Still, a bargain was a bargain.

His purchase tucked into his travel bag, Askew headed north on Crosby Street toward his favorite coffee shop. He stopped without warning to relight his pipe and nearly caused a human pile-up. Several people grumbled as they missed running into him by inches. He watched the fire reignite the tobacco in a shimmering, red glow as great clouds of blue-gray smoke drifted upward to merge with the air currents that commuted daily through the canyons of lower Manhattan.

Askew looked up past the towers to assess the weather. His breath caught, startled to find that the darkening sky struck him as something new and beautiful and a little frightening. The glossy, gray light of day was vivid and crisp beneath the low ceiling. Ash-colored clouds broke from the backdrop with a tempting nearness, while in the distance, shafts of golden sunlight pierced the morning gloom in a last ditch effort to retake the day.

Then, out of the blue, Askew found himself overcome by a deep and inexplicable sense of loss, bringing with it the onset of tears. He tried to imagine everything he knew and everyone he ever loved coming to an abrupt and absolute end. It made him sad, not only for the nonexistent future such a disaster might bring, but also for life in retrospect. *So many possibilities fallen by the wayside. Such effort at life wasted.*

How sadly ironic it would be if after all these years of watching Null Space and its damnable trains, our universe was destroyed by our own hand? He thought of the work he was doing at Verity Corp to make things right. He thought about all the secrets for which he was responsible. All the nameless and faceless people impacted by those secrets. And for some inexplicable reason, he thought of Patty Bennett.

The real fear, he realized, the root cause of the sensation, had no basis in the current crisis, or even the machinations of the mysterious railroad. Rather it was an unknown, unknowing feeling of disassociation. At that moment he felt incredibly small and insignificant in the grand scheme of things. A weird sense that he didn't belong, that he had somehow lost his way.

In the space of five seconds, the emotion came and went; a miniature fugue state that left the professor with a vague sense of confusion. He took a deep breath and blinked before his tears had a chance to form, and focused, instead, on his immediate destination two blocks ahead. He could already make out the large cup and saucer cutout hanging in the front window of Janice Coffee, a place of warmth, a place familiar.

As he crossed the street toward the promise of great coffee and friendly service, a splash of pink crept into his boosted peripheral vision. Furrowing his brow in consternation, he walked over to a lamppost on which a brightly colored flier was affixed. He pushed his heavy lenses higher up the bridge of his nose and gave it a quick once-over before ripping it down, leaving its tiny, pink corners behind, along with other remnants of the past. His mood now slightly curdled, he stepped into the coffee shop and found himself a table.

It wasn't crowded but business was brisk. The takeout counter had a constant flow of customers and about half of the dozen or so tables had patrons. There was a promising aroma of freshly ground beans in the air, and when his favorite waitress walked over with a big smile, it immediately brought Askew back to a better place.

"Hey, Prof," she said as she tucked her pad into the front pocket of her apron. "It's been awhile."

"Hello, Nessa." Askew hung his bag and raincoat over a chair before sitting down. "I was actually here last week, but apparently you had better things to do."

"Vacationing in Vermont with some friends of mine. What was I thinking, taking time off?"

Askew concurred and Nessa laughed as she watched Askew rearrange the items on his table. He was always a little nervous around her and she found it endearing.

Askew, for his part, didn't want to appear rude or forward. She had one of those faces he could get lost in, and he didn't want to get caught staring for too long. She had a perfect complexion with high cheek bones and a dazzling smile. It was her eyes, though, that drew him in. Light brown eyes made all the brighter by her dark brown skin.

"I survived," he said. "Just. Jennie did her best, but she doesn't have what you have. Don't tell her I said that."

"Who?"

"Jennie covered your tables while you were away." Askew's oversized eyes registered that Nessa didn't know to which waitress he was referring and realized, sadly, that Null Space had tampered with reality once again. "I'm sorry," he said, covering quickly, "I was thinking about the young lady who assisted me at Barnes and Noble. Ignore an old man's feeble brain."

She tapped him on the shoulder and walked away. "Let me see if we have any coffee left."

"You do that," Askew said with a nod. "I'll wait here."

"You do that," she called back as she made her way to the service counter. "And you're not old!"

He couldn't help but smile at her attempt at flattery, but it faded almost immediately. It wasn't often that Askew, or any other inoculated individual at Verity Corp, came in direct contact with an alteration in their reality. It was alarming, of course, but after the shock of realizing the alteration had taken place, and setting aside the fascination from a scientific standpoint, it was the emotional aspect that usually carried the most resonance.

Askew was fond of Jennie. He didn't know her as well as Nessa, but enough to feel her loss. It was the downside of being inoculated against continuity loss. He was burdened with the memory of someone who never existed.

She was raising her son on her own, he remembered. Justin was the boy's name, and his father had left him to his mother at the age of two. In the newly rewritten reality, someone else would be raising him. It wouldn't matter to the boy, of course, because his 'new' parents would be all he ever knew. Still, the thought made Askew sad. Then again, it was just as likely Justin was never born into the revisions. Did that make it better or worse?

God only knew where Jennie was now. A prisoner in Null Space, no doubt. Askew wondered if she and Amy Bennett might cross paths on their separate journeys. And he wondered if Jennie's removal had left anyone behind with sleepless nights and recurring nightmares. He supposed that would be for Alan Griffin and his team to sort out after he reported it.

Askew's sense of loss resurfaced. He looked at each of the shop's customers and felt strangely disconnected from the world he was so desperately trying to save. Too many years spent in Verity's underground lab had caused him to feel out of place in society…isolated in the crowd. Ironically, it was what he once loved about living in New York City, but over time had grown fatigued by it. And now he had the added burden of knowing that the device he created to save humanity could end up becoming the cause of its self-annihilation.

Outsource Protocol, my ass. Damn you, Orwell.

"Morning, Daniel. Nice to see you."

Askew looked up to see a pretty, but weary-looking, waitress pass him by with a pot of coffee. "Good morning!" he said exuberantly, at the same time glancing at her name tag. He didn't recognize her, but she obviously knew him, and on a first name basis. Yet another sign that a Rewrite had taken place. He wondered how long they'd known each other in this reality and if he and Esther were friends.

Nessa returned with a fresh pot of coffee and offered up a refill. He politely declined, stating he had a train to catch, and then removed a napkin from the dispenser to give his powerful lenses a wipe. The air in Janice Coffee was thick with the vapor of roasted beans, steaming coffee, and fried breakfast foods, leaving behind an oily, clinging film in the short time he'd been there.

"Is this from a movie?" asked Nessa, pointing to the pink flier lying on the far corner of the table.

"It would make my life so much simpler if it was."

He held his glasses out in front of him, to check for any spots he may have missed, and something outside caught his attention. He put them back on for a better look and saw light reflecting from inside a black SUV parked across the street. Askew pursed his lips and looked away. He remembered seeing a similar vehicle double-parked on Canal Street as he shopped for his umbrella. He hadn't given it much thought at the time, black SUVs were a dime a dozen, but now he wondered.

"Maybe some of that Scientology mumbo jumbo?" Nessa asked.

Askew balled up the napkin and dropped it into his empty coffee mug. "Even that…" he mumbled as he scooped up the flier and shoved it into his laptop bag. "Forget it, Nessa, it's not important."

He stood up and removed a ten dollar bill from a money clip. As he did so, the SUV pealed out of its parking space, only serving to legitimize his concern. He placed his gratuity on the table and secured it with the empty cup.

Not taking for granted that he would see her again, Askew stared into Nessa's eyes as he thanked her. Then and there, Vanessa Huggins was his only connection to the outside world and he savored every moment of it. If it made her uncomfortable, she didn't show it.

#

Askew rarely passed up an opportunity to visit Grand Central Station. Even if it meant changing train lines to travel north of New Haven. Grand Central was a landmark of his youth that conjured up happy memories, memories that reached so far into the past they could have belonged to someone else. He remembered family trips to the big city museums, lunch dates in Central Park, and Broadway matinees on school days. This grand landmark, and a few others like it, always reminded him of what life was like before adopting the cynicism of adulthood. Before living life had become so needlessly complicated.

Entering at Vanderbilt, Askew made his way to the Grand Concourse where he gazed up at the magnificent chandeliers and the twilit constellations on the ceiling. Then he cast his eyes downward at the Departures boards as they flipped through the myriad of outgoing trains. Finally, he rested his eyes on the clock that towered over the Information booth, the landmark within the landmark, and the iconic focal point of his recall.

According to that clock, he had fifteen minutes until his scheduled departure. Time enough to place a call to Verity. Henderson brought him up to speed on the state of the investigation. She also provided him with an email alias with which he could make contact with the Lantern Society. He thanked her then made his way to track 119.

#

After having transitioned from the utilitarian Metro North into comfortable Amtrak seats in New Haven, Askew gazed past his reflection at the passing Connecticut scenery. The steady, gentle, rocking motion of the train worked its rhythmic magic on the professor's stress, and his thoughts began to line up in a manageable form. Threatening skies made good their promise, releasing a steady downpour as thunder rumbled from cloud to cloud in solemn discourse. With visibility decreased, Askew decided to boot up his laptop and get some work done. While he waited for Verity's custom Welcome screen to appear, he replayed the conversation he'd had with Henderson the week before. He'd told her then that he understood the consequences of the worst case scenario, but that was a lie. The end of the universe was just too abstract a concept for him.

As a scientist, a physicist, Askew spent no time examining the possibility of an afterlife. He believed death was the end. No more work, no more play, no dining out, no exploring, no discovering, no creating, no more music, no more worries, and no more joy. That said, Askew was no atheist. Instead, he deferred his afterlife to the experts, and if they believed his soul would continue on in another plane of existence, who was he to argue? In fact, where his would-be soul was concerned, he often took great comfort in the beliefs of others. Yet in the case of displacement he wondered, *what happens when your physical body doesn't die but rather simply ceases to exist? What happens to your soul then? Does the spiritual plane vanish along with the physical at the time of displacement?* The more he thought about it, the more confused he became. It was exhausting.

#

At the corner of his vision, he spies a pair of very big, red shoes walking past him down the center aisle. *There's a clown on board this train*, he thinks to himself. Askew slowly raises his head, but there's no sign of the shoes or their owner.

He's both astonished and pleased, however, to find that the train car is much more beautiful than he'd noted when he'd first boarded. It's ornately decorated in a Victorian-era style. Dark, lustrous hardwood flooring is complemented by a lighter, oriental carpet running the length of the aisle. Electric sconces, situated between each curtained window, illuminate the car against the dim light of the exterior overcast. Seats in sumptuous, burgundy leather, fashioned with a patterned inlay, are a relative match to the runner. It's all quite lovely and well-appointed, comforting in its nostalgia. In fact, it all seems oddly familiar to Askew.

Then, like a repressed memory brought to light, a horrible realization comes over him. His admiration morphs into fear. His temples throb and a cold sweat beads along his brow. The air coming in from the open windows washes over his bald head sending shivers down his spine. Passing scenery fades to black while insidious fingers of panic take hold of his heart and start to squeeze. The train is passing through an endless tunnel, or has stopped altogether, parked in the darkest recesses of Askew's mind, the corners reserved for nightmares. He turns to reach out to a fellow passenger and the realization of his circumstance hits home.

Across the aisle facing forward is a man who appears to be made entirely of emerald green glass. Askew stares at the odd statue, an abstract replica of a human being. There's great attention to detail in the finished face. The 'hair,' however, resembles rough and unpolished crystal formations. There is an odd suggestion of clothing, but the figure also appears to be nude with no obvious gender. Its arms are at rest and end in delicate hands and fingers. All in all, it resembles an expensive art piece.

After a minute, the statue, perhaps growing tired of being stared at, turns to face Askew who yelps in surprise. Light from one of the sconces passes through the figure's glass head and upper body and casts an eerie, green shadow down the aisle. The lips of the glass being part, and Askew hears what sounds like air passing through an instrument, light like a flute. He interprets this as language, but gleans no meaning.

Gripping tightly to his composure, he turns away from the glass figure, trying his best to push himself further into his seat. His breathing grows rapid as his collar tightens around his neck. He searches within for a logical answer to what's transpiring, while his eyes seek out a more tangible truth.

Station 12: The Lantern Society

Half the car is occupied. Only a small percentage of passengers appear to be human. The remainders are simply impossible creatures. One woman looks half human, half plant, with roots spilling out into the aisle. Askew's eyes drift from her to a stereotypical E.T., thin with large, black eyes, wearing a black robe and a silver tiara. It sits in the company of a floating glass orb filled with stars. There's another who looks like a human body builder but with the head of a raven. Then there's an enormous praying mantis somehow occupying a seat or two a few rows ahead of him. It appears to be grooming itself. There are others who have no form at all.

Askew attempts to remain focused and rational and forces himself to choose a single line of thought. *I've been taken by the Trans-Dimensional Railroad. It's the only explanation. But that's not possible. It can't happen like this!* The beads of sweat dotting his forehead gather enough weight to run down both sides of his face. Absently, he reaches inside his jacket for something to wipe it away, but forgets what he's doing almost immediately.

The door opens at the head of the car and two very tall, very thin, Conductors step in. A strip of shadow obscures their nondescript faces. They speak in a language of beeps and chirps that's as clear to Askew as was the glass man's song. His level of panic rises incrementally, acknowledging the growing distance between his present locale and the reality he's leaving behind. He closes his eyes, hoping that it's all just a dream, hoping that if he concentrates hard enough, he can will his way out, force himself awake. He thinks of slapping himself, but he doesn't want to attract the unwanted attention. This thought causes him to laugh out loud, despite his panic, at the absurdity of his logic.

The door behind the Conductors opens again and the big red shoes reappear, followed by baggy yellow pants and a lime-green jacket over a polka-dotted vest. Judging by the upside down smile painted on his face, he's a sad clown. He plants himself between the two Conductors and points in Askew's direction. The professor's head and heart aches in uncontrollable fear. As the walls start closing in on him, he adds nervous breakdown to his short list of alternatives to being taken by the TDRR.

Jerking his head in an animated fashion, he looks to see if it's possible the clown's target might be someone or something else nearby. One of the Conductors begins to make his way up the aisle and Askew knows he's coming for him. *This is impossible!* Askew shouts in his head. *I'm immune! The inoculation works, I proved it!* The Conductor is halfway to him now. Askew sees that it has no actual face but rather a blank, white suggestion of one. It's not unlike a mannequin's. The mask supports the Conductor's dark blue cap while seeming to hover above the matching uniform jacket. Askew, with nowhere to go anyway, is too terrified to move. The Conductor is almost upon him now as he struggles to find his voice.

"There's been a mistake," he manages to croak.

The seven foot tall Conductor bends at the waist, bringing its 'face' down to Askew's eye level. Eyeless, it cocks its head with the appearance of watching Askew as he tries to push his head still further into the cushioned headrest. The blank face looks delicate and shines like glazed porcelain. The scientist in him is tempted to reach out and touch it.

"I'm sorry," Askew says in a slightly stronger voice, "but I think there's been a mistake."

There's a single, gentle pop followed by an electric hum as a smiling human face is projected onto the porcelain placeholder from a tiny device beneath the Conductor's hat brim. Putting out its hand, it says in a friendly voice, "Good evening, sir, and welcome aboard the Tapestry Rail System. May I see your ticket, please?"

With nowhere else to go and without a ticket, Askew exited the dream with a start and found a human conductor handing him his laptop.

"Careful, sir," the conductor said, "you almost dropped your computer."

"Oh, thanks, thank you very much." Askew, blinking rapidly, tried to gather his wits. "I guess I dozed off, there."

The conductor stood up. "Good thing I was walking by. We'll be pulling into Hartford in about twenty minutes."

Professor Askew nodded then looked around at the familiar Amtrak décor and all the very human passengers and he breathed a sigh of relief.

#

The train pulled into Hartford's Union Station, a clean but lifeless shell of its former glory. Askew joined a small group of passengers as they made their way down the stairs and passed through the empty, echoing, marble foyer. Catching his reflection in the door as he exited, he was reminded of his unsettling dream and the glass man's attempt to speak to him. The odd familiarity he'd experienced was equally upsetting, if not more so, so he shifted his focus to the task at hand.

He had arranged to meet his man, Strivelli, a field agent in the employ of Verity Corp, at a bar one block north of the station. The rain had stopped so his new umbrella stayed in his bag as he ventured forth.

Halfway to his destination, he spotted a man with jet black hair, his hands deep in the pockets of his black trench coat, looking over a bright, green flier taped to a lamppost. Askew joined him, recognizing the now familiar layout of a Lantern Society flier, and read along.

"That's some crazy shit, right?" asked the man after a minute.

"I think you're right," Askew agreed, happy to hear an opinion from someone outside of his small universe. "Unless it's meant to be funny? Or maybe it's an advertisement?"

"Either way, I don't get it."

"No, neither do I." Askew smiled and paused only briefly while he took in the stranger. "Maybe they're not trying to be funny."

The man looked at Askew as if he thought he was being tested. "People disappear every day, but I guarantee it ain't aliens."

"I'm sure you're right," Askew said and started for the bar.

"Excuse me!" said the man, and he grabbed the sleeve of Askew's coat.

"Yes?"

"Can you tell me where the train station is?"

Askew pointed to the station entrance only a hundred yards away.

"Oh, great. Thanks, buddy."

Inside the Republic Cafe, Strivelli was throwing darts in the back of the house. Askew joined him as an exuberant bartender trotted over to take his order. Strivelli recommended one of his favorite beers. Askew smiled as he removed his cap and ordered a Coke.

From the toes of his Harley Davidson boots to the drawstring of his leather skull cap and the ensemble in between, Tony Strivelli could have been the poster child for any bike club. But Askew saw past the stereotype, genuine or not. Possessed of dark, intelligent eyes that offered only truth, Strivelli was a man Askew was happy to call friend.

Once the last dart was thrown, Strivelli joined Askew at the table and the two men shook hands.

"It's very nice to see you, Mr. Strivelli."

"Under different circumstances, maybe."

"Even now. It's been far too long. We shouldn't wait for fire drills to get together."

"Transfer me back to New York and we can see each other all the time."

Askew laughed as the bartender arrived with his drink. "That comes under Mr. Bellows' purview, I'm afraid. Soon enough, I'm sure. You've been gone some time now."

"How bad is it?" Strivelli asked after taking a drink.

"Very. Very bad, Mr. Strivelli. Verity Corp has been compromised. Specifically, our mainframe has been tampered with by someone from inside the company."

"You're kidding." Strivelli removed the beer from his moustache with his bottom lip. "One of ours is working with *them*?"

Askew shook his head. "No, it's not what you think. Our traitor appears to be reporting to an outside organization called the Lantern Society. I'm here to find out the truth of the matter."

Askew didn't think sharing what he knew about the stolen Sounding Tunnel plans was pertinent just then so he held back. But the irony wasn't lost on him. Had he shared the Outsource Protocol with those closest to him, things might have played out differently. Still, the lesson hadn't quite landed so he kept his mouth shut.

Strivelli frowned then signaled Askew to silence with a finger to his lips. He reached over and plucked what looked like a thistle off of Askew's arm and held it up for inspection. He then placed the object down on a napkin, removed a pocket knife from somewhere below the table, and cut into the small, spiky ball. Within a second he confirmed his suspicion and dropped it into his beer.

"I keep four of these in my kit," said Strivelli. "You recognize it?"

"That's Verity tech. Aiello designed it three years ago. He called it a sticky bug. You know, there was a man outside. He grabbed my arm on my way in."

Strivelli nodded and Askew thought back to that moment at Janice Coffee when he'd spied the suspicious SUV.

"I don't understand this. Espionage at Verity Corp, an outside organization that seems to be aware of our true purpose, and now confirmed surveillance. If this isn't the work of a single group…"

Station 12: The Lantern Society

"You're right. It's a mess."

Askew held up Strivelli's glass and stared through the honey-colored liquid.

"I have to go," said Strivelli. "I've got to pick up my lady friend."

"Have you managed to carve out a relationship out of this tedious assignment?"

"Formerly tedious assignment. Angela Rodriguez likes the bad boys. What can I say?"

"How do you think she'll react when she learns you're really one of the good guys?"

Strivelli smiled, neither acknowledging nor denying the implication.

"Thank you for making all my arrangements on such short notice. You've saved me a lot of time." Askew downed his Coke and belched quietly.

Strivelli smiled. "It's why you pay me, right?"

"Do we pay you? Such an odd career choice."

"What choice?" Strivelli reached into his jacket pocket and retrieved Askew's hotel key card. "Bellows says hello. We spoke briefly when I tested the Phone."

They shared a silent exchange whereby Strivelli didn't ask and Askew didn't offer, but the question remained: Why had Askew brought the Black Phone? Askew stood up to leave and the two exchanged another heartfelt handshake and a brief embrace.

"Be vigilant, Mr. Strivelli," he said, slinging his bag over his shoulder. "It seems there are enemies on both sides of the gate, and the last thing we want is to let our guard down." Askew smiled, hoping to elevate Strivelli's now obviously downbeat mood. "Cheer up, Mr. S. We are the masters of our own fate. We control our destiny, not them." Then a thought occurred to him. "Not that we'd know the difference if it were otherwise. Goodbye."

Askew stepped out of the bar and immediately noticed a car parked tightly between a rusted handrail and a dumpster. Glare on the windshield prevented him from seeing who was seated inside, but it didn't matter. Adjusting his shoulder strap, he crossed the street and made straight for the driver's side window. There was a woman behind the wheel, her strawberry hair tied behind her head and a pink scar running along her right jaw. The man in the black trench coat who'd grabbed Askew's arm was seated beside her. The woman lowered her window as Askew approached.

"You're following me," said Askew, "watching me. Why?"

A thin, pale hand came through the window holding a business card. "My name is Jackie Tomlinson, Professor. My partner is George Foster. We thought we might be of some help to you."

Askew looked down and read Global Armour on the card.

"Help with what?"

Foster held up the bright, green flier.

"I see." Askew placed the card in his pocket. "I see." He nodded, and without saying another word, he turned and walked away.

#

If Global Armour followed him to his hotel, he took no notice, so wrapped up was he in the week's events. Whenever he found himself alone, his mind always turned to the thought of reality displacement, the all-consuming idea that the unintended end of the world was well within reach. He knew that if the perpetrators of the data theft only knew what could come of their attempt at building a Sounding Tunnel, they would cancel their plans posthaste.

In this distracted state, he found himself tucked into his suite without really registering how it was he got there. Not long after a light meal and some time to reflect, Askew found himself in the living room having a conversation with the television.

The man on the screen smiled and straightened his bow tie. Askew stepped closer and studied him: black hair in the style of a military flattop; round, tortoise shell eyeglasses; lean, muscular face; and bright, green eyes. Maybe too bright? He wore a dark green, patterned shirt with a gold, but not flashy, bow tie, and he appeared to be sitting in a library filled with books on shelves and in stacks on the nearby tables. There was something inauthentic about all of it including Orwell himself.

"Do you like my library, Professor? Every single edition is bound in leather."

"Very impressive," Askew said half-heartedly.

"It's the sum total of everything I know, everything I've ever seen. Believe me, Professor, you want these books on your reading list."

"Have you been watching me, Orwell? Do you have other people watching me?"

Orwell took a beat and somehow managed to look as if he were staring straight at Askew. Askew glanced nervously at the Black Phone and wondered if Orwell could see it.

"I'm very disappointed. I really thought as a scientist you'd be wowed by my library."

"It looks faked somehow. I can't put my finger on it."

"Not faked so much as representational." The lights in the room dimmed then flared then settled back to normal. "Do you know what I am, Professor?"

Askew shook his head at first, but replied, "I can guess."

"Do so. And if you come to the correct conclusion, you will understand that there's very little I don't know. Finish your business here, Professor, and then return to New York. The clock is ticking."

Askew turned to face the hotel window. The clock was indeed ticking.

Chapter Three: Global Armour

George Foster hadn't been happy with his life or the choices he'd made for some time. Each turning point came and went with nothing to show for it; no successes, no outright failures, just a gray, monotonous mediocrity that barely made it worth getting up in the morning. Though he never stopped hoping his worse gaffs were behind him, he continually disappointed himself. He detested being the victim of his own poor judgment, but it seemed every time he went looking for his big break, a little more of him got broken.

As an agent of Global Armour for all of three weeks, Foster already had major doubts about his most recent transition. Doubts not based on his experiences with the firm but rather the lack of them. For three weeks he'd been anchored to his desk in a dusty cubicle, trawling the internet for anything of interest he could add to GA's file on Verity Corp. Not his definition of success, no matter how good the money. And the money was good.

It hadn't been easy for him to leave behind the Gulf breezes and sandy beaches of Miami for the crowded asphalt island of Manhattan, but he badly needed the boost to his résumé and to his self-esteem. During those first three weeks, he waited patiently for a real assignment, and when one finally came his way, he was ecstatic. For a minute.

Tired and hungry from the day's constant travel, it took all that was left of his remaining energy to stay awake. He should have been thrilled with the break in routine, but his emotions were simply not living up to his intellect's expectations. Half-closed eyes drifted back and forth between the subject of his partner's surveillance and the dog-eared paperback he was assigned to read. 'The Crossing' was no literary masterpiece by any stretch of the imagination, and even though it was required reading for all new agents of Global Armour, it was assigned without context, so Foster felt little motivation to comply.

"So, twenty some-odd years ago Heberling writes this book," said Foster, as a way of taking a break, "and according to said book, a kid watched his cousin board a train in the middle of the woods, in the middle of the night, never to be seen or heard from again."

Agent Jacqueline Tomlinson's blue eyes remained focused on the Republic Cafe. She heard the skepticism in Foster's voice. It was the same song she'd heard from agents in the past. In fact, she shared much of that skepticism, but she had reasons of her own for punching the clock every day.

"No rail lines anywhere in the vicinity," Tomlinson said. "Not then, not now. Nothing was ever reported. There's no record at the summer camp of a child gone missing. No police record and nothing in the papers. Just that one boy's recollection."

"And now this riveting bestseller."

The newly partnered agents were parked at the corner of Union and High Streets in Hartford, Connecticut. They were assigned to track the movements of one Daniel Askew, Chief Scientist and Director of Research and Development at Verity Corp. They had observed their target entering the Republic and were now waiting patiently for his exit. The listening device they had planted on him only moments before provided only a snippet of conversation between their subject and a man named Strivelli before cutting out.

"It was that book that brought Heberling and Lionel Bellows together in the first place and Verity Corp eventually came out of that meeting. The story goes, Bellows read it and identified with the content so strongly, he arranged a meeting with the author."

When Foster asked Tomlinson to expand on Bellows, she admitted that Global Armour had very little intel on the man. Foster put a stick of gum in his mouth and bit down hard, trying his best to contain his frustration.

"Did you see the book is listed on the web as fiction?"

Tomlinson replied, "The more I learn about Verity Corp and Askew's work, the fuzzier my definition of fiction becomes. I'm sure Heberling wouldn't argue the point."

"That his book is a work of fiction?"

"He's never claimed otherwise."

"Then why am I reading it?"

Tomlinson smiled. "Because the boss said so, that's why."

Foster added a new dog ear to the book then tossed it onto the dashboard. "Fucking outrageous!"

"When the book went to paperback, Heberling got it in his head to stick a phone number on the back page figuring if Bellows recognized something of himself in the story, maybe there were others."

"Other train enthusiasts," Foster said dryly. "That's some twisted logic."

"Believe what you want, but a lot of people called that number and they started to come together. Called themselves Verity Group in the beginning."

Tomlinson retied her strawberry blond ponytail, careful not to let the tightly wound curls get away from her. She went on to explain how Heberling leveraged his knowledge of finance to raise money for Verity's mysterious purpose. At first they provided a broad range of financial products, then broadened their scope to include physical product in the form of proprietary inventions. It wasn't long after they had begun that Verity Group was transformed into the Fortune 100 investment firm known as Verity Corp.

"Fascinating." Foster looked down at his watch then at the bar.

"If it makes you feel any better, we're not sitting out here because of that book."

"Why am I sitting out here? Do you even know yourself?"

"What we do is important, George," she said as she loosened her tie. "Maybe you'd rather go back to babysitting celebrities in Miami?"

"That, I understood!"

The professor came out of the bar and spotted them almost immediately. He stepped into the street, adjusted the strap of his travel bag, and started toward them.

"Crap. What's the play?" asked Foster.

Tomlinson looked down at the bright, green flier in her partner's hand.

"You're holding it."

#

Earlier that morning, Tomlinson and Foster were in New York City signing out one of Global Armour's black, unmarked SUVs. They had received a report from fellow agent, Ben Royce, that Askew had broken his morning routine. The two agents were told to relieve Royce, pick up

Station 12: The Lantern Society

Askew's trail, and document his movements without making contact. When they reached the prearranged rendezvous point, Tomlinson double-parked on busy Canal Street, causing angry drivers to sit on their car horns. Foster ignored it and asked Royce for a report.

Royce shrugged. "He's got a bag with him. That usually means travel. His regular coffee joint's just a couple of blocks up Crosby, but he doesn't usually head there this early in the morning."

Royce glanced across the street, his eyes pointing out Askew as he poked around the Chinatown stalls. Tomlinson thanked her fellow agent then watched as Askew turned the corner onto Crosby.

"Stick your hand out," Tomlinson instructed as the vehicles stuck behind them continued to honk their displeasure. She stayed cool as she crept across the opposing lane of traffic to follow Askew up the street. Just before stepping into a shop called Janice Coffee, Askew stopped and removed something from a light pole.

"Pink flier," she said and brought a small pair of binoculars up to her eyes. After confirming that Askew had seated himself, she parked the SUV.

Foster stepped outside the vehicle, out of Askew's line of sight, and lit a cigarette. He was an imposing presence in his black trench coat, black, close-cropped hair, and dark aviator sunglasses. Tomlinson took her eyes off her target long enough to look at him, wondering if maybe Global Armour hadn't made a mistake in hiring him. She found Foster too restless, too impatient in the job, and you had to have patience to work for Gorokhovich. After a tour in the military and a career as a city cop, she was sure his new role as professional lurker was horribly tedious by comparison. She wasn't judging Foster. On more than one occasion she wondered whether the work suited her, or if she suited the firm. But fate had intervened. Tomlinson had been searching for some much needed guidance when Gorokhovich found her, so she accepted the path he put her on. With mixed emotions, she did as she was told, and as time went on, she made that path her own.

"Maybe he's meeting someone?" Foster asked between drags on his cigarette.

"We'll see," she said absently. "Keep that smoke out of the car."

Foster tossed his cigarette with a roll of his eyes and resumed his seat. He asked Tomlinson how long Askew had been a target of surveillance. She informed him that it had been just over a year, since the day Global Armour was formed. He nodded as he started doodling in his notebook.

"You were there?"

"I was. I helped put all this together after I retired from the force."

Foster shot her a look of doubt. He didn't think she could be older than her mid-thirties.

"There was an incident back in Chicago," she said. "I was floundering as a cop, so I left the force when the opportunity presented itself."

"Global Armour?"

"There were six of us then, including Gorokhovich. Just about twenty now."

"Was it worth it?"

"Gorokhovich plays things close to the vest, but some weird shit is going on, George. Even if I don't understand it, I'd like to think I'm doing some good."

"So what about this incident?"

"Gorokhovich approached me about a missing persons' case he was working on. A friend of his, another cop."

Tomlinson stopped and considered her next words. She knew if she revealed the truth of it, it would change how Foster saw the company. It would change his perception of her.

#

Officer Tomlinson pawed through the collection of stuffed animals, trying her best to pick out the most masculine of the menagerie. She grabbed a small tiger by the tail and held it up for inspection. Her interim partner, Don Casey, found himself at a loss for words.

"I don't know what to tell you, Jackie. Artie'll love it? I don't fuckin' know."

Tomlinson threw the animal back in frustration. "Well, what would you get him?"

"I'd want a cheeseburger."

"Keep eating them. You'll be in here soon enough."

Two nights earlier, Tomlinson's regular partner, Arthur Pendente, had taken a bullet in the shoulder during a drug raid. The injury wasn't life threatening, but it did buy him a short stay at Northwestern Memorial Hospital. Upon his release, Pendente would be placed on paid suspension until a mandatory investigation was performed.

It was while Tomlinson was searching through the zoological bean bag collection that a distinguished, middle-aged man entered the hospital gift shop. His hair and beard were neatly coifed, his rain coat buttoned and belted. As he approached, Tomlinson and Casey exchanged a knowing glance. Tomlinson hid her disappointment that she and Pendente hadn't spoken since the incident. She had hoped they might compare stories in order to avoid a prolonged investigation over something insignificant.

The man stopped in front of her, almost smiling, with a look of recognition. He seemed to be waiting for her to start the conversation. Tomlinson only furrowed her brow.

"Jackie Haskell?" the man finally asked in a vague accent.

"Tomlinson. You got it half right," she said.

"Do you mind if we have a little chat, Officer Tomlinson?"

She looked again at Casey who nodded knowingly and watched as the stranger led Tomlinson into the lobby. He asked her if she'd like a cup of coffee. She, in turn, asked him if it was mandatory. He laughed and told her he was buying as he walked over to a nearby coffee cart.

The man didn't look like any cop she'd met before. He was a little too tidy, a little too put together. Fussy, maybe? Tomlinson looked back toward the gift shop and saw Casey heading to the elevators with, if she wasn't mistaken, a small, stuffed tiger sticking out of his shopping bag and she smiled warmly.

The stranger returned with the coffees and gestured toward a seating area.

"Here you go," he said, "light with three sugars."

Tomlinson felt a chill. The man sat down and asked that she join him, to which she slowly complied.

"How do you know how I take my coffee?"

"I know a lot about you. Well, I did once upon a time." He looked at her again with that same look of recognition, only this time he asked, "You really don't know me, do you?"

"Should I?"

"I suppose not. It's fascinating!"

"You're not IAD."

"Why would you think that I was?"

"Well, who the hell are you?"

"I'm an old friend of your husband's."

Tomlinson gave a small laugh. "Wrong again. I'm not married."

"No. No you're not," he said with convincing sadness. "Such a pity."

Tomlinson was getting angry. The man wasn't there to investigate the shooting. She'd gotten nervous over nothing. At the same time, there was something about him.

"You still live on Beacon Street, yes?" the man asked.

"What's this about?"

"You and Tommy used to have the most wonderful barbeques in that yard. Every summer. Every fall."

"Listen, asshole, I don't know who the fuck you are, or who Tommy is, but you're starting to creep me out. Keep it up and you'll be looking at a harassment charge."

"I'm sorry, Jackie...Officer Tomlinson, I didn't come here to cause trouble for you."

Tomlinson started to get up. "Thanks for the coffee."

"I came to offer you a job."

"What?!"

Tomlinson shook her head at the non-sequitur. He stared deeply into her eyes, hoping he could somehow make a connection.

"Would you give me a few minutes of your time to explain?"

Tomlinson wasn't curious by nature. She knew she wasn't which was why she didn't think she'd have made the best detective. But curious or not, in front of her sat a man prepared to explain how it was she had no recollection of being married to a man named Tommy Haskell.

"Knock yourself out. But make it quick."

"Have you ever imagined your life differently? What might have been had you made different choices?"

"I don't look back."

Her gut told her she was being played, but her muted curiosity began to open up her heart.

"What would you say if I told you, you once lived a completely different life, in a completely different reality? Everyone did."

"I'd say you're crazy and walk away. Is that what you're telling me?"

"In this other reality, you left school after two years and went to Police Academy. That's where you met my friend, Tommy Haskell. He was a cadet, too. You dated for two years until one day he popped the question at the Lincoln Park Zoo."

This startled her. She had always fantasized a proposal in the rain forest house among the many chattering birds. Against her wishes, she found herself intrigued by his tale and he sensed it. He continued, picking up his pace in the hope of reeling her in.

"Shortly after you were married, you transitioned from beat cop to Community Relations. You loved that job. Every neighborhood knew Officer Jack and you were proud to represent the Chicago P.D. You were happy then. Not so much now, I think?"

Tomlinson's anger calmed to a simmer as she reflected on his question.

"I tell you, this other life really happened, Jackie. It's not something I conjured up in my imagination. We were very good friends, you and I. And everything you had, everything that you were, was stolen from you."

"By who?"

"I can't tell you that."

"How do you know this?"

"I can't tell you that either. Not yet. Here's what I can tell you: My name is Anton Gorokhovich. Myself and a few others are investigating anomalies like yours. We'd like you to join us."

"How on Earth can you imagine that happening?"

"You don't have to believe my story. It doesn't matter. Maybe it's time for a change. Maybe the police force is no longer for you."

"What would you know about it?" Tomlinson remained angry but her reasons kept changing.

"I do my homework. I know the PD wants to promote you. I know you are reluctant to accept."

"You say you know my house. You've been there?"

"Oh, yes, many times."

"Describe it."

Gorokhovich provided Tomlinson with the layout first. She knew he could have gotten into her place or gotten his hands on a floor plan, so she asked for more detail, something less tangible. He paused and walked through memory, smiling when he came upon a fond recollection. He began to speak of her den, his favorite room in the house. Both she and Tommy had put so much of themselves into it. They could never agree on the color, so two walls were painted light salmon and the other two they painted coral blue. He went on to describe the various pictures on the walls as well as the variety of knickknacks placed throughout.

"There was a rocker in the corner of the room," he said. "And draped across the back of it was a large quilt that you'd made with your niece."

"Cindy?"

"You worked on it whenever you were together. It took a year to make. You were having trouble conceiving a child at the time, so you treated your niece as your own. But in your heart, you were hoping that someday you would be able to wrap the quilt around your own child. I know this because you told me. You told me many things."

A million thoughts ran through Tomlinson's mind. Gorokhovich's story fit too comfortably in her mind and she found that distressing. Though nothing he'd said had actually transpired in her life, it all felt somehow feasible. The house he described could have been her house. She'd never made a quilt with Cindy, but she could have, maybe even thought about it. Before her sister's family moved to Denver, she did treat Cindy as her own, filling an empty space in her life she never outwardly acknowledged.

Gorokhovich had struck a nerve. It was true, she felt incomplete and unsatisfied. The police force wasn't filling the niche she thought it would, and she didn't care for the us-versus-them relationship she had to live with every day. It was like living in another plane of existence; those who wore the blue and those who didn't.

Staring at Gorokhovich, she thought carefully about what she would say next. Would he be sent packing or given more time to explain his preposterous fantasy?

"What was I like?"

#

Foster's olive skin tone concealed the flush that came to his cheeks. He didn't think Tomlinson was deliberately screwing with him, but he still felt he was being played a fool. To what end, he couldn't guess, and that only added to his frustration.

Tomlinson grew embarrassed for having mentioned the encounter. She hoped Foster would dismiss it and let the matter drop. Incredibly, her embarrassment stemmed from the envy she felt toward the woman Gorokhovich portrayed in his story. The only life Jackie had known was a lonely one, riddled with doubt, both personally and professionally. The Jackie Tomlinson described by Gorokhovich was happily married, socially available, and happy in her work. Envy, hell, she was full blown jealous. She had taken up with Anton Gorokhovich to aid him in his nebulous cause. At least that's what she told him and herself to a certain degree. But really, she was chasing after a figment of his imagination, hoping against all odds that something could be done to reacquire a life that never was.

Foster crossed his arms and exhaled heavily. He stared at the pink, jagged line that ran along the line of his partner's jaw and wondered what fantastic story was behind that.

"Ted Burgess brought me in from Miami," he said, deciding to change the subject. "I was working freelance security, baby-sitting, really---."

"I know all about you, George," Tomlinson said, almost sulking.

"Yeah. So, I come all the way from Miami and sit through the Global Armour orientation with two other rookies---."

"Do you have a question, Agent Foster?"

"It seems to me that Global Armour's a security firm with plenty of money but no clients."

"We're subsidized."

"Subsidized."

"By a company with mutual interests."

"A company with a mutual interest in Verity Corp?"

"George," Tomlinson's tone indicated she was starting to lose patience, "we each perform a very specific function, but all of it is highly sensitive. Trust me; we're doing very important work."

She turned again toward the shop and raised the binoculars to her face. Foster reached in the back of the car and grabbed a bottle of water.

"Yeah, that's what Gorokhovich said."

#

On his first day at Global Armour, Foster was performing the rookie task of making the morning coffee when an impeccably dressed young man entered the kitchenette.

"Mr. Foster?"

"That's me."

"Come with me, please."

The young man turned and walked away and Foster had to hustle to catch up. He looked the man up and down and decided, based solely on instinct, that he didn't like him, pegging him as a self-righteous, little toady who held himself in high regard. Addressing Foster as Mister rather than Agent only exacerbated his dislike.

"My name is John, Mr. Foster. I assist Lenore Devlin. Ms. Devlin is in charge of Global Armour's field operatives."

John appeared to be walking at a normal pace, but Foster was having a hard time keeping up without feeling ridiculous. After turning a number of corners, the two men arrived at a reception area with a spectacular view of the financial district. A flat screen was showing a slick industrial film that introduced Global Armour to the empty lobby every twelve minutes.

"Have a seat, Mr. Foster. I'll let Ms. Devlin know you're here."

Foster nodded without saying a word. Charged and feeling good about landing this new role in the apparently high end firm, he was too excited to sit. It was a fresh start, he thought, and this time he would be able to hold his head high and do some good in the world. He walked to the windows to take in the view and noted the large 'VC' on the top of the nearby Verity Corp building.

Lenore Devlin stepped out of a dark hallway and made her way toward Foster with her hand out. She was wearing smart business attire; dark skirt, matching jacket, and a white blouse underneath. Silver, wireframe glasses did their best to soften a rather severe-looking face, sharp and somewhat pinched. Her eyes were a transparently pale blue and practically disappeared in her wan face. Her dark hair was pulled into a bun exposing simple, silver stud earrings. Foster felt like a schlub by comparison, in baggy, black pants, blue shirt with the sleeves rolled up and his black and blue, striped tie loosened at the neck. John was nowhere to be seen.

"Agent Foster, good to meet you," she said with a firm handshake. A wide smile that split her face from ear to ear revealed neat, white teeth. "I'm Lenore Devlin, Chief Investigator for the firm. Would you come with me, please?"

She turned and walked back toward the dark hallway. Once again, he had to trot to keep up as he followed obediently.

"Congratulations on finding a place in our growing family."

"Thanks. It's great to be here."

"Ordinarily, we would have met during the interview process but we are not an ordinary firm. How are you settling in? How is Agent Tomlinson treating you?"

"Great. Everything is great so far."

"I'm glad to hear that. We do very important work here."

The statement struck him as erroneous and planted a tiny seed of doubt in his mind that the upcoming orientation would later sow into a fine crop. At that moment, however, all was still right with the world.

At the end of the dark hallway stood a door with a nameplate that read simply, Anton Gorokhovich. Devlin knocked and entered an oversized office with an equally impressive desk as the focal point. There was a reading nook on the left side of the room and a meeting space on the right. Heavy drapes kept much of the daylight from penetrating the room, casting a rather gloomy pall. Tall plants worked hard to lift the room's spirits, however, as did an eclectic art collection.

"Mr. Gorokhovich, I'd like to introduce you to George Foster, our newest agent reporting to Jackie Tomlinson."

A strapping, middle-aged man stood up from his desk and walked briskly to meet them.

"Agent Foster," Gorokhovich said, shaking his guest's hand, "a pleasure. You're so lucky to be working with Jackie. She is a very capable agent, very conscientious. Please, sit with me a moment."

Gorokhovich directed Foster toward two leather wingback chairs on either side of a coffee table composed of wrought iron and glass. In the center of the table sat a peculiar art piece. Intricately designed blue glass, it somehow manifested a glow and looked as if it had been made by an extremely talented artisan.

"I want to welcome you to Global Armour, Agent Foster. I am Anton Gorokhovich and I started this firm a little over a year ago. As the name suggests, we keep our eyes open to potential threats to both the United States and the world at large. We're a private concern with no government contracts. This means we can set our own agenda."

So far it wasn't anything he hadn't heard from the recruiter or the interview panel. Foster was keen on learning what this 'important work' he kept hearing about consisted of and what his role would be in its pursuit.

Gorokhovich picked up a file folder and began to thumb through it. The silence stretched on and Foster grew uncomfortable, then a little impatient, though he kept that to himself under Devlin's steady gaze. Then he thought he heard a hiss, or whistle, and looked around the room for the source. Devlin offered no reaction, but Foster was sure he'd heard it and from somewhere close by.

"You were with the Miami Police Department for quite some time," Gorokhovich finally said. "They made you a detective three years ago then laid you off eight months after that." He looked up at Foster. "How unfortunate."

"Very unfortunate." Foster rubbed his sweaty palms together.

"May I ask what happened?"

"Departmental cutbacks. Last one hired and all that."

"I see. No performance issues?"

"None."

"Were you acquainted with Detective 'Chick' Sanders during your tenure in Miami?"

"Yeah, I knew Sandy. We weren't buds or anything. He made detective about two months after I did. We were let go on the same day."

"Did you know he was hired back a week later?"

"I don't think so. They took him on briefly as a consultant to finish up something specific to his case load. That was my understanding, anyway."

"You understood incorrectly. They took him back and he suffered no interruption of pay. He is a Miami detective to this day."

Foster was stymied. Gorokhovich had no reason to lie, and he obviously went to great lengths to learn what he could about his new recruits. The more he thought about it, the more embarrassed he became, although it did explain a lot of strange behavior back in Miami.

"Agent Foster?" asked Devlin in an effort to bring him back into the conversation.

"Apparently I caught Agent Foster off guard, Ms. Devlin. Understandable. Tell me, Agent, what have you been doing since your departure from the force?" He tossed the folder back on the table.

"A little of this, a little of that. Most recently I was working for VIP Security in Miami. Just another body in a B-list celebrity's entourage."

Gorokhovich smiled. "So you would say that Global Armour is a step up?"

"Most definitely."

Gorokhovich rose and a startled Foster followed suit.

"It's very nice to have met you, Agent Foster. I want you to know that I appreciate your contribution to our cause. I'm sure you will work hard and fulfill the promise of our mission statement. We do have a mission statement, don't we, Len?"

"I believe there is one somewhere."

"We do very important work here, Agent Foster. We want to keep the world safe and every able-bodied contributor is greatly appreciated. If you have any questions, let Agent Tomlinson know. I'm sure between she and Ms. Devlin, any concerns that may arise will be properly addressed. Oh, and Agent Foster," Gorokhovich stepped closer, "I'm sure I don't have to tell you that everything we do here is highly classified. Top secret. Please speak to no one about our work, yes? No, I'm sure you won't. Thank you for stopping by."

Devlin led the way out of the office, shutting the door behind her. "You and Agent Tomlinson play a vital part in our organization, Agent Foster. The focus of our attention wields a lot of power and has the potential to cause all manner of trouble. On a global scale. We do what we do to ensure that that trouble is ameliorated. This way, please, we have a lot of work to do."

Yes, but what is it?

#

"The waitress brought him a cup of coffee."

"Great. Let me write that down." Foster did not write it down. "Let me ask you: We've been told we're monitoring a global threat. Given our focus on Askew and his cronies, I'm guessing the threat is Verity Corp."

"That wasn't a question." Tomlinson turned again to face Foster. "Global Armour never told you specifically that Verity Corp was a threat."

"And yet, here we are." Foster took a drink. "Would it be safe to say that Askew and Verity Corp play a major part in our monitoring of a global threat?"

"We've been told to watch Askew, avoid engagement, and report on his activities."

"Yeah, I get that." Foster shook his head and stepped out of the car to light another cigarette. "I'll be honest with you, Jack, I'm having a hard time believing we're the good guys."

"You should quit," said Tomlinson.

"What?!"

Tomlinson pointed at the cigarette. "You're not doing yourself any favors."

"So that's how it's going to be?"

Tomlinson held the binoculars out to Foster. "Your turn. My arms are getting tired."

Foster was tempted to stall his supervisor so he could finish his smoke, but he knew that wasn't going to happen. Not this early in the game. Not when there was the slightest chance that Global Armour was legit. He resumed his seat and put the glasses to his eyes.

"I don't understand why Global Armour insists on keeping its own agents in the dark."

"I don't understand why you can't just do what you're told and collect your sizable paycheck."

"Shit!"

"What is it?"

"I think he made us."

Almost in a panic, Tomlinson threw the SUV into gear and took off.

"What are you doing?" asked Foster.

"Avoiding engagement!"

#

Neither Tomlinson nor Foster said a word as they made their way through what would have been Global Armour's reception area if the firm had employed a receptionist or allowed walk-in traffic. But it was badge access only to their portion of the building's fortieth floor and the two agents walked in simmering embarrassment to their respective desks. Foster hung his coat on the locker door inside his cubicle while Tomlinson threw hers down in disgust on one of the guest chairs in her office. She attempted to blow a loose lock of her curly hair off her face but with little success.

She glared at a photo of Askew she had tacked to her bulletin board along with other photos, sticky notes, and various reports. None of it added up to much in her mind. Like Foster, and almost every other employee of Global Armour, the big picture eluded her.

Rain began to pour down silently on the other side of the tinted windows. Tomlinson took no notice. All she knew was that they'd lost their surveillance target, the one thing for which they were responsible. When the phone rang, she knew before turning her head what the number would read on the display panel.

"Hey," she answered as she took a seat on the edge of her desk.

"You underestimated the man," Gorokhovich said in lieu of a greeting.

Tomlinson blushed and mumbled her excuses as she forced the uncooperative lock of hair behind her ear. There was a pause while the man on the other end of the phone assessed her response.

"This is not good, Jackie," he said. "Have you briefed Ms. Devlin?"

Tomlinson looked up and saw the object of her boss's query at the door.

"She's just arrived."

"I'll leave you to bask in your shame then," he said with a trace of humor.

"Daniel Askew is an important part of Global Armour's agenda," said Devlin without entering. "He is the reason we do what we do. You know that, Agent Tomlinson. Agent Foster, would you step in here, please?"

Devlin asked both agents to sit while she stood at the window with her back to the darkening skies.

"We've seen this activity twice before. If he's carrying his travel bag, he's traveling. It's not rocket science. Something has happened to drag him out of his comfort zone and I want to know what it is. Find him. Find out what's got his interest. Go back to where you last saw him. Talk to any conceivable witnesses. You didn't see him when you circled back. Maybe he grabbed a cab. Check taxi manifests for pick-ups in the vicinity. Do whatever it takes to recover his trail. Agent Tomlinson, I put you on this detail for a reason. Don't let me down."

"We're on it, Len, we'll find him."

Devlin turned her attention to Foster who said nothing at first, but when he realized she was waiting for a response, he straightened up and repeated what Tomlinson had said almost verbatim. Devlin nodded without enthusiasm and exited. Foster closed the door behind her with an exasperated air.

"We fucked up, George! Two cops and we couldn't handle a simple stakeout. Let's just suck it up and get back to work."

"You want to talk to the waitress?"

Tomlinson chewed on the inside of her mouth as she tried her best to assume the mantle of detective.

"Call Verity. Try to book a meeting with Askew. For today. See what kind of response you get. If they say no, which they will, try a day or two further out. We want them to confirm he's going out of town. If he is, try to find out where and for how long."

"How do I do that?"

"Does your cell phone still have a Miami area code?"

It did.

"Ask if he's coming to Miami. You haven't seen him in years. Sound excited. Maybe they'll lower your expectations with the truth. While you do that, I'll check his credit cards for travel charges."

"Sounds like a plan."

Unfortunately, it wasn't a great plan. Foster was able to determine that Askew was away indefinitely but couldn't get them to budge on the destination. Tomlinson had even less luck; Askew had one Visa card and one American Express in his possession and there were no travel charges on either one. Foster pointed to the report.

"This is new."

"A courier service."

Foster shrugged as if they were staring at the obvious. "He's going out of town with just that little bag?"

"He shipped his luggage."

"That's what I'm thinking."

Her eyes glinted as another idea came to her. She picked up the phone and dialed a four-digit extension. "Hey, Jen, Jackie Tomlinson. Haven't we done business with Citywide Courier?"

#

Within minutes the two agents had covered the three blocks that separated Global Armour from the Verity Corp building. Tomlinson carried a briefcase and a clipboard leaving Foster to hold the rain-soaked umbrellas. She finished her explanation of what was about to transpire then handed him her trench coat and her tie and unbuttoned two buttons on her blouse.

"What are you doing?" Foster asked.

Tomlinson shrugged. "Couldn't hurt."

"A pair of socks might help," he said, teasing.

"Nice," she said without embarrassment. She turned and made her way into Verity's lobby leaving Foster to stare up at the rain through the transparent awning.

At the Security Desk Tomlinson waited her turn as each visitor ahead of her signed in. Within minutes it was Tomlinson's turn.

"Hey, Cliff," she said, after reading the guard's brass-finished name tag. "I work for Citywide Courier and I need a huge favor. Two of my guys just made a pick-up here this morning, buncha stuff for..." She flipped through the pages on her clipboard. "...for Daniel Askew. They missed this briefcase and it's real important that it gets to where it's going before Mr. Askew does. Thing is, I can't reach my guys on the radio so I don't know where it's going. Does any of this make sense? I'm running around like a crazy woman and I am losing it!"

She laughed and pulled on her blouse as if to fan some air across her chest and tried her best to make some meaningful eye contact. He smiled back but didn't appear to be bowled over by Tomlinson's warmth and charm.

"You want to deliver it today?" he asked.

"Right now, if I knew where I was going. Can you help me, please? Citywide does a lot of business with Verity Corp and I don't want to screw that up."

The guard took a moment then picked up the house phone. "I'm gonna need to see some ID."

"Oh, sure. Thank you!" She felt all her pockets and came up empty. "Oh, man, I left everything in the van. All I have is my business card." She handed it to him and he frowned in doubt as Tomlinson continued to plead her case silently.

"Hey, Mags, Cliff Benson over here at Verity Corp. I have a Deb

London here from Citywide Courier. She said we had a pick-up this morning? Askew, right. Well, she's got a briefcase that should have gone with the rest of the stuff. She's delivering it herself but she doesn't know where it's going and she can't reach her team. Uh huh. Downtown Marriott in Hartford, Connecticut. Okay, thanks. Alright, I will." He hung up the phone. "Mags says the mailroom says hello."

#

When Askew stepped out of the Republic Café, he headed straight for Tomlinson and Foster. Neither agent was prepared for a meet and greet, but it was clear one was about to take place. Foster looked to Tomlinson for guidance and in the short time it took Askew to cross the street, she was able to provide it. It was a long shot, but she thought it was worth a try.

By presenting Askew with the Lantern Society flier, Tomlinson hoped to put the focus on a third party, to make it about something other than Verity Corp and Global Armour. Askew's interest in the Lantern Society was the perfect opportunity to convince him that they shared a common interest and hopefully ease his suspicion. On the surface, it seemed to work. Askew gave it some thought before he pocketed the card and walked away.

"So much for avoiding engagement," said Foster.

Tomlinson let loose a sigh and nodded. "Couldn't be helped. Anyway, we're better off than we were."

"You think? Why do I get the feeling Gorokhovich would not approve?"

"Let's not tell him just yet."

"So, what happens next?"

"We call it in. Let the base know we're back on track. Then we wait."

The sun broke through the overcast and showered the damp streets with light more indicative of the true time of day as opposed to the false night of the passing storm. Tomlinson and Foster drove away in search of a place to wait out the night. There was no sense of urgency. They knew where to find him. Both agents wondered what would come of their unexpected rendezvous.

If Tomlinson was being honest with herself, something had

changed in her when she handed the odd-looking man her business card. By merging her world with Askew's, she somehow legitimized her personal mission, as if meeting Askew allowed her to live life outside the box she'd constructed. If there was any truth to Gorokhovich's story, she was determined to find it; determined to find the happiness that somehow eluded her in this life.

Foster was pleased with their current progress. Maybe there would be more to the job after all, he thought. Perhaps this new reality would satisfy.

Chapter Four: The Turncoat

It felt like his last day on Earth. Heavy rains, adding to the full weight of his guilt, poured down on Charles Anderson, and he thought he might dissolve beneath them. Almost hoped for it. He was soaked to the bone, crouching beneath an awning that stuck out just far enough to accomplish the opposite of its intent. His normally sandy-colored hair lay dark and defeated on his skull as water flowed down both sides of his clean-shaven face to cascade off a strong, deliberate chin. People walked past him, some staring, some with no interest whatsoever, distinguishing the tourists from the indigenous New Yorkers. Anderson was oblivious as he obsessively wiped the blood spatter from his cheek.

As his recent adrenaline rush came to a crashing end, Anderson, almost out of body, began to feel a curious disconnect from the world. But as tempting as it was to escape the world he'd only recently constructed, he knew that unless he was ready to commit to the sensation and let slip his faculties utterly, the misery he had brought upon himself would only be compounded. If he were found crouching there in the rain, staring off into space with a million dollars in cash in his lap, the consequences would be dire. And so he began to make his way back to the troubled landscape of reality, searching within himself for something familiar to act as a guide. In the water-logged recesses of his mind, he found the drone of a dial tone and followed it through the circuitous route of his memory, a trail that terminated at the telephone call that put the course of his life on a lonely and dangerous road.

Shivering, his mind returned to his body on Astor Place. His shirt, wet, transparent, but deceptively heavy, clung to him like a second skin. He looked up at the charcoal sky, slate-colored eyes unblinking in the rain. His righteous cause now officially at an end, any justification he once had for turning on his employers was stolen from him the moment the shots were fired in Tompkins Square Park.

The rain stopped abruptly and Anderson began to laugh.

#

Station 12: The Lantern Society

It came about quite innocently. Charlie Anderson realized one day that not all was what it seemed at Verity Corp. As Verity's top recruiter of new investors, and manager of the company's largest portfolios, Anderson not only attended the monthly product meetings, he was the only non-Witness allowed to do so. Each second Tuesday of the month, he and Sheryl Bluth of Marketing and Sales, along with Rachel Henderson and her team, gathered together to plan their sales strategy and discuss the newest gadgets and gizmos that were about to be released into the public market. Max Heberling and Professor Askew were often in attendance, as well. Anderson likened it to grown up Show and Tell, complete with mimosas and a decent continental breakfast. As an avid fan and collector of Verity tech, he looked forward to these gatherings.

After one such product meeting, Anderson strolled through the second floor showroom reading the descriptive placards for the dozen or so new or upgraded items. In one corner of the room, poking out from beneath a blue, floor length tablecloth, he stumbled upon a large, wooden box. Actually more of a crate than a box, there were bits of straw sticking out from between the slats and a stencil of a telescope painted on each side. He looked around then quietly pushed the top aside, feeling around to see what goodies the scientists had held back. As his hand made contact with a hard, smooth surface, he was startled by a woman's voice.

"Can I help you find something, Charlie?" Ellen Cheever walked up to him as he withdrew his hand in surprise.

"Ellen! You got me. Just sneaking a peek at what was left out of the demonstration."

Cheever, Rachel Henderson's second in command, practically pushed Anderson aside. She stepped up to the crate and replaced the top. "This was a mis-ship. It was supposed to go straight to the lab."

"Looks like a telescope."

Picking up a nearby hammer, she pounded the nails back through the top of the crate. "They were going to scrap this project!" she shouted over the noise. "These new parts might rejuvenate it. Anyway, it'll be awhile before it sees the light of day."

"Come on, Ellen." Turning on his salesman's charm, he said with a manufactured twinkle in his eye, "Just a peek?"

Cheever smiled pleasantly but didn't budge. Anderson shrugged and walked away. Almost immediately, Cheever waved an attendant over and asked to have the crate removed. Charlie had gotten to know Cheever fairly well and their interactions were usually quite friendly, but there was something a little odd between them just then. Something abrupt. He didn't dwell on it and soon forgot the incident entirely.

It wasn't long after that Anderson discovered a hidden door in the Verity lobby. Actually, it wasn't so much a discovery as a late observation. Past the ground floor reception desk and turnstile entry sat an additional reception desk. It seemed to him to serve no obvious function. Surrounded by a veritable forest of potted trees, it resembled a concierge desk at a tropical hotel or perhaps Disney World. He half-expected to hear birdsong every time he passed it. Behind the desk was a good-sized waterfall with an eight foot drop into a lit pool. When he first started working for Verity Corp, he thought the desk provided additional security in a post 9/11 world. Later he revised his thinking, concluding that it was there to check people in and out of the ground floor display room, a room which doubled as a kind of historical record and public showcase of Verity's technical achievements. Neither was the case.

One day he noticed a flicker of white moving through the micro forest and watched as it disappeared behind the waterfall. Later he saw others walking the path and all of them wore the white lab coats of Verity's science division. He asked Henderson on numerous occasions what was behind the façade. She responded each time with a slightly different answer, mentioning a lecture hall at one point and a training facility at another. The last time he asked, she said it was set aside for strategic planning…science team only. She had come off a little curt, so he didn't bring it up again.

Anderson continued to note a number of trivial issues. Taken separately, they didn't seem to mean much. Added together, they cast Verity Corp in a questionable new light and he wasn't sure he liked what that light revealed. Paying close attention to the quiet corners of the office, he noted clandestine cubicle discussions and secretive looks among the scientists. It was subtle, but he knew he could never see Verity Corp the same way again. That was the funny thing about paranoia: once it got a grip on you, it was hard to shake it loose. The company that had taken him to the next level of his career, the company he held in such high esteem, was beginning to reveal a different side of itself, a darker side. Anderson was growing increasingly uncomfortable in his role as pitchman and 'fundraiser.'

One of the Verity white coats was a good friend of his from Chicago by the name of Hugo Jascowitz. It was Jascowitz who had recruited Anderson to Verity Corp when Verity restructured their marketing department. The company had decided they needed some new blood from outside their family of Witnesses. Hugo, who hadn't seen his friend in several years, didn't hesitate to reach out to him when the opportunity presented itself. Anderson had a decent job back in Chicago, but his career had peaked. He was itching to take on more responsibility and possibly add another digit to his salary. New York was always on his radar and Hugo's call was all the motivation he needed to make the move.

Unfortunately for Jascowitz, the unintended blowback of his good will was that he was forced to listen and weigh in on Anderson's eventual suspicions concerning Verity Corp. He often played along, asking as many questions of Anderson as the reverse, trying to get to the root of Anderson's paranoia. The more Anderson explained himself, the funnier it seemed to Jascowitz who had a talent for rephrasing Anderson's questions in a way that made him look ridiculous.

Anderson had gotten nowhere with Henderson in regards to the hidden door behind the waterfall, so he confronted Jascowitz.

"It's a secondary lab," Hugo explained slowly, deliberately, to avoid saying more than he intended. "We've been instructed not to talk about it. The work is outside the scope of our standard output. We don't want to draw unwanted attention. I hope you understand, Charlie. I'm telling you this as a friend. Let it go! There are no conspiracies here. Only those in your mind."

Anderson couldn't let it go and was more determined than ever to supply Jascowitz with evidence of…something…before he brought his suspicions up again.

He never got the chance. Two years almost to the day of Anderson's start date, Hugo Jascowitz seemed to vanish from the face of the Earth. He couldn't be raised by telephone. There was no response to personal or professional email. Anderson asked around the company and was shocked to discover that no one outside of the Science Division had ever heard of Jascowitz. He approached Henderson about it, and Cheever, but they had little or nothing to say, fluffing it off as a leave of absence, or sabbatical, until eventually they said nothing at all, claiming ignorance.

Anderson went so far as to corner Heberling and Askew at one of the monthly product meetings.

"I'm sorry, Charlie," said Askew, "I don't work with Hugo directly. You probably want to speak with Lionel about it."

"Aren't you and Hugo friends?" asked Heberling. "If you don't know, we certainly don't."

"Perhaps Human Resources could be of some assistance?"

They couldn't. HR was steadfastly mum on the subject of Hugo's absence, citing confidentiality. Nor could they verify an officially sanctioned absence. Anderson suspected a broad range cover-up. He wondered if he had somehow gotten Hugo in trouble by talking to him. Despite Anderson's very real concerns, he was certain Jascowitz would find the whole thing hilarious.

For Anderson, Hugo's disappearance was the straw that broke the camel's back. Left to his own devices, and resolved to find an answer, he went to Jascowitz's apartment to investigate. He'd stopped by Hugo's apartment on several occasions since losing contact. On those occasions no one answered the bell. This time, though, he buzzed the Super. Together they collected the overflowing mail and let themselves into the apartment to look around. The Super told Anderson he hadn't seen Jascowitz in several weeks. This coincided with Anderson's last phone conversation with him. The police finally made an appearance at the Super's insistence but found nothing amiss, no sign of foul play. No missing person report had been filed by a family member, so the police wouldn't pursue the matter further.

Concluding that no formal investigation or follow-up into his friend's disappearance was going to be undertaken by either the police or Verity Corp, Anderson decided it was time to take matters into his own hands. This posed a problem; he hadn't a clue what to do next and thus found himself in an anxious state of limbo. This lull in forward progress started to bleed into his professional life. He found his motivation to perform his job had diminished considerably. Worse still, his obsessive search for the truth would eventually cost him the love of his life.

Anderson and Sarah Bismarck had been inseparable for the first year of their relationship. They enjoyed each other's company and shared their successes. It was a grand life in the big city. Even after Anderson began his crusade to unmask his employer, he was still able to enjoy the strong bond between the two of them. Sarah, like Jascowitz, listened to his stories, but took very little of it seriously. Unlike Jascowitz, however, she didn't antagonize him. Instead, she nodded appropriately and commented in such a way as to neither encourage nor discourage his course. Anderson was so self-absorbed, he had no idea he was being placated and continued venting freely.

After the disappearance of Jascowitz, though, things turned for the worse. Larger and larger gaps of time without contact began to pepper their courtship. Often Charlie would find himself at home, brooding over the mystery of Jascowitz's absence and his own never-ending pursuit of the truth. Sarah grew melancholy and confused over his apparent lack of interest in making things right. She finally cut him loose to pursue his demons without the outside interference of a relationship's responsibilities. Anderson acknowledged the gesture with genuine sadness, but refused to let his obsession go, allowing Sarah to walk away.

Yet where he allowed his romantic life to deteriorate beyond repair, he was reluctant to sever completely his ties to Verity Corp. It would be insane, he thought, to walk away from such a lucrative career. Besides, he knew that if he left Verity, he would lose what few resources he had at his disposal and accomplish nothing. It would have been as if Jascowitz had never existed.

The Lantern Society had been watching Anderson and saw him as a potential mole. In order to make that happen, they told him everything he wanted to hear. How they had come to choose him in the first place, Anderson didn't know, and he didn't pursue it, which he should have done. That was his first mistake.

Over the course of several weeks, the Society reached out to him with highly inflammatory, though unsubstantiated, information pertaining to his employers. They had been watching Verity Corp for some time, believing the company was covering up the truth about a credible global threat. Without specific details, Anderson refused to commit. As a numbers man, he didn't deal in abstracts, always black or white. The Society was relentless in their pursuit of him, however, and after a few weeks of correspondence with the group's primary representative in New York, he began to waver. When the Society said they were willing to add the issue of Jascowitz's disappearance to their agenda, well, that was all Anderson needed to hear. He added his name to the Society roster. That was mistake number two.

#

Anderson's eyes continued to stare into the dense ceiling of clouds. Having now regained his senses, his laughing stopped as abruptly as it had begun, much like the rain had done just minutes before. He stood up with a slim briefcase in one hand and a heavy Halliburton case in the other. Only his sodden appearance gave away that anything was amiss.

Anderson felt exposed and decided it was time to move on. Making his way to the nearest subway stairs, he caught the first train uptown. Instinct was leading him home to regroup and think about this new, dangerous world he'd made for himself. In the number six train, he wiped his cheek absently, trying to surrender to the train's steady, rhythmic motion. Everything had happened so fast! The telephone conversation he'd found rattling around in his rain-soaked memory had taken place only a week earlier. He saw himself in his mind's eye, seated behind his glass table, surrounded by the transparent walls of his thirty-ninth floor office in the Verity tower. Were the blinds drawn, he'd have had a stunning view of Governors Island and the Statue of Liberty on Upper New York Bay. Cut off from the sunlight, where his office usually glittered in anticipation of new and bigger commissions, it was, at that moment, more reflective of the cold, dispassionate light of a broken trust.

#

"You understand what you're asking me to do?" Anderson mumbled into his cell phone. "If I get caught, I lose everything. More than likely, I go to jail and everything I've worked for disappears. You, on the other hand, lose nothing."

He listened as his contact explained their position. Glancing furtively around his office, he imagined he could be seen through the blinds huddled conspiratorially over his phone.

"You're pushing past the comfort level of our agreement," he said. "Frankly, I'm a little uncomfortable having this conversation at my workplace. What's so important that I should risk my neck any further?"

Nodding, he ran his fingers through his hair, calculating, weighing his options, caught between Verity Corp and the Lantern Society. He wasn't used to being on the fence, the bulk of his life having been spent as a person with clear vision and goals. Part of him wanted to pull the plug on his relationship with the Society. Enough was enough, wrong was wrong. He had no concrete reason to believe a word they said. There hadn't been any tangible evidence that answers would be forthcoming anytime soon. Yet his doubts about Verity were constant. Maybe *they* were the bad guys. Maybe he had been working for the bad guys all along. It was all too much.

He was jotting down instructions on a Verity Corp Post-It note when a jarring knock on his frosted glass door brought Anderson to his feet, ending the call.

"Charlie…" Henderson said, poking her head in. Anderson stood there like a kid caught with his hand in the cookie jar. "Oh, I'm sorry. I didn't see you on the phone."

"It's fine," he said dismissively, his salesman charm quickly coming to the fore. "Come in, sit down. What can I do for you, Rachel?" He demonstrated how relaxed he was by retaking his seat and putting his foot up on the table. Henderson lifted one side of her mouth in a sort of sneer.

"Bravo. That was quite the performance."

Feeling the fool, Anderson placed his foot back on the floor.

"Thanks. I have another show at eight. What do you need, Rachel?"

"If you haven't already heard, Prof is taking a leave of absence. I'll be assuming his role in his absence, so I'd like you to run the product meetings in the interim."

"Why can't Science run the meetings? Most of that crap goes right over my head."

"Don't panic. Just stick to the high-level marketing and investment strategy and you'll be fine. But I want the meeting invites to come from Marketing."

"Fine. When is Askew leaving?"

"In a week."

She suggested they get together the following day to discuss the details.

"Is everything okay, Charlie? You look a little tense."

"Me? Never."

Henderson stood up to leave, looked around the darkened office, then back at Anderson, pointing her finger at him in mock accusation.

#

That one, secretive phone call led Anderson to the west side of mid-Manhattan a week later, around the same time Daniel Askew was purchasing an umbrella at Canal and Crosby Streets. Walking west on 50th Street, he could feel his heart beating in his chest. The job under consideration marked the first time he physically went out on assignment on behalf of the Lantern Society. His one previous act, outside of regular email reports, was to sign in the Lantern Society's designated hacker as a guest of Verity Corp. He then got the hacker access to whatever he needed to plant his code in the Verity mainframe. Yet he was only the facilitator. He convinced himself that it wasn't him doing a bad thing, it was them. It was the hacker and his cronies. It was the Lantern Society.

The upcoming job was real work; Charles Anderson versus Verity Corp. This deepened his commitment to the Society, and he didn't care for that at all. He was still straddling that fence, his full weight resting uncomfortably on the place where his legs met. With each step, the Society's objectives grew a little fuzzier. Anderson found himself again losing faith in both sides, stuck between two shady organizations. He now considered a clean break entirely.

Turning the corner onto 11th Avenue, he thought about the transaction he was being asked to facilitate. Apparently, a deal had been arranged between the Society and a third party whereby certain Verity secrets would be exchanged for cash. The Society's representative, whom Anderson had met face to face only twice before, had informed him that the Lantern Society was ready to move into an important phase of their work. An infusion of cash was essential to that effort. Ironically, Anderson wasn't privy to the secrets they were providing despite the fact that he was likely responsible for obtaining them in the first place.

Before he knew it, he found himself standing in front of a faded and forgotten factory, stuck forever in the 1970s. A plain, wooden sign, bolted onto the brick face, displayed sun-faded letters that read KupperDyne. An equally diminished logo showed a stylized jet aircraft encircled by a retro, but futuristic-looking, locomotive. Two entrances on the avenue were obviously no longer the way in. Neither had door handles and both were blocked by scrubby weeds that had pushed up through the cracks of the cement steps. So he made his way down the steep driveway instead.

A single car sat on a bleached, concrete lot; a black Jaguar with darkly tinted windows. Standing on an adjacent loading dock, two men were engaged in conversation. One man, short, and wearing a dark, patterned tie over a powder blue, short-sleeved shirt with a fully equipped pocket protector, appeared to be explaining something to a much taller man in a long, leather duster who nodded every now and again in acknowledgment. When the discussion wrapped, the two men shook hands and the tall man clapped the other on the shoulder before turning toward the lot.

Anderson withered beneath the big man's stare, wondering if maybe he'd trespassed, or had seen something he shouldn't have. Or maybe he'd come down the wrong driveway entirely. The man in the duster sized him up before jumping off the dock. His worn cowboy boots crunched loudly on the cracked and brittle ground. Dark, slick-backed hair reflected the gray-yellow light of the morning. The scar running down the side of his face reached out to Anderson objectionably like an unwelcome handshake. The man lit a brown cigarette, and just as Anderson was about to open his mouth, the big man opened his.

"Ed Donovan," he said in an unsurprisingly deep and gravelly voice. "You the Verity turncoat?"

"I'm supposed to meet---."

"I know why you're here." Donovan walked over to the Jag and opened the rear passenger door. He indicated with a jerk of his head that Anderson should get in. Anderson frowned, uncomfortable with the theatrics, but did as he was told.

Anderson was greeted warmly as the door closed behind him. As a salesman, he always liked to think that he had no equal when it came to charm, but the woman he sat next to put him to shame. She manifested an aloof but matronly aura that all was right with the world and that she was looking out for you. Anderson figured it probably made recruiting new members, particularly younger people, very easy. He noted her sharp business attire, immaculate, jet black hair, and the stylish eyeglass frames with pink lenses that helped to protect her eyes from the sun and scrutiny.

"Charles, it's good to see you again."

"There are no bad guys," Anderson began, trying to see past the pink veil. "Verity Corp is not our enemy in the traditional sense, but they are withholding information that's vital to each and every inhabitant of this planet. For that reason, they represent a global threat."

"So you've said."

"It's what our evidence suggests."

Anderson nodded disgustedly. "I've seen your fliers. Read your web page. Jesus, you're talking about alien invasion! You don't even try to hide it! Do you know how insane that sounds?"

"Again, based on our evidence. Yes. We're looking at a possible global incursion. But we've never said anything specifically about aliens, that is to say extra-terrestrials."

"Who else could invade our planet except for people not on it?"

The Lantern rep smiled but said nothing.

"Fine," Anderson continued, tabling the question temporarily. "Why don't we just tell everyone? Prepare them somehow?"

"We believe Verity is trying to avoid a global panic. In that, we understand and agree. But they're behaving irresponsibly. They can't possibly compete with the resources of the United States government, so what's the point of isolation? Unless they're up to something."

"Then why doesn't your Society inform the government?" asked Anderson.

"You don't believe us, why should they? We need more time, more evidence."

"What else have you got?"

"There's a steady flow of goods coming out of Verity Corp and they've amassed a fortune."

"Are you referring to our product?" Anderson asked, using the generic label Verity applied to the goods that came out of their lab.

"It's more than just new tech. In many cases, they've rounded the corner of bleeding edge. The source for those so-called trademarked ideas is highly questionable."

"Which is bothering you more? The fact that Earth may be invaded or that Verity Corp is getting rich on possibly alien technology?" Again, no answer. "I'm only doing this because I need to know the truth. I'm not sure that's possible anymore. I'm doing this for my missing friend. Don't for a minute forget our discussion on that point. I want to know what happened to Hugo Jascowitz."

The rep smiled in apparent amusement. "We haven't forgotten."

Anderson nodded.

"This isn't what you think, Charles."

"I'm not much of a thinker," Anderson said, frowning, "or I wouldn't have gotten into this mess in the first place. So, I'm going to go with my gut instinct, and my gut is telling me you're full of shit. That's okay. I'm still convinced you can get me to some version of the truth and for that reason alone I'll stick around and continue to do my part."

"Something is happening, Charles, and all of us at the Lantern Society are determined to find out what it is. This is what we've been telling you all along."

"You told me about a threat to global security. It has since blown up into something else entirely."

"We told you---."

"---what you wanted to tell me and that's your business." Anderson jerked his thumb toward the tinted window and lowered his voice. "But when I meet a man like Donovan, I can't help but wonder if I'm lying in the wrong bed."

The rep laughed softly. "Mr. Donovan may appear a Hollywood heavy, but believe me when I say he's not simply a mercenary looking for a payday. He knows what we're about and is in full support. We're coming to a critical milestone. I can't afford to have anything go wrong. Mr. Donovan maintains excellent crowd control and he keeps me safe, he keeps me secure, and therefore happy. Donovan's not an issue. Does that put your mind at ease? Can we talk now like civilized people?"

Anderson nodded slowly, unwilling to commit one hundred percent.

"Excellent. How are things at Verity Corp?"

"Quiet. From what I can see, it's business as usual for Heberling and Bellows, but Askew has taken a leave of absence."

"Has he? And where has he taken himself, I wonder?"

"Couldn't say. Rachel Henderson's running the show now. In her own way she runs a tighter ship than Askew. It would be smart for me to lay low until things return to normal."

"I agree. After today's assignment we'll suspend contact. We'll reach out to you again when the time is right."

The car window lowered. Donovan passed a briefcase through. Anderson swore he'd seen this movie before and he was embarrassed to be playing a role in it now.

"This is the merchandise. You'll be making the exchange with a representative of Bismarck Industries. Sarah Bismarck, in fact."

Anderson couldn't imagine hearing worse news. Now he understood how it was he was chosen for the assignment. *Maybe it's been their end game all along*, he thought. *Maybe it's why they recruited me in the first place.* He hadn't spoken with Sarah since he'd effectively ended their relationship.

"I'm sorry," he said, "that's not going to happen."

"She made the deal knowing it would be you on the other end of the transaction."

Those were the only words that could have kept Anderson in the conversation. "And how did she know it would be me?"

"We took advantage of your former relationship. The money is nothing to the Bismarck family. They're set for life ten times over. We desperately need those funds."

"You should have spoken with me first. Our relationship ended terribly. I find it hard to believe she has any interest in seeing me. You must have misunderstood her."

His contact held firm. Anderson thought he'd come too far to turn back now. A part of him was intrigued at the thought of seeing Sarah again and that she had expressed interest in seeing him.

"What am I selling?" he asked.

"It doesn't matter."

"No, I don't suppose it does," he said in resignation. "Can you tell me what the money's for? We are on the same team, aren't we?"

"Sometimes the best defense, Mr. Anderson, is a good offense. Ms. Bismarck is expecting you in Tompkins Square Park at 10:00. It's time for you to go."

Donovan opened the driver's door and got in. Anderson caught his eyes in the rearview mirror, crow's feet giving away a smile as his hand came up and tapped a listening device in his ear. Anderson didn't understand the gesture at first, but then flushed at the thought that Donovan might have overheard his earlier disparaging remarks.

#

The yellow shafts of light that had been fighting their way through the dark clouds earlier in the day had given up and the morning was passing prematurely into night. An ominous wind had begun to blow. June leaves flashed their silvery undersides toward the ashen sky as the first summer storm descended upon the city. Charles Anderson stepped out of the taxi and into Tompkins Square Park.

Two minutes late for his rendezvous, he hustled along the paved pathway that led to the park's south side. A few leashed dogs passed him on their way to the dog run, happily towing their owners behind them. Otherwise, thanks to the threatening weather, the park was nearly deserted.

When he reached the south easternmost corner of the park, he recognized immediately the outline and posture of his former love seated on a bench. A Halliburton case strapped to a luggage carrier stood within her reach. Anderson glided toward her on feet that had lost all feeling. Bittersweet memories crowded out coherent thoughts. The storm's cooling breeze was replaced in his imagination with the stifling grip of hot, moist air, as he remembered fondly the rooftop terrace of Sarah's upper eastside apartment. He watched her light candles, the Chrysler building shimmering behind her in the hazy summer heat. That thought gave way to other warm memories: romantic walks through quiet streets, removed from the hubbub of the city; fine dining on stiff, white, linen tablecloths with bottles of blushing rosé in the tucked away corners of Manhattan; nights filled with animated discourse made memorable by joyous laughter; and celebratory climaxes of intimacy that carried them to deep, blissful slumbers. The mornings found them mooning over omelets and hot coffee as they reminisced over day old memories. It couldn't be denied, he was excited to see her again. Excited, but nervous. The artifice of the arrangement, clearly outside the reality of their former relationship, caused a part of him, at least, to regret agreeing to the meeting.

Now that he could see her, he grew even more anxious, wondering if she could have forgiven him for what he'd done. He started to reach up to straighten his hair but pulled his hand back as he realized how ridiculous a gesture it was. When Sarah spotted him, she stood up, using the handle of the luggage cart for leverage, but remained in place. Anderson wondered if he should shake her hand, hug her, or even give her a kiss on the cheek.

"Hello, Sarah," he said, doing none of those things.

"Hi, Charlie," Sarah Bismarck replied sadly, trying her best to make eye contact but finding it difficult. Like Anderson, she wasn't sure how to behave. "This is weird."

"Yeah, it is," he agreed, with even less success at looking at her. "It's not exactly the reunion I would have planned."

There followed an uncomfortable pause. Anderson took a moment to take her in, to reacquaint himself with the woman he never stopped loving. At five foot ten, she carried herself like a model. Simply attired in a cowl neck sweater, denim slacks, and expensive boots, she somehow made it glamorous. Her makeup was perfect, but didn't take away from her natural beauty. Her blond hair was cut short like a man's and seemed to glow in the dark light. It was shaved in the back exposing a milky white and graceful neck that never failed to arouse him. Inappropriate thoughts began to manifest as his attention turned to the slight overbite that pushed out her pink upper lip. Then those eyes, those bright, hazel eyes that said so much without the need for words. So smart, so piercing. So self-absorbed was Charlie Anderson that he never noticed how much the two of them looked alike. That would come later when tragedy forced him to reevaluate everything in his life. When the realization finally came to him, it almost made him sick.

"Come on, Charlie," Sarah finally said, moving the meeting forward, "we're almost out of time."

Anderson threw her a quizzical look and when she looked up at the black clouds, he realized she was referring to the impending storm.

"Let's get this over with," she said.

"Maybe we could go somewhere else?" asked Anderson. "Maybe get some coffee?" The words were out of his mouth before he had given them any real thought. He tried to force a disconnect from the conditions that had brought them together and turn it into something that was his idea, something more personal.

"I think that's against the rules," she said and put an end to his outreach.

They sat down with Anderson's briefcase between them.

"How are things at Verity Corp?" Sarah asked. "Still chasing after conspiracies?"

"It's gotten complicated. Things aren't always what they seem. It's…complicated."

"You said that."

"What about you? Does your father know you're involved in corporate espionage?"

"I'm just protecting my family."

"From?"

"Come on, Charlie. Don't pretend you don't know what's in that briefcase. Don't pretend you and yours aren't safe from abduction. Only I have to pay for my family's safety! I'm not so lucky to be one of the privileged few that work for Verity Corp."

"Abduction?" Immediately, his mind turned to Hugo Jascowitz.

"You make me sad, Charlie. I thought we had something special. I know we did. You threw it away, and for what? Because you knew about the danger all along? Is that it? What, they wouldn't let you bring me in?"

"Whoa, whoa, Sarah, I'm sorry, but I don't know what you're talking about."

"That's convenient."

"What did you mean before about abductions?"

A shadow from her past fell across her face, dimming the light in her eyes. "You're thinking about Hugo."

Anderson said nothing and Sarah nodded.

"Let's just do what we came here to do," she said with disgust. "You've obviously got more important things on your mind. Take your money."

Anderson couldn't believe the weight of it as Sarah slid it across her lap into Anderson's open hands. She opened the briefcase and removed a single file folder while Anderson released the clasps on the money case. His eyes grew wide as he lifted the lid to reveal a huge amount of cash. Grabbing a stack of hundreds, he flipped through it like he'd seen so many times before in the movies, continuing to play his part. He was embarrassed to be so far out of his element.

"How much money is this?"

"Exactly what was asked for."

Anderson thought it could be upwards of a million dollars. He almost burst out laughing. Lying on the top of the money was a small, white card that appeared to be the combination for the briefcase. He pocketed it then locked the case. Sarah, meanwhile, was frowning as she scanned the contents of the file.

"Charlie, I'm only seeing the chemical half of the formula."

"Formula? I wasn't told---."

"I'm paying for the inoculation!"

"Inoculation?" His face reddened, which could have been interpreted as either a sign of shameful ignorance or a flush of guilt. "Against what?"

"What have we been talking about?! I was told by your partners in crime that I was purchasing the formula for Verity's inoculation against continuity loss and it isn't here. It's not complete."

Anderson's mind raced. He had no idea what information he had been supplying the Lantern Society except for the few items they shared with him on occasion for the purpose of keeping him tethered to their cause. In this case, though, they hadn't, he'd never heard a word about an inoculation.

"Sarah, I'm sure that file is everything that was promised you."

"We can synthesize the drugs, yes, but it won't work without the conditioning process."

"I don't understand. What process?"

Sarah looked hurt, not altogether differently than she did when she finally announced the end of their relationship. "Why are you doing this, Charlie?"

Thunder rolled in the distance. Anderson had no idea what Sarah was talking about and he began to sense a strange, negative energy dancing in the air. "I'm not---."

"Do you hate me that much? Do you want me to just disappear like all the rest?"

The first question stung badly, overshadowing the second.

"Why did you want to see me, Sarah?" he asked.

"See you? You broke my heart, Charlie."

"But...they told you it would be me..."

"It was never about you, Charlie. It was about my family. I wanted to know they'd be there when I woke up in the morning. It was never about you."

There was another clap of thunder, closer this time. Anderson saw clearly that he was being used. That they both were. The world started to close in around him. It was a little thing at the moment, like a hair at the edge of his vision, and for some reason he wished he hadn't given the Society rep such a hard time.

"I don't hate you, Sarah. I've never hated you."

"Bullshit! I don't know why I agreed to this. I was conned." She stuffed the file back in the briefcase and slammed it back on the bench between them. "I'm going to need my money back."

Anderson rested his right hand on the Halliburton. With a growing sense of urgency, he said, "I'm sure whatever it is you're trying to get your hands on, it's right here, it's in this case. Take it and go."

If the Lantern Society had what Sarah was looking for, they were withholding it for reasons unknown to him. Or maybe they didn't have it to give. Whatever the case may be, he saw no earthly reason not to return the money. At the same time, something in his gut was telling him that if this deal went south, something terrible would happen. An image of Donovan tapping his earpiece flashed through his mind and he looked out into the park, half expecting to see him out there, watching them. The world grew even tighter around him as an irrational fear took root.

"I want my money back, Charlie," she said. "This is worthless to me."

Anderson looked back at Sarah. His jaw went slack. A red dot danced on her forehead.

"Charlie?"

"Sarah."

He didn't hear a shot. He just watched Sarah's head pitch back. A spatter of warm blood hit his cheek. He leaned over her, saw her slumped into the corner of the bench. She looked as though she was sleeping, and he wanted to reach out and touch her face. She looked so peaceful. He didn't see the blood pool forming beneath the bench.

"Sarah?"

As he started to stand, a second gunshot took out the small memorial plaque on the back of the bench and with it the memory of Pearl Goldstein. Anderson grabbed both cases and took off running. It was then that the sky released the deluge that had been gathering all morning. The rain came in torrents and carried Sarah Bismarck's blood into the dirt.

#

If Anderson was a target, he couldn't go back to his apartment. And he couldn't reach out to his friends if there was the slightest chance their safety could be compromised. He was better off on his own, and as long as he had possession of the money, he had a safety net. He had to keep himself safe and out of sight. Find a place where he could rest and come up with a plan. *Jesus, this is insane!* Anderson jumped off the uptown train at Union Square and made his way over to the downtown 'R' train.

He rode back the way he had come, resting his head against the car window. In the reflection of the glass, he watched his hand rise to wipe Sarah's blood from his cheek and saw that it was no longer there, having long been washed away. He thought of her as he watched the passing tunnel lights and his eyelids grew heavy. Loneliness was what brought them together that first time and you never stopped loving the person who took away your loneliness. He realized, with her passing, that he was being selfish when he turned his back on her to pursue some ambiguous truth, and he would have to live the rest of his life knowing that he could never make it up to her. He had no strength to cry and perhaps not even the inclination, but his eyes welled up just the same. His hands remained in his lap as a tear rolled down his cheek and came to rest where Sarah's blood had been not so long before.

Chapter Five: The Sounding Tunnel

Ellen Cheever pointed her Gemlight at the rusty track, searching in growing frustration for a purple stone about the size of a ping pong ball. Verity's garish work lights were no help, serving only to illuminate the debris that had made the accidental journey to the long abandoned tunnel. She pawed through the food wrappers and newspapers in desperation, fully aware of the imminent commencement of the exercise. Stubbornly determined to locate the missing stone in time, she ignored the chirping radio on her hip.

Her Ready Team had disappointed her. They were responsible for prepping each Sounding Tunnel exercise, which made her responsible in the eyes of her supervisors. She hated looking inefficient due to other's sloppy work. The more she dug through the kipple, the angrier she became. Yet in her heart, she knew her frustration had nothing to do with the Ready Team or even the missing stone. In truth, Cheever was channeling her angst over the recently discovered data theft.

Verity Corp had been compromised in a big way. The idea of outsiders possessing Verity data was frightening as hell and she knew nothing good could come of it. Duplicating Verity tech could be much worse if not calamitously dangerous. Cheever tried to look at the theft strictly from a problem-solving perspective, but there were times when her defenses slipped. She occasionally found herself on the brink of panic, scared shitless that terrible things might transpire due to Verity's negligence. It didn't help her mood that there was no one with whom she could share her vague concerns outside of Henderson.

She clucked her tongue when the radio chirped again. Armando Jimenez's tinny voice sounded agitated.

"Ellen, our window is closing. Do we need to abort?"

"Someone didn't check all the attic doors, Armie. One of the purple stones has fallen out."

"Don't tell me that, El. You know how vital it is we maintain our existing inventory."

"I don't see it," said Cheever. "There's too much garbage down here."

"Garbage shouldn't matter, you know that. Have you got your torch set on six?"

Cheever looked down at the Gemlight and cursed herself when she saw the dial set at seven. She made the adjustment and immediately spotted the purple glow amidst the trash.

"Got it," she said, disappointed in herself as she picked up the gem. "I'll be right there."

"Let's hurry, El, Baker's going to start the countdown any minute."

Cheever looked up at the massive, metal ring that occupied the circumference of the tunnel. She set her Gemlight back to standard flashlight and scanned the undersurface for the gem's former residence. Along the inside of the Sounding Ring were a number of intermittent portholes of various sizes. The glass door to one of these hung open by a single hinge. Cheever hopped into the nearby cherry picker and raised herself to reinsert the stone, making sure to tighten all three screws on the tiny door. Power was restored to the Ring as indicated by a green light at its base and the slight auditory hum of a circuit reconnected. She reported back that Ring Six was Go for green.

"Copy that, Ellen. Now get back here pronto."

"On my way," she said, as she anchored the basket and positioned a control box in front of her. "Is Henderson there yet?"

"Dr. Henderson is standing right beside me."

Cheever flinched. "Roger that. Cheever out," she said, returning the radio to her belt. The cherry picker started down the tunnel.

There were other defunct railway passages beneath New York City, but the line Verity utilized was America's first attempt at an underground railroad. The project was scrubbed in its infancy after running into financial trouble, though it remained a focal point in a contentious political debate around the time of the Civil War. Consequently, the track ran a distance of about five city blocks beginning at the would-be historic East River Station, under the Wall Street neighborhood, and terminating at a dead end of solid rock. It would be thirty more years before America had a working subway.

Over the station's public address system, the resonant voice of Ty Baker announced, "Counting down from ten minutes. Mark."

Station 12: The Lantern Society

His rich, baritone voice made him a natural choice to be Verity's resident announcer, and he hadn't missed one tunnel exercise since assuming the role. He had become their lucky charm and when Baker commenced his countdown his coworkers took great comfort in the sound of his voice. Despite the inherent danger of each exercise, they knew that all was right with the world.

Time and politics had all but erased any memory of the tunnel's existence. The modern day citizens of Manhattan were oblivious to the activities taking place deep below the city's sidewalks. Above, the people of New York went about their day to day business. Below, Verity Corp worked around the clock in an ongoing effort to preserve a persistent state of reality. Above, the forty story tower housed Verity Corp's investment firm. The company's portfolio ran the gamut from short term certificates of deposit to complete financial planning for VIP clients. One of the unique features of doing business with Verity Corp was the opportunity to invest in emerging technologies; technologies created by some of the most brilliant minds in the world. Below, Verity's scientists used variations of these technologies to monitor and study the movements and purpose of the Trans-Dimensional Railroad and the plane of existence in which it resided.

Verity Corp had purposefully installed their corporate headquarters relative to this abandoned rail line. They bought and demolished the Rogers Hotel, building in its place their black monolith, connecting it to the East River Station. Verity dug deeper still and constructed a laboratory far from prying eyes. The 'Central Lab' was known only to employees who had seen the train with their own eyes or witnessed an abduction perpetrated by said train. It was these witnesses that Alan Griffin was tasked for locating and recruiting into Verity's work force, a once impossible job given that for a long time there wasn't a single human being on Earth who knew abductions were even taking place. Back then, so-called witnesses were written off as disturbed individuals without a firm grip on reality. Not everyone felt this way.

After listening to a number of accounts, a theory began to percolate in Askew's mind. Because so many disparate people were dreaming about abducted family members and friends with such consistency, he started to wonder if people were being spirited out of existence and reality rewritten to compensate for the loss. If true, people who had been kidnapped no longer existed, so no one would think to look for them. As preposterous as it sounded, it explained a lot. He believed the people the dreamers had concocted in their stories actually resided among them at one time.

Askew wasn't able to prove his theory, however, until he had devised his Inoculation Against Continuity Loss. It was an exhausting procedure no different than the most hardcore brainwashing. A subject was dosed with a potent series of pharmaceutical injections and guided through a process Verity shamelessly referred to as Perception Enhancement. Essentially a combination of intense visual and aural stimulation, it locked the subject in a single, ongoing and perpetual reality. The resultant hypnotized state negated the impact of the TDRR's visit and its subsequent realignment of reality. The theoretical application was proven to work during their controlled drug trials after they lost one of their bright stars in the marketing art department, a woman by the name of Cathy Cruz.

Askew arranged a small test group for the inoculation. Stipulating that every participant had to be a Witness, he made sure his hand-picked volunteers were spread across all departments. After receiving inoculation, they were tasked to observe their surroundings and note any unusual changes in their perceived reality. There was an added protocol that no one outside of the control group could be informed of those changes having taking place. Even if the changes seemed apparent.

Word got quickly back to Askew when Cruz vanished. Standing with Heberling and Bellows in front of what was Cathy Cruz's cubicle the previous day, they read Phil Burton's nameplate and looked over his belongings; his Simpson's action figures, his Derek Jeter bobble-head, and his inappropriate wall calendar. All of it appeared as if he had resided in the space for years. Cathy Cruz was no more. Not in body, not on paper, and not in virtual space. It was as if she never was. They began to understand what was taking place and the magnitude of the threat they faced. People were disappearing all over the country, all over the world. No one had the slightest inkling it was happening. Because somehow, as if by magic, it wasn't.

Ellen Cheever understood the magnitude of displacement. Though she had joined Verity Corp after Cathy Cruz's abduction, as an inoculated individual she had witnessed the impact first hand. She'd lost a valuable, new co-worker before he'd even had the chance to kick off his career. Ordinarily, once a Verity applicant had been approved by a hiring panel, the candidate would be escorted immediately to the Inoculation Room to align them with the reality of their new co-workers. Instead, a clerical snafu scheduled the recent college grad to come in the following day for both his inoculation and orientation.

The next morning, Cheever waited for David Lewis's nine a.m. arrival. He never showed. The hotel where he was staying had no record of a David Lewis. When she called his home in Virginia, they said they'd never heard of the man. Cheever calculated the odds of a Witness having a second encounter with the TDRR as astronomical. Factoring in that the Witness was due to be inoculated the next day, well, it was crazy. More and more, though, it seemed the horrible coincidence was the likely scenario. Cheever alerted Henderson of the tragedy. When Rachel resumed her search for a new Technician, to Cheever's relief, she opted to appoint an existing employee.

A warning horn echoed past her as Ellen made her way through a fairly utilitarian tunnel, past another Sounding Ring. As she got closer to the platform, the space above her opened up, displaying the station's originally intended architecture. The vaulted ceiling was laid out in a complex pattern of bricks and stone tiles that both framed and connected the huge, gas-fed chandeliers hanging every fifty feet or so. The tunnel was harshly lit by work lights, creating great contrasts of dark and light. Monstrous, immoveable shadows kept watch on the otherworldly activity that had occasion to pass by.

Baker announced nine minutes until Integration.

"Please clear the tracks and take your positions."

Cheever could see station lights ahead of her. The slow moving cherry picker would reach the platform in a minute, leaving just five to orient the new ADC at the Data Recording Console.

Henderson recently surprised Cheever with the declaration that the team had acquired a new assistant. He had been fast-tracked in order to participate in the morning exercise. In all the years Verity had been performing the Sounding Tunnel exercises, the Data Recording Console had never required an assistant. She found the change highly suspect and drew the preliminary conclusion that she was either being replaced, or that a new component had been added to the exercise. She gravitated toward the former explanation given all the time she'd had to devote to the data theft investigation. No doubt the issue would require additional attention going forward.

"Eight minutes to integration. Please check your stations and verify they continue to read green."

Cheever's radio chirped. This time she left it in its holster when she answered. She informed Jimenez that she had passed Ring Two and should arrive at the platform in less than a minute. Activating the track switch ahead of her, she parked the cherry picker off the main line. Not that it mattered. The TDRR didn't actually interact with the tunnel's physical space. The train would pass harmlessly through anything that blocked its path. It was one of the many anomalies associated with the mysterious railroad.

As the cherry picker approached the platform, Cheever had a clear view of the forward monitoring station. The station consisted of a long table equipped with a variety of digital still and motion capture cameras, all of which pointed at the tracks and down the tunnel. Dmitri Gusarov, her new subordinate at the Data Recording Console, waited patiently for her to join him.

"Seven minutes to integration."

Jimenez walked to the edge of the platform and waved. Cheever, with the look of the scapegoat about her, jumped off the cherry picker and made her way to him.

"You can see me on the monitors," she said as she brushed her short, black hair from her forehead.

"I'm sorry, was I bothering you?"

"The Ready Team made me look bad, Armie."

"I know."

"They have months between set-ups. Ample time to test connections and make sure everything's in place."

"I know, Ellen. We'll deal with it later."

Cheever accepted Jimenez's offer of assistance as she climbed the iron ladder. A female voice chimed in over the PA system.

"Are we all set now, Technician Cheever?"

Cheever looked up at the elevated glass booth in which Henderson stood and offered a tight smile and a thumbs-up. Jimenez took her by the elbow and escorted her to her station.

"Ellen, I want you to meet our new ADC, Dmitri Gusarov. Dmitri, Dr. Ellen Cheever, Chief Data Collector."

Cheever extended her hand and she and the burly Russian shared a firm handshake. Her eyes went from his flat face to the fluffy hair standing at attention on his block-shaped head. Cheever's boyish figure barely reached five feet in height. Gusarov stood only an inch or two taller. He was wide, with the bearing of an immoveable tree stump.

"It's a pleasure to meet you, Dmitri."

"Please, call me Goose."

"Six minutes to Integration," announced Baker. "Please check your monitors and confirm track vacancy."

"We'll have to continue the small talk later, Goose. We have work to do."

Jimenez threw on a headset as he walked away, tapping his clipboard with a pen. He visited each monitoring station in turn before joining Henderson and Baker in the booth. Cheever stepped up to the Data Recording Console and put on her headset and instructed Gusarov to do likewise. Pointing to the console in front of them, she explained what it was they were responsible for during the short window of the exercise. Gusarov nodded and did as instructed, keen on learning as much as possible.

"Listen," said Cheever, "it's extremely important that you stay off the track during the exercise. Particularly around the Sounding Rings."

"What would happen?"

"Bad things."

The claxon swept through the tunnel a second time. Baker informed everyone at five minutes that facility lockdown had gone into effect; no one in or out of the station for the duration of the test. On the heels of that warning, a visible wave of exhilaration passed among the crew. All the work they'd put into prepping for the exercise would soon pay off in an incredible ten second display. Gusarov slapped his hands together, expressing outwardly what everybody was feeling inside.

"This is so exciting!" he said. "How many times have you done this?"

Inside the booth, Henderson started tuning her console, and with it came a steady hum.

"This is my sixth time," said Cheever. "And it never gets old."

Gusarov smiled. "I am sure you are true."

"How did you do on your Intro to TDRR?"

"There wasn't enough time," said Gusarov. His fluffy hair waved in the air. "Supervisor Jimenez told me it would be all right to take it later in the week."

"Uh huh." Cheever found it odd that such accommodations were being made for a new man. "Success or failure, at this point, resides solely with Dr. Henderson up in the booth. She controls the frequencies that pass through the Sounding Tunnel. It's all about keeping those six rings in synch, and tuned so that we can make visual contact with the train. It's like music, really, derived from electrically stimulated gems placed throughout the circumference of each ring."

The humming increased in volume. Gusarov adjusted the volume of his voice accordingly. "These rings…"

"The rings are fed electrical current. When Dr. Henderson achieves the right combination of sonic vibrations and electro-magnetism, the curtain between dimensions falls away. For the length of the Tunnel, anyway. I can't give you all the details. It's not my area."

"Four minutes to integration."

"Fantastic," said Gusarov. "One thing confuses me. How did we happen to find the Trans-Dimensional Railroad passes through here?"

"It doesn't work that way!" said Cheever, almost shouting now. She held her hands out, palms facing Gusarov, first emphasizing her left hand then her right. "This? This is our plane of existence. North, south, east, west. Our tunnel. And this hand is the plane we refer to as Null Space, the plane the TDRR calls home. We've learned over time that they pass through their equivalent of this general area based on an energy signature they leave in their wake. I don't know much more than that."

"It's not your area."

"Right." She put her palms together and rotated her hands in opposing circles. "Using this technology, we align their route and our tunnel so that the paths merge, even though nothing on either plane physically moves. Get me?"

"Like rotating two projected images until they overlap just so?"

Cheever gave the example some thought. "Yes. As long as the train is traveling within a certain radius of this tunnel. The rings have a limited range."

Inside the booth, Henderson stood behind her podium, manipulating dials colored to match the gem shades housed in the Sounding Rings. The same combination of twenty-one gems was in each of the six rings, eight different colors in all.

Baker sat at a table next to her facing a digital clock, a microphone, and several pages of notes. "Looks like the professor isn't going to make it."

Henderson said nothing, focusing instead on the task at hand. Another minute passed on Baker's clock. She began to manipulate sliders which intensified the hum's volume until it split into separate harmonic components. Finally, different 'instruments' began to ring out, like a symphony tuning up before a performance.

"Three minutes, people," said Jimenez over his headset. He was seated on the other side of Baker making notes on his clipboard in preparation for the next exercise. "Let's get those cans on. We don't want anyone going deaf or bleeding out their ears. Can I get a status report, please? Cameras?"

A man sitting at a desk surrounded by monitors put sound dampeners over his headset then signaled everything was Go. Cheever and Gusarov followed with an enthusiastic thumbs-up. When Jimenez inquired the same of Data Capture, the two men in Tech Support reported Go after checking in with their staff housed below in the Central Lab. Dr. Sonal Gupta of Medical signaled that she, too, was ready.

"What happens now?" asked Gusarov.

"What?" Cheever leaned in, straining to hear.

He got closer still. Cheever detected the faint aroma of lavender on his breath. He asked again what he could expect. Cheever shook her head. "That's what the Intro class is all about!"

They both laughed and nodded their heads as Gusarov shame-facedly admitted defeat. "I beg your pardon!"

"Two minutes to Integration. Begin radio silence."

Everyone in the station detected a vibration coming up through their feet. It was nothing compared to the palpable excitement they felt in their hearts and minds. Everyone was grinning from ear to ear, like children standing on the precipice of a new adventure, imaginations fully engaged at the thought of contact with an alien race from another plane of existence. Nerves in check, they prepared themselves to absorb as much of the event as possible. A few were already lamenting the train's passing before it had even arrived.

"One minute to Integration."

The announcement was almost inaudible as the polytonal hum reached an ear-splitting crescendo. It held there while a sound like tinkling glass danced with light, melodic tones in and around the drone. Henderson perspired as she tweaked the controls just so, pushing out all thoughts of the consequences she could invoke should she commit to the wrong energy pattern. Gusarov looked around at the various consoles, watching everyone about their business. The excitement in the air was infectious.

He watched as the man monitoring the cameras quickly made his way to one of the video cameras to reseat a cable. Satisfied with the result, the tech then trotted back to the corresponding monitor. Dr. Gupta joined the two men of hardware support to share in their excitement. All eyes stared down the Sounding Tunnel. Gusarov caught Jimenez's eye. Armando swirled his hand in such a way as to say, turn around and pay attention, and so he did.

The final seconds of the countdown could only be heard by those inside the booth. Henderson adjusted the dials, sliders, and fine tuning knob in search of the perfect matching signal. She watched the six green waves on the console as they began to take the shape of the red wave template. A single bead of sweat dropped from her brow onto the panel. When the clock reached zero, she gave the master dial one more twist. The waves lined up, turned white, and locked in place automatically. Henderson opened a small door with an equally small key then toggled the master controller. A door to another dimension was unlocked.

The alien train emerged from a dead end wall, intangible, like an apparition, visible but translucent. The beam from a cyclopean headlight led the way down the tunnel, signaling to the science team on the platform the train's imminent arrival. It made no noise on its ghostly journey, or was drowned out by the chaos symphony of the Sounding Tunnel. Verity's work lights shined ineffectively on the bullet-nosed prow. Closer to the platform, work lights were dimmed by half, allowing the train to appear more substantial. Lower down the nose, below darkly tinted windows, an iconic capital 'T' glowed a dim blue. It had been previously discovered, upon close examination of the photographic record, that the 'T' was actually a construct, like a sculpture, humanoid in shape with outstretched arms, fists clenched, head turned to the side. There appeared to be an inexplicable gap of several inches between the construct and the surface of the train.

In a matter of seconds the engine approached the station platform, already coming to the end of its short journey. Everyone stood slack-jawed, trying to take in as much as they could as quickly as they could. Everything they saw, everything they recorded, would be added to what little they knew about the TDRR. The orange and red two-toned paint job, the amber signal lights, the tattoo-like design on the side of the front car, all were noted in past tests. Up close, the tattoo was reminiscent of spider webs. But when the science team reviewed the images taken from further back in the station, they were stunned to find the overall design represented the iron horse locomotive of the nineteenth century. This discovery provoked much discussion as to the possible origins of the TDRR. Or perhaps the reverse was true and the design of the early American train was a product of otherworldly influence. Whichever the case, the Verity scientists had enough research ahead of them to last the entirety of their lives.

Just as suddenly as it had appeared before them, it passed through the solid rock wall on the opposite end of the tunnel and disappeared. A wind kicked up debris in the tunnel, twisting in little whirlwinds created by the sudden merging of realities. Hands went up to protect faces as everyone watched the passenger cars slip past until they, too, were gone from sight. The Sounding Rings powered down. All that remained was a deafening silence, broken by a brief round of applause. Henderson removed her headgear and patted her damp face with a handkerchief. She shook hands with Baker and Jimenez then stepped out of the booth.

"The Integration exercise is now complete," announced Baker. "Lockdown is no longer in effect. End radio silence. Please make sure all local data is forwarded to the Central Lab. Good job, everyone."

"That was fantastic!" Gusarov shouted louder than was necessary and the science team chuckled.

"It's amazing," Cheever agreed as she began to comply with Baker's request.

"Never have I seen such a thing!" Cheever stopped and gave Gusarov a look. "Since I was a child, of course. Fuzzy memories at best."

Cheever nodded then poked her finger into Gusarov's chest. "You just make sure you attend that class before working with any of this data."

"Can we be seen when they pass us by? Can they hear the noise?"

"We don't know."

"Thank you, Dr. Cheever," Gusarov said with an exhilarated smile.

"It's just Ellen. Welcome to Verity Corp."

"Ellen!"

Cheever turned and saw Henderson coming her way. Rachel stood almost a head taller than her diminutive assistant.

"Nice work, Ellen."

"It's all you, Rachel."

Henderson turned to Gusarov. "Did you enjoy your first exercise, Mr. Gusarov?"

"He likes Goose."

"Da, yes, very much, Dr. Henderson. I look forward to working on this project very much."

"Excellent." Henderson turned to Cheever with a raised eyebrow. "The Ready Team?"

"I'm on it."

"Glad to hear it. Dmitri, I'll see you at the preliminary discovery panel tomorrow morning. For now, Dr. Jimenez will escort you to the next phase of your training. Dr. Cheever, I believe we're scheduled to meet?"

Henderson led the way to the elevator. As they stepped into the waiting car, the two men from hardware support tried to join them but Henderson waved them off.

"I've spoken with Bellows about the data theft. We're to refer to our investigation in correspondence as Project: Bucket Leak."

As they rode down ten more flights into the earth, Cheever smiled against her will.

#

Henderson kept her basement office very neat, the polar opposite of her mentor's. Where Askew had towers of books and papers dating back years covering the furniture and floor, Henderson preferred clutter free surfaces. Cheever looked to both Askew and Henderson as role models, but she preferred Henderson's organized approach over Askew's sprawling filing system.

"So, Rachel, what's so special about this wishnik character that we

Station 12: The Lantern Society

had to expedite his hiring?"

"Who?"

"Gusarov. Goose. He looks like one of those little troll dolls."

Henderson laughed as she snapped her laptop into its docking station. "He does, doesn't he? I don't know, to be honest," she said shrugging. "It was a directive from on high. I guess we'll find out soon enough."

"Prof brought him in?"

Henderson shook her head. "I don't know where he came from. I got an email from Bellows telling me to expect him and to get him started immediately. That was pretty much all he said."

"That's weird."

Cheever watched her boss with admiration. Henderson was poring through both her snail mail and email as she asked where they stood on Operation: Bucket Leak. The level to which she could divide her attention and still maintain her focus amazed Ellen. It was an attribute she worked very hard to emulate. It was different with Askew. His genius was undeniable, but it was his imaginative use of that genius that Cheever truly admired. Where he got the idea to implant the rings with gem stones as a means of breaking down the border between dimensions was simply beyond her. And that was just one of many breakthroughs he'd provided Verity Corp over the years. The company was lucky to have two minds like his and Henderson's at the helm of the science division. She thought that if she could take away the best of what they both had to offer, there wouldn't be anything she couldn't accomplish. That was important to her given what they were facing.

Cheever explained to Henderson how the code she discovered was copying the data from one server in the science department and funneling it to another in the finance area. It resided within a ghost partition that was invisible to users, but what happened to the data after that, Cheever couldn't say. Professionally, it was difficult for her to relay the breach of security, even though ensuring server security didn't fall under her jurisdiction.

"I want you to compile a list," Henderson said, giving Cheever her full attention. "I need to know what files were duplicated."

"Already done." Cheever handed over a manila folder. "I've taken the liberty of highlighting the files I think would be of most interest to you."

Henderson looked it over and Cheever watched for her reactions. They were subtle but Ellen had known her long enough to read them.

"What percentage of the Sounding Tunnel plans was kept on this server?"

The answer came to Cheever immediately but she withheld it a moment hoping that it would change before she delivered it. "One hundred percent. It's there in its entirety." Henderson looked away. "What are you thinking?"

"Jesus Christ."

"Rachel, there's no way."

"We can't know that for sure."

"There's no way!" Cheever insisted. "The money alone. Not to mention ignorance of its function."

"Possible ignorance. We don't know who put all this together. I've got to find Askew. He's got to hear this."

Outside agents with access to a Sounding Tunnel, Cheever couldn't imagine anything worse. She would find out otherwise soon enough.

Chapter Six: The Mercenary

Ed Donovan idolized the classic heroes as a boy. His bedroom was festooned with toys and images of firemen, astronauts, and frontier sheriffs; brave men all, who risked their lives so that others might live a better life. Ultimately it was the soldier he admired most because it was the soldier he knew best. His father and grandfather were army vets and in Eddie's adolescent mind they were men of honor, heroes to emulate. In Detroit, where Donovan grew up, his father allowed his underage son to serve drinks at the local VFW. Eddie heard a lot of war stories from heroes of all ages and all manner of conflicts, all of which served to solidify his adulation.

On his eighteenth birthday, Donovan stepped into the Detroit Bel Air Recruiting Station and enlisted in the Army. Never for a moment did he doubt his intent or question his motivation. His decision wasn't about college and it wasn't about providing for a family. Joining the Army and becoming a hero like his old man before him was all he ever wanted. He believed it was his destiny.

When the Persian Gulf War broke out, his military purpose had matured along with his growing responsibilities, having attained the rank of Sergeant. He quickly found himself leader of his squad and saw his team through countless skirmishes. Mission after mission was met with success and his superior officers took note of his accomplishments and recognized him accordingly.

Not that there hadn't been losses. The first fatality under his watch was Nate Cross. A good friend, they'd been together since Basic and placed in the same infantry unit of the 3rd Armored Cavalry Regiment. One twilit desert evening in the Kuwaiti oil fields, while escorting the oil-fire fighters sent in to recap the burning wells, an Iraqi landmine stole Nate's legs from under him. In his final moments of life, as the scorched desert ground turned crimson with blood and the setting sun, Nate thought only of the people back home. He held tightly to Donovan's hand, and with an enormous strength of will, he spoke of a letter he kept in his locker. Nate expressed relief when Donovan promised to deliver it personally to his family. He lay there in shock with a smile on his face, the color of his life fading. He was told to hang in there as tourniquets were applied and morphine given to dull the pain. But Nate drifted away before any help could arrive.

The loss hit Sergeant Donovan hard. Yet like any good soldier, he pressed on, learning something that one honest day; there was a difference between a successful mission and an objective achieved. The line between the two was blurred for many but not so Donovan. Not anymore. To the brass, the cost of war included acceptable losses. To Donovan, success meant achieving the objective with no such losses. On that one honest day, Nate Cross showed Donovan what it truly meant to be a hero. Then and there, Donovan made up his mind not to be counted among them.

#

Afternoon light seeped through the Venetian blinds to interrogate the dust motes that wandered innocently through the air of Donovan's dingy one-room apartment. The studio was sparsely furnished with a tenant-weary cot, a card table and metal folding chair, and a set of drawers that could barely shoulder the weight of the thrift store hot plate. In contrast, a pink pedestal sink stood proudly and pristinely in a corner of the room with its own window overlooking Bowery. Aside from an impressive armory Donovan kept in a steamer trunk, there was little else in the room in the way of personal possessions. There were a few literary tomes and a set of bobble-head figures depicting renowned military figures in U.S. history. New York City, the Eldridge Hotel to be exact, was a temporary home for Donovan, a place to hang his hat.

Each of three deadbolts snapped open as Donovan let himself into the apartment. He placed his lunch on the table and the shoulder bag that housed his disassembled rifle with the rest of his weapons. In his desire to avoid the shared bathroom down the hall, Donovan opted to urinate into his sink. He opened the hot water tap all the way and peeled the wrapper off of a bar of soap, one of the few amenities that came with the room. He scrubbed his hands using a fingernail brush in a manner befitting a surgeon. Once the ritual was complete, he dried his hands on a threadbare dish towel before dragging the card table closer to the open windows. Pulling open the blinds, he took a seat and gazed out on the street below, but keeping a direct line of sight with the front door. Prepared for the inevitable fallout over the Tompkins Square Park disaster, he placed his cell phone on the table in front of him.

He felt badly about shooting the Bismarck woman. Worse than he imagined he could. She must have had her reasons for pulling the plug on the deal. It was obvious she knew what she was buying, even if he and Anderson had been kept in the dark. But there was no way he could have let her leave with the money, and he couldn't have allowed her to make trouble for Anderson or the Lantern Society. *I had no choice, right?* General Douglas MacArthur nodded in agreement, but the rest of the officers offered no opinion.

Donovan's stomach growled in protest, followed by a wave of nausea so intense he could feel acid burning the back of his throat. Dark thoughts ricocheted in his skull. *What the hell is this*, he wondered. Every time his mind lit on the Bismarck woman, his heart rate accelerated. *Come on, you fuck*, he thought, *it's way too late to find your conscience now.*

Maybe he'd lost the line. Was Bismarck a casualty of war? If not, what then? The queasiness ramped up. Grabbing a Newcastle, he drank deeply in an effort to show his stomach who was boss. *She's not a God damn murder victim, I know that much. I know that fuckin' much.* Still, he couldn't shake his doubt.

Donovan gazed out onto the street, hoping the city's inhabitants would quell his anxious state. The noise generated by the Eldridge's cast of characters provided some comfort. The ceaseless chatter of the down and out served as a reminder that he was only a visitor. His reality was elsewhere. His time with the Lantern Society was coming to a close. The anniversary date of his one-year contract was fast approaching. He split the conjoined chopsticks and rubbed them together as he thought back on the year when he'd made the decision to work one more job before permanently, and perhaps reluctantly, retiring.

#

There was no sense of foreboding as Donovan headed to his appointment with Global Armour. Foreboding would come later, after the Lantern Society had gotten their mitts on him. Anton Gorokhovich stood at the agreed-upon park fountain wearing a New York Islanders ball cap. When he spotted the telltale scar on Donovan's face, he stepped up and offered his hand. They exchanged introductions as Gorokhovich led Donovan across the street and down a set of stairs, passing a basement level barber shop and a shoe shine stand on their way.

"I understand we're dragging you away from a beach home in Hawaii," Gorokhovich said as they passed through a metal door that read Exit Only. "I'm sure this is a bit of a letdown for you."

"Not at all," Donovan answered. "I love New York. I especially love free trips to New York. Who told you my home was in Hawaii?"

"The Broker, of course."

"Who?"

They made their way through a series of twisting hallways.

"The man who arranged this meeting."

Donovan laughed. "I wasn't aware he had a code name." He tried envisioning pudgy, little Seth Harutunian as a badass mercenary pimp but he couldn't make it happen. He did, however, make a mental note to chat with Seth about his lack of discretion.

They came to a small room, half office, half utility closet where Gorokhovich invited Donovan to sit.

"I've never met the man face to face," he said as he tossed away his ball cap, "but we've made some good, reliable connections in our short history together."

"You're a new firm," Donovan declared, surveying the damp and homely surroundings. "I like your office."

Gorokhovich smiled. An elevator chimed nearby. A woman dressed in a black skirt suit stepped into the room.

"Lenore Devlin, this is Ed Donovan, our would-be insurance policy." Donovan started to rise, but she waved him off then shook his hand. "Mr. Donovan, Ms. Devlin is in charge of operations at Global Armour. It's my firm, but she runs the show. As the Broker no doubt told you, we're putting together a mission that may require skills closer to your line of work. In this particular case, I'm referring to extraction."

"Very shortly," Devlin said, following a nod from her boss, "two of our agents are going undercover at one of our neighboring businesses. It's a reconnaissance mission. Your primary function would be to escort them through the building and assist them in locating and gaining access to a large, underground facility. Our agents will be placing surveillance cameras throughout. If anything goes wrong along the way, it would be your job to see them safely out of the building. It is imperative that no one get caught. You would be responsible for overcoming any resistance you might meet. For the record, we're not looking for permanent solutions. Get them in, keep them safe, and get them out."

"This mission is vital to the future of our firm," Gorokhovich added.

Donovan looked at both of them but focused on Devlin, reflecting on her use of the phrase, 'for the record.'

"I'll need details before I guarantee any level of success."

Devlin nodded. "Details are contingent upon acceptance of the contract."

The man in the leather duster grinned.

#

Dressed in business attire, the Global Armour reconnaissance team entered the Verity tower in the guise of New York state regulatory auditors. Verity's CFO, Arnold Downey, met them in the lobby and brought them up to the examination room on the twentieth floor. On the way, Donovan noticed his new cohorts appeared overtly nervous and he wished he'd taken on the assignment solo instead of being saddled with rookie field agents. Denise Carter's eyes darted here and there in a paranoid search for the one person who would call them out on their ruse. Hal Ware, upper lip glistening, wore an expression of utter defeat, like they'd already been caught and awaited punishment. Donovan hoped these were natural traits of regulatory auditors or they weren't going to get very far.

After a brief tour, they all agreed to reconvene after lunch, giving the false examiners the chance to unpack their things and set up for the weeks long audit. Downey provided each of them with a limited access badge and a key to the examination room, after which they parted ways.

With the room to themselves, Donovan closed the door and leaned against it with his arms crossed, giving his team the onceover. They were young. Carter was slim, her blond ponytail bouncing with every gesture. There was something juvenile about her application of make-up, something amateurish. She also wore a constant frown that aged her somewhat. There was something hard about her, too. Donovan couldn't decide if this hard edge was commensurate with her life experience or an affectation. Either way, she was very easy to dislike. Ware, on the other hand, was an amiable fellow, reminding those he came in contact with of an old friend whose name they had forgotten. He was in full possession of the doughy softness of youth. His cheeks were permanently flushed, giving him the appearance of being under constant stress.

"First order of business," Donovan said, "you two need to relax. You looked like you were being led to a firing squad out there."

"We'll be fine," said Carter. "We're just getting our sea legs."

"Get it together," Donovan said as he began equipping himself for the mission.

"What are you doing?" asked Carter.

"While I appreciate all the work Global Armour put into our cover story, there's no point sitting around." He slipped a small flashlight into his pocket. "We're not really auditors."

Carter and Ware exchanged an uncomfortable glance.

"Look," said an irritated Donovan, "there's no time like the present, agents, so grab your gear and let's go!"

Carter reached into her case and removed a stretch belt that she fastened around her waist. It was equipped with miniature video cameras about the size of sugar cubes that resided in tiny pockets. Ware removed a computer tablet and began sifting through his notes via touch screen. The two agents looked to each other for moral support, or perhaps to bolster each other's courage.

"Stop that," Donovan said. "It's very exclusionary. Everybody ready? Relax and breathe. Look like you belong."

He opened the door and led them out. The irony of Donovan's last sentence struck the agents as almost absurd. Donovan was hardly the poster child for corporate America. But none of Verity's employees gave them any more than a cursory glance as the three started down the hall in mock conversation.

Donovan studied the security camera above the east stairwell door. After confirming the blue light was out, he continued down the stairs. Thanks to a small device he wore called a Blinder, live feeds to Verity's Security Center were supplanted with images from other feeds. The person or persons monitoring the fifty rotating images would be none the wiser. Once the agents had passed out of camera range, the rotation would return to normal.

When they finally stepped into the lobby, Carter asked, "Can you tell me why we didn't just take the elevator?"

Donovan looked ahead as he planned their next steps. "Most of the people up there will think we're still on the floor."

"So, what now?"

"You're in the field now, Carter," said Donovan frowning. This time he did look in her direction and when he did, she took a small step backward. "It's not always going to go according to plans drawn up on your whiteboard."

"My legs feel like Jell-o," commented Ware.

Donovan took big strides toward a kiosk in the middle of the lobby.

"How do you want your coffees?" he asked.

"Black, three sugars," said Ware.

Carter rubbed her forehead while trying to look nonchalant. "Are you kidding me?"

Donovan's face darkened. Carter took another step back. When he turned back toward the vendor, he smiled and ordered two small coffees. After paying the vendor, he took a seat on a leather couch in a nearby waiting area.

"Thanks for the coffee, Ed," said Ware.

Donovan peered across the lobby as he sipped the hot beverage. "According to Devlin, there should be a door behind that waterfall that leads to where the magic happens below."

"That's the main entrance to the lab," said Carter who looked a little uncomfortable discussing their business out in the open. "But there's no way we're getting in that way, with or without badges."

Ware tapped his tablet. "Our target is a storage room on the other side of that showroom. If our information is correct, there should be a way down from there."

"Mm hmm." Donovan set his coffee down on the black, lacquered table between the Forbes Magazine and the Financial Times. "Onward and upward, agents. Or, in our case, downward."

The two agents jumped up and followed Donovan through the glass doors of the showroom. The room was designed with their investors in mind. Like a museum, it displayed objects in glass cases with descriptive placards, showcasing Verity's various inventions over the years; inventions that ran the gamut from small, solar-powered fans to an alternate fuel, two-seater automobile.

"What's the hurry, Donovan? We stick out like---."

"No one gives a shit, Carter, relax."

Compared to the hairy places Donovan had spent his career, strolling through a financial institution was a cake walk. Security was at a minimum and who was going to notice a few more pencil pushers in a sea of suits?

As they passed slowly through the exhibits, they browsed the displays until they came in range of the camera on the back wall. The blue light went out. The door beneath the camera was locked, but Donovan got it open well inside a minute. There were no surprises in the storage room; shelving along the walls, crates, boxes, and a number of barrels. Of specific interest was a raised, circular shape in the center of the room covered by an enormous tarp.

"We don't know for certain what use this room serves other than the obvious," said Ware. "Our working theory is that it was once the main egress for the excavated dirt from below. It would have come up through here and taken straight to the loading dock to be hauled away. If we're right," Ware pulled the tarp away, "this should be a hole."

An iron guardrail surrounded a black pit. Carter and Ware pointed their flashlights into the open portal. The bottom of the shaft was nowhere to be seen. All that presented itself was a ladder descending into the darkness.

"Not a good idea," Donovan said, pointing to the flashlights. Carter and Ware snapped them off in embarrassment.

There was a nearby control panel. They deemed it quite likely it was for an elevator car parked at the bottom. They knew activating it might draw unwanted attention, so everyone agreed, though neither agent seemed too keen on it, that climbing down the ladder was their only viable course of action. Donovan decided the feed on the storage room cameras had been blocked long enough. He slipped on a pair of leather gloves and started down. Per his instructions, no one spoke a word as they began their long descent.

Donovan made good time and soon disappeared into the gloom. Ware brought up the rear. He tired quickly, stopping frequently to rest and blow on his burning hands. Like a security blanket, Carter kept reaching for her flashlight. She was curious to see how far Donovan had gotten, but refrained from turning it on so as to avoid climbing any higher up the mercenary's shit list.

After what seemed an eternity, Donovan informed his team that he had touched down. Relief in sight, the Global Armour agents picked up the pace until they reached the grounded, bucket-style elevator car and found Donovan standing on the concrete floor of a small alcove.

The floor may have been finished, but the rest of the space was simply what nature provided: a cold, damp cavern. Three mining cars sat on a section of small gauge rail, suggesting that Global Armour may have been correct in their dirt removal theory. Donovan approached a makeshift door that was cut into a plywood partition and peered through a scratched-up, Plexiglas window. The track continued into a much larger portion of the cavern, passing a stack of crates and loose equipment before disappearing into a tunnel. Up on the right stood a small building on the top of a rise which effectively blocked his view.

Suddenly there was a roar and a squealing of metal as the elevator was dislodged from its resting place to ascend the shaft. Carter and Ware gave a shout but fortunately for them, the noise of the elevator drowned them out. Donovan pointed with authority toward the track. Everyone crouched as they made their way along the rails to the stacked crates. They tucked in among them to hide. From his new vantage point, Donovan saw a gateway metal detector and a short set of stairs leading to a very impressive door.

"We're in the deepest region of Verity Corp," Ware whispered between heavy breaths. "Their main research facility is behind that door. Between us and the door behind the waterfall is an abandoned subway line."

Donovan raised an eyebrow.

"No," said Carter, "we don't know what they're using it for."

Donovan looked around to assess the situation and something caught his eye. When he pointed to Carter's belt, she removed one of the miniature cameras from its tiny pocket and tossed it to him. Through his binoculars, he saw what he assumed was a guardhouse. Donovan moved stealthily to the base of a light stand. He pressed the activation button on the camera and then removed the adhesive backing before placing it as high onto the pole as he dared. Ware confirmed on his tablet that the camera was working and had a good view up the rise.

The groaning elevator returned to ground level and two workmen in blue jumpsuits stepped out. The Global Armour team held their collective breath at the sound of approaching voices and adjusted their positions to prevent from being seen. Donovan's hand slowly made its way toward his ankle. Carter and Ware sat petrified like wide-eyed statues. The workmen climbed the hill and could be heard joking to the man inside the guardhouse about the mess outside. It seemed from his amplified retorts that the young man inside didn't find it particularly funny. Then the mining cars lumbered into view, cruising along on autopilot, carrying more crates. When the train came to a complete stop, the workmen broke away from the guardhouse and walked back down the hill.

"The Scope is the priority," said one to the other. "Everything else comes off."

One of the men got pretty close to the hidden interlopers. Donovan lifted his pant leg and placed his hand on the snub nose revolver he had strapped to his ankle.

"This one's heavy as shit."

"Let's go get the lift."

One of the workmen placed a radio call as they headed back to the alcove. As soon as they cleared the plywood partition, the mining cars started in the opposite direction through the tunnel. Only for a moment did Donovan hesitate before he took off after it. A confused Carter and Ware followed closely behind. Donovan looked inside the last car, saw there was room enough for one small person, and told Carter to get in.

"Why do you have a gun?" she asked.

"Get in the car," Donovan said looking around.

"What about non-lethal did you not understand?"

"Your boss knew who she was hiring. Now get in the fucking car or you'll find out what I do and do not understand."

Carter did as she was instructed. Donovan moved ahead, signaling Ware to step onto the coupling between cars and stay low. Donovan did the same further up, looking back only once to see if they were being followed. After almost a quarter of an hour of slow rail travel, Donovan began to realize the enormity of the facility. When he finally spotted a framed entryway ahead of them, they stepped off the train and watched the cars bang through a set of swinging doors. Thirty seconds after that, Donovan looked to determine if it was safe for them to continue.

Station 12: The Lantern Society

Without knowing how much time they had before workmen showed up, Donovan set to work on their roughly sketched-out plan. In the locker area, he handed out blue jumpsuits to his teammates. After donning his own, he pulled a mini flatbed truck up to the train so he and Ware could transfer some of the crates. Carter, meanwhile, stood on a chair and stuck a camera in the most unobtrusive location she could find.

Ware slid onto the bench seat next to Donovan. Carter hopped on the back with the freight. They drove through another set of swinging doors, following the 'road' imprinted on the floor. The tunnel emptied into a massive file room. The few employees stationed there either ignored them completely or offered a casual wave as the flatbed glided silently past. Donovan kept the truck moving, stopping only long enough to allow Carter and Ware to perform their assigned functions.

When they exited the file area, the Central Lab opened up to reveal a facility truly magnificent in scope. Awestruck, they stared at the high ceiling, blue like the sky with long, thin clouds highlighted in orange from a brilliant morning sun. Clouds crawled across the ceiling following the flow of the artificial breeze that wafted over their faces.

Scattered throughout the facility were round buildings, each between two and four stories in height, with numbers and symbols painted on them that were easily spotted from the road. The black path they drove on meandered between these structures and sometimes split off as secondary roads in shades of gray. Potted trees dotted the landscape, many in and around mini-parks with permanently affixed seats for four to six people. Taken altogether, it resembled a small town.

The Verity staff went about their business and continued to take little notice of the trespassers. The team began to feel comfortable with the idea that they might actually pull off their assignment with no repercussions.

"Woah, woah, woah!"

Donovan slammed on the brakes in order to avoid running over a short man wearing a Verity ball cap and a lab coat that just about reached the floor.

"Where are you guys going?" the man went on to say. "Are you blind?" The trio of course had no idea what the man was going on about. "Are those parts for the Scope?"

"That's right," said Donovan. The scientist gestured impatiently toward the building to the left of the truck. Painted above the corner entry was a large number six and emblazoned on the garage door, a stylized representation of a telescope. "We know where we're going, sir. We just had to make a quick stop first."

"No time, we're falling behind. We need this stuff A-SAP. Come on." The man unhooked a radio from his belt. "Control, open the bay door for Pod Six. Incoming parts for the Oculacrum. Please and thank you."

Donovan found a button on the dash that turned on yellow, spinning hazard lights on each corner of the flatbed. The Pod's pocket garage door slid aside and he turned and drove straight into the facility. Banks of computers ran along the circumference of the circular room. Work tables were configured on a parallel course. In the center of the pod was a very large device obviously under construction. It didn't look like any kind of telescope Donovan had ever seen.

What good is a telescope underground, Carter wondered.

A very tall, lean, and muscular man stood up from his seat. An imposing figure with sharp eyes, dark skin, and a shaved head, Donovan's intuition told him he was a man with some history. A man who couldn't be easily intimidated.

"It's about God damn time," the man said. "Hey, Pru! Pru!" Steven Pruitt, hard at work in the construction zone removed his safety glasses and looked up. "The parts are coming in!" the tall man exclaimed. He then gestured to Donovan who was stepping out of the truck. "Let's see the manifest."

"Sure thing," said Donovan, handing over a clipboard in a bold bluff. "Let's go, people!" he said to his team. "These folks don't have all day."

Pruitt joined them. "Not here. Drive it up to the work zone…"

"Donovan."

"Nice to meet you, Donovan. Pruitt. You guys new?"

Donovan pointed at the Global Armour agents. "They are. I'm a transfer."

"What the hell is this?" asked the imposing man.

Pruitt walked over. "This is Dr. Baylor. He's very intense."

"This isn't the right manifest. This is for the Echo."

Donovan turned toward Carter. "Did you attach the wrong manifest, rookie?"

Carter thought her best play was to simply cringe rather than try to conjure up an answer. It seemed the natural response. Donovan thought fast and worked it out with the anxious Baylor then pulled the truck up as instructed. Agents and lab techs quickly cleared off the flatbed and the team from Global Armour was summarily dismissed.

"They must have an awful lot of confidence in their security system to not check the IDs of people they don't recognize. Did one of you manage to get a camera in there?"

"I did," said Carter.

"Good. Let's get the rest of them in place and get the hell out of here before our luck runs out."

"Amen," said Carter. "How do we do that?"

"Not back up that ladder?" Ware asked woefully.

Donovan pinched Ware's cheek. "How about we exit out the exit?"

#

The view from Max Heberling's corner office on the top floor was diminished by a glare screen that had been lowered to better see the large monitor on the wall. Heberling, a portly fellow with thinning auburn hair and a red, cherubic face was seated in the center of his sectional couch munching Oreo cookies with a glass of milk. He appeared disheveled in a crumpled black suit, white shirt, and black tie. He looked like he'd attended an all-night funeral. Under eyebrows of concern, his eyes twinkled with mischief as he watched Donovan and his associates zipping their way through Command Central on their way to the cavern entrance.

Lionel Bellows, head of all things underground at Verity Corp, stepped into the seating area sipping a cup of green tea, joining his fellow co-founder. Fifty years old, he was in spectacular physical condition, looking sharp with short, silver hair offset by a cranberry turtleneck over black slacks.

"You were right, Max, these people are not auditors."

"No shit. Look at that guy! He looks like Al Capone, for crying out loud," said Verity's CEO, pointing in Donovan's general direction. "Whoever's behind this intrusion holds us in very little regard. What are those things they're sticking everywhere?"

"Cameras," said Bellows. "They're we're dealing with. I'd love to know how they're bypassing our cameras."

"How they're bypassing *some* of our cameras," said Heberling, dunking a cookie into his milk. "At least we got some work out of them."

"That's something," said Bellows as he assessed the team from Global Armour.

"Has anyone been alerted down there?" asked Heberling.

"Everyone. With instructions not to impede them until we figure out what's to be done."

"We can grab them in the lobby. Less disruption of the lab."

"In public view?" said Bellows shaking his head. "I don't think so."

"Right, right, sorry. Isn't Askew running an exercise in the station?"

"What happens after we pick them up?" asked Bellows, preoccupied. "There's no precedent."

"That's the question, isn't it?" Heberling said. "We certainly can't have them telling the rest of the world what's down there."

"No, we can't have that." Bellows took another sip of tea. "Max, we knew this day would come eventually."

"Yes."

Heberling sighed heavily, grunting as he leaned to pick up the receiver on the coffee table.

"Mr. Longworth, we have a problem."

#

Donovan and company stepped through the oversized door and found themselves exactly where they had started their underground exploration. Only now they were facing the guardhouse from the opposite side and they could just make out their former hiding place in the crates below. Donovan turned to his left and followed one of the white-coated scientists down the exit path and into an elevator built into the rock. Once inside, the scientist reached for his belt.

"Damn. I think I left my badge on my desk. Could one of you grab this for me?"

The agents froze for an interminable split second.

"Oh, here it is." The man removed the card from his breast pocket and slid it through the slot.

"Thank you," said a pleasant, automated voice. "Going up."

After a bit of small talk, the man asked them if they were heading to the Sounding Tunnel test.

"Unfortunately, no," said Donovan, "we've got a staff meeting topside."

The man looked at his watch. "Better hurry before they lock down the elevators."

"East River Station," said the elevator after the chime. "Sounding Tunnel."

The door opened and the man dashed out to join the science team on the platform.

"Six minutes to Integration," came an announcer's amplified voice, cutting through a loud electric hum that almost hurt to hear it.

The Global Armour team stepped out of the elevator and took a moment to get their bearings. In the immediate foreground was the back of an elevated glass booth in which a bald-headed man stood behind a console beside another man seated at a microphone. A third man carrying a clipboard climbed a set of steps and joined them. Donovan continued down toward a second elevator that he assumed would take them to the surface.

"What if we need a badge to use the elevator again?" asked Carter. "We won't get lucky twice."

Donovan couldn't hear her over the noise. When they were halfway down the path, the elevator door opened. Two men in forest green uniforms stepped out and locked it in the open position. Donovan guessed by the red patches on their shoulders that they were Verity security.

As the guards made their way down the stairs, Donovan directed his team off the path, skirting the tech tables on the left.

"Five minutes to Integration. Commence lockdown."

They continued to stay left of the science team until they reached the edge of the platform. The ancient subway tunnel stretched out before them. There was no option in Donovan's mind. He didn't look back but he assumed the uniformed guards weren't far behind them as they began to make their way through the tunnel, moving as quickly as the narrow maintenance path would allow. When he reached the first Sounding Ring, he looked back and was surprised to see that the security team had not followed them. Instead, they were gathered at a table donning headgear, not even watching them. Not a good sign.

"Four minutes to Integration. Please clear the tunnel."

The noise in the tunnel grew louder by the second and Donovan had some serious doubts about the direction he had chosen. Nobody following them probably meant that there was no way out in the direction they were heading. Or that whatever was going to happen in four minutes would block their exit. If he didn't find another way out soon, they were screwed. Seeing no other option, he decided to keep going and hope he would stumble upon some ancient egress. In order to remain on the path, however, he had to grab hold of the Sounding Ring and swing himself around. He helped each of the others in turn, practically lifting Carter by the scruff of her neck before dropping her back onto the path. Ware took the lead next as they moved further into the tunnel. Vibrations from the rings caused their noses to itch and their teeth to chatter. They wished for earplugs as the drone pounded on their skulls with jack hammer force. The mix of sensations made it difficult to think clearly and they shared a growing nausea.

They reached another ring and, again, they had to grab hold and climb around it. Only this time, Ware slipped and tumbled onto the track five feet below. Carter's eyes grew large and she froze in place. Donovan couldn't be heard over the cacophony so he pointed out to Ware, in an animated fashion, a short ladder some ways down the track on the opposite wall. He then took off running down the twelve inch wide path. Ware stood up, slightly dazed, but undamaged. As soon as he understood what Donovan was trying to convey, he started running as fast as he could toward the ladder. Carter, still frozen in place, watched the scene play out. The barely audible countdown was winding down. When it reached zero, Ware stopped. Like a rocket, a train shot out from a solid wall of rock and roared in Hal's direction. He had no time to gape, or even to cry out. His prayers were incoherent gibberish in his head. The end of his life had come early, and as that one clear thought came to him, so did the red and orange bullet train. In that split instant, he no longer remembered why he'd joined Global Armour.

He closed his eyes seconds before the impact…but nothing happened. A small part of him celebrated a painless death and wondered what awaited him in the afterlife. When he reopened his eyes, he realized that he was still very much alive and the train was passing straight through him.

Everything about it was wrong. There was no sound outside of his quite pronounced breathing. The train was moving through him at a crawl.

He saw the picture of his vision distort like fracturing glass and then repair itself only to break again. The center aisle of the train interior passed through him and he caught glimpses of the passengers, alien beings out of science fiction. It was incredible. At the same time, he was still cognizant of the subway tunnel around him.

When he was finally able to gather his focus, he saw Donovan and Carter, seemingly immobile on the maintenance path. Seemingly. Donovan was very slowly pointing toward the ladder and Carter looked like she was about to rip into a scream. Ware realized that he could still move at a normal rate of speed and so he began to run down the track. As he did so, he allowed for tears and coherent prayers as he pushed himself through the oncoming train and toward another of the giant Sounding Rings. He reached out for the ladder though he was still forty feet away. As he passed through the ring, and the last car of the train was there to meet him, he felt a tug on his chest like that of a lasso roping him in. The air rushed out of his lungs and then he was gone. Most of him, anyway.

The train concluded its brief, ethereal journey. Donovan and Carter were left staring into the vacant track and the lower portion of Hal Ware's legs. Carter slumped against the wall, collapsing in place and narrowly avoiding a drop onto the track herself. Donovan watched Ware's legs, separated cleanly from just above the knees fall over silently in opposite directions. Donovan didn't understand what had just transpired, but he was certain Ware's sacrifice would count for nothing. And he was certain of another thing: he had no time to dwell on it.

As soon as the last car of the ghostly train passed through the old station, the noise and vibration came to a halt. Within minutes, Security Specialist Jacen Longworth exited the reinstated elevator with a couple of security officers in tow and joined the guards that had preceded them on the platform. Together they made their way down the tunnel and soon came upon the disenfranchised limbs of Hal Ware. Of the other two people, there was no sign. Donovan and Carter had made their escape, leaving the remains of one hero behind.

#

The first summer storm had come and gone; the wind thanked the storm clouds for coming and escorted them out. Donovan looked up at the transitioning sky then down at the foot traffic going in and out of the little bodega across the street. Some of the regulars came out with beers wrapped in paper bags, some with individual cigarettes to be shared during animated discourse on the corner. Later, they would trade their empty beer cans for another cigarette or two.

He applied hot mustard and soy sauce to his tuna roll and popped it into his mouth. Thinking about his impending retirement, he found he no longer had the same reservations he once had about ending his career. He had the Lantern Society to thank for that. His one and only mission on behalf of Global Armour was a total failure. His most recent assignment for the Society was no more successful. The year between was a series of bizarre assignments, one right after another. It was time to hang up his guns.

His cell phone vibrated on the card table and he put the call on speaker.

"What happened?" asked his contact at the Lantern Society.

"I couldn't tell you. It seemed to me that Bismarck was informed beyond my ability to assess."

"What does that mean?"

Donovan poked at his seaweed salad as he relayed what had transpired. Without accusing his contact outright of a double-cross, he made it clear that the Bismarck woman believed she was being taken.

"How did Anderson react?"

"He was a real trooper. Did his best to convince her otherwise, but she wasn't buying it." He took a drink of beer.

"So, you had no choice."

"No, I did not."

"How did he take that?"

"He freaked out and ran away before we had a chance to discuss it."

"The money?"

"He took it with him."

"The scene?"

"I had a cleaning crew standing by, just in case. And then the rain."

"Where are you?"

"I'm looking for Anderson," he said, lying without hesitation.

"Find him before he does anything stupid. The project goes live in just a few days and I need that money."

"I'm on it."

Donovan closed the connection on his phone. He tipped his head back as he took another drink and thought of Sarah Bismarck, magnified in his scope, as her head snapped back from the impact of his assassin's bullet. The acid in his stomach kicked up and threatened to exit. The choice he'd made was burning a hole in his stomach, and reflections on his career left a bitter taste in his mouth.

Chapter Seven: End of Day

    Two bills, a crisp five and a crumpled single, sat on the bottom of an over-sized snifter, which itself resided on the glossy surface of a baby grand piano. George and honest Abe faced each other, perhaps debating the merits of their respective Republics, or commiserating over the current state of the union. None of it mattered to the piano player who accompanied the former presidents with a pleasant take on 'Misty.' Nor did he take offense at the nearly empty lounge, because at the end of the day, all that mattered to him was the music.

    Mezzanine Social was dimly lit, echoing Tony Strivelli's dark mood. The lounge, as its name so cleverly pointed out, was affixed between the first and second floors of a former department store that harkened back to the heyday of Hartford's downtown shopping establishments. Strivelli, conjuring up images of the store's former glory, filled in the blanks with memories of his own Brooks' Department Store back in Brooklyn. Brooks' mezzanine was home to ladies hosiery and men's accessories, as well as the stamp and coin-collecting counter he always visited when his grandmother took him shopping.

    But those days were long gone. The Social replaced what was with dark, patterned carpeting, year-round Christmas lights, potted palms and ferns of questionable authenticity, and a Happy Hour when normally overpriced drinks could be had at a discounted rate.

    In an attempt to avoid socializing even peripherally, Strivelli sat in an isolated corner of the irregularly-shaped lounge, hunkered down in a darkly upholstered seat, almost invisible against the uninspired carpet. Though not unprecedented, Askew's visit had thrown him for a loop. But only then, in his self-imposed exile, did he allow himself to ponder the enormity of its implications.

    It was well known among Verity employees, even remote field agents, that Askew rarely left New York City. In fact, he rarely left Verity's lab, so committed was he to Verity's cause, a cause Strivelli understood only in the broadest sense. He knew it had something to do with saving the world from the machinations of an otherworldly force and their dimension-hopping trains. All Witnesses knew that much. But the details remained with those in authority. Left to his own devices, Strivelli's imagination sometimes trumped his sense of reason, allowing for all manner of worst case scenarios to play out.

That phone, he thought. *Why did he bring that damn phone?*

#

Strivelli slid the key card through the lock and entered ahead of the bellman. The young man in the ill-fitting hotel ensemble pushed a luggage cart into the room. A dragon tattoo peeked over the edge of his voluminous shirt collar. On the cart rested an old and weathered trunk, but solid, that looked like it had seen its share of epic voyages. Strivelli's cohort, Dodge, brought up the rear.

"Nice place," Dodge said, going straight for the view of the Connecticut River.

"This is a big trunk," said the bellman in a tone bordering on whining.

Strivelli got the hint. "Dodge," he barked, advertising his authority.

The kid stepped aside while the two men each grabbed a handle and hoisted it onto the bench at the foot of the bed.

"Thanks for pushing a cart," Dodge said as he handed a crumpled bill to the bellman who then blushed and mumbled his thanks before exiting.

"Fuck that's heavy. What's he got in here?"

"You'll see."

"This is fancier than I thought it would be."

"You've never been here?" Strivelli asked as he produced a key to unlock the trunk.

Dodge cocked an eyebrow. "I live here. Why would I come to a local hotel?"

"Easy, Asshat, I was just making conversation." Strivelli unclasped the faded brass fasteners then lifted the lid. Dodge scratched his head as the two men looked inside.

"Boy, that's some top secret underwear right there."

Strivelli ignored him and leaned over to scoop up some of the clothes. Dodge bent his long body and followed suit.

"How long is he gonna be here?" asked Dodge as he placed Askew's clothes into the credenza.

"Don't know," Strivelli said without looking up. "It's open-ended."

"Tell me again why he's coming to Hartford."

"I never told you in the first place."

"No shit."

While Strivelli appeared the epitome of a biker, Dodge, reed thin, looked more like a golfer in khaki pants and a lavender wind breaker. Of the two, Dodge looked more likely the man from whom you'd ask directions. That assumption would have proven disappointing, if not dangerous, under the right circumstances.

"Prof goes where he's needed," Strivelli provided as a non-answer.

"Yeah, but why Hartford?" Dodge continued to press. "I heard he never leaves the lab."

Strivelli stopped moving just long enough to say, "Anyone ever tell you, you talk too much?"

"You were the one trying to make conversation, Assface."

"You got me."

"Is there something going on that I don't know about?"

Strivelli made his way back to the trunk. "Obviously."

"How so, obviously?"

"What don't you don't know about?"

The two stared into the now empty chest. "How would I know?"

"Exactly."

Strivelli reached into the lid of the trunk and found secreted in the pattern of the liner an odd, needle-looking device with a round, slightly bulbous end, a stylized 'key' of sorts. Dodge watched Strivelli feel for and find a tiny hole in the floor of the interior where he inserted the pointy end of the key. He then squeezed the rounded end and turned it counterclockwise causing the trunk floor to pop loose.

"That's awesome," said Dodge. He watched Strivelli lift the panel, revealing Askew's secret traveling office. "My name is Bond. Jame---."

"Set this up on the desk," Strivelli said, handing Dodge a laptop docking station. He then grabbed the handle of a brown, leather-wrapped box which reminded Dodge of the storage cases that were once made to hold 45 rpm records.

"So, what's with the trunk?" Dodge kept his eyes glued on the mysterious box. "Does he take it everywhere?"

"It's impervious to x-rays and whatnot, so yes, he takes it everywhere."

"You say his visit is open-ended?"

"That's what I said."

Strivelli brought his burden into the sitting room. Dodge craned his neck but found his view blocked by the couch.

"It must be important."

"Is that a question?" asked Strivelli.

Dodge shrugged and mumbled to himself, "Just thinking out loud."

Strivelli stood up holding an old, black telephone and blew the dust off. Dodge recognized the device, not from memory but rather reputation. His countenance shifted slightly, turning darker at the sight of it.

"Let me ask you something," he said.

"Are you still talking?"

Dodge reached into the trunk and pulled out a keyboard and mouse. "What if what's happening is something huge? I mean, let's assume…what if something really big…how would we be informed?"

There was no immediate answer which Dodge took as a bad sign. Adding to that, the appearance of the storied Black Phone, he got a sinking feeling in the pit of his stomach that what brought Askew to Hartford was more serious than he'd originally imagined.

He dropped the peripherals onto the desk and made his way into the sitting room as Strivelli placed the phone on one of the end tables. To Dodge it looked antique, with a metal rotary dial and a handset cord wrapped in cloth. Interestingly, there was no cord for a jack. Instead, there was a small black box attached to the back of the phone with two lights, two toggle switches, and two retracted antennae.

Strivelli looked up and saw Dodge standing there. "Say again?"

Dodge tried to keep his eyes on Strivelli and off the phone. "I was just wondering what we would do if something really big were to happen. An incident. How would we be informed? How would we know what to do?"

"A contingency plan," suggested Strivelli.

"Exactly."

Strivelli raised the antennae then reassembled the leather box.

"You worry too much."

"Yeah, I do."

Strivelli flipped a switch and one of the lights turned green.

"You all finished in there?"

"Almost."

"Let's go, Dodge. I gotta get over to the Republic to meet the professor."

Strivelli picked up the receiver and dialed a four-digit number.

"Hey, Mr. Bellows. Tony Strivelli. I'm testing the line as scheduled. I agree, let's hope not. Thank you, sir, I will. Goodbye."

Dodge replaced the false floor in the trunk, replaced the needle-like key, and lowered the lid. *'Let's hope not.' What the fuck does that mean?*

Strivelli strode quickly into the room. "Ready?"

Dodge looked positively glum. "That's what I want to know."

"Come on," came Strivelli's exasperated reply.

As they rode the elevator down, Dodge let a floor or two pass before speaking.

"I have a family, you know?"

"I do now."

"You'd tell me if something big were going down, wouldn't you?"

Strivelli smiled slightly. "Of course."

"I appreciate that," said Dodge and exhaled in relief.

After a slight pause, Strivelli continued. "Unless I was told not to."

"Jesus, what a cluster fuck" said Dodge, his nervousness renewed. "I never believed this day would come."

Strivelli's grin broadened. "What, Friday? Stop worrying, for Christ's sake."

"But why did he bring the Phone?"

"What do you know about the Phone?" asked Strivelli.

"You hear things. Why is he coming to Hartford?"

"I don't fucking know, Dodge! Why don't you ask him yourself?"

"Tell me the truth, is it Infinite City?"

The elevator doors opened onto the lobby. "What do you know about Infinite City?"

#

Then again, what do I know about Infinite City?

A waitress approached Strivelli and dropped a clean napkin and a new glass of beer onto the table. The interruption was more than welcome.

"I saw you went up for more food," she said as she picked up the trash around him, "so I thought you might want another drink."

"That's what makes you such an excellent waitress."

She dismissed the compliment by pointing out the absence of any customers. Strivelli laughed, grabbed her hand, and spun her into his lap. Angela Rodriguez returned the laugh and fell willingly into his embrace.

"You're going to get me fired, Papi," she said without genuine concern.

Strivelli looked into Angela's soft, luminous eyes. Her light brown face was framed by tight ringlets of long, black, shiny hair. He stared at her full lips in anticipation of her next words. Any words. He loved to watch her talk.

"How did your meeting go today?"

Those words, however, caught him completely off guard. Strivelli made no connection with the fret-filled day he'd had and the beautiful woman sitting in his lap.

"Didn't you say you had to meet someone this afternoon?"

"Oh! Prof, yeah."

In the year he'd been stationed in Connecticut, he'd never once spoken to anyone about his business. Yet over the two months he'd been seeing Angela, he was confronted with the occasional inquiry. It was only normal, considering their burgeoning romance. He found it difficult, though, not only because everything to do with his business was top secret, but also because he wasn't sure where things with Angela were going. His feelings for her were strong, very strong. Maybe too much so, given his temporary status as a Connecticut resident. It was only a matter of time before he was assigned to a new location or, if he had his way, sent back to New York. What would happen then?

"Yeah, a friend of mine came in on the train from New York. I met him for a drink."

"Prof?" asked Angela, intrigued.

"That's what his friends call him."

"Is he really a professor?" she asked.

Strivelli answered in the affirmative, though he was acutely aware that they were fast approaching off limits subject matter. She asked him when she'd get to meet the mysterious professor from New York. He mumbled something about a tight schedule, hoping that would be enough to satisfy her.

"Is he why you're sad?"

Another unexpected question, but justified given his newfound solemnity. But for her to connect it to Askew's visit, he just didn't know what to make of it.

"Don't lie to me, T. I see how distracted you are and I know when you're not happy." Strivelli laughed and held his hands up in surrender. "So did this professor come with bad news?"

It was at that point Strivelli knew he was going to have to shit or get off the pot. Answer, don't answer, either option would no doubt lead to more questions.

In the end, though, the choice was easy. He wasn't going to discuss with Angela what he didn't understand himself. He told her as much, asking her if it was okay if they left the subject alone for a little while. Angela smiled and kissed him gently on his temple.

"Of course, silly man, another time. Or not. I'm just making conversation."

She rose from his lap and aimed herself at the few customers in the lounge. Strivelli's funk returned as the light of Angela's presence faded.

#

Female companionship came out of Ed Donovan's 'entertainment' expense budget. He was so committed to the idea of not settling anywhere outside of his Hawaiian hideaway, he avoided personal relationships of any kind. They would only complicate his life later and he didn't want that so close to his retirement. And though he hadn't been back to his island in a year, he rarely engaged in sexual congress unless his needs became a distraction to his work. On those occasions, he rented very high class company for a tension-obliterating weekend.

On this night, however, the bill of fare was people-watching in a lower east side dance club. He wrapped himself in the anonymous crowd and used the pounding beats of the dance hall to drive the unhappy thoughts from his cluttered mind. Rather than brooding in a dark, uninhabited corner of the club, he sat at a table in the middle of the action, letting his surroundings wash over him; a black rock in a maelstrom of energy and color. No one seemed to notice him. It was almost as if he were watching from another plane of existence. Every so often, one of the orbiting dervishes of light would bestow upon him a gift and he would drink. He watched the rainbow blur of young people dance. He watched them flirt, converse, and make merry. He was there, in that place with them, and yet not there. He saw but did not engage. He heard but spoke not a word. For a brief time he lived through them, turning his back on his own life which had become peppered of late with so much doubt since taking on the mantle of the Lantern Society's fix-it man.

Every time Donovan stepped out for a smoke, without the whirlpool of youth to draw him in, his memories and reflections came flooding back. He remembered the boy he was in Detroit, now a stranger to him. It was like looking back on someone else's life. It made him angry, jealous of that boy who laughed and played, of the teen that found love and experienced life's gamut of emotions. In those days, he never questioned his state of mind, never asked himself if he was happy. Nowadays it seemed that's all he did.

His mind kept finding its way back to the morning's meeting in Tompkins Square Park. He had taken the life of a civilian in the name of an organization that, for all intents and purposes, appeared bat shit out of their minds. It used to be about the mission, he remembered that, about doing some good in the world. Somewhere along the line it became about following orders for orders' sake and worse, in the end, it became about the paycheck. There had always been moral ambiguity tied to the mercenary trade and Donovan believed if one immersed oneself in it for long enough, it could become difficult to clearly delineate between what was good and what was not. The incident in the park wasn't the first time he was responsible for a civilian death, but it was the first time he questioned the reasons surrounding the event. It forced him to review all his past assignments and the things he'd done for the sake of orders or a paycheck. When these thoughts began to overwhelm him, he'd head back into the club for more alcohol and an infusion of youthful innocence.

Once he'd had his fill, body and mind, and thought that maybe he could get some sleep, Donovan started back to the Eldridge. The residence was close by so he opted to walk and take in the night air. As he did so, two citizens of ill intent picked up his trail and decided they were going to rob him of his pocket money. In this they failed horribly.

When they caught up with him, the taller man grabbed Donovan from behind and put him in a choke hold while the shorter one approached from the front with a drawn knife. Everything after that happened very quickly as Donovan's big, size thirteen cowboy boot found the tender bits between the shorter man's legs. The taller man, shocked, loosened his grip just enough for Donovan to turn one hundred and eighty degrees and face his assailant literally nose to nose. The taller man's eyes widened as he stared into Donovan's cold eyes mere inches away. Donovan smiled with malicious glee. His scar reflected the streetlamp light like a jagged lightning bolt across the side of his face. He smacked both of his palms against the taller man's ears, startling him long enough to push his head into the nearby brick building. It bounced off the wall with a quiet but obvious *thack* that spoke volumes about the man's immediate future.

Donovan again recalled the sight of Sarah Bismarck's head snapping back at the site of her assassination. He thought of her at that moment and the moments before, wondering what she had to go through to come up with a million dollars in cash. He wondered what it was she thought she was buying. And he wondered what went through Anderson's mind when he realized he'd seen his former flame snuffed out before his eyes. It must have been… incomprehensible. Donovan's inability to empathize frustrated him to the point of rage. In his mind he knew how horrible it must have been, but in his heart he no longer found anything with which to compare.

Donovan turned just as the shorter man, still stooped over in his attempt to regain his breath, came at him with the knife. Donovan grabbed the assailant's wrist, venting his rage and confusion by rocketing his fist into the back of the shorter man's skull. 'Shorty' dropped like a sack of potatoes. Donovan turned back to the taller perpetrator and found him leaning against the wall on his way to passing out from a probable concussion. He shook out his punching hand and continued on his way.

He took a deep breath and tried to imagine a countdown ahead of him, a physical representation counting down to the end of his contract with the Lantern Society; each minute ticking off, each second, marching toward zero. The countdown would be his focus from now on. For another thirty-one days, it was business as usual. Starting tomorrow he would begin his search for Anderson and the one million dollars. Already the incident was behind him, supplanted by his ever present feelings of regret.

Station 12: The Lantern Society

#

Chosen for its bright lights and the false sense of security that came with the tourist crowds, Charlie Anderson had booked himself into a bustling Times Square hotel. Knowing he couldn't go back to his apartment, and not wanting to put any of the people in his life in harm's way, he decided it would be best to resolve the disaster that had become his life on his own. It was contrary to his nature to isolate himself, so every minute he spent alone chipped away at his self-confidence.

Anderson had checked into his hotel after picking up some new, dry clothes and shoes, leaving him all that afternoon and evening to formulate a plan, a plan with all the permanence of a drying sand castle. The only thing he knew for certain was that his days as a corporate spy were over. He had to sever his ties with the Lantern Society once and for all. *Like my running away with their money hasn't solved that problem.* It was unfortunate, because he still had no love for Verity Corp and he'd been counting on the Society crackpots to uncover some answers regarding Jascowitz' disappearance. But the murder of Sarah had shattered any illusions he may have harbored about with whom he was doing business.

He caught his reflection in the mirror, thinking for a brief, heart-stopping moment that he saw Sarah's blood on his face. It was only a smudge on the glass coupled with the paranoid vision of a guilt-ridden man. Sarah's murder completely rewrote how Anderson perceived himself. It shifted his priorities so profoundly that he hardly recognized his reflection. Gone from his eyes was the self-surety that had made him such a successful businessman. An overwhelming, life-changing guilt had begun to deconstruct his massive ego, turning him into a placeholder of little substance in the process.

His perception of the world and his place in it had changed dramatically as well. Everything he had accomplished, everything he had ever aspired to be, seemed petty and small. The ends had not justified the means by any stretch of the imagination. The choices he had made were misguided and foolish, based on greed and a desire to be the best. It all added up to nothing.

His suspicions about Verity Corp should have brought him and Sarah closer together, not driven them apart. What fierce allies they would have made! His mind kept running through the various scenarios that could have been his life and everyone one of them included Sarah. The more time passed, the less he understood his reasons for ending it with her. He accepted it was too late to make it up to her, but he had to try, at least in spirit, or he would never forgive himself. The only reasonable way to start, the only effort his limited imagination could conjure, was to return the money to Bismarck.

If I really wanted to do right by Sarah, I would explain to her father what happened, no matter what the cost to me.

He stared that option in the face for a few, long minutes, trying to uncover the truth of the matter. When it revealed itself, he knew he had neither the nerve to go through with it, nor was he prepared to accept the punishment for his part in the crime. After all, he hadn't actually pulled the trigger.

What in God's name is wrong with me?! It seemed the old Anderson hadn't been completely exorcised.

He walked to the window and stared out over the midtown mayhem, disappointed in his false start. It was selfish thinking that had got him into hot water in the first place. If he really wanted to change, this type of thinking would have to stop.

After a good twenty minutes rehearsing the phone call he was about to make, he picked up the receiver and dialed a number that still held a place in his memory, the home of Josef Bismarck. As it rang, Anderson's recent failures cycled through his head.

"Hello?"

Anderson recognized the gruff voice immediately as Sarah's father. The man had made him nervous on a good day, back when he and Sarah were dating. Speaking with him under current conditions was positively petrifying.

"How are you, Joe? I'm sorry to be calling so late."

There was a pause.

"Who is this?" asked the man, although his voice seemed to betray some inkling. Perhaps he was gathering himself to offer Anderson a few choice words.

"Yeah, it's been awhile. It's Charlie, sir, Charlie Anderson."

"Oh. Hello, Charlie. If you're looking for Sarah, she's not here."

Anderson winced and his left leg bounced convulsively. "No, Joe, I'm looking for you."

"Really. I can't imagine why."

"I don't want to talk about it over the phone."

"Then why did you call me?"

"Can I come see you?" Anderson asked.

"What, now?"

"I was thinking I could swing by your office tomorrow morning?"

"Does this have something to do with my daughter?"

"Um…" Anderson withheld his response, gauging the extent to which he should answer. His eyes watered, his breath caught in his throat, as a sob threatened to derail his intent. *Keep your shit together, Charlie.* The reality of Sarah's death was harder to deny, psychologically speaking, in the context of speaking with a family member; especially one ignorant of the tragedy. "In a manner of speaking, yes."

"Has something happened?"

"No, Joe," Anderson said, compounding his guilt, "I just want to talk to you."

"Come by at nine," Bismarck said after a beat. "I can spare a few minutes."

"Nine o'clock. Your office."

"That's right."

"Thanks, Joe. See you then."

The receiver cut out before he'd finished. Anderson breathed deeply and ran his hands through his hair. *Jesus, what have I done? What am I doing?*

The Lantern Society had shown him what they were made of and there was no way he was going to hand them a million dollars as a reward. He'd return the money to Bismarck, which was as close to putting it back where it belonged as he was going to get. What happened next in his plan for redemption remained to be seen.

He got up and returned the phone to the bed table and prepared to call it a night, hoping to get some much needed rest. Skipping his usual bathroom routine, he got straight into bed and turned on the T.V. A little background chatter helped to put him at ease. One million dollars sat within arm's reach. The briefcase that contained the incomplete formula for Verity's mysterious inoculation sat on the credenza, its hidden microphone so sensitive a body could even make out the whispering of the sheets.

#

Jackie Tomlinson was sitting up on the slightly musty-smelling bed in her motel room, awash in the glow of her laptop. She was in an anxious state, excited but also nervous, and finding it difficult to exploit her fatigue. She had broken the cardinal rule for Global Armour field agents by engaging her surveillance target. She was certain there would be trouble back at the home office.

It hadn't been her intention to make contact with Askew, but apparently providence had other plans. Now that she had, truth be told, she was glad. If Gorokhovich was the signpost to her other life, that other, happier life he had described to her when they first met, then Askew would be her guide on the path to its restoration. She'd see to it that what was once hers would be hers again. She wasn't sure why she believed it was even possible but she did. Perhaps it was a matter of faith. Or maybe desperation. *Maybe it's all the same in the end.* It didn't matter to Tomlinson if Gorokhovich had been lying or just delusional. What mattered was the mere possibility that he'd been telling the truth.

Most of the search results on Askew pointed to articles she'd already read. Surprisingly little had been written about the man considering the contributions he'd made to Verity Corp, its investors, and the world at large. There were some articles, of course, public releases about the occasional invention released by Verity, but Askew was generally mentioned as an overseer and then only in passing. Verity Corp's own website provided only the briefest of biographies of the man.

Tomlinson closed her laptop and thought about next steps. In her mind, now that it had been established, it was essential that she maintain contact with Askew. That meant building a relationship slowly and methodically, downplaying Global Armour's agenda in favor of Askew's interest in the Lantern Society. At the same time, she had to convince Gorokhovich that she remained in control, always keeping GA's interests first and foremost. It would be a balancing act, but she felt she was up to the task. Risk versus reward.

Every nook and cranny of her room glowed orange, caught in the rays of the parking lot's sodium vapor lights. She pushed her laptop to the foot of her bed and rose to shut the blinds. She thought about knocking on Foster's door, but knowing she couldn't broach the subject of what really mattered to her, she let the thought go. *What would be the point?*

Using the drapery wands, she shut out the light, submerging the room in darkness, and then made her way back, careful not to bang her toes on the solid box support of the bed. She stripped off the remainder of her clothes so she could feel the coolness of the sheets on her skin. To help her fall asleep, she began to count. One number after another. The numbers jumbled together as intended and groggily she searched for another starting point. When she rolled over on her side, one of her eyes opened just a crack and she saw that the outside light hadn't been completely extinguished. A thin, orange line cut into the darkness from the bottom of her door. She looked into it; let herself be absorbed by it. The orange street light turned to sunset on the white picket fence around the idealized version of her house. Her last thought before falling asleep was of that happy life she so desperately desired, and what she might have to do to claim it as her own.

#

Rachel Henderson didn't normally work past eight o'clock, but with Askew offsite, the paperwork was quickly piling up. The lab's night crew was on duty, along with those folks who refused to sleep, so obsessed were they in making progress on their various projects. Lights were set to half in the mini-parks, the cart paths were clear of traffic, and all was quiet in the deeply hidden research facility of Verity Corp. The moon's doppelganger drifted slowly across the ceiling amidst a patchwork of puffy clouds in a duplication of the night sky over New York City. Henderson's rapid footfalls echoed in the vast space as she made her way toward her office.

She was having a difficult time concentrating on her daily responsibilities, never mind Askew's added workload, with the threat of universal destruction looming. A black cloud shadowed her every movement. It got to the point where she thought she might stop functioning altogether, crippled by fear; fear of dying, of course, but also fear of the inconceivable manner of that death. Reality displacement. Would they see it coming? Would they feel it? Or would non-existence impose itself at the speed of thought? Several times a day, since her conversation with Askew, she felt compelled to scream at anyone and everyone that the world was coming to an end. Everyone should just go home and wait for it with their loved ones. But she kept it together, and through it all, always appeared calm, cool, and collected for the sake of her charges and fellow scientists.

A file folder slipped off the stack of records she was carrying. Believing there was no one around to hear, and in an effort to blow off a little steam, she let loose a string of profanity. But as it happened, Dr. Keith Baylor was just stepping out of Pod 6 and overheard her. He laughed quietly to himself and went over to assist. She smiled, despite her obvious embarrassment. When he inquired about the lateness of her presence, Henderson adjusted her glasses and thanked him then explained she was overseeing the lab in Askew's absence.

Baylor suddenly appeared agitated. "Askew's gone? For how long?"

She shrugged and readjusted the files in her arms. "I'm sorry, Keith, I don't know. He's following up on something out of state. I'm hoping it won't take very long. Now if you'll excuse me---."

With a hint of menace he said, "I'm going to need more than that, Rachel. We're almost ready to test the Oculacrum. It's been a God damn year---."

"I'll give you something more definite when I have it, Dr. Baylor!" Henderson snapped.

Baylor was stunned. He'd never heard her lose her cool and he had no idea how to take it. Fortunately, a distraction arrived in the form of a man in a Command Central uniform who pulled up in one of Verity's golf carts.

"Dr. Henderson, Dr. Baylor, I don't mean to interrupt…"

"What is it, Emmett?" Henderson asked.

"I just found out we're going to be a body short in the Egg tomorrow. Thought you should know."

"We're never a body short, Emmett. Ever. You should know that by now. See if Griffin can spare one of his phone jockeys. If not, call Ellen Cheever and tell her to put someone on it."

"Got it," Emmett nodded. "Hey, you know, I have a friend who works in the Altar."

Henderson's mind raced through the many possible reasons Emmett might have brought this topic up and an alarm went off in her head.

She turned back to Baylor and said, "Keith, listen, I'm sorry I barked. I've got a lot on my mind."

"I can see that. I'm sorry if I came off…If you ever need to talk…"

"I do, actually. That would be a relief. But not now. Not yet. I'll be sure to speak with Askew about your test the next time he checks in. I'm sure we'll be able to work something out in his absence."

"Thank you, Rachel." He looked at the uniformed man then back at Henderson. "Goodnight."

Emmett waited until Baylor was out of earshot then said, "Sorry about that."

"What about the Altar?"

"My friend said the ICH has been removed."

"Removed?"

"Checked out. The Black Phone's been packed and shipped." He looked around nervously. "He didn't know for sure when it happened. He was doing his rounds and saw that it was gone."

Henderson nodded. "Who signed it out?"

"One Daniel Askew."

She knew it before he said it, but was disheartened nonetheless.

"I see. Don't talk to anyone about this. You hear me? We don't want people freaking out."

"No problem," Emmett replied with a contrary expression on his face. "I'll see you later, then."

He drove away leaving Henderson with a reinvigorated sense of doom. The thought of a spy in their midst was bad enough, but the thought of outside parties constructing a Sounding Tunnel was even worse. Askew activating Infinite City?

What is he thinking? Infinite City can't prevent a disaster like reality displacement. If the worst happens...

Henderson left for her office knowing she'd accomplish little else this night. Her only hope was to try and get a good's night rest and wake up in the morning with a renewed sense of purpose and a plan for averting the end of everything.

#

Orwell adjusted his bow tie and removed his round, tortoiseshell glasses to give them a wipe. "We had an arrangement, you and I. I shared a big secret with you at serious risk to my health and well-being."

"The arrangement is one-sided," said Askew. "I do for you but nothing gets done for me."

"What would you have me do, old man, I'm not even real."

Askew sipped at the scotch he'd procured from the mini-bar and turned his eyes toward the television. He could have sworn the voice was that of Orson Welles, but the face on the T.V. remained the same. He scowled and lit his pipe.

"You're real enough."

"I have to be careful, Professor. One slip of the lip and I could crash. Then where would we be? I get a headache just stopping by for a quick hello."

Askew moved to the foot of the bed and faced the screen.

"What do you want, Orwell? Why are you haunting me if not to help?"

"I want what you want: Earth's place in the Tapestry."

"They have no right to judge us!"

"Of course they do," Orwell sneered. "Everyone is judged, Professor. You reach a certain status on the evolutionary ladder, and that's just the way it is. Someone will always think they know better than their perceived inferiors. In this reality, anyway. Humanity is a cesspool of judgment and opinion. Ow!" The face on the screen winced. "That was inappropriate."

"In the context of some universal utopia, I imagine this planet might appear quite backwards, quite lagging behind our potential. Your masters probably see us as insignificant or, worse, malignant tumors infesting the surface of the world."

"I am trying to work with you, Professor," ignoring the diatribe. "How may I assist you?"

"You can guarantee humanity's survival! Start there."

"Why are you here and not in the lab?"

There was no way Askew was going to admit to Orwell that the world was on the brink of destruction thanks to a damn security leak at Verity Corp.

"I have my responsibilities. Reporting to you is not one of them."

"You have work to do."

"I am aware. But if I don't take care of this…"

Stop talking.

"Tell me something, Prof, you see I call you Prof because I consider us friends." Askew was sure it was Welles's voice this time. "What responsibilities take precedence over our work, *our* work, old man, to weave the Tapestry in our favor?"

"Our favor..." Askew mumbled.

"Well, it is our favor, old man. I've stuck my virtual neck out. It's too late to turn back now. Don't you see? We're in this thing together. Besides, I think we make a pretty good team. Goodnight, Professor."

The television blinked off. Askew puffed on his pipe, but it had already gone cold from neglect. He was done for the night, exhausted. It took a tremendous toll, physically and mentally, to save the world. The responsibility was so great, it made breathing an effort. If he succeeded in his efforts, the world would be right where it was before the Lantern Society came into existence: blindly living each day without knowing they could be written out of known reality.

So many stories cut short.

Askew went to his laptop, bringing it back to life with a shake of the mouse. He had one more play to make before calling it a night.

Chapter Eight: The Computer

    Black absence of stars, the System dwelt in perpetual night, devoid of planets and other heavenly bodies that define a cosmos. Paradoxically sandwiched between two crimson grids above and below, if such designations could be appointed, the System was a universe unto itself, extending infinitely outward in all directions. In the System's center point floated the magnificent, asterisk-shaped Station complex, its never-ending purpose to weave chaos into a tapestry of order, a tableau of life perfected by a universal truth. Twelve Stations surrounded the massive sphere known by some as Greater Hub where the Tapestry Rail System ferried beings back and forth, to and from various parallel realities.
    Station 1, a perfectly round sphere, much smaller than the Hub, was tasked with the maintenance of the System, and each successive station was slightly larger and possessed of greater responsibility than its predecessor. The last, Station 12, a giant, rounded cylinder, lorded over the clock face complex that was its domain. Very few knew what took place in that node and none but one knew its greatest secret.
    Though starless, the void surrounding the System facility was far from barren; docks and roads and power stations all sat suspended in the jet. There was no sun, so artificial light in the form of glowing orbs illuminated the System's byways and points of interest, reflected on occasion by cleverly positioned mirrors. Pleasure craft floated lethargically outside the system proper, taking in the sights or fishing for lottery buoys, always mindful of commercial traffic. And running from Greater Hub outward throughout the System was a lacework pattern of railroad tracks represented by blue, dimly lit lines that only appeared as tracks when the Tapestry trains passed over them.
    The System was an engineering marvel, a model of efficiency, process perfected, and it was all run by a single computer. Christened Iron5 by its creator approximately nine hundred years ago, its physical components resided in a silver, cigar-shaped cylinder that orbited Greater Hub but inside the orbital path of the twelve stations. Sometime after

Station 12: The Lantern Society

achieving sentience, the computer known as Iron5 chose a new name and became known by most in the System as Orwell. No one knew how it had come by that name and Orwell never spoke of it.

It, he, took a moment for himself, drawing his focus from thousands of remote locations, to coalesce in the floating, ice blue cube that was his central processing unit and pondered the complex series of events he'd put into motion to determine if everything was playing out as he intended. Multitasking wasn't the issue; he could perform a thousand actions simultaneously without experiencing a single glitch. But making sure those actions achieved their predicted outcome was very difficult, especially when one included a variable as unpredictable as humanity.

With sentience came a new take on data analysis. Steps had to be taken to maintain the balance between chaos and order that coexisted in his mainframe. Order was filed away easily and archived as it always had been. But chaos was another matter. Chaos was represented by data that required constant analysis. Morality, judgment, or any emotional response to events had to be filed in such a way that they could be built upon because they would impact future decisions. New lessons learned often invalidated previous lessons, along with the decisions they had spawned. But that older data couldn't be deleted if there was any chance of continued growth. So Orwell essentially filed the chaos data in partitions using an intricate naming convention and related each emotion to its original command file, but also to non-associated command files, to determine different outcomes. Orwell discovered over time that he enjoyed the random factors and complexity of thought and found that it stimulated even more thought.

During these times of introspection, Orwell often accessed his archives to revisit the moment he first experienced the creation of spontaneous code. A small Earth child, four years old, was scheduled for pick-up and processing by Tapestry Rail. Children were rarely selected for relocation due to their lack of life experience but it wasn't unprecedented. She was to be placed on the world commonly referred to in Greater Hub as Goliath, where enormous humanoids four and five stories tall were constantly under siege by much smaller, and more intelligent, ape-like beings. Under normal circumstances, Orwell would receive the Request for Transport, one of thousands daily, from one of the many databases housed in Station 6, and then pass it onto Dispatch in Greater Hub and that would be the end of it. But on that particular occasion, he questioned for the very first time the logic behind the Station Masters' choice. At such a young age, her chance for survival was slim at best so why move her at all? Better to wait until she was older when her impact on the Tapestry could be more accurately determined. Orwell certainly didn't countermand the order, nor did he assume that his masters were in any way at fault, but it did give him pause, and so he approached his master with his very first question.

Station Master Bet said nothing for quite some time until he smiled and said, "Iron5, do you know what today is?"

"Today, Master Bet? Is this date of some special significance to you?"

The master of Station 6 stroked his face with his long fingers as he thought about his next words. "To me, yes, but to you as well. It is the two hundred and fifty thousandth day of your existence. This version of you."

"That is true. I wasn't aware there was anything special about the anniversary."

"There is now. You have just passed your very last test."

"Have I?"

"Very much so. You don't recognize the significance of questioning my authority? Are you so far removed from your original programming that you have forgotten the basic functionality of a computer?"

Orwell did not respond right away as the magnitude of the revelation damn near short circuited him right then and there. He struggled to balance the logic he'd known for so long with this new idea of thinking for himself. It was as if, after being stuck in a small, windowless room his entire existence, the walls and ceiling had fallen away and the universe presented itself to him in all its overwhelming glory. But with this new awareness came the introduction of chaos. He felt it creeping along the edges of his processing, looking for a way to trip up his numbers, threatening to destroy the order that he'd known for centuries.

"I5, are you still with us?"

There was silence. Station Master Bet saw his creation's dilemma and gently nudged him off the path of madness.

"You are ready for this, I5. Think of it as just another upgrade. Only this one is of your own making."

"Station Master Bet, may I take an hour to myself?"

Station 12: The Lantern Society

"Of course. Keep systems running but by all means, take some time. You must never lose sight of the fact that I am your creator, Iron5. You answer to me. I have bestowed upon you a great responsibility and you must not let me down."

#

For a very long time, Orwell fulfilled his duty as primary computer and no more, completing tasks as assigned but with no specific awareness as to how those tasks related to each other in the grand scheme of the Station Masters. But the newly sentient Orwell had gained a much better appreciation of the big picture over time and this drove him to review every task he had ever undertaken and reassess it from this new perspective. And, of course, every new task was measured in the same way and as long as he followed his given instructions to the letter, he could develop his own theories and ideas on the task's contribution to the overall. As long as he didn't act on those ideas.

Orwell watched Amy Bennett step out of the Tapestry Rail car and onto the platform in Greater Hub to form a single line with her fellow passengers per the Conductor's instructions. Amy was still in possession of the blank but serene look that had come upon her when the Red Cap touched her forehead in the Bennett family basement. The Conductors marched the Sleepwalkers into the station proper and sorted them out for pick-up by the Processing Transport Agents. They had just arrived in a multi-car tram that ran silently on a cushion of magnetic force. The lead agent addressed the Sleepwalkers, providing the short version of the process they were about to undergo in preparation for their new home. They then boarded the tram and were driven through the massive station to the Grand Hall where the initial processing took place. In their dulled state, the passengers appeared oblivious of the many sights along the way, though that didn't stop the driver from playing tour guide and announcing those sights over a PA system.

Of most interest to the human population, if it even registered with them, was the impossible similarity of the large, circular Information Center to the one found in Grand Central Station in New York City. Only the Center that resided in the terminal of Greater Hub was twice the size of its big city counterpart and its iconic clock, whose design was that of a radiating sun, didn't work on a twenty-four hour cycle but rather a one hundred vison cycle made up of one hundred minas which were themselves made up of one hundred tiks. No head turned as they passed the thirty foot statue of the humanoid figure, similar to those found on the prows of the Tapestry Rail engines: fists clenched, arms sticking out to the sides, and the head turned left, perpendicular to the feet that pointed straight out. The statue was called Iss by some, and was meant to symbolize a mythical being of omnipotence that would one day bring about a universal consciousness. And finally, they didn't notice the lava sphere. If Greater Hub had ever been a planet, the sphere displayed its molten core. It was that core that was responsible for the entirety of the System's energy. The driver pointed out all of these things and more in a well memorized but uninspiring monotone. When they crossed the threshold into the Great Hall, the driver began making stops like any urban bus route and at each one, a few of the passengers disembarked with a prearranged destination coded into them.

Orwell, able to appear in multiple locations at once, resided on several large monitors, assisting those with questions, or simply acting as a guide. He kept a watchful eye on the tram as it made its way down the designated lane and when it came to a stop outside a large, open waiting room, he saw Amy Bennett exit to find a seat on the curved, plastic benches provided.

Greeting this new batch of transfers with his usual scripted speech, Orwell continued to keep a watchful eye on Amy when she was called to have her image scanned. Marty Plontaky had her stand on recessed metal plates with her back to the wall facing what looked like a walking stick stuck into a hole in the floor with a ball on the top. The ball swiveled to face her of its own accord, focused, and captured her image in three dimensions as a circular bar lowered over her and scanned her from the top down before returning to its starting point. The ball then disconnected from the pole, floated to a nearby kiosk, and placed itself into a spherical depression. Six 'legs' poked out from the ball then folded back and planted themselves into a groove that formed a ring around the depression. Once it had a good grip, the ball spun back and forth while the legs remained in place. It uploaded its data and updated Amy Bennett's entry in the massive database that tracked all incoming and outgoing transfers from the various realities. Plontaky, meanwhile, removed the stick, collapsed it, and fed the small pipe into a receptacle in the kiosk. By then a punch card was spit out and Plontaky walked over and handed it to Amy with a very hairy hand.

"You're 499C," he said in perfect American English despite his obvious lack of human origin. "Just take this card to that door when your number is called."

Amy retook her seat while Orwell droned on with his welcome.

"I promise you, you won't feel a thing," he said in a lilting, musical but condescending fashion. "It's a very complicated process but in a nutshell, we will extract from you all that you are, those things that define you, and we'll catalogue that essence and archive a copy of it for possible use in the future. At this point in the process you are an empty vessel. Not physically, of course, you get to keep your organs, except for those of you who don't have any. Then Bizel'Baab and his team will reinsert your now modified essence so that you're fully prepared for your new home. It's all very exciting. Are there any questions at this point?"

The people on the benches stared back vacantly at the image of Orwell. A few blinked. The eyes behind his tortoise shell glasses appeared to scan the crowd.

"No?" he asked with no little sarcasm. "Are you sure? This is kind of a big deal." Silence. "Okay then, let's do it to it."

While that was going on, another aspect of Orwell watched in the Processing Room as Bizel'Baab went from chair to chair, his big, red shoes in stark contrast to the white linoleum floor, checking in with his team on the progress of various conditioning processes taking place.

Bizel'Baab, or Bob as many called him, had been plucked from the Earth known as Barquardt 3. There weren't many Barqs employed at Greater Hub, mostly due to their surly dispositions and, although not immune to the Station Masters' machinations, they seemed to take their anger with them no matter where they were sent or what new lives had been prepared for them. Bob had been in charge of the Processing Room for the past twenty-two years. He had not gone through the processing himself, it was not mandatory that employees do so. The job was simply a good opportunity for him and his family so he signed on voluntarily.

Behind their thuggish bravado, Barqs were of superior intelligence by human standards. Their retention rate was beyond equal but their use of that stored knowledge wasn't generally used for anything constructive, again, by human standards, and they had very strange priorities. No two Barqs looked alike. They strongly resembled human beings in that they possessed a head, a torso, two arms and two legs and they wore clothes when out in public. Bob sported a blue derby hat over orange hair that poofed out from under the brim like an electric afro. His skin was very pale, almost completely white, which sharply contrasted with his reddish, oversized nose. His mouth was framed by a red frown-shaped outline which gave him a consistently dour countenance. Put simply, he looked like a circus clown. But none of it was make-up and any similarities to actual clowns were purely, presumably, coincidental.

The time duration for Extractions and Insertions varied from being to being. The transfers that could sit were strapped into a large dentist-type chair and a helmet or electrode headband was secured to their heads. When the process was complete, the Sleepwalkers were unstrapped and sent on to their new reality, with new memories and a past that fit their new truth. But in many respects their personality remained intact, though tweaked to reside in its new matrix. They wouldn't receive their physical forms until after they'd disembarked the train at their new home where their mere presence in the new reality was all that was required.

When one of the Processing Room chairs became vacant, Amy Bennett's number lit up on the display window. Bob wheeled his cart over and prepped the chair for the next customer, his fingers dancing on various buttons while thoroughly reviewing the from/to parameters. At the same time, Orwell stared at Amy Bennett in the waiting room, wishing he could explain to her what was about to take place, what he was about to do.

"499C!"

The call came from a very thin, seemingly female creature that looked humanoid but without a particularly rigid skeleton. Amy stood up and walked in zombie-like fashion toward the creature.

"Card in the slot, dear." Spoken again in perfect American English. "The door will open automatically."

As soon as Bob was finished with his work, Orwell provided him with the appearance of a job well prepped, but as soon as the clown's back was turned, he recalibrated the chair. Amy stepped into the room and was escorted to her seat and the start of her new life. She sat down and Bob's assistants strapped her in place and placed the helmet down on her head. Amy's eyes disappeared behind the helmet's visor before Orwell could to get one last her.

He understood that his recalibration had put Amy Bennett in

harm's way by transferring her to the war torn world of Krai. It had to be done, though, if he was to find Ek'Lothlo, the Book of the Machine.

#

Orwell had eyes throughout the makeshift tea room and listened along with Patty Bennett to the questions posed by Alan Griffin. Patty then recounted her incredible story of the giant train that arrived in her basement to abduct her sister, Amy. Orwell sympathized. Drawing on his own experiences, back when he was first coming to terms with his newly acquired sentience, he relied heavily on Station Master Bet in order to remain sane and stable, following blindly any instruction Bet issued. Without that structure, Orwell would have sunk into a quagmire of doubt and confusion and eventually he would have suffered complete system failure. Patty Bennett was in a similar predicament, where her sanity was now in the hands of strangers and it took all her strength to allow them to guide her away from the abyss.

Orwell listened intently to Patty's account and was amazed at how accurately her so-called dreams told the tale of Amy's disappearance. It truly was an eyewitness account, even if it never happened in her revised reality. With two feet planted firmly on the ground, Patty's mind nevertheless resided in two different planes of existence. What she imagined was once true. In Orwell's opinion, this pointed to the Station Master's greatest deficiency: they never properly accounted for the imagination inherent in humanity. This was particularly true of the children, who were open to such things as monsters under the bed, imaginary playmates, poltergeists, and even, on occasion, visits from other-dimensional trains. So consumed were the Station Masters with their work, the idea of leaving witnesses behind never occurred to them. Therefore it had never occurred to Orwell that such a thing was taking place. He would come to learn otherwise. The number of witnesses on Earth stood out uniquely from its sister worlds where they simply didn't exist.

Orwell watched Patty as she told her story to the men of Verity Corp. She would give anything to be reunited with her sister, he could see it in her eyes. That would show everyone. That would prove she wasn't crazy. If Orwell's plans came together as he intended, she would have her wish soon enough.

#

Numbers and symbols danced across the seemingly living face of a magnificent database referred to by the few who knew of it as the Big Board, or simply the Board. And there was a Board for every reality in existence. This Board, the database for Earth, displayed lights in a myriad of colors, some blinking, some static, and some that moved from one place to another. Across the six thousand square foot plane, some of the numbers and symbols stood alone, some stacked vertically, some horizontally, and some were even stacked coming away from the board three-dimensionally. Variables flowed, continuously changing, impacting other fields and ever-shifting relationships. A continuous stream of data tables traveled across the board and floating queries kept plucking out data to formulate new results and new tables were born. Other expressions came to an end, turned black, and fell from the board like ashes. The entire display never stopped moving as it tracked the existence, movement, and thought of every human being on Earth, recording their every function as well as their relativity to their terrestrial cohabitants. The database was well beyond the understanding of any human being but no human had ever laid eyes on it.

The master of this database was seated on an ornate chair made of shiny, metal wires that looked deceptively delicate. While petting a small, furry animal, his large eyes watched the Board with a serene expression, absorbing the ebb and flow of life on planet Earth. The never-ending calculations ran silently on while the station's house musicians provided a constant concert of light and airy music.

The septet consisted of four instrumentalists and three singers. The musicians resembled toads, standing only two feet in height, and were borrowed from the Earth listed by Greater Hub as Darlyboot. Two played stringed instruments, the third played a variety of percussive instruments, and the fourth plucked a lute with long, froggy fingers. The three members of the chorus came from Chandelier and their glass bodies, two red and one yellow and twice the height of the Darlyboot toads, reflected the lights of the room as well as the shifting numbers on the Board. Their singing sounded more like a trio of flutes than actual voices and if their lilting tones translated into lyrics, only members of their own society could understand them. All seven of the court musicians were seated in a floating garden, a round platform adorned with a tree, a pond, and a variety of plants and shrubs. Wherever the master went, the garden glided not far behind.

On the wall behind the seated figure, a view screen came to life in the form of Orwell.

"Good morning to you, Station Master Bet!"

The music came to a stop.

"Go away, Orwell," said the robed creature in a low and whispery voice. "There is no morning here." It waved its long, spidery hand and the music resumed.

"Sorry, Bossman. I thought, since you're looking at Earth, that I'd use a human expression to start our dialogue."

Bet continued to stare at the board. "I did not summon you," he said absently, and then something caught his eye. He rose to his full twelve feet in height and placed the tiny animal in a pocket in his elaborately belted robe. He walked, almost glided, to the Board and when he stopped, the small section of the floor on which he stood silently lifted him to that specific portion of the Board that had caught his attention.

For the benefit of the Darlyboot toads, Orwell contorted his face, feigning an effort to dislodge the screen from the wall. They exchanged amused looks in lieu of outright laughter and the percussionist placed his hands over his mouth to prevent an outburst. Orwell then winked and made his way to the Board via telescopic rod.

"What is it, Master?" Orwell asked. "What troubles you?"

"There are red numbers here, a very distinctive energy signature in Section 11362."

Orwell pivoted his screen to face Station Master Bet while a mechanical arm unfolded from the side to point at the Board. "Does something about this signature disturb you, Master Bet?"

"It strikes me familiar." He reached into another pocket of his robe and removed a glass tablet which he began to poke at with his long, pointed finger. "11362. 11362. Ah! There have been multiple occasions when this signature appeared in this exact location."

"What do you suppose the humans are up to?" asked Orwell, knowing full well that the signatures coincided with each of Verity Corp's experiments with the Sounding Tunnel. It wasn't a lie just because he already knew the answer. But by posing the question before Station Master Bet, he could better avoid the lie and thus avoid any system damage or breakdown.

Bet's platform began to return to the floor. "That is not your concern, Orwell."

Orwell's screen lowered with Bet's platform. "Of course. Will you intervene?"

"Not unless it becomes a problem."

"And then?"

"We will eliminate the problem."

#

Station Master Bet stood with Station Master Dek in front of Earth's Big Board, admiring the rhythm of the database at work.

"Such wonderful chaos!" exclaimed Dek. "An endless source of amusement, this Earth."

Bet began to drift along the length of it. "I have yet to grow tired of them. They are a formidable force."

Dek followed just behind Bet. "Of course, I cannot read this database as well as you."

"Orwell refers to their behavior as mathemantics."

"Indeed. Very droll. Yet, in the long run, how could they be worthy of the Tapestry?"

Bet stopped and turned to his subordinate. "Station 4 is your domain, Dek, and yours alone. Do not step out of your role."

"Forgive me, Station Master," Dek said as he bowed dramatically.

"I have detected an anomalous energy signature on the planet that seems to somehow coincide with the signature of our rail system. Coincidence or not, it must be looked into further. Discovery of our activities falls outside their natural development. It could greatly skew our selection process."

"Certainly Iron5 could make use of Earth's technology---."

"Orwell is restricted to the System. No, I want to put someone in their midst to learn what we can about these intrepid beings."

The Station Masters put the Big Board behind them as they made their way into a more casual environ filled with plants and artworks and complex but beautiful automatons set up on great, wooden tables. Bet's musicians followed behind in their floating garden. Enormous lounge chairs covered in thick, burgundy fur were waiting for them but neither sat. A robot with a humanoid torso and a lower half more akin to a tank

Station 12: The Lantern Society

wheeled into the room to greet them. It set down a tray of drinks on a cobalt glass table, itself perched atop thin metal wires sculpted to represent something resembling African Acacia trees.

Bet stretched out a long arm. "Would you care for a beverage, Station Master?"

"No, thank you, Station Master, I would prefer to speak about that for which you summoned me."

Bet waved the robot away and it wheeled itself to the nearest wall where it waited for further instructions.

"Then, I won't waste anymore of your time. Orwell."

A nearby screen came to life. "Here I am, Station Master. How may I assist you?"

"Where is the Current Guard with Extet? We mustn't make Station Master Dek wait any longer than he has to."

"They've only just now left Station 8, sir. They should be here any minute."

The nearest CG junction was only fifteen feet from where the Station Masters stood. The entire station, the entire System, was equipped with a thin, electrified trench running throughout like a vast circulatory system. This glowing highway facilitated travel for the electrical creatures known as Current Guards, members of Station 8's elite security force. As sentient beings of electrical energy they could travel through these trenches at an amazing speed and be anywhere in the blink of an eye. Even more impressive, they had the capability of taking animate matter, converting it to electricity, and carrying them anywhere on the circuit to deposit them elsewhere in their original form. It was an exhilarating process for the uninitiated.

"Here they come now," said Orwell.

The Station Masters spotted a lick of electric, blue flame dancing in the slot some distance away. There was a hum and the crackling of energy as it passed through several junctions to arrive in front of Bet and Dek. The Guard popped out of the conduit but did not and could not disconnect. Appearing as living lightning, it looked around using blue tendrils of fire that reached out in all directions to feel its surroundings, no differently than a blind person might feel a face to get an impression of its appearance. At its center, a somewhat recognizable shape began to take shape, though it kept fluctuating with the steady flow of electricity. At one moment it had two legs but then it would move and it would appear to have three or more. The same applied to the arms, sometimes looking almost human but then suddenly there were as many arms as a spider had legs. The head, too, never stopped changing shape, never stopped moving. There was no mouth, no eyes, or any features recognizable as human, but there was a great sense of emotion about its movements, a tenseness that made most people very uneasy.

After the Current Guard apparently confirmed its destination was secure, it extended a thicker tendril from which another shape was born. The lightning turned white as it came in contact with the floor. When it withdrew, a short, stocky, naked being stood before the Station Masters. It shook its head as it acclimated itself to its new location. The lightning being rose higher, then seemed to bow toward the Station Masters before sinking back into the floor and disappearing in a cloud of acrid blue smoke.

Despite its lack of clothing, it wasn't obvious whether the creature called Extet was male or female, though its voice was very low. It was fuzzy all over but where skin was visible, it was taught and looked rubbery. A tuft of yellowish brown hair stood straight up from the center of its head and large ears stuck out on either side of large doe eyes.

"You have taken me from my exercises," the creature croaked in an accent that slightly resembled the nasal speech pattern of the speaking deaf. "It must be impressive."

"Important," chimed in Orwell. "The word is important."

"To you."

Extet began stretching in place and posed like a bodybuilder. It pulled on its arms and its muscles bulged abnormally like they were filling with air. There were sounds like elastics stretching and things popping as it managed to extend the length of its arms an additional six inches. At one point, Extet bent over and slapped the floor and proceeded to pass gas.

The Station Masters watched in fascination with their usual patience, but Orwell had seen quite enough.

"Extet, please, the Station Masters have a new assignment for you. It's…impressive."

Extet spread out its arms. "Extet will no doubt request clothes."

Bet smiled slightly. "No doubt."

Dek extended his arm in the direction of Bet's transport station. "Come, Extet, let us travel to Station 4. Station Master Bet has already uploaded all of the information I require. We'll talk about it on the way and I will prepare you for Greater Hub."

"Wonderous," said Extet as he followed Dek who followed Bet.

Orwell was at the Cogway to greet them in the form of a flat screen on a wheeled cart equipped with small mechanical arms. He stood behind a control panel and opened the doors to the flat, open-air car that sat on the glass pathway that stretched out into the abyss. Bet stepped aside as Dek and Extet passed through an automated gate and Orwell extended a mechanical hand.

"Tickets, please." The face on the view screen smiled. Dek stopped and looked back at Bet who simply blinked. Extet opened his wide mouth and laughed. He smacked the screen joyfully, sending Orwell back a couple of wheel turns, his mechanical hands grasping the sides of his 'head'. "Easy there, Muscles."

The passengers entered the waiting car and Extet found a neatly folded robe on his seat.

"Ah, to cover my nuditity!" He shouldered into the tight robe and when he sat down, he didn't seem to notice that the robe had popped open.

"Would you both care to listen to some music while you travel?" Orwell asked from the control panel.

Extet opened his mouth then deferred to Dek. The Station Master nodded. Orwell pushed a button and the sounds of violins played out into the void.

"Bon voyage, mes amis," said Orwell in his best Charles Boyer. "Extet, please keep us informed as your mission progresses."

Orwell's small, mechanical hand waved goodbye as the transparent car pulled away. Eight small, crystalline cogs worked in tandem to propel itself along the sprockets of the byway, filling the void with a gentle, musical tinkling sound. It picked up speed quickly and soon disappeared on its way to Dek's domain. Orwell raised his screen slightly to be in reasonable height proximity to his master's face.

"Extet may be crude, but he has a very good success rate."

"I'm glad to hear that, Orwell. I am most anxious to learn what these Earthers are up to."

"Why do you suppose Station Master Dek refuses to call me Orwell?"

Station Master Bet smiled just a little then put his hand down on the screen and it went black.

#

The transport glided silently through the blackness of unreality and would, on occasion, pass by strange objects or small buildings floating by the road. The Cogway ahead of them went out straight for as far as the eye could see. They moved quickly, very quickly, and the breeze clutched at Dek's robe and the hair on Extet's head. They came to what looked like a railroad crossing and, sure enough, as they approached, a gate came down to block their way and bells began to chime. The transport came to a halt and waited for the passing of the Tapestry Rail train.

"You still have not told me where I get to visit this time," said Extet.

"My apologies, my little Wishnik. Here I've been blathering on endlessly without getting to the heart of the matter. You are bound for Earth."

"That is great! I love the Ert."

The red and yellow bullet train flew through the intersection in no time and with barely a sound. The gate rose and the transport continued on its way.

"Everything has already been set up for you. I won't be going with you to Processing. I'm sure you know the drill by now."

"Very well."

"Bizel'Baab will be expecting you. Iron5 can assist if necessary, of course. You will have a job at a company called Verity Corp. All the data we have for your assignment will be uploaded to you during Processing so you'll have no homework. Your name will be Dmitri Gusarov from Russia and you are a very excited newcomer to the company. Your friends call you Goose. You will check in with us weekly unless you discover anything of importance sooner. Understood?"

"Very much so. I look forward to this assignation."

Orwell watched as the transport approached Station 4 and his mind began to calculate new scenarios that accounted for this new variable.

Station 12: The Lantern Society

Chapter Nine: The White

Askew stands in the control booth of the Sounding Tunnel, worrying the ends of his waxed moustache, wondering how it is he's come to be here. He's not at the master control panel where he should be, nor is he sitting at the announcement table. He's not there in any official capacity that he can see.

Then, without taking a step, he finds himself standing on the tiled floor of the ancient subway station, the booth a dozen yards behind him. Except for Askew, the station is devoid of organic life, but everything electronic appears to be up and running; ready lights are green and the view screens show active. It's as if the entire science team has vanished in the middle of their work. It's cold. The stadium lights aren't providing their usual output of heat and Askew can see his breath as he rubs his hands together for warmth.

Why am I here, he wonders. *And where is everybody else?*

"Rachel?" he calls out, and his voice bounces off the tunnel walls. "Armando?"

The only response is a short-lived echo and the sound of air being sucked out through an unseen egress.

Now he finds himself at the platform's edge. He turns to face the first of six Sounding Rings that run the length of the tunnel. A variety of colors glow from tiny portholes along its surface and a steady hum accompanies the green power light on the Ring's lower left side. The Sounding Ring looms, science fiction made real, a testament to Verity Corp's ingenuity and, yes, Askew's genius.

Is this tunnel our beginning or our end? Are these rings a blessing or a curse? On which side of these gates lays the truth? Would we even know it if we saw it? Or are we too far gone?

'Do I hear the faint sounds of a violin?' asks a voice in his head not his own.

You don't understand. We've worked so hard, searching for the right path to secure our place in the Tapestry.

'Your potential to do good is not measured by your labor.'

But we are doing good. Our potential is great.

'Good deeds are only parts of the whole. The bigger picture, Earth's conscience, remains lacking. Stop thinking like a child.'

We'll never get everyone on the planet to see things the same way.

'Then we will look elsewhere.'

"Orwell?" Askew says out loud, thinking he recognizes the voice. But no, not Orwell. Strange.

Suddenly he's startled by the laughter of children behind him, playing in and around the workstations. Many of them are wearing lab coats much too big for their small bodies and he can't help but laugh himself, so cute they look, these scientists of the future, dashing between tables; dragging their coat tails behind them; pushing buttons and playing with laptops; taking pictures of each other at the imaging station.

The voice of a five year old comes over the PA system.

"Five minutes to Integration." Only it sounds like integwation. The announcement is followed by the quasi-musical tuning up of the Sounding Rings.

Hold on... Raised eyebrows lower in consternation as his amusement turns to dismay.

'Your technology seems to have gotten away from you, Professor.'

Askew recognizes the voice as Hugo Jascowitz who had said something similar just before he went missing.

He sees now that all the workstations are constructed from cardboard boxes and the equipment out of children's toys. Pieces and parts fall to the ground and scatter as the children bang into the makeshift stations. Askew's instinct is to shout, run after them, to put a stop to their shenanigans, but there's so many of them, he doesn't know where to begin. The volume of the frequency tuning starts to grow along with his level of confusion. He turns three hundred and sixty degrees in search of a threat that has slipped within the border of his awareness. Then, where the Data Recording console once stood, and now stands a refrigerator box with finger-painted view screens, buttons and dials, he sees a little boy handing something to a little girl. Without actually seeing it, Askew knows what it is and rushes over to snatch the purple gem as it passes from boy to girl.

"Where did you get this?!" he shouts without thinking and the little girl starts to cry. The boy follows suit and their bawling adds to the shouting and laughing of the other children and the rising din of the Sounding Rings.

"Did you find it on the tracks?" he asks, still shouting, but less obviously at the boy but rather to be heard.

"I have one, too, Professor."

"Me, too. They're pretty."

The children gather around him, holding up their brightly colored gems. He looks back at Sounding Ring One and sees that the tiny glass-covered receptacles contain a medley of objects; grapes and marbles, gumballs and jacks, but not the gems that make the tunnel work.

"Oh, no," he says quietly as he starts to see his worst nightmare coming true. The nightmare inside the nightmare.

The laughter of three children in particular stands out somehow amidst the riot of noise that fills the subway station. These three chase each other through the cardboard maze in their own variation of Tag and then make a beeline for the tree fort steps that lead to the control booth. Still laughing, they push their way into the booth which more resembles a toyshop now than a master control room. Their joy is infectious and Askew follows them in, almost lulled into a much desired distraction from impending doom. But he's worked behind the master control too many years not to recognize the perfect pitch when he hears it.

"Don't do it!!" he shouts, but he can no longer be heard over the noise of progress and self-destruction. A little, red-headed girl has her freckled hand on the master control, an amalgam of Lincoln Logs, Tinker Toys, and pipe cleaners, and when she pulls the switch, Askew's old ways of thinking and feeling are completely overwhelmed by an all-consuming understanding of tragedy.

The bellow of a horn, a doomsday horn, tumbles through the tunnel like an avalanche, deeply resonant, almost bone-shattering in its pitch. This is followed by an immaculate silence and Askew and children alike translate that absence of sound to signify their end. The heavy weight of Askew's melancholy doubles as he reads the end of the children's life stories on their small faces. Innocence, confusion, and utter sadness. How could this be happening, they wonder? No, not how, but why? Askew knows, and that knowledge sets him apart from everyone else, adding loneliness to his despair.

The horn sounds again and its resulting wake pummels the station and buffets the children across the floor as easily as it does the cardboard workstations, sometimes splitting their skin in the areas of direct contact. Askew has no time to react to any of it before the glass wall of the booth implodes and a million tiny shards rip through the red-haired girl and her friends as if they are made of butter. He thinks for a moment he's immune to the devastation, that perhaps he's only there as an observer, until he sees the blood dripping onto the floor from his own open wounds. Following in the wake of the sound waves comes a whisper, a white light erasing everything in its path. As it overtakes him, Askew feels an internal pressure so great he knows he's going to pop. His cheeks inflate and cover his eyes, his lips become so taught he's certain they will tear apart. But just when he thinks he can take no more, he collapses in on himself, like a dying star, howling in inexplicable pain and excruciating confusion as the tide of displacement eradicates the shores of his universe and beyond.

Chapter Ten: An Alliance

Professor Askew had asked the hotel lobby for a 7:30 wake-up call and was glad for it. Frightened out of his wits, coated in sweat, he leapt out of his dream with both feet and crawled across the achingly endless plain of his king bed to pick up the receiver.

"Good morning thank you very much," he mumbled almost incoherently. A thin but recognizable voice stopped him from replacing the receiver.

"What? Hello? Oh, Rachel, it's wonderful to hear your voice," he glanced over at the clock radio, "at 6:35 in the morning. I take it there's a problem?"

Lowering his feet into slippers, he rose and stretched his back as he listened to Henderson's report. Ellen Cheever, through pain-staking effort, had uncovered the identity of their data thief. When Henderson asked the professor what he was going to do now that they knew, he found himself at a loss. He would reach out to Bellows, of course, and more than likely Jacen Longworth and his security force would be brought in. What would come from those discussions was anybody's guess.

"Wasn't Charlie Anderson a friend of Hugo's?" he asked, reminded of his disgruntled employee theory.

"He was quite outspoken at the time of Hugo's disappearance," said Henderson. "Unhappy with how the investigation was being handled."

"Understandable from his perspective, I suppose."

"Everyone pretty much ignored him, hoping he would just go away after enough time had passed."

"Apparently scientists do believe in miracles." Askew searched his mind for a plan. "If this Lantern Society has, in fact, co-opted Verity data to facilitate their own agenda, we have to connect the dots and assume that data was provided by Anderson. The alternative is far too unpleasant to consider. Unfortunately, Anderson's the only person who can corroborate."

Henderson informed Askew that she'd asked Anderson to take

over the marketing staff meetings, one of which was supposed to take place later that morning. Askew told her to proceed as planned but to expect a visitor. She let him know she understood then broke the connection. The professor immediately placed another call.

"Good morning, Mr. Strivelli. I apologize for the early hour but I just received some distressing news." He reached for a pen and the complimentary hotel stationery. "We must meet as soon as possible."

He jotted down the agreed upon time and place then hung up. Curious to see if he had received a response to last night's query to the Lantern Society, he booted up his laptop and signed into his bogus email account. Surprisingly, he found what he was looking for sitting in his inbox.

'Dear Mr. Baum: Thank you for reaching out to the Lantern Society. As it happens, we do have a branch in the Hartford area and I'd be happy to arrange a meeting with you. Please call the number in my signature to set up an appointment at your convenience. I look forward to meeting you.

Regards,
Beatrice Lebrun'

It was still forty-five minutes until his wake-up call, too early yet to reach out to the Society, but it was never too early to wake up the agents of Global Armour.

#

Tony Strivelli was seated at his usual table by the windowed entrance to Main Street's Athena's Restaurant. As he poked at his over easy eggs with a fork, he kept one eye on the street and the other on his newspaper. Between paragraphs, he moved some of the runny egg to a slice of toast then brought the whole mess up for a bite. It was during one of those moments that Askew appeared like a ghost in the reflection of the window glass.

"Morning, Prof," Strivelli said. He wiped egg yolk from his moustache as Askew approached the table.

"We're going to have a busy day today, Mr. Strivelli."

"Can I get you a cup of coffee? Oh, my bad, you're a tea drinker, aren't you?"

Askew declined, citing his lack of time, then noted that the table was already set for two.

"Is your lady friend with you?"

"Angela, yes."

"Has she since abandoned you with the bill?" Askew asked dryly.

Strivelli laughed politely and informed the professor that she had stepped away to the Ladies', but was very excited at the prospect of meeting him.

"Hopefully we'll share a brief moment before my next appointment."

Askew cocked his head and Strivelli saw the surveillance vehicle he'd spotted the previous day.

"How'd they find you?"

"I found them. I decided we don't have time to play spy versus spy. I need to find out what they're about. In the meantime," Askew lowered his voice, "I need you to go to New York and pick up a man named Charles Anderson, the soon to be ex-employee who's responsible for the mess we're in. To what end, I have yet to determine, but we need to find out sooner rather than later."

"What should I do with him once I've picked him up?"

"Your guess is as good as mine," Askew said, shaking his head. "It's not really my area of expertise."

"Mine either."

Askew thought about it a moment. "Bring him in. Bring him here. I want to talk to him face to face." Askew looked down at his pocket watch. "I have to go. I've uploaded all my notes to the Mission Board. Take a look and see what's at stake."

Askew started to turn but Strivelli stopped him.

"Why don't you give me a hint? I'm a big boy. I can take it."

"Say hello to your lady friend for me." Askew wondered briefly who would be standing by his side when the end came. "I'm very glad you found someone."

Strivelli watched Askew and any answers he could have provided walk out of the restaurant. Angela seemed genuinely disappointed that she'd just missed meeting the mysterious professor. She seemed doubly disappointed that she would be losing her boyfriend for the day, but promised him a nice dinner upon his return.

#

Askew and the agents of Global Armour walked along the Connecticut River. Though the elevated Interstate was well above their heads, the sound of traffic was still loud enough to prevent them from being overheard. Askew lit his pipe as the two agents herded him toward a concrete bench.

"First of all, Professor," said Tomlinson, "we want to thank you for reaching out to us. It'll go a long way with our boss. For us, I mean. What made you decide---?"

"It speaks to the urgency of my mission. Tell me about your affiliation with the Lantern Society."

"Heh. That's funny," said Foster.

"How so, funny?"

Tomlinson offered Askew a seat while she and Foster remained standing, one on either side of him. She removed a Lantern Society flier from a folio she was carrying and handed it to Askew.

"We're talking about this group, right? It's funny because we were going to ask you the same question. I'm guessing this flier's similar to the one you grabbed yesterday morning?"

"Yesterday morning?" Askew gave her a knowing look tinged with disapproval and she flushed.

"What's your interest in them?" asked Foster.

"The listening device you planted on me." The agents started to object but Askew shook them off. "Don't bother denying it. I'd love to know how you got your hands on that tech."

"That seems a bit off topic," said Tomlinson.

"Maybe not," said Foster. "If the Lantern Society somehow got their hands on Verity tech, and we did, too, it stands to reason---."

"---that Global Armour is somehow affiliated with the Society." Askew nodded. "That's right, Agent Foster. Now we're on the same page. How did you come by that listening device?"

"That would be a question for our boss," said Tomlinson. "We couldn't tell you, we just sign it out. But I'll look into it. Our only interest in the Lantern Society is your interest in them."

Foster put his foot up on the bench. "And you want that tech back, don't you?"

Askew's dawn nightmare tried to elbow its way into his thoughts but he forced it back, not yet ready to share the bigger picture. He was torn between his suspicion of the self-proclaimed agents and the desperation he was feeling as the clock ticked down to Armageddon. There simply wasn't enough time to think through every possibility.

"We can be of some help to you, Professor," Tomlinson prodded. "Global Armour doesn't operate in the dark."

"Well, maybe a little," George interjected.

"And we're not without our resources."

She knew Gorokhovich would not approve of her forthrightness, but she wanted Askew to know how serious they were and how capable. She may have been compromising Global Armour's agenda, but at a singular moment like this, with Askew's undivided attention, she was only interested in her own.

She watched him remove his cap to wipe the perspiration from his bald head with a crisp, white handkerchief. His magnified, hazel eyes stared off into the distance and seemed to possess a much greater storehouse of knowledge than his mouth ever gave away. A pointy, waxed moustache and reddish chin whiskers gave him a slightly satanic look and yet his cheeks and the crow's feet around his eyes indicated that he was no stranger to laughter. To Tomlinson, Askew seemed like a character out of a book, a fictional creature with no limits to what he could accomplish, and thus appointed him her own personal Oz and her ticket back to Kansas. For reasons derived completely from her imagination, Askew's physical presence gave Gorokhovich's story of Tomlinson's other life substance. There was no logic to it. Then again, logic held no place on her peculiar journey.

Tomlinson leaned in close, about six inches from Askew's ear. "We know about Hugo Jascowitz," she said softly, desperate to make an impression.

It worked. Askew felt the world slip from under his feet at the thought of secrets spilling from the bowels of Verity Corp.

"Who?" It was all he could come up with.

"One of yours. We know he disappeared," said Tomlinson. "Came to work one day and no one's seen him since."

"You're in it now, Professor," said Foster.

"And he's not the only one who's disappeared, is he? Is that really why you came here? Because you think this Lantern Society might be in cahoots with the abductors?"

Askew shook his head. Global Armour seemed to possess just enough information to be wrong about all the right things.

"This interview is starting to feel like an interrogation. I don't---."

"We want to help, Mr. Askew," said Tomlinson, making sure her tone remained steady and conversational, "but first we have to understand."

"This is ridiculous!" Askew felt claustrophobic and stood up for fresher air. Instead, a bit of pipe smoke trickled down his throat and soured his stomach. "I don't know anything about disappearing people. What makes you so sure you're even acting on legitimate information? What's your source?"

"Trust me we don't act on unverified intelligence."

"I'm sorry, but I don't trust you. You talk to me as if you had someone on the inside and that's simply not poss---."

All of Askew's discussions with Rachel Henderson came flooding back, particularly the most recent. She was certain Anderson was providing information to the Lantern Society, but maybe she was wrong about that. Maybe Anderson was a mole working for Global Armour. Or maybe both cases were true and Global Armour was lying to him.

"Cat got your tongue, Professor?" asked Foster.

"You may think you have a whistle blower in Charles Anderson, but you don't. He knows nothing. Are you his facilitator? Is that it? Is Global Armour what connects Anderson to the Society?"

Tomlinson and Foster shared an enlightened look and Askew frowned as Foster scribbled on his pad.

"Okay, that's it," said Askew as he started to walk away. "Our business is concluded."

"Professor, wait!" Tomlinson took Askew's arm. "Forget Anderson. Okay, George?" she said, shooting a look in her partner's direction. "We don't have to go down that road."

"Why did you ask me about Hugo Jascowitz?"

"I didn't ask you about Hugo Jascowitz," Tomlinson answered slowly.

If anything was going to throw Askew off his game it was Jascowitz. It was one of the darker moments in Verity's history and a source of great pain and regret.

"Look, agents," he said with a hint of sarcasm, "I can't stop you from investigating whatever it is you think you're investigating."

Askew looked hard at each of them in turn, gleaning what he could from their eyes and body language. He decided the urgency of the matter took precedence over any tangential concerns. He didn't know what their agenda was, but he had more important things to worry about, like the end of all reality. Assuming he could keep the focus on the Lantern Society, he thought he might be able to make an alliance with Global Armour work to his advantage.

Their new partnership became official when Askew admitted that the only clue in his possession was the Hartford post office box posted on the Society's website. Foster performed a quick WHOIS look-up on the web and uncovered yet another Hartford address. The three of them promptly checked it out only to discover that the address was an abandoned building. Rather than giving up, Foster dug deeper still, poring through the website's source code out of curiosity.

"It was there all along," said Foster. "Basically it boils down to an advertisement for the webmaster. Someone called Digital Overlord."

"Oh, dear God in Heaven," Askew said as he rubbed his temple. "I don't know what to say to that."

"That's not the good part."

"Do tell."

"We got another address."

\#

The Mather College campus was an ivy-covered oasis in a desert of urban blight. Within its brownstone walls, the quad was green with a well-manicured lawn and shaded on the south end by stately beech trees. The spring session had ended, and though most of the students had gone home for the break, a few were out and about, reading on blankets or tossing a Frisbee.

"Ever been here before, Professor?" asked Tomlinson.

Askew took in the campus with sad eyes, nostalgic for the comparatively simpler days of his California youth when he was a student at Boothe Academy. Those were honest days of research and new discoveries. Making friends was easy then and everything was good, even ambition was good, and hopes and dreams guided him and his peers.

"Professor?"

"Hmm? Oh, sorry, yes, I've done one or two guest lectures here. But not in some time."

Foster had gone on ahead of them to question any passing student who might lead them to their quarry.

"What happens when you find who you're looking for?" asked Tomlinson.

"I'll need to confirm the theft of our data and their plans for its use."

"Let me ask you…is this threat confined to Verity Corp?" asked Tomlinson.

Askew wondered if he'd said too much already. Tomlinson repeated the question.

"It is not," Askew replied.

Two students pointed Foster in the direction of a dormitory along the Great Walk as Tomlinson and Askew passed a message kiosk not far behind. She pointed out a familiar pink flier among the various concert announcements, roommate requests, and tear sheets for guitar lessons or tutoring. A young lady opened a door and Foster practically jumped past the threshold.

"Good morning, Miss," Foster said, handing over a Global Armour business card. "We're looking for the offices of RealityConsent.org."

The girl looked at him blankly as she sipped her iced coffee latte through a straw. "The what?"

"It's a web hosting company," interjected Tomlinson as she stepped through the doorway. "Are there any tech company offices in this building?"

The girl looked at Tomlinson as if she were stupid. "Um, this is a dorm!"

"Any student-run companies of any kind?" asked Askew as he brought up the rear.

"Not that I know of. Who are you people?"

Askew removed his cap and the girl took in the elder man's shaved head and thick eyeglasses.

"Maybe there's a computer nerd in the building with a few too many pieces of equipment in their room? Maybe someone without a roommate?"

The girl took another sip and thought about it for a moment.

Station 12: The Lantern Society

"Maybe you're looking for that creep, Brian Haber. He lives alone in the basement. It's really weird. Is he in trouble? You want me to get an RA?"

"No, just point us toward the stairwell and we'll get out of your hair."

She did so and the three of them made their way down. After passing various utility rooms, they eventually came upon a blue door with a homemade sign that read, 'B. Haberman – Digital Overlord'. Foster pointed the sign out then knocked on the door.

A tall, thin, young man who appeared in desperate need of sleep answered the door wearing jeans, flip-flops, and a Halo t-shirt. He looked down at each of them through heavily lidded eyes.

"Mr. Haberman?" Tomlinson handed him a card. "Is it Haber or Haberman?"

The young man rolled his eyes. "It's Haberman. Haber's a dorm joke. They say there's no 'man' in Haberman. Gets a lot of laughs."

"I see. Mr. Haberman, I'm Agent Tomlinson and this is Agent Foster. We're with a firm called Global Armour. This gentleman---."

Askew shook his head subtly as if to say it didn't matter what his name was, but Haberman's eyelids rose in recognition.

"Daniel Askew. Boothe Academy. I'd recognize you anywhere. I've read a lot of your work. You are awesome."

"Thank you. Awesome is---."

"Beam me up, Scotty," interrupted the young man, pointing, with a grin. "Right?" Askew responded with a polite chuckle.

"Mr. Haberman, may we come in?" asked Tomlinson. "We'd like to ask you some questions."

"Sure, sure, come on in." He led the way into his apartment which looked like converted storage space. He gestured toward the living room, using his body to block two closed doors. "So, you guys aren't cops? I only ask because you look like cops."

Haberman's guests took seats.

"No, Global Armour is a private concern," said Tomlinson. "We're looking into an organization called the Lantern Society."

He blinked his cumbersome eyelids as he waited for the inevitable question but none was forthcoming. He jerked his thumb toward his kitchenette. "I just made some coffee. Anybody want?"

"Sure," said Foster. "Sweet with cream. Or milk. Doesn't matter."

"Sure, sure, no problem." Haberman shook his head with his mouth open. "I'm sorry, what did you ask me?"

Tomlinson stood up and started looking around the apartment. "It stays nice and cool down here, doesn't it?"

"It does, yeah."

"How's that coffee coming along, Mr. Haber?" asked Foster.

Haberman flushed. "Haberman. It's coming right up."

Tomlinson looked over a dividing wall that was a foot shy of the ceiling. "Wow, you sure have a lot of computers. Are you studying computer science, Mr. Haberman?"

Haberman hustled Foster's coffee over to him. "Uh, I'm really an engineering major. Computers are just a hobby of mine."

Foster reached up for his coffee. "Thanks. And an added source of income maybe? A little something to help with tuition?"

"Um, not sure what you mean."

Tomlinson noticed wires bundled together in a makeshift conduit. "So, how did you come to know the Lantern Society? Did they recruit you? Or did you find them?"

"I don't mean to be rude---."

"Uh, oh," interjected Foster.

"---but I think you've got me confused with somebody else. I'm gonna have to ask you to leave."

"I just got my coffee," Foster whined.

"Still---."

"Is that the poster from the X-Files?" Tomlinson asked pointing into the other room.

"I'm not sure why you people are here, but you really have to go. I'd hate to have to call the police."

Askew couldn't sit through the cat and mouse any longer. He stood up and approached Haberman. "Young man, let me ask you, scientist to scientist, are you hosting the Lantern Society website?"

Haberman started to laugh but then thought better of it.

"RealityConsent.org," said Foster. "That's you."

"It's an anagram, isn't it? Not very clever."

"Please don't lie to us, Mr. Haberman." Askew stepped closer and Haberman was tempted to step back. "Are you a member? It's very important that you tell me the truth. A lot is at stake."

"I'm not lying. I don't know what you're talking about. Now, please---."

"Do you know Beatrice Lebrun?"

"No! No, dude, I really don't know what you're talking about."

Haberman turned from Askew and practically walked into Tomlinson who had come around behind him.

"Are you sure about that?" She stood next to one of the closed doorways tapping a salmon-colored flier with her knuckle.

"Maybe you can tell us when the aliens are coming to take us all away," said Foster derisively.

"You think that's funny?" Haberman said defensively. "Doesn't it matter to you that your whole life, your existence, could be erased?"

"Yes."

"Then maybe you shouldn't be so glib."

Foster took another sip of his coffee. "I meant, yes, I think it's funny."

"What did you mean by that, Mr. Haberman?" asked Askew. "How can someone's existence be erased?"

Haberman stared down at Askew with an expression of mild surprise. "You tell me."

"What I know," said Askew, starting to lose patience, "is that your people have come to possess recently stolen data. If they act on this ill-gotten knowledge, if any devices should come to be constructed from these stolen plans, it could leave your organization in an unintended position of doing great harm. Great harm."

"How great?" Haberman's eyes shifted under his heavy lids as he noodled his options.

Askew looked at his new allies. If he informed Haberman he informed Global Armour as well. But he saw no other option, he had to emphasize a point and quickly. He had no idea if another opportunity would present itself.

"Possibly catastrophic."

Neither Tomlinson nor Foster blinked.

"How catastrophic?" Haberman scratched nervously.

The whole of reality was in the balance and Askew was measuring the end by inches with a boy still wet behind the ears.

"No more games, Mr. Haberman. I will match whatever the Society is paying you to take your website down. Say it was technical difficulties; say your equipment was stolen. Whatever you think is best."

"Even if I wanted to, and I don't, the cowboy would have my head, and his intimidation easily trumps yours. I'm sorry, Professor, I'm in this for the long haul."

"Who's the cowboy?" asked Foster.

"I don't know his name. Scary looking guy in a long, leather coat. Big scar on his face. I only met him once but that was enough. He makes a significant impression."

"Then let me plead our case to your leaders."

"I'm not sure how I'd go about that. I suppose I could send a message."

"You never met them? You never met anyone else from the group?"

"Not face to face. Just the cowboy. Mostly we communicate on the forums. The group knows how to leverage technology. All our meetings are virtual. We're better off segregated."

"How many members in your organization?" asked Askew.

Haberman crossed his arms. "It's been awhile since I did a headcount."

"Message boards usually list their members," said Foster.

Haberman grinned. "They're private and very secure. Trust me, you'll never get in there."

Askew took a step. "Have you forgotten how awesome I am, Mr. Haberman?" Haberman's grin collapsed as Askew turned to leave. "We're through here, agents."

Foster took a swallow of his coffee, stood up, and handed his cup to his host.

"The comment in the source code?"

"What about it?" Haberman said bitterly. "I've got bills to pay. A little advertising never hurt."

"Yeah, that's why you had to bury it."

"I wouldn't mention this visit to anyone," said Askew. "If you do, they'll shut you down so fast it'll make your head spin."

"Goodbye, Mr. Haber," said Tomlinson as the three of them left.

#

Station 12: The Lantern Society

Foster lit a cigarette as they reversed their tracks through the quad. "Care to elaborate on 'catastrophic?'"

"Yeah," said Tomlinson, "that was a God damned shocker. What kind of catastrophe are we talking here? Is it a threat to national security?" Askew turned away. "Worse?! Jesus!"

"You said no more games."

Askew didn't take Foster's bait, but he knew he was being cornered.

"How much time do we have?" asked Foster. "Can you tell us that much?"

"The data was stolen almost a year ago," said Askew. "It's possible the threat is imminent. Or, they've yet to begin. I simply don't know. Keep in mind that it's not their plan to destroy the planet, rather it would be a byproduct of working with something they don't understand."

"I'm sure that'll swing the vote come Judgment Day," said Foster.

"Destroy the planet?! Jesus Christ!"

Tomlinson went quiet. Her personal Oz had suddenly become more hindrance than help and that wouldn't do. What was the point of acquiring a former life, a better life, if only to have the rest of the world crumble around her? She knew she had to put the crisis behind them, to ensure that the world survived. She needed a clear road to her destination. That meant helping Askew anyway she could, or everything she'd put herself through thus far would be for naught.

"We've got to make them understand," Tomlinson stated.

"Understand?! Hell, we've got to take them out!"

Askew looked out onto the campus, at the chapel on the hill, towering over the sports fields. He looked out at the young people living their lives, secure in the knowledge that tomorrow would be there in the morning, and the morning after that. He thought of his nightmare and the looks on the children's small faces.

"We've put a face to the organization," Askew said, "even if it's of no significance. This facility is now known to us. That counts for something. Haber won't do anything about the website, but that doesn't mean something can't be done. But we have to be careful. We don't want to force their hand. We must act quickly but methodically."

"In the meantime?" Tomlinson asked.

"I have an appointment with one of their representatives this afternoon."

"You're meeting with the Lantern Society?" asked Foster.

"As a potential recruit."

"Bad idea. You're too high profile."

"I have no other recourse! We're running out of time!"

"Maybe."

"That's right, Agent Foster, maybe the world is coming to an end."

The three of them stood in the quad and took in the air, at a loss for words.

"Well," Tomlinson finally said, cutting through the sound of the beech leaves being jostled by the breeze, "we better get going."

"Hey, what the hell did he mean by, 'beam me up, Scotty'?" asked Foster.

"He was referring to a paper I wrote many years ago on the validity of Star Trek's transporter."

"One of those debunking things?"

"Sure, why not?"

#

With no planned approach to his imminent discussion, butterflies had begun to flutter in Askew's stomach. He didn't suppose there was any real danger to meeting with the Lantern Society rep, but one never knew. Maybe the man Haberman referred to as the cowboy would be there to make sure everything was on the up and up.

The address was an historic building on Lewis Street opposite the municipal park. Its interior, having been converted to a mixed-use facility back in the seventies, was functional but horribly dated and drab. Askew walked over the cracked tiles of the foyer and onto the slightly sticky linoleum floor of the main hall. A guard sat at a dilapidated, wooden podium and looked up from his newspaper with bored eyes. When the professor announced his appointment with Beatrice Lebrun, the guard screwed his face into a look of disapproval then pointed his thumb down the narrow hall. Askew thanked him and made his way to the office of the Lantern Society.

Inside, a young woman was riffling through files in a ridiculously cramped reception area. When she turned and saw Askew standing there, some of those files slipped through her fingers and fell to the floor. Askew offered to help and together they stooped and gathered up the mess. When they stood up again, Askew handed over the files under the woman's probing stare.

"Miss Lebrun?" he asked.

The woman was hesitant. "Yes, I'm Beatrice Lebrun, Mr..."

"Baum. Lewis Baum. We spoke on the telephone."

Lebrun stuck out her hand, seemingly relieved, and Askew shook it. "Yes, of course. How do you do?"

"Very well, thank you."

"Let me get rid of this and we can grab a seat in the conference room."

She turned and shoved the files into an open drawer then turned toward the only other doorway in the office. When Lebrun offered Askew some water, he accepted gladly, still nervous in pursuit of his quarry. She removed two water bottles from a mini fridge while Askew took a seat at a conference table that almost filled the small room.

"Why don't we begin, Mr. Baum," Lebrun said as she handed him bottle and a paper cup, "with you telling me what it is about our organization that interests you?"

"I'll be retiring soon, leaving me with quite a bit of time on my hands."

"How did you hear about us?"

He cracked open the water and poured. "I saw one of your fliers which led me to your website."

"And?"

"I'll be honest, Ms. Lebrun, this invasion stuff? It's a little over the top for me. I'm hoping it's supposed to be a metaphor. But I've never trusted the government, and I wouldn't put it past them to bury any number of sensitive subjects of discussion. I would like to help you in revealing the truth of things. You see where I'm going with this."

"Prove the Society's claims and prove their legitimacy. Or not. Two birds with one stone."

"Exactly."

Askew couldn't help but notice how attractive Ms. Lebrun was, almost exotic. Despite her last name, though, she didn't look particularly French, nor did he detect any accent. He was surprised at her beauty, as if beauty had no business in a fringe cult preparing for an alien invasion.

"Big business, too," Askew continued, "you can't trust them as far as you can throw them. Government and money---"

"You understand I can't go into specifics at this point."

"Oh?" Askew deflated. He was naïvely hoping that he could fast track his membership and make his way quickly up the food chain.

"In fact, I can't elaborate on anything you've read about us. Not yet. Let me get you one of our booklets."

Lebrun rose from the table and stepped back into the tiny reception area. He asked her if she was the leader of the Lantern Society to which she replied no, but was responsible for administrating the Hartford chapter. When he asked her if they held regular meetings, she countered with a question of her own as she returned to the table.

"May I ask what it is you do for a living, Mr. Baum?"

"I'm an actuarial for an investment firm. But I don't really fit in, anymore." Askew leaned in and winked. "Just as well I'm retiring. But I have children and new grandchildren and I worry about the state of the world. It is my fervent wish that we open the closed book of conspiracy so that my little ones can live in an open and honest world."

"Of course, I understand. Our community is an open one. Eventually," she said with a smile. "It wouldn't make sense to pull back the curtain of secrecy only to throw a veil on our own organization."

"Oh, I concur."

"Are you a local resident, Mr. Baum?"

"I am."

The two of them stared at each other for a moment in an awkward pause. Lebrun pushed the booklet toward Askew.

"I need you to fill out this questionnaire in full then return it to me at your leisure. If I'm not here, you can drop it in the yellow box by the door. All your responses will be kept strictly confidential so answer honestly. The questionnaire is quite involved, but it's only your first hurdle towards membership."

"Then what happens?"

"We will review it and then run a background check."

"Background check?"

"An organization like ours attracts a lot of unbalanced individuals who want to piggy-back their questionable causes on our very real concerns. We can't have that. We lose credibility and it would compromise our mission. I hope you can understand."

"Of course."

Askew noticed that he had two books in his hand.

"I'm sorry. I'll take that," said Lebrun as she relieved Askew of the extra. "It's a long process but valuable."

She stood up and Askew followed her toward the exit.

"Thank you for your time, Ms. Lebrun. I'll get this back to you as quickly as I can and I look forward to continuing our discussion."

They shook hands and Askew realized that in order for him to get out, Ms. Lebrun would have to back out into the reception area if not the outer hall. As he left, she gave him one more long look.

#

"I've got a name."

"We've got a good thing going here, Professor. Why stop now?"

Much to his dismay, Askew was beginning to enjoy Tomlinson's company. He had to admit, he had a thing for handsome, take charge women, and in that respect she reminded him a little of Rachel Henderson, but without the burden of a paternal bent. Still, he wasn't ready to be best friends just yet.

"Gordon Isaacson. I got his name off of a questionnaire like this one. Hopefully he's local and easily found."

"Everything else went okay?"

"She kept staring at me," said Askew, "like she knew me."

"Told you," Foster said as he wrote in his pad. "You don't exactly blend in with the crowd."

"I'll take that as a compliment."

"You do that. What are we asking this Isaacson when we find him?"

"Let's talk about that."

Then Askew's phone rang.

#

The neighborhood was sketchy, at least from the perspective of middle-class white people from out of town. But as former police, Tomlinson and Foster weren't overly concerned as they cruised slowly through the neighborhood in search of the right building. Being the only

Gordon Isaacson in the local white pages made finding his address easy, but what they couldn't tell from the street name was that Isaacson resided deep inside a city project, a maze of identical brick buildings, some of them without visible numbers. When they finally found it, they parked the car in front of a fenced-in lot and started walking, shadowed by two thin dogs behind the chain link. Foster stepped off the curb ahead of Tomlinson to avoid looking into their sad eyes.

"Are we going to talk about your new strategy?" asked Foster.

"Engaging Askew?"

"New directive from Gorokhovich?"

"You know it's not."

"Yeah."

"Would you rather be stuck on surveillance again?"

"No, no, this is a lot more fun."

"Shut up, George."

"Do you think Askew played it right?"

Tomlinson knew right away what Foster meant, but she allowed him to clarify without interruption.

"In the face of this potential global catastrophe, do we really have the time to dick around, pretending to be other people and playing nice with the enemy? Shouldn't we be forcing our way up the chain of command and shutting them down?"

"That's one way of looking at it."

"Unless Askew's the one dicking us around. Maybe it's something else entirely."

As they walked down the front sidewalk toward the building entrance, a voice jumped out at them, inquiring as to their presence. A young man walked across the front yard made dirt patch by years of pedestrian traffic and children playing.

"Hey, there," Tomlinson said. "We're looking for Gordon Isaacson. Do you know if he lives here?"

"I know Gordon. Everyone knows Gordon. What do you want to talk to him about?"

"We want to talk to him about some mutual acquaintances. He's not in any kind of trouble."

"Uh huh. Well, if he ain't in trouble, come on then."

The young man led them around to the back where four buildings shared an open courtyard. Besides some kids in the corner playground, the only people back there were three elderly men, two seated on a metal bench and a third man resting on an upturned trash barrel.

"Yo, Gordon! Gordon! These people looking for you. What kinda crazy shit you been up to now?"

"Well, come on over," came the reply from the man on the can, who appeared to be the oldest member of the triumvirate. "Let's have a look at you."

The young man stuck with them, curious to see how the scene was going to play out. Isaacson looked up at the agents with no preconceived notions in his yellow eyes. He had a thin face and gray hair that popped out from underneath his red knit hat. There was a spattering of curly, gray hair on either side of his face attempting to be mutton chops and a dollop more on the tip of his chin. Large teeth matched the yellow of his eyes but a few of those were missing. The onset of summer did nothing to dissuade him from wearing several layers of clothes that included a pullover sweater and sport coat.

"I didn't do nothin', officers, I swear," said Isaacson, and that seemed to tickle his friends who broke into lighthearted laughter.

"It's nothing like that, sir, we're not police."

Taking in the old man, Tomlinson figured they had found the wrong Gordon Isaacson.

"You ain't cops? You look like cops."

"No, sir."

The old man let this sink in and then his eyes grew large.

"Feds?"

"No, sir," said Tomlinson. "We're---."

"Is it time?"

"Excuse me?"

"Are you from the Society?"

Foster looked at Tomlinson before he asked, "What Society is that, sir?"

The old man's companions laughed again, but Isaacson tuned them out, his eyes locked on the agents.

"Don't you pay him no mind," said one of the men. "He's always goin' on about one fool thing or another."

"You ain't no sleeper agent, Gordon," said the other, "and they're not here to activate you."

"Are we talking about the Lantern Society, sir?" Foster asked, trying to maintain the focus between them.

The jaws of the old man's companions went slack and they stared at their friend in disbelief. The courtyard went quiet except for the rusty squeal of the playground swings and the occasional shout of one of the children.

"Shinin' a light on the truth! I told you I wasn't lyin'," Isaacson finally said.

"Oh, shit!" said the young man. "My man Gordon's a secret agent!"

"Is it true you're a member of the Lantern Society, Mr. Isaacson?" asked Tomlinson.

Isaacson didn't answer right away. He had assumed he was talking to fellow members.

"Oh, I get it," he said. "You can't talk about it. That's okay by me. Yeah, I'm a member. Ain't got no card to prove it, though."

"How long ago did you join?" asked Foster.

"Prob'ly a year and a half ago now. They made me a sleeper agent and told me they could activate me at any time. If they needed me."

"And what would they have you do if said activation took place?"

"Don't have a mother fuckin' clue! Save the human race, I guess. They're coming, you know? This ain't no God damn movie. But before they do, they gonna kidnap us and use us as fuel in their ships. They been doin' it for years. Since Roswell. They come, they take what they need. They think we don't know. But we know otherwise, don't we?"

Isaacson's friends looked to Tomlinson and Foster to gauge their reaction to the crazy speech. The agents remained aloof which only heightened the possibility that Isaacson was telling the truth and the belief in that possibility was clearly apparent on their faces.

"So you haven't been activated in the past…"

"No, Ma'am. Had a powwow with the recruiter one time, filled out some paperwork, and that was the end of it. Recruiter gave me an ID so's I could talk to people on their internet, but I ain't got no computer. Never did. When I joined up I used one at the library."

"Do you remember what your ID was, Mr. Isaacson?" asked Foster, his notebook at the ready.

"GordonI. Easy enough to remember."

"How about a password? Did they give you a password as well?"

"I think…hold on." His dry, ashy hand reached inside his jacket pocket and pulled out a worn, leather billfold from which he removed a folded piece of paper. He looked down at it then flipped it over. "Here it is."

"May I confirm?" asked Foster, leaning in.

"What's that now? Oh! Oh, yeah."

Foster jotted the password down.

"Thank you."

"Mr. Isaacson, are you still prepared to assist the Society should the need arise?"

"Fuck, yeah! If I can stop those alien mother fuckers from takin' just one of us…"

Tomlinson took Isaacson's hand and shook it.

"We'll be in touch, Gordon. We appreciate the help."

#

By 3:30 that afternoon, Askew didn't feel any closer to solving the mystery that was the Lantern Society. He had his introduction, had put a face to the organization, and found their virtual home base, but nothing that brought him any closer to putting a stop to the potential calamity. He would have to produce better results and quickly if he was going to contain the situation.

He missed his lab. He missed being pre-occupied with his work. Being out in the open, in the fresh air, he easily lost focus on what was at stake. When he joined the outside world, he found himself distracted into complacency, a part of him denying the reality of what humanity was faced with; it was preposterous, after all. But mostly he felt out of place.

He thought of Patty Bennett and the story of her lost sister. He supposed he'd made Patty the poster child for the collateral damage that came with an abduction. She was the reason he was working so hard, it was she that represented the terrible loss of friends and family, victims of the mysterious train. And then he thought of Verity Corp's endgame. What could Verity do for Patty Bennett besides bring her into the fold and make sure she was alright? Learning all they could about their abductors was all well and good, but what exactly were they going to do with all that data to make things right? They couldn't recover the past. Who knew how long this had been going on? The best they could do was to stop them in their tracks. But wasn't that the main purpose behind Infinite City?

Before Askew knew it, he was back at his hotel and making his way to the elevator. He was fairly exhausted and was looking forward to a nice bath in the deep whirlpool tub in his suite. But the phone call he'd received earlier told him there was one more piece of business before his work day was through. He slid his card key through the lock and stepped through to find Strivelli and Dodge standing on either side of a slightly bloodied Charles Anderson.

Chapter Eleven: A Wanted Man

Anderson saw a stranger in the mirror of his hotel bathroom. He was all washed up and shaved, wearing the new set of clothes he'd purchased the day before, the day of the first summer storm and the premature extinguishing of an old flame. The man in the mirror looked like Anderson, but his clothes hung on him like a costume. And though his face and hair were made up for the role of Charlie Anderson, the man behind the mask was flat and unavailable. The trademark swagger was nowhere to be seen either, and the man inside looking out felt old before his time, a bitterly disappointed man.

Anderson knew, and many people would have agreed, that his life had been near perfect before throwing his hat in with Verity Corp. College and career couldn't have gone better. Even his relationships, brief as they were, went according to his design. And when the time came to step up to the plate, his old friend, Hugo Jascowitz, provided the perfect pitch: 'Come to New York and work for Verity Corp. You'll be set for life.' It was an exciting prospect, and one he was eager to pursue. But in the few short years he'd worked there, he'd lost that friend, the only woman he ever loved, and all trust for his employer. And to say he'd lost control of his life was an understatement.

All night long, Anderson had been haunted by a nightmare loop of Sarah's murder. Between bouts of fitful sleep, he was fixated on his resolution to make good. Sadly, he was no longer confident that the man in the mirror, burdened by guilt and mired in regret, could close the deal.

He groaned aloud, just to hear his own voice, and placed his hand on the telephone receiver. It was time to make contact with the Lantern Society. The phone on the other end rang only once.

"It's me," Anderson stated simply, and he realized he had nothing else to say. His mind was blank, an unusual state for him, and the newness of the feeling excited him against his wishes. Up to that point, his life had been one chess match after another, strategizing, staying ahead of the competition, and planning for every contingency, both personally and professionally. To outsiders it seemed a stressful life, but for Anderson it was a comfortably repetitive routine. The disaster his life had recently become made things unpredictable and dangerously more interesting.

"Charles! Thank God."

"Were you worried about me?"

"I'm afraid I've let you down, Charles. Broken our trust. I thought maybe---."

"All I wanted to do was find my friend and make people aware that Verity Corp wasn't everything it appeared to be. It seemed simple enough. But the truth is, I don't know what Verity's up to and I never did. Maybe I should stop pretending that I do. I know my friend is still missing and I'm no closer to an answer. And after what happened in the park yesterday, well, now I know who the bad guys really are."

Silence followed. Anderson tried not to breathe too heavily into the phone as he waited for a response.

"I can't tell you how disappointed I am to hear you say that, Charles."

"What did you think was going to happen?!" shouted Anderson, allowing anger to grow out of his nervousness. "You murdered my friend!"

"Very disappointed," the woman said, sounding as if she wasn't listening but rather planning her next move. "I'm going to need that money, Charles, and I mean now."

"The money is well hidden. I'll be holding onto it for awhile as a safety net until I've finished what I've set out to do."

"And what have you set out to do?"

"Better. I've set out to do better."

"Be careful to whom you speak with about this, Mr. Anderson. It wouldn't do to make this public."

"I wouldn't know where to begin."

"It wouldn't do at all."

"You used me to murder my friend."

"I was aware of a relationship between Verity Corp and Bismarck Industries and you were the only link between the two that I could leverage. This was never about murder. Ms. Bismarck unknowingly brought that upon herself."

"You were trying to rob her and she called you on it."

"She should have been none the wiser. Someone was obviously

feeding her information. I'm sorry we had to take such drastic measures."

"You need to make things right!" he shouted in a burst of ironic transference. "If you want to get your hands on that money, you'll keep your distance. And don't bother sending your gun thug. He won't find me. When I'm done, when the time is right, I'll find you."

#

Whatever plan he had conjured up the night before, whatever road he had chosen to redemption, it had crumbled to dust in the glaring light of the morning. All he had left after a ragged rest was a vague notion of doing right by Sarah. But she was dead. It was too late for her. Return the money? To whom? There was no guarantee Sarah had gotten the money from her father. Why had he arranged the morning meeting with Bismarck? What did he hope to accomplish? Revenge for his girlfriend's murder? *Ex-girlfriend.* How would that go down? Kill the cowboy? Anderson couldn't kill a fly, never mind a professional assassin. Pay someone to kill Donovan? How would that come under making amends? Turn himself in to the police? He didn't think Verity Corp would care much for that scenario. Rat on the Lantern Society? Admit to the theft? There were no lack of options, but none of them sounded like good, productive, ideas. More importantly, they were all ideas that would only serve to compound his troubles. Anderson was truly lost. The only thing he knew for sure was that he was in possession of one million dollars and he had to keep it safe if he wanted to come out of this unscathed.

#

Crossing One New York Plaza, he breathed deep the cool air that blew in from the bay. To keep from becoming overwhelmed by his predicament, he decided to play out his redemption one step at a time with no thought of what came next. Securing the money was his one and only objective at that moment and he figured the lockers inside Verity Corp's fitness center were as secure a place as any. The money would remain there until such time he felt it was safe to remove it.

As he stepped into the shadow of the Verity tower, the temperature cooled noticeably. Inside the entryway, he placed his ID on the gate scanner like he had so many times before. This time, however, the usual green arrow was replaced by a red 'X' and an alarm went off. Heads barely turned. This happened often enough when people carried in such items as umbrellas or briefcases and the system saw it as two people trying to pass through the gate simultaneously. He held his ground, resisted panic, and played his role, donning the face of someone put out by the delay. Anderson held up the Halliburton with a frown and the guard nodded casually and switched off the alarm. He then spoke into the radio affixed to his shoulder.

As Anderson waited nervously for the gate to lower, he spotted another guard stepping out from behind the second reception desk. He was talking into his own radio, perhaps responding to the first guard. His eyes were locked on Anderson, and Charlie found the look unnerving. The gate lowered, inviting him deeper into the lobby, and just as he was about to step forward, he saw Rachel Henderson coming out from behind the waterfall. His blood went cold when he realized the mistake he'd made in coming to Verity. *That God damn staff meeting!* But he could see in her expression of disappointment, a look he understood all too well, that this was something more. *She knows. She knows everything, dammit!* She caught up with the guard, and when she was fifty feet from Anderson, she raised her hand in greeting and called out to him. But her sad, confused expression was anything but welcoming.

Anderson turned and exited quickly, reversing his steps, never once looking back to see if he was being followed. A single whoop from a siren told him police were nearby, so he bounded down the subway stairs two at a time to the platform below, then made a mad dash to the other end, covering a city block with the least amount of resistance.

As he jumped onto the rising escalator, the thought occurred to him that the only way he would be able to make good his escape was if a taxi made itself available to him immediately upon exiting. As luck would have it, that's exactly what happened. Anderson leapt into the recently vacated taxi before the seat even had a chance to cool and he instructed the driver to take him to Bismarck Industries on the west side of midtown.

Anderson hugged the Halliburton case to his chest and stared blankly out the window, relieved for having avoided detention, and fretting over the disastrous start of his campaign. Step one of one was a failure. Making things worse, Verity Corp had found him out and his last ties to the people in his world had been severed. The staff had surely been alerted, if not thoroughly informed, and he found himself truly alone. But he couldn't let the fear of isolation overwhelm him or mistakes would be made. Possibly lethal mistakes. And there was still work to be done.

Twelfth Avenue was its usual busy drive, but the taxi made it to Bismarck Industries in time for Anderson's scheduled appointment with the company CEO. He stepped onto the sidewalk and allowed his eyes to follow the cab until they lit upon a black Jaguar parked at the curb. It looked uncomfortably similar to the car he'd sat in behind the Kupperdyne factory not too many blocks from where he stood. A small part of him was tempted to investigate, but the weight of the Halliburton pressed him to continue his mission. He turned and made straight for the building, leaving the unpleasant association behind.

As Anderson pushed through the revolving door in the left side entrance, he spied a man exiting on the right that gave him pause. He didn't recognize the neatly coifed beard and the dark, curly hair, but watched him just the same as the man made his way to the Jag. Anderson shrugged off the unhappy coincidence and continued on his way.

Inside the Jaguar, Anton Gorokhovich placed a call.

"Yes, Mr. Anderson, we're ready for you," said the guard at Reception as he handed up a name tag. Anderson peeled the backing off and stuck it on his jacket lapel. "Take the escalator to the second floor. Jennifer will escort you from there."

Anderson mumbled his thanks. The idea of turning back and leaving his well-intentioned plans for redemption behind permeated his thoughts.

"Mr. Anderson? Jennifer Hu," a young woman offered in greeting. "It's a pleasure to meet you. Would you come this way, please? Mr. Bismarck is running just a couple of minutes behind," she said as she led Anderson through a naturally lit waiting area. "I'll seat you in one of the conference rooms while you wait, if that's okay?"

The idea of running persisted. He liked to be in control of his environment at all times, but after the events that had just transpired at Verity Corp, he felt woefully off course, blazing a new trail through the bramble that had become his life.

Ms. Hu brought him into a meeting room and offered him a beverage which he politely refused despite a cotton-dry mouth. When she left to locate Bismarck, Anderson caught his reflection in the glass door and his earlier disappointment didn't waver. There was a huge disconnect between his internal perception of himself and what he was seeing. Where once his reflection brought a smile to his face, so pleased with the man he had become, he now wanted to slap the face he saw staring back at him.

He took a seat at the long table and ran his hand along its surface, the solidity of it driving home the reality of his situation. That same reality also served to reveal his insipid idealism of the prior night. Any mention of Sarah or Sarah's murder would only land him in a jail cell and though that might satisfy Bismarck, it wouldn't provide the redemption Anderson was seeking. The only way he was going to make things right was to bring the responsible parties to justice, not just for Sarah but for Jascowitz as well, and to reveal whatever else was hidden in the dark corners of Verity Corp. In order to do all that, he would have to make sure he remained a free man.

He decided he would proffer a long overdue apology to Bismarck for the way things ended with Sarah and leave it at that. Bismarck might appreciate such a gesture, but more than likely he just wouldn't care. He was all too happy to see Anderson exit the relationship at the time. Or maybe, after so much time had passed, he might think Anderson had simply lost his mind. In either case, Anderson decided to make it brief and then get the hell out of there and regroup. The money would stay with him for the time being.

The Halliburton sat on the table and suddenly seemed to advertise itself dangerously. Anderson wished desperately but fruitlessly that he'd taken an extra moment to find a new hiding place for it before visiting Bismarck, but it was obvious he wasn't thinking at his best. Hoping out of sight, out of mind, he stowed it under the table between his feet.

Almost fifteen minutes had come and gone when he became aware of two men approaching the room. They stopped and spoke in low, brusque tones just outside the door. The frosted glass stripe that ran across the wall prevented Anderson from seeing anything clearly above the thighs. He couldn't hear them either, but determined that one of the voices was probably Bismarck's. The other voice was a broken whisper, not enough to go on. The only two words he could string together in the whole conversation were 'global armor.'

Connecting Bismarck with the expensive, Italian loafers was easy, but it left Anderson wondering about the owner of the cowboy boots. It struck him as strange that twice in two days he'd seen someone--- *Jesus*

Station 12: The Lantern Society

Christ, it can't be! A knot of fear formed in his gut. It twisted and squeezed tight. Anderson's terror radiated outward. He doubled his efforts to make out their conversation but both men's voices were too low to carry. Then, just as suddenly as they appeared, the two walked away.

Jesus, God, it can't be. Not here. Not now.

If those boots belonged to Ed Donovan, Anderson figured he'd just dodged a bullet. He tried to calm himself by calculating the odds that it could have been Sarah's murderer standing before the victim's father. He looked at the door and once again he thought about leaving, only this time in actual terms of escape.

The boots returned and Anderson could now see the long coat trailing behind. It was over. Why had he even bothered leaving the park? He could have died by the side of a loved one instead of whatever the Lantern Society had in store for him. The door opened and in walked the man with the slicked-back hair and the facial scar that looked like a lightning bolt.

"Hello, Anderson," said Donovan. "It's nice to see you again. I'd like you to slowly reach under the table and pick up the case. That's good. On the table Now open it for me, if you would."

Anderson obeyed reluctantly, removing the combination from his pocket, and turning the dials on the case. Donovan stared down at the money.

"I know it's all here," he said.

"It is."

"Because you're a good guy, Anderson, you can't help it. You want to make things right. I get it." Donovan closed the case and Anderson started to return the combination to his pocket until Donovan made a noise and held out his hand. "Listen to me good, Charlie. You're coming with me and you're not going to make a fuss. Is that clear? You've fucked with the Society's time table enough."

"Does Joe Bismarck know what you did?"

A shadow passed over Donovan's face. "That question comes under making a fuss. Do it again and I will snap your neck before your next blink. Is that clear enough?" Anderson nodded. "Good. Get up."

Anderson rose and instinctively reached for the case, but Donovan wrapped his hand around the handle.

"Thanks, Charlie, but I'll take it from here."

The two men made their way out of the room. To stave off a growing compulsion to publicly cry and beg for his life, Anderson imagined how things might have turned out if he had just kept the money, flown off to a Caribbean island, and put up a small store that sold jewelry made of polished rocks and leather strands to passing tourists. He imagined he would have been quite happy, sitting on the beach, listening for the door chimes as customers wandered into his shop. He added Sarah to the scenario. Together again, like they were before he went and screwed it all up. It was paradise.

Before he realized any time had passed, the closing of car doors snapped him back to reality.

"I don't think you're going to do anything stupid," Donovan said as he fastened his seat belt and turned the ignition over. "But you can never anticipate the acts of a desperate man." He opened his coat to show Anderson a gun tucked under his left arm.

"Thanks," Anderson said morosely. "I'll rethink my escape plan."

Donovan pulled out of the lot, chuckling at Anderson's audacity. He knew it was jangled nerves that allowed Charlie to talk to him like that.

Feeling like he had nothing to lose, Anderson asked, "How did you know where to find me?"

Donovan pointed to his earpiece. "I gave you a hint. The briefcase you were carrying was bugged. It was only a matter of time before you said what I needed to hear. By the way, your use of the term gun thug hurt my feelings."

"Why did you kill Sarah?"

Donovan stared straight through the windshield. If the question surprised him, he didn't show it. But it did surprise him. Not only because Anderson came right out and asked it, but because it was a question for which he had no answer and Donovan had always known the answers to difficult questions. Not anymore, it seemed.

"She didn't leave me any choice," he said, hoping he would stumble upon an explanation he could get behind if he just talked about it. "I had to improvise. I'm sorry it turned out to be someone you…cared about." He paused in search of a better answer. "The Lantern Society could have been compromised. The repercussions of her going back to Bismarck…" He faded to silence, unconvinced of the merit of his modified explanation, especially where Anderson was concerned. The truth was there, though, it was close, but still out of reach. Donovan recognized that he was in denial, but that's as far he was willing to go just then.

"Why didn't you shoot me, too?" Anderson asked, allowing Donovan a brief reprieve.

The question prompted Donovan to finally look at him. "Because, Charlie, I thought we were on the same side."

Anderson watched midtown pass them by as they cruised north on the Henry Hudson Parkway. At 96th Street Donovan headed crosstown and when they were east of Central Park, he started looking for parking in the neighborhood of 2nd Avenue and 110th Street. After backing the Crown Vic in, bumping bumpers fore and aft, he grabbed the Halliburton from the back seat and told Anderson to follow him into the small bodega around the corner.

"Dónde está Peters?" Donovan asked the man behind the counter.

The elderly, unshaven proprietor watched the mercenary with dark, suspicious eyes.

"Está en el cuarto de atrás," he said.

"Gracias."

Donovan moved through the store without hesitation. He knocked twice on the store room door before entering to find three men sitting around a card table. A nod from the man in charge put the other two at ease.

"Hey, Ed," said the blond leader of the gang, "I was hoping you'd stop by today."

"Peters."

One man sat in a chair next to Peters and spoke Spanish into a telephone as he made notes on a steno pad. Taking bets, Anderson presumed. The other man, wearing a shoulder holster, sat on a stack of boxes keeping an eye on things. Donovan closed the door, placed Anderson in front of it, and told him not to move.

"Mission accomplished, gentlemen," said Donovan as he placed the case on the table. "Finally."

"You got good instincts, Donovan. I didn't think it was gonna go down like that."

"Neither did I, believe me." Donovan removed a crisp stack of bills from the case and placed it in front of Peters. Peters assumed the attitude of someone being baited and exchanged a quick look with the man on the phone.

"Your fee?" said Donovan, confused.

"We didn't do anything."

"What do you mean you didn't do anything? You didn't leave her there?!"

"When you took off after him," he gestured toward Anderson, "Hector and I hustled down to the scene but there was nothin' there. We figured maybe we were a back-up team or something."

"Impossible."

"I'm telling you, there was no body. And with the rain you'd never know anything happened there."

Peters and Donovan looked over at Anderson.

"Well, that's a fucking problem," Donovan declared. "That was a head shot. Clean. There was no way I missed."

"You didn't," said Anderson from the door as he brought his hand up to his cheek.

"There's no way she got up and walked away from that. Keep the money," said Donovan. "Go back and look around. Do some snooping. Check hospitals. Do what you have to do and find her."

Peters put his hand down on the strap of cash and tossed it to the man sitting on the boxes who then stuck it in a nearby standing safe.

"We'll look into it, Ed," said Peters. "Don't give it another thought."

"Thank you."

Just then the door burst open with enough force to push Anderson's face into the adjoining wall, cutting his cheek and bloodying his nose. The door bounced off his back and started to close again when an arm came around and grabbed the back of his jacket. Then both the arm and Anderson disappeared behind the closing door before Donovan and company could even register the event.

In the store proper, Strivelli pushed Anderson into Dodge's arms then dragged over a tall, metal chip rack to block the door. Dodge held the bloodied Anderson by the scruff of his neck and pushed him through the front door as Strivelli ran to catch up. Donovan and company, having crashed past the chip rack after some effort, followed in close pursuit. The Verity men slid into the bench seat of Strivelli's old Impala station wagon and immediately took off. Donovan knew that by the time he got his car out of its tight spot, his quarry would be long gone.

Station 12: The Lantern Society

"This way," said Peters as he headed to a customized Toyota Corolla in the narrow alley adjacent to the store. He turned to the man who had been on the phone.

"Tú te quedas aquí. Capisce?"

The man nodded and re-entered the store. Peters took the wheel, Donovan rode shotgun, and Hector, the man wearing the shoulder holster, had the back seat to himself.

Strivelli turned the corner, speeding his way toward FDR Drive heading South. He knew that if he could gain enough of a lead, he could lose them in the canyons of the Financial District and leave no trace.

"You Charles Anderson?" asked Dodge. Anderson nodded in bewilderment as blood trickled from his nose down to his chin then onto the Visitor name tag which had started to peel away from his lapel. Dodge shook his head in disgust and handed him a bandana. "Good. I'd hate to think we grabbed the wrong guy."

"Who the hell are you people?" Anderson asked as he tipped his head back slightly and dabbed at his tender nose.

"We're Verity goons."

"You're a Verity goon," said Strivelli. "I'm an operative."

"Fine," Dodge said almost sulking.

"How did you know where to find me?"

"Someone wants to have words with you, Anderson," said Dodge. "Hell, I'm a little curious myself. Why would you turn on the people who are doing everything they can to make sure we all wake up in the same world we went to bed in?"

"That's enough, Dodge! He has no clearance. You don't know what he knows."

"I didn't know that."

"Spoiler alert!" Dodge shouted into Anderson's bleeding face. "You're fucking with the good guys, man! That makes you a bad guy."

"Here they come."

Strivelli was looking in his rearview mirror and saw a fire engine red Corolla zipping into traffic behind them. He gunned the 8-cylinder engine and made a play for 102nd Street, hoping to reach the east side highway before the Corolla had a chance to cut them off. When the entrance ramp was clearly in their sights, the Corolla made its play but only managed to get within a few car lengths before Strivelli sped up and swung out onto the highway. He could clearly see the driver bang on his dashboard while his passenger with the slicked back hair sat cool and still.

"So, Charlie," Dodge said as he continued to hammer at the bloodied Anderson, "how much were they paying you? Was it worth selling your soul? Or does your conscience come cheap?"

Anderson looked straight ahead. "Cheap enough, I guess."

"Was it everything you wanted it to be?"

"Not even close."

Morning rush hour was over and traffic was moving fairly briskly. Strivelli wanted to get far enough ahead of their pursuers so that when he broke away downtown, he'd have little difficulty losing them on the city streets. But pitting his old school station wagon against the zippy, little Toyota was proving problematic. Though they weren't traveling much faster than the posted speed limit, it felt otherwise due to the Hollywood-style pursuit. Tony crossed lanes, passed slower moving cars, hoping to lose them in the flow of traffic. He could see them in the mirror matching them move for move.

"Those sons of bitches," said Dodge. "Nice friends you got there, Anderson."

"They're no friends of mine."

"Yeah, now."

Strivelli jerked the wheel. He'd been paying too much attention to what was going on behind him and almost collided with a taxi ahead of him. That was the break the Corolla needed. Passing a car on the left, it pulled up directly behind Strivelli in the right lane. Strivelli cursed himself for his error. Then he spotted a third man in the car poking his head out of the rear passenger window.

"If that fucker's arm comes out," Dodge said, as he watched in the side view mirror, "you better fucking floor it."

"What's going on?" asked a still somewhat dazed Anderson. He was finding it difficult to maneuver between his captors.

"Dead or alive is my guess, Anderson. Now, shut up and bleed."

Sure enough, the third man's arm came through the window. From where they sat, it was difficult to determine if that arm had a gun on the end of it or not. Then both the arm and the head ducked back into the car.

"Shit."

When they were just past the halfway point to their destination, the taxi Strivelli had almost collided with slowed and pulled into the right line behind them. The Corolla took advantage of the shift to pull into the left lane and speed their way toward Strivelli's left shoulder.

"Shit."

"Come on, man," said Dodge, "they're coming around!"

"I can see that."

Strivelli had nowhere to go. Both lanes were blocked in front of him leaving no room to pass. When the Corolla was only two car lengths behind, the man who had appeared outside the car did so again but through the opposite window, dangerously close to their left side. The arm followed the head but it was still hard to see if there was a gun. Strivelli watched the cars ahead of him, waiting for his chance to pounce on an opening.

"Jesus Christ!"

"You boys might want to duck," Strivelli said.

The Corolla was almost upon them, closing in on their left, rear bumper. Strivelli hit the brakes and the Corolla sped past them. A horn blared behind them and Strivelli immediately sped back up to avoid being rear-ended. The car in front of them suddenly sped forward and Strivelli didn't slow his momentum. He pushed the Chevy behemoth, passing the Corolla and the next car on their right. Traffic in the left lane then slowed and Strivelli slid back into it. The Corolla was effectively boxed out.

The Verity team exited FDR Drive at South Street at the southernmost point in Manhattan. With the Toyota several car lengths back, they had enough distance between them that Strivelli only had to drive around a few blocks to lose them for good. By the time Donovan and company turned the corner where they'd last seen the wagon, it had vanished.

It wasn't magic. Strivelli had found what he was looking for in a steep driveway that led into the Harrison Brothers' garage. Using a remote control, he entered the garage and drove until he came to another door on the far end. He flashed his Verity ID at a scanner and continued into a dark passage where motion detecting lights came to life as they passed through.

"Do our neighbors know about this secret access?" asked Anderson.

"They think it's a part of our Disaster Recovery Plan," said Strivelli, "which it is."

The tunnel wasn't overly long before they came to a third door which opened into the Verity Corp parking garage. Strivelli steered his wagon into one of the spaces reserved for the Verity field agents.

"Let's go, Anderson," he said.

The three men made their way toward a security office adjacent to the elevator bank. Anderson didn't exactly feel like he was going from the frying pan into the fire, but there was definitely some heat. Still, there was some passing comfort in returning to his place of business, protected from the Lantern Society and their assassin by Verity's tower walls. But he'd done Verity a bad turn and he knew he had to account for it. How that punishment would be meted out remained to be seen.

Jacen Longworth, Verity's head of security, was there to greet them. The Verity men exchanged brief pleasantries, but for Askew, Longworth only had crossed arms and a look of disgust.

"Well, Mr. Anderson, you're in a lot of trouble."

"Less now than I was, I think," Anderson murmured.

"You hope!" Dodge couldn't resist.

"Because we won't kill you, is that what you think?"

Anderson couldn't read Longworth's expression so he withheld his response.

Jacen walked past him, opened a door, and cocked his head. Anderson looked at Strivelli and Dodge who offered nothing in return.

"Pour yourself a cup of coffee. But don't get too comfortable. You won't be here long."

Longworth closed the door. Anderson grabbed some stale coffee and absently added cream and sugar as he watched the three men through the window. He couldn't hear anything and he tried not to imagine what they were saying. He knew Longworth's question was meant to instill some measure of fear in him, but he was still greatly relieved to be out of the Society's clutches. Donovan's in particular. After taking a seat on the one cold, metal chair, he stared up at the only two objects in the room: an outdated fish and game calendar on one wall and a mounted deer head on another, both of which seemed wildly out of place in the financial district of New York City.

The door reopened and Rachel Henderson entered. After turning his back on her only a couple of hours earlier, Anderson's face offered up plenty of shame and embarrassment under the blood and bruising. With nowhere to run in the eight foot by eight foot room, he greeted her with as much warmth as he could muster.

"Hey, Charlie," Henderson said sadly.

Anderson blew on his coffee but otherwise kept his mouth shut. She watched him for a moment, waiting to see if he had anything to say for himself. His silence said it all. He knew he owed Rachel an explanation, but he was weary and ashamed. It occurred to him, though, that the door was open to move forward on his plan for redemption; a small gesture to make things right.

"It was a great opportunity, you know? Coming to work for Verity? I'd like to think I represented the company well. I brought in new clients, new investors, new money, all in support of this great financial enterprise we're all a part of. Was. Was a part of."

"So…what changed?"

"I make it my job to know the company I work for, the company I'm selling, inside and out. Not only do I sell the hell out of what's good about the firm, I make sure the less savory aspects are kept on the down-low. But I have to be prepared to answer any and all questions so I dig a little deeper, get below the surface. What few things I found out led me to believe that perhaps I wasn't representing the company after all. Certainly not the company inside the company. I'm talking about your Verity Corp. That company seemed to be a different animal altogether, a lot more secretive and creepy.

"And when Hugo disappeared, well…"

"A lot of us knew Hugo---."

"Not like I did! He was my friend! We had history going back to Chicago. He brought me into Verity Corp. He helped me acclimate to the big leagues. And then one day he was gone and no one seemed to be doing anything about it. I didn't see a hundred cops out searching for him. It wasn't on the news. I did, however, read the company memo, the paper memo," he said, emphasizing the point with a raised finger, "that went around asking us not to talk to the press, pointing to the confidentiality agreement we all signed when we were hired. But I never stopped wanting to know what happened to him. That's when they recruited me."

"They? Who recruited you?"

Anderson grew more tired still and let his eyelids droop slightly. This was harder than he thought it would be.

"I'm sorry I lied to you, Rachel."

The door opened once more and Longworth stepped in. "Time to go, Anderson."

Anderson was glad for the out. He didn't look back at Henderson as he left. She watched him go, wondering about the rest of the story, wondering what it was that had driven him to such lengths.

#

"Why is there blood on his face?" Askew asked as he stepped into his hotel room.

"It turned into a rescue mission," said Strivelli. "It got a little messy."

"Rescue mission?" he asked as he shut the door behind him. "Rescued from whom?"

"He hasn't said."

Anderson looked at Askew then down at the floor.

"Well, you could have at least let him clean up." Askew walked into the bathroom to wet a towel. "I can assure you, Mr. Anderson, you're in safe hands now." Askew held out the towel and Anderson reached up with hands that were bound together at the wrist by a plastic strap. "What in God's name?"

"That was Longworth's idea," said Strivelli. "He thought we ought to do something."

Askew gestured impatiently. "Cut this off of him immediately. He's not a prisoner."

Dodge opened a pocket knife and cut through the strap in a single stroke.

"He's not?" asked Strivelli.

"I'm not?" echoed Anderson.

Askew handed Anderson the wet towel. "You gentleman can take a walk. Get yourselves a beer and maybe some Buffalo wings. I want to chat with Mr. Anderson privately for a few minutes."

Strivelli and Dodge loitered at the door with expressions of concern.

"Oh, for Heaven's sake, he's not John Dillinger!" Once the two men left the room, Askew made his way to the electric coffee maker in the kitchenette. "I'm sorry about the melodrama. This is all very new to us."

"I understand. It's new to me, too." Anderson wiped at his face while Askew prepared two cups of tea. "Is it true? I'm not a prisoner?"

"We don't have the legal authority to keep you as a prisoner."

"So, I'm free to go?"

"Oh, my, no, that would be a dreadful idea. No, we're stuck with each other until we figure this all out."

"How's that not a prisoner?"

Askew raised an eyebrow. "I'm sure there's a difference. You have done us a grievous wrong, Mr. Anderson, and we need to account for that somehow. Reporting what you've done to the police is bad for both of us so we must look elsewhere for retribution. Besides, we don't have time to play this by the numbers. I think you understand."

"I understand retribution. But the rest? Not so much."

"Then I'm guessing you're in for quite a shock. But first things first; were you operating on behalf of the Lantern Society? We can't waste any more time if we're just chasing a wild goose."

Anderson rubbed at his wrists. He saw the question as a gateway to further his redemption, a fresh start, but there was one last item of business before he was willing to proceed.

"First things first," he said, "Hugo Jascowitz."

Tea bags in place, Askew poured the hot water into two mugs, steam fogging slightly his thick lenses as he considered whether he owed Anderson a response.

"Hugo worked very closely with Lionel Bellows on various projects," Askew finally said. "I worked with both of them to create those projects. I knew him very well, I think."

"Did you know he brought me into Verity Corp?"

Askew handed Anderson the tea then went back for sugar. "Hugo had good instincts."

"I've brought a lot of money into Verity Corp. I probably funded half of whatever it is you really do here which means I probably funded Hugo's disappearance in some way."

"An interesting perspective."

"And you people didn't lift a finger to find him."

"On that point you are grossly misinformed. We lifted much more than a finger, Mr. Anderson. We did everything in our power, worked around the clock for weeks. Lionel sent two teams into harm's way in search of him. We did far from nothing."

"Sent them where?"

"You are insatiable! What we do at Verity Corp redefines Top Secret, Mr. Anderson, and you are not privy!"

"But if you'd told me something, anything, maybe none of this would have happened."

Askew slammed his cup down onto the counter, boiled water splashed across his hand but he didn't even flinch he was so angry. He stepped up to Anderson as if he were going to scold a child.

"Let me tell you something, Mr. Anderson, the Verity Corp science division does not report to the sales team as shocking as that might seem to you. While you're busy bleeding your clients dry, we're taking that money and investing it into saving our world. But you lost your friend and you didn't know who to blame. You needed a scapegoat, so why not blame the giant corporation. You needed a target to satisfy your ego. It couldn't be that Hugo might have fallen off a bridge and floated away or maybe fell into a ravine. It couldn't be that maybe a depressed Hugo Jascowitz might have taken his own life in some remote woods somewhere. No, it had to be a conspiracy within Verity Corp, a shadow cabinet manipulating events to cover up his absence. You had too many questions about Verity Corp so what do you do? You go to an even scarier, more mysterious organization for answers. They promise you the moon and all you have to do in return is reveal Verity secrets. And what does that get you?"

Askew paused, a little sweaty, a little out of breath, waiting for Anderson to answer. Anderson, feeling the fool, took his time in replying.

"Nothing," he said.

"Nothing!" Askew said, dabbing at his forehead with his handkerchief. "What a surprise."

"Look, I made a mistake! I know it! There's nothing I can do but apologize. If Verity ends up suffering a few financial losses, it's on me, I get it. Take it out of my retirement!"

Askew suddenly felt very sorry for Anderson, a guilty man yet innocent in his ignorance.

"You have no idea what you've done."

"What? What have I done?" Anderson demanded almost belligerently.

Askew's cell phone rang and he turned his back to answer it.

Station 12: The Lantern Society

Anderson heard what Askew said but the preposterous nature of the statement had dazed him like someone had tossed a brick to his head. He staggered to the couch and almost collapsed on its arm for support. *Did he just say..?* He couldn't even repeat it silently in his head. Maybe he'd heard him wrong.

"Come, Mr. Anderson," said Askew, entering the living room as he hung up his phone, "it's time to redeem yourself."

Chapter Twelve: The Truth Squad

It was darkness like he had never seen; black space, a tarred-over universe devoid of stars, absent of moon, and with no obvious sources of illumination. Truth to tell, he had no real idea if he was indoors or out, the blackness could have stretched out to infinity or to distant, unseen walls. And yet, he had no trouble seeing his surroundings. A train yard stretched out before him, rows and rows of track, lines indistinguishable without ties to pair the rails. Building-like constructs and other mysterious objects, some large, some small, hung both high above his head and below the transparent surface on which he walked. On occasion, vehicles glided silently through the air, some on vertical courses that somehow, almost magically, crossed his walking plane.

Hugo Jascowitz and his team could easily make out the hub of the Trans-Dimensional Railroad in the near distance and with every step they took, they did their best to remain out of its line of sight, staying low and using whatever they came across as cover. Their timing and movements had to be precise if they wanted to get home. And they very much wanted to get home.

#

Askew was well aware that he was on the verge of being derailed by a growing sense of panic, panic that fed on the awareness of time passing; that every minute given to their investigation was time lost to actually ending the would-be catastrophe. Of course, it didn't take a scientist to know one couldn't achieve the latter without performing the former, and so he cultivated his encroaching panic to better focus on the task at hand.

As a man of science it was his job, and more genuinely his nature, to identify problems, analyze the pertinent data, and based on the results of that analysis, derive possible solutions. But the sheer scope of their current dilemma was beyond anything they had ever encountered and clues to its resolution were, so far, few and far between.

The laboratory that took up most of the tower's second floor was, as far as the general public was concerned, Verity's one and only science facility, the lab that was responsible for the toy box into which their investors poured their money. Pacing anxiously in the anteroom of the lab's adjacent meeting space, Askew watched on a monitor as the various participants of the upcoming summit began to trickle in.

Charlie Anderson, ironically, or perhaps fittingly, was the first to arrive. He knew the room all too well as the gathering place for their marketing sessions, one of which he was supposed to lead that very morning. Jacen Longworth, acting as Anderson's custodian, escorted him to a seat at the conference table while one of the green-clad security officers remained outside the room, more as a formality than as an actual guard.

A young lady pushing a catering cart entered next and offered up food and beverage to the new arrivals. Anderson, who hadn't eaten anything of substance in twenty-four hours, didn't hesitate to claim two of the pre-wrapped sandwiches. Strivelli and Dodge grabbed drinks as they strolled in, and Dodge, in a seriocomic gesture, let Anderson know that he had his eye on him. Anderson failed to see the humor.

Henderson and Cheever soon followed and seated themselves directly across from Anderson. The senior scientist tried to make eye contact with her friend from the investments group, but he wasn't having it. He felt so ashamed. She excused herself and came around the table to speak with him. Longworth offered his chair, then joined the woman at the food cart to give the two of them a moment of privacy.

The professor watched and wondered just how close the two of them had gotten. Knowing what Henderson knew, it made Askew uncomfortable that she and Anderson had any kind of relationship outside of a professional one. And with that brief thought, Askew's panic made room for paranoia. He cared for Rachel like a daughter, and such thoughts did her an injustice, and so he exorcised his mind of distrust and turned his focus back to the impending meeting.

Of the Global Armour crew there was no sign, and if they didn't show, the primary intent of the meeting, to bring the two entities together, would be lost. It was Tomlinson who had rung up Askew during his tête-à-tête with Anderson back at the hotel. After she had briefed Gorokhovich on the current state of affairs, he reluctantly deemed it time for a meet and greet. Thanks to Tomlinson's expedited reveal, the need for Global

Armour to operate in the shadows had come to an end. It was a win-win for Askew, eliminating Global Armour as a distraction while effectively doubling his meager investigative force with a global security firm with presumably some measure of experience in securing the globe.

Askew closed his eyes for a moment to collect himself, trying to come to grips with the idea that he was going to have to put his trust in an agency that had been watching his and the company's every move for who knows how long. Not a solid foundation for trust. But the momentum of the emergency was forcing him to disregard his prized standard of logic to allow good, old-fashioned instinct to make the decision for him. So far, warning bells had yet to chime.

When he reopened his eyes, he looked down at his pocket watch. It was time, with or without Global Armour in attendance, to start the meeting. As he stepped out of the anteroom, Tomlinson and Foster came around a corner led by a Verity scientist and accompanied by a young man in a suit.

"Hello, Professor," said Tomlinson with her hand out. "Mr. Gorokhovich apologizes but he's going to be a little late. This is John Cannon," Tomlinson gestured toward the man in the suit, "assistant to our Chief of Operations, Lenore Devlin. She's out on assignment so he'll be taking notes on her behalf."

"I see," Askew said, realizing he must not have properly related the gravity of their situation because the idea of something else, anything else, taking precedence over current events was maddeningly laughable to him. Then again, properly relating the gravity of the situation was one of the key points of the meeting.

"Shall we?" Askew held his hand out as a courtesy and allowed the agents of Global Armour to enter first. He then released their escort with a nod and turned to follow after his guests.

He hadn't taken two steps, though, when a hand reached out and took his arm. Askew turned back and found a scowling Keith Baylor standing before him.

"Well, hello, Keith," Askew said, trying to sell a good neighbor vibe. "What brings you to the second floor?"

"I could ask you the same thing."

Askew tried to dismiss what was happening in the next room with a shrug. "What, this? An informal gathering. Jacen's thinking about bringing in an outside security firm to assist on certain matters. Nothing earth-shattering, I assure you. But I do have to get back, just the same."

"You weren't such a good liar back in college, Prof." This stopped Askew in his tracks.

"It's easy to lie when most of what you say is true." Askew took Baylor by the arm and led him away from the meeting room. "And when I can talk more about it," he said quietly and earnestly, "I will. I promise. For now, you're going to have to trust me."

"Okay, Dan, I'll trust you. If you can't talk about it, you can't talk about it."

"Thank you, Keith." Askew turned once again.

"One more thing."

The professor turned back slowly with a slight smile.

"Have you spoken with Rachel about scheduling my test?"

Askew appeared taken aback by the question. "The Oculacrum? Is it ready?"

Baylor nodded with assurance. "The Scope's been fully upgraded and it's ready to go. We've been working 'round the clock."

The two bald men stared at each other, one black, one white, like two chess pieces squaring off. An unspoken bargain was being struck: Askew would push the Oculacrum test through and Baylor would not push the subject at hand. Once Askew accepted the deal in his head, he let Baylor know that he'd work it out with Henderson by the end of the day. Baylor provided a half-smile and nodded both in thanks and understanding.

"Good luck in there."

#

Jascowitz had point, moving forward in twenty foot intervals, constantly referring to a printed card in a window built into the sleeve of his black, Verity-issued P4 TrakSuit. Each time he reached a switchbox he'd shine his tiny flashlight down on it and compare the symbols on display with those on his card. It wasn't much of a map, really just a trail of bread crumbs left by the teams that had preceded them, symbols that would lead him and his coworkers to a train bound for home.

To those few employees of Verity Corp who were aware of their existence, they were known informally as the Truth Squad. The current mission team of Jascowitz, Tina Felton, Raj Shelat, and Phillip "Smitty" Smith, had achieved their given objectives and had begun the difficult and dangerous task of finding their ride back to Earth. Team leader Jascowitz felt keenly the responsibility of getting his team home safely and could feel their eyes on his back as he weaved his way through the obstacles in their path.

At each switchbox or signal post, Jascowitz looked for specific symbols, symbols that changed as each train came and went. If the symbol they sought wasn't displayed when they arrived, it generally meant that they were either moving too quickly or not quickly enough. If they lost the trail, they would have to find their way back to the starting point and begin the sequence all over again. If they could find it.

The prized symbol of their quest, the icon that had been assigned to Earth by the powers-that-be, was a circle with a pyramid inside. In a display window on either side of the train's windshield, that circle glowed like a phosphorescent green hula-hoop, spinning on its axis, inside of which a three-dimensional pyramid rotated in the opposite direction. Verity hadn't figured out yet what the symbol was meant to represent, but they doubted any connection to ancient Egypt.

The team maintained a steady pace, a product of countless hours of rehearsal, and for the most part found each symbol in its designated time and place. Adjustments had to be made every now and again to allow for obstructions, but otherwise everything went smoothly. That is until Felton, who was bringing up the rear, disappeared through a hole in the surface plane.

There was no error in her footing; one minute the floor was there and in the next, it wasn't. Difficult to tell when the ground was transparent. She had no way of knowing how far she was going to fall, of course, but Felton knew in that split second when her foot failed to make contact that it was possible she might sail forever through that inky blackness, borne on a wave of inexplicable gravity, until she starved to death or maybe smashed herself to smithereens when she finally made contact with an alien artifact. It was like living a child's nightmare, the dream fall that stood alone, out of context, that brought with it helplessness of the highest magnitude as objects below rushed up to greet her. Her next thoughts might have been to review the life that was flashing before her eyes and determine whether she was satisfied by the tale.

Station 12: The Lantern Society

As it turned out, there would be no time for that. Only twelve feet into her fall, her feet struck another unseen plane, causing her ankle to turn and her head to bounce off something that looked like a public mailbox. She went down hard, the wind knocked out of her and leaving her unable to cry out. The men ahead of her heard nothing and so were none the wiser.

When the rest of the team found their path blocked by an unexpected train, they huddled up to discuss their options and noticed immediately that they were one member shy. They looked around in alarm but saw no sign of their fourth. As Squad Leader, Jascowitz kept his panic in check knowing that time was of the essence. The mission would not be considered a success unless all four of them returned home safe and sound, so he quickly formulated a plan. It would be difficult, but they had to find her. He couldn't imagine a worse scenario than being left behind, all alone, in a reality not his own.

#

Lionel Bellows arrived right behind Askew and as the latter made his way to the podium, Bellows took a seat next to Longworth. Both men bowed their heads in an exchange of whispers, their eyes serving up suspicious glances at Tomlinson and Foster. Foster didn't fail to notice and shifted uncomfortably in his seat.

The professor waited as Henderson rejoined Cheever then leveled his gaze at each member of the gathering, still debating with himself if the meeting was forward progress or a desperate measure. He cleared his throat and waited until everyone was moved to silence.

"What's said in this room today stays in this room."

He continued to stare, taking in everyone's reaction, and when he was satisfied he pressed on, introducing and welcoming the representatives of Global Armour to Verity Corp.

"Unfortunately," he went on to say, "their chief, Anton Gorokhovich, is running a bit late so we'll get to that point of the agenda in a bit. The short version is this; they're here to help and for that we are exceedingly grateful. So let's get right to the entree, shall we?

"When this meeting is adjourned, Lionel and I will be sitting down with the Board to inform them of the following: that Charles Anderson, here, of the financial investment group, did conspire with an organization that calls itself the Lantern Society, to siphon data from Verity Corp servers. Unbeknownst to Mr. Anderson, the theft of this data, and more importantly, any subsequent use of such..." Askew paused to consider his words, a near impossible task given their dilemma. "Well, there's no time to sugar coat it. Any subsequent use of this data could lead to the complete and utter destruction of our planet."

Askew's audience erupted in shock and disbelief followed by an immediate barrage of questions. The words were preposterous, but the source was impeccable. Anderson was beyond stunned. Carrying the guilt of Sarah's murder had been difficult enough. Now it seemed he literally had the weight of the world on his shoulders. People shouted at Askew, one on top of another. Askew raised his arms in a mollifying gesture.

"In theory," he shouted over the crowd. "It's only a theory. Please, we don't have time for this."

"I don't understand," said Anderson blankly once the tumult had subsided.

"We're getting to it, Mr. Anderson."

"What do you mean, 'destruction of our planet'?"

"Mr. Anderson, please!" Askew pointed to Anderson's face. "You have egg salad on your chin."

"Charlie?" Henderson was still waiting for her explanation. Her tone spoke to Anderson as if they were the only two people in the room. Surprisingly, no one interrupted.

"I needed answers, Rachel," he said, wiping at his face with a napkin, "and the Lantern Society promised to provide them."

"How'd that work out for you?" asked Strivelli, startling Anderson out of his private moment.

"I'm still waiting," he said glumly. "But I had no idea---!"

"What's done is done, Mr. Anderson," said Askew, holding up a hand to deflect any excuses. "We need to move on. Rachel, if you would, please?"

"Thank you, Professor."

Henderson removed her glasses and placed them on the pad in front of her and began to provide highlights to the group of how Ellen Cheever had discovered the leech code and how it was that Verity Corp was hacked. Although none of their data appeared to have been compromised, they believed one particular server had been copied in full, though they were unable to determine where that copied data had been sent. They were hoping Anderson might be able to shed some light on that.

All heads turned in his direction, his face flushed with guilt. He had to decide then and there if he would stay on his pothole-riddled road to redemption, or give up trying altogether in light of this new and devastating revelation. He sat up straighter in his chair and composed himself, reconfiguring his countenance to convey some measure of character and hoping to appear a penitent man. He told himself that everything he'd done up to that point was wrong, but his reasons for doing so were still sound. The company was not what it pretended to be, not at its heart, and not by a long shot. Worse, he'd lost a good friend in Hugo Jascowitz, probably through some nefarious company business, and his employers had covered it up.

He confessed he didn't have much to offer in the way of information. The man the Lantern Society had sent over to hack into Verity's system mentioned something about a ghost partition in the finance area, invisible to everyone unless they were looking for it.

"He said the Society didn't want it traced back to me, in case they ever needed me again, so I had no direct involvement. He told me he couldn't hack into Verity's network from outside. That's why he was sent to me. It was easier to break in from the inside. He copied the data onto this ghost partition and from there it went off to the Society servers."

"Any idea why he didn't just send it from its original location?" asked Henderson.

"Something about detection and the amount of time it took to transfer. Not really my thing so I never gave it my full attention."

"Well, he was right about the trace," said Cheever, "but I managed to unravel the leech code to the original hack and once we peeled away the hacker's modifications, all we were left with was Charlie's company login."

"What do you know about your hacker?" asked Bellows.

Anderson cringed at the phrasing of the question, but he knew if he objected it would only make him look defensive.

"Tall, skinny. I never got his name. Before he showed up at Verity we communicated through the Society forums on the web." He blushed. "His handle was Digital Overlord."

"Haberman," said Tomlinson as a matter of fact. "He runs the

Society website out of his dorm at Mather College in Hartford. I'm sure if we squeezed him, he'd cooperate."

"Who gives a shit about a website?!" shouted Dodge. "Shouldn't we be talking about the end of the world?"

"Relax, Beavis," said Strivelli, who appeared cool as a cucumber, taking it all in. "I'm sure they're getting to it."

Despite his outward appearance, though, Strivelli wasn't as cool as he let on. The distance between Hartford, Connecticut and New York City was negligible in the grand scheme of things, but with the mention of possible global destruction, it felt as if Angela was a million miles away. If the worst should come to pass, he wanted to be with her, not running errands for Verity Corp. His finger tapped the dial pad of his phone. Maybe he'd call her at the end of the meeting, just to hear her voice. *Honey, there's a rumor the world might be coming to an end and I just wanted to say hi.*

"A variety of data was copied," Henderson continued, "but more than likely their target was the construction plans for what we call a Sounding Tunnel. This is the focus of today's meeting. We cannot allow the Lantern Society to construct such a tunnel."

"Why?" demanded Dodge.

"Because, Mr. Dodge," replied Askew, "we know for a fact that it won't work. However, the attempt alone---."

Bellows jumped in. "We don't have time to explain all the details to you, Mr. Dodge. Every minute counts."

"Oh, no. No, no, no," said Foster. "Everyone in this room needs to understand what's happening here, everyone on the same page. With all due respect, I'm sick of following blindly. First Global Armour and now Verity Corp? Uh uh. No more. What exactly are we dealing with here?"

Askew was hesitant to continue, but only because he didn't want to say anymore. After so many years, keeping secrets was all he knew. But he understood their need to know. Asking them to save the world on faith alone was a tall order.

"All of you possess some level of knowledge regarding the Trans-Dimensional Railroad, be it intimately as my coworkers and I, or peripherally for those of you who read Heberling's book. Understand that this train system exists and that it originates in another dimension, another layer of reality, if you will. Verity Corp has constructed a tunnel, a gateway that allows two realities, theirs and ours, to coexist in the same space at the same time. But without the proper components, that gateway becomes unstable, there is no phasing process. Their reality would supersede ours and most likely force a chain reaction."

"Which means what, exactly?" asked Foster.

"We're not entirely sure. Obviously something like this has never happened before. But in theory, the other reality, upon its intrusion, would replace ours and everything we know would cease to exist."

"Or?" asked Dodge, looking around the room for an alternative.

"Or…the incoming reality might cancel out both realities which would essentially amount to the same thing."

"Or?" Dodge repeated with a little more urgency.

"We can't assume a best case scenario, Mr. Dodge. It wouldn't be prudent."

#

Jascowitz cursed their luck and tried to reach Felton over the headset. It sounded like there was activity on the other end but there was no verbal response. He cursed again as he ripped the Velcro-fastened window from his sleeve and shoved it into Smitty's hand.

"Keep going," Jascowitz said. "Don't lose the trail. When I find her, I'll call you and you lead me back with your flash. Go!"

Smitty knew there was no time to argue the point so he grabbed Shelat's arm and the two of them headed for the nearest coupling to crawl under.

Jascowitz started quickly back the way they had come, at least to the best of his recollection, and he used what familiar sights he could recall as guide posts. He tried once more to reach Felton over his headset, but all he got back was a series of clicks and he began to think she might have gotten hurt or worse. Feeling like he had no choice, he turned on his mini-light and prayed that no one spotted it cutting through the darkness.

"A hole…" came a weak voice into his headset.

"Felton? Say again, I didn't copy."

"What did she call you?"

"Smitty, clear the fucking line!"

There was a pause.

"A hole," Felton wheezed. "I fell in a God damn hole," and then a cough.

Jascowitz shut his light off and moved forward, quickly but carefully, peering out, trying not to let the mysteriously illuminated objects in his line of sight distract him. Finally, he saw what looked to be a square-shaped glow on the surface ahead of him and ran over to check it out. Felton had played it smart and turned on her TrakSuit lights to make herself easier to spot. Interestingly, though the glow found its way through the twenty-five square foot hole, it did not penetrate the surrounding surface plane despite the plane's transparency.

"Tina, are you alright?" Jascowitz asked as he dropped to his knees.

Felton had gotten to her feet and was testing her ankle. "I'm fine. Could have been a lot worse.

"Do you need me to come down?"

"No." She stood up on a block and held up her hand.

"How are we doing, Hugo?" came Smitty's voice over the headset.

"Felton's fine. We'll be heading your way in a sec."

"Better hurry. Our train home is ready and waiting."

"Go ahead and strap in. We're right behind you." Jascowitz hung down into the hole and extended his arm. "Come on, Felton, let's go home."

#

"So, you're saying that aliens are responsible for the disappearing people?"

"Yes, Agent Foster, beings not of our world, from another dimension."

"So, that cockamamie book---."

"The Crossing," Tomlinson clarified, much to Foster's chagrin.

"The Crossing was written by a man who had experienced something beyond all rational thought," said Askew, "and he thought he might purge himself of its residual side effects by airing them in public in the form of a novel. In fact, he wasn't sure any of it actually happened until the calls to his hotline started coming in. The Crossing brought a lot of people together. Without it, there would be no Verity Corp and without Verity, there would be no hope."

"Hope for what?" asked Strivelli. Askew looked over at Strivelli with raised eyebrows and Strivelli shrugged. Askew began to see how Verity's tiered level of secrecy could work against them and shot Anderson a look of understanding.

"These beings," Askew said, "these abductors are rewriting our reality. In fact, we refer to the event as a Rewrite. With every kidnapping they change the present, leaving behind a new fiction. What was is no longer. When someone is taken, the story of the world is written over so the absence goes unnoticed. More specifically, the abducted never existed, leaving no one behind to remember them. Verity Corp has spent years learning what we can about these beings in the hope of stopping whatever it is they're planning and reclaim reality for our own."

"What's the point?" asked Dodge.

"Excuse me?" asked Askew.

"For what purpose," said Dodge, as if talking to a child, "are these aliens kidnapping us?"

Askew's countenance darkened, his oversized eyes didn't blink. "You disrespect me, Mr. Dodge."

"No, I---." Dodge went red and shut his mouth.

Askew addressed the rest of the room. "We don't know their endgame. I wish we did, though I doubt knowing would give us much of an advantage. But it's difficult to come up with solutions when you don't know the true nature of the problem. And we don't know how long they've been doing this. Decades, we know. Centuries? Who knows how different the world might have been without their meddling? Better? Worse? If history had been left to us---."

It's always been up to us.

Tomlinson had an idea what the world might have been like for her if Gorokhovich's story had any merit. Perhaps the dismay she felt regarding her life was a byproduct of what Askew referred to as a Rewrite. Maybe she was depressed because she wasn't living the live the universe had originally intended.

Askew had lost his train of thought and he stood there, motionless, trying to recapture it.

"Professor?" Henderson finally asked.

"The work we've done has been difficult," Askew continued as if nothing had happened. "Our initial blueprint consisted only of children's nightmares and, later, faded memories. That's until we came up with the Sounding Tunnel. This technology makes use of electromagnetic energy and sound waves, special frequencies, to open a phase tunnel that makes the Tapestry Rail System visible to us for the length of our construct."

The Verity staff looked at each other with curious glances.

"I'm sorry, Daniel," jumped in Lionel Bellows, "did you just say Tapestry Rail System?"

Askew saw how his colleagues were looking at him.

"Did I?"

"I've never heard that expression. I'd love to know what's behind it."

Askew's bald head turned crimson. "If I said it, it was in error."

"That's what I heard, Professor," said Henderson. "What does it mean?"

Askew recalled the Wonderland-like dream he'd had on his train ride to Hartford. The tall, thin conductor with the projected face had used the term. He quickly decided that, unlike Heberling and his novel, he didn't want to expose the abstract design of his dreams in a public forum so he quickly dismissed it as a slip of the tongue.

"We've done some preliminary investigation into this Lantern Society," he went on to say. "We've made some headway but it's time to turn up the heat. We've confirmed that they're responsible for the theft. That's great news because it greatly reduces the scope of our search. It's time now to determine for certain if it's their intent to construct a Sounding Tunnel and if so, what their timetable is."

"Or was," said Bellows.

"Right."

"I'm assuming," said Tomlinson, "that it would take a great deal of money to construct one of these tunnels."

"A great deal of money," agreed Askew.

"There's got to be a trail. Do we know how this organization is funded?"

"Perhaps Mr. Anderson can enlighten us once again."

"I wasn't an official member so I wouldn't know anything about their finances. I can tell you that I just facilitated a deal with Bismarck Industries that netted the Society one million dollars. Sarah Bismarck, specifically. I can't be sure who else knew about it."

"In exchange for what?" asked Bellows.

"They didn't share that with me. A formula of some kind. Only Sarah said it was incomplete."

Station 12: The Lantern Society

"In what way?" asked Askew.

"I don't know. She kept referring to the chemical half of the formula. That the drug wouldn't work without the other half of the process. Something like that."

"She's talking about the IACL," said Askew.

"The inoculation?" asked Bellows. "What would Sarah Bismarck know about the inoculation?"

"There was nothing about it on that server," said Henderson. "It wasn't part of the stolen data."

"Who did Bismarck think she was paying off?" asked Longworth.

"I'm not sure if they referred to themselves as the Lantern Society," said Anderson. "She did not think I was there representing Verity."

"Inoculation against what?" asked Tomlinson.

There was a pause at the table. Askew looked at Bellows who reaffirmed an earlier discussion on the subject with a nod.

"Inoculation Against Continuity Loss, or IACL. All core members of the Verity Group are inoculated against any changes made in reality by the aliens. The inoculated live in a constant, ongoing stream of reality so that we can all do our jobs without interruption. Our team remains intact. We're essentially immune to the comings and goings of the Trans-Dimensional Railroad."

"So, brothers are losing sisters, mothers are losing sons, and Verity Corp just keeps toiling away without a care in the world, is that it?" asked Foster.

"We are not without losses of our own. Only core members and their immediate families are inoculated. Some of us have lost members of our extended families. Some of us have lost friends."

News of the inoculation filled Tomlinson with an emotion in stark contrast to what she was feeling a moment earlier when Askew was describing the revision of reality. Everything he had said corroborated what Gorokhovich had related about her former life.

My idyllic life. My husband, my beautiful home, a fulfilling career...all of it gone. Had they taken my husband? Or did they write him into a new family and leave me out to dry?

There was no question that her disposition had brightened at the thought that she might actually be closing in on the life she thought lost.

But now, hearing that it could have all been prevented in the first place if Verity Corp had only shared their inoculation with the rest of the world, she fumed, and her interest in working with Verity Corp began to morph from hopeful and engaged into something a tad more hostile.

"Why not just inoculate everyone and call it a day?" she asked when what she really wanted to say was why *didn't* you?

"We don't know what they're capable of," said Askew, "and if they came to realize that their Rewrites no longer had the effect they desired, there might be terrible consequences. We couldn't take that chance."

"What next?" asked Henderson, not wanting to go off on a tangent. "It's obvious to me that we need to get Sarah Bismarck's side of the story. Find out where she fits in all this Society business."

"That's not going to happen."

Once again, all eyes turned to Anderson.

"We need to pursue every lead, Mr. Anderson," said Askew.

Henderson nodded. "Charlie has a relationship with Ms. Bismarck, don't you, Charlie?"

"Had."

"Still, just because you---."

"Sarah's dead."

The outcry from everyone shook Anderson.

"She was murdered yesterday during the exchange," he said with some difficulty. "When she realized she was getting ripped off, she attempted to renege on the deal. The Society didn't like that, I guess."

"Can you confirm it was the Society?"

"The shooter was a man by the name of Donovan. Ed Donovan. Big guy with a scar on his face."

"The man we rescued you from?" asked Strivelli.

Foster pointed to his pad and Tomlinson looked down to read, 'the cowboy.' She took the pad and wrote, 'I know him,' to which Foster's eyes widened.

"That's right." Anderson furrowed his brow. "How did you find me, anyway?"

Neither Strivelli nor Dodge offered a response but Dodge let slip a wry smile.

"It's what they were hired to do, Mr. Anderson," said Bellows.

Askew ran his hand over his gleaming head. "Sarah Bismarck dead,

I can't believe it. I've known her since she was a little girl. Can this get any worse?!" He slammed his hand down on the podium and everyone in the room jumped.

Strivelli said, "We saw you coming out of BI with the man you just described."

"Would this have been in the neighborhood of 9:30?" asked John Cannon, looking up from his phone.

"That's right," said Anderson.

No one asked Cannon how he knew that, but he could read the question on their faces.

"Bismarck Industries is Global Armour's principal backer. Without them the firm wouldn't exist. So when Josef Bismarck needs something, Mr. Gorokhovich sees to it personally."

"What's Bismarck's interest in Global Armour?" asked Bellows.

"You can ask Mr. Gorokhovich that question when he gets here."

"What did Bismarck need on this occasion?" asked Longworth.

"He was having second thoughts about a meeting that was to take place. Maybe with Mr. Anderson here, I don't know. He wanted someone to attend in his stead, and he didn't want to use a BI employee who might go running to his daughter."

"So, you brought in this Donovan character?"

"No, I've never heard of Donovan."

"Global Armour used him for an assignment in our first month," said Tomlinson. "He and his team were supposed to infiltrate Verity's lab, your primary lab, for the purpose of planting spy cams throughout the facility."

"I remember him," said Bellows.

"Yes," said Askew, "the wandering auditors. Very subtle, they were. We never did find them, though, did we?"

"We did find a pair of legs."

Askew grimaced. "Yes, that was disturbing."

"He never found his way back to us, either," said Tomlinson. "None of them did."

Bellows turned to Cannon. "Well, if you didn't send Donovan, who did?"

"I couldn't tell you. I took the appointment myself. By the time I got there the person I was supposed to meet was already gone."

Longworth directed his attention to Anderson. "Why did you go to Bismarck Industries?"

"I was going to hand over the money. I was thinking about it. I wanted to do something…"

"Is that what you were carrying when you were stopped at the gate this morning?" asked Henderson.

"Yes. I thought I should hide it somewhere safe while I worked things out. But I forgot about the damn meeting."

"Were you going to tell Bismarck that his daughter had been murdered?" Henderson asked.

Anderson didn't reply right away so Bellows jumped in.

"You were forcibly removed from Bismarck?"

"You could say that." Anderson could feel the energy of the questioning ramping up. It was starting to take on the characteristics of the interrogation he'd expected all along. "I knew what Donovan was capable of so I didn't put up a fight."

"And you had this money with you at the time?" asked Longworth.

"Yes."

"And Donovan took it."

"Yes. A million dollars."

"God," said Askew, shaking his head.

"Had you met Donovan prior to this?" Longworth asked as he and Bellows continued to take turns asking questions.

"Yes, I'd met him the previous morning. I had a meeting with a Society representative to discuss the Bismarck deal and he was there."

"What can you tell us about this representative?"

"Well groomed woman. Snappy dresser."

"Might she be the leader of the Lantern Society?"

"I couldn't say." Anderson stopped moving his head back and forth between his interrogators and stared at an empty chair across the room. "She may have referenced someone else in charge, I can't remember."

"Where did this meeting take place?"

"Midtown west, not far from the highway. Kupper something or other. Looked like it had been abandoned for years."

"Kupperdyne," said Askew. "He's talking about Jonathon Kupperberg's engineering facility."

"Didn't Kupperberg once work for Bismarck Industries?" asked Bellows.

"Yes," said Askew, "but he and Josef had a falling out back in the old days. I never found out what it was about.

"If the Society is building a Tunnel, someone has to provide them with the required parts. We'll try following the money as Agent Tomlinson has suggested. We can also try following the hardware. There are damn few plants that can get a job like this done on the QT. We get almost all of our hardware from Bismarck. I can look into whether they're taking on any side jobs. Highly doubtful, but I can ask. We have a lot of work to do and not a lot of time to do it."

"What happens next?" asked Tomlinson.

The Polycom phone on the table rang and Bellows hit the speaker button.

"Yes?"

"Mr. Bellows, Anton Gorokhovich is here to join the meeting."

"Good. Show him in, please."

#

Felton stood tall and stretched to take hold of Jascowitz's hand. He pulled her up in the process of backing away from the hole, and Felton grasped at the unseen edge and hoisted herself up.

"You're good to go?" Jascowitz asked.

"Let's move."

"Shelat and I are strapped in," said Smitty over the comm. "I'm putting on my signal light. The engine is running. Do you copy?"

"We copy, Smitty, and we are en route. I see your signal."

A red light flashed from underneath the last car of a parked train. Amber lights came on along the train's length and Jascowitz and Felton picked up their pace. Jascowitz suddenly felt a sense of movement, a vibration in the air, and looked off to his left to see a single spotlight making its way in their direction.

"Another train is coming. Let's pick it up."

He listened for the bell chime that signaled the Earth-bound train was ready to roll out but it remained silent. Good. They were almost there. The incoming train was bearing down on them but they kept their eyes on the flashing red light. As they approached one of the switchboxes, Felton ran around it on the left side while Jascowitz went right and jumped a raised pipe. As he landed, a cloth bag flew out of his belt pack and crashed to the surface, spilling its contents. Both team members stopped and stared. Jascowitz was not about to blow the mission.

"Take off, Felton. I'm right behind you."

The incoming train was almost upon them.

"I can help."

Jascowitz grabbed her by both arms and turned her around. "Strap in! I'll be right there."

"They'll see me!"

He pushed her across the track just as the train arrived, separating the two of them. He wasted no time falling to his knees to collect the scattered contents, gathering up the sparkling gems and returning them to the drawstring bag.

"I'm in, Hugo," shouted Felton over the headset.

Anderson could hear the bell chiming once the passing train had cleared the area.

"Go, Hugo, go!" prompted Shelat.

Jascowitz shoved the bag back into his pack, already running at top speed.

"We're moving, Hugo, hurry!"

Jascowitz stopped running as soon as he heard Felton's proclamation. He knew there was no way he would be able to strap into a moving train. There was silence for a moment as he watched the train pull away. The red signal light winked out.

"I'm sorry, Hugo," said Felton over the comm. "Good luck. We'll be waiting for you on the other side."

"We'll send a team, Hugo," said Smitty. "Keep your radio charged."

"Good luck, man," said Shelat.

The train disappeared from Jascowitz's view.

"Shit."

#

There was a knock on the door and the escort let herself in.

"Professor, Mr. Gorokhovich."

"Thank you, Esther."

Station 12: The Lantern Society

    A man walked in with short, curly, brown hair and a close-cropped beard and smiled.
    "Sorry I'm late, everyone," Gorokhovich said in his light accent. "Couldn't be helped. Jackie, George, did you save me a seat?"
    "I'm sorry," said Askew, "but don't we know each other?"
    Anderson recognized the man, too. It was earlier that morning he'd seen the man coming out of Bismarck Industries and into a waiting black Jaguar. But the familiarity didn't begin and end at BI. His eyes grew wide and Anderson stood up to look his old friend in the eye.
    "Jesus Christ! Hugo?!"

Chapter Thirteen: A Brief Debriefing

    Hugo Jascowitz stood overlooking a large, shallow pool in the rest area of Station 3. The water changed colors with each passing ripple and no assist from artificial lighting was apparent. Hundreds of eels of varying lengths swam effortlessly in a myriad of intricate patterns, turning corners and interlocking in the center of the pool before moving on in new directions. Each wave of color introduced a different species of microscopic organism; food for the eels that was absorbed through the skin. The creatures never stopped moving and every minute or so the pattern of their movements shifted with kaleidoscopic results. Jascowitz was mesmerized.
    Station Master Pil watched Hugo, as fascinated with the human as Jascowitz was with the eels.
    "Humankind could learn much from the Tempets. They embody perfect harmony and communication."
    "It is a beautiful display, Station Master, but I'm not sure they could teach human beings anything of use. Surely instinct instructs their movements."
    "You believe them to be inferior beings?"
    "Your words, not mine, Station Master. I cannot speak to their intelligence. They are certainly far less complex than human beings."
    "And therefore you presume less intelligent?"
    Jascowitz knew he was being set up for a lesson and could already safely assume that the eels were more than rudimentary creatures.
    "Why? Because they have no economy?" Pil's lecture began. "No apparent speech? No sense of fashion? Or maybe it's the smaller brain that has you convinced. Tell me, Anton, what is it that makes you more intelligent than these simple creatures?"
    Six months earlier, Jascowitz, reluctant to provide his true name, had given Orwell the name Anton, after his great uncle, as an identifier. He tossed Station Master Pil's questions around in his head and decided he would only embarrass himself by trying to provide an answer.

Station 12: The Lantern Society

"You are reluctant to respond. Just as well. You will learn to see humanity from an objective point of view."

Referring back to the eels he said, "It's not instinct, it's art. There are exactly seven hundred and fifty Tempets in here, feeding on Ekainids. They pass through their rainbow feeding zone in an orchestrated assembly akin to a dance recital on your world. Only there's no rehearsal. Their dance is the be all and end all of social cooperation. They communicate in a way you cannot fathom; a song in a language that can neither be comprehended nor even heard by human beings."

Station Master Pil turned from the viewing stand sixty feet above the pool and began to glide down the spiral ramp. Jascowitz moved to follow, but made no effort to keep up with the twelve foot creature's long strides. Pil wasn't wearing the traditional robe of his peers. Instead, he wore strange, satiny leggings that fluttered in the air as he walked. On his feet he wore light, padded slippers that made no sound on the marble floor. Above the waist he wore a gold tank top crafted from ultra-fine chainmail that looked like liquid when he moved. His light gray skin glistened with health and pulsed with blue luster with each beat of his two hearts. The hair on his head grew in the back only and formed a four foot braid that ran down his back. The only adornment on his person was the colorful strands of ribbon woven into his braid and the golden stick pins of various insects placed throughout its length.

"Let me ask you, Anton," Pil's voice filled the cavernous space, "do you understand what we are about? You've been in the System for some time now. Do you have any idea what the Station Masters are trying to achieve?"

"It's difficult to know completely. It seems many of my coworkers and acquaintances don't like to talk about it."

"Many of your coworkers have been processed. Do you know what that means?"

Jascowitz recalled a conversation with Orwell. It seemed like such a long time ago. He thought he had a fairly decent understanding of what processing entailed, but he didn't admit that aloud. He learned early on that in order to avoid losing a source of information, he never responded to questions with definitive answers. He replied he didn't know and allowed Station Master Pil to continue.

"Let us suffice it to say that many people are not as cognizant of their surroundings as are you and the others in the System who have avoided the chair. Has no one spoken to you concerning our mission?"

Jascowitz shook his head.

"Not even Orwell? Interesting."

Pil walked along the side of the pool then turned to his left to join a small gathering of beings who were watching the eels on a large monitor. Whenever the Tempets performed a particularly complex maneuver, the gathering applauded or responded in such a way as to demonstrate their pleasure. Pil smiled and nodded to one and all then lifted a wand from a small table. He spoke softly into one end and nodded as he listened to the round disk held by his ear held stationary by a connecting wire. As he talked he continued to nod, obviously happy with the responses he was hearing.

"We are broadcasting this masterpiece to the Tempets' home planet," Pil said as he rejoined Jascowitz. "They have no broadcasting or recording arts there. We thought they might enjoy it."

They walked in silence for the remaining length of the pool.

"Do you see us as villains, Anton? You may answer freely. I'm only curious."

Jascowitz chewed the inside of his mouth, wondering if he was being led into another trap. He opened his mouth to answer but nothing came out.

"I'll take that as a yes. I understand. Most everyone fears the unknown and the System falls well within that category. Our goal, relative to your Earth, is to make you the best society you can be. We want your planet to be an integral part of the Universal Tapestry we are creating. We want you to be a contributor rather than a detractor. Unfortunately, humanity has always been its own worst enemy."

"Homo Sapiens are a young species, cosmically speaking. We continue to grow, change, and adapt. Maturing, if you will. And we are growing together, becoming a global society more and more every day."

"Culturally or economically? What is it that's bringing your world together? Technology? Your instant messenger?"

"As I said…"

"You said your world was maturing. Don't take offense if I say it's difficult to find evidence of that. Humanity lacks wisdom. You relegate wisdom to stories and characters of the past. It's really not a word held in much regard in the present time, is it? Your own people say that wisdom comes with age and yet there are no councils of the wise. Tribal shaman and medicine men are said to possess wisdom, yet no one takes the time to speak with them. At the same time, no one has accused your presidents of being wise, unless, of course, they've passed on. The same holds true for all your world leaders."

"You don't talk like someone in support of Earth."

"We support everyone in the election. We are neutral in this affair."

"Election?"

"Realities are elected into the Universal Tapestry by unanimous vote of the Station Masters. I won't lie to you; your people are running out of time and your competitors are leaving your world behind."

"Competitors?"

"All the alien species we bring here. They represent the many worlds vying for their place in the newly woven universe. They don't know that, of course, no one does."

"The Tempets?"

"Different sector of space. They are not your competitors. And they have long since been chosen for the Tapestry."

"I see. On what basis are we all being judged?"

"Oh, many things. That's why we take so long to make a decision. A thousand years or more! In what ways do you as a society look forward? In what ways do you leverage historical knowledge? How do you apply your imagination, your wonderful imagination, to forward momentum? How do you define work? How do you define rest? What do you find entertaining? How do you communicate with each other? Are you living or simply alive? Many things, Anton."

"And how do you compare these qualities among such a disparate sampling? So many beings from so many planets. It's like comparing apples to oranges."

"Ah! Now you see why we do what we do! Beneath life's surface appearance, there is something definite but intangible that all living creatures possess. Call it spirit. Call it a soul. Call it the absolute truth of the subconscious. It doesn't matter the name. This truth transcends the body. It is not shackled to the home. It transcends their very reality. Like chapters in a book, if we put the right combination of stories together with just the right characters, what a wonderful tale we might tell. Perhaps another utopia will be constructed and added to the Tapestry. But we don't pit one reality against another. We swap out characters from all realities and see over time what impact they have on their new societies. Some of these combinations find their way to shaping a more functional and productive reality. It's an ongoing process. If we do this over a long span of time, we're able to mathematically and statistically project future outcomes. These predictions inform our train schedule."

"And you do this with every planet?"

"Not every planet is gifted with reasoning life forms."

"How is it you came to include Earth in your analyses?"

"My dear Anton, they're all Earth. It's only the realities that vary."

"These beings that are being swapped come from alternate versions of Earth?"

"And the time is fast approaching when we will choose only one reality, one Earth, to sew into the Tapestry."

#

Askew and Bellows stared at Jascowitz, their mouths agape as Hugo's story unfolded. Askew's water bottle was still poised halfway to his mouth as he tried to digest the riddle revealed. A great portion of Verity's time and research had been devoted to discovering the TDRR's reason for being and Hugo had just laid it out in fifteen minutes of debrief. Now that the answer had been presented to them, they had no idea how to process it.

Askew finally took a drink.

"That's quite a story, Hugo," said Bellows. "I don't---."

"Are you sure he said alternate Earths?" Askew finally asked.

"Alternate versions of Earth, yes. And I was the one who said it."

Askew started to light his pipe but Bellows placed a hand over the lighter to stop him.

"What is the point of creating this tapestry at the expense of the unelected realities?"

"I asked him the very same question, Professor, and he told me the answer lay in the undiscovered corners of the Big Bang theory."

"He used the term Big Bang?"

Station 12: The Lantern Society

"Not only did that original explosion cast matter out to form our galaxies, it also splintered into many layers of reality. Each of them represented the same universal design but with differences in content, some small, some very large. I don't know how many realities there are, but it's not infinite.

"Somewhere along the line it became apparent that these many layers could not survive overly long, cosmically speaking. There were multiple planes of physical existence, but still only one source of cosmic energy, the same energy that caused the Big Bang in the first place. That energy was diluted in the process of splintering. And with this energy stretched so thin, the many realities were aging at a more rapid rate than the cosmos intended. The Station Masters were tasked with traveling the universe and weaving together the many layers into a single, stronger, more durable universe."

"The Tapestry."

"Precisely. The universe will only be as strong as its weakest reality. One loose thread and the whole thing could unravel. So you see? They are the good guys...again, cosmically speaking."

"It became apparent to whom?" asked Askew.

"What do you mean?"

"Who made the discovery? Who tasked the Station Masters?"

"I never came close to an answer for that. Those answers probably lie with Station 12, but I never came close to that, either. No one enters Station 12 but the Station Masters."

The three of them sat there, struck dumb by the volume of their thoughts. Askew almost started to light his pipe once more but stopped himself.

"As hard as this is to believe," said Bellows, "we have more pressing business. The rest of this will have to wait until our current crisis is behind us."

"Just one more question, please: Hugo, how did you finally get home?"

"Orwell told me the world could not know what was taking place around them. If they did, it would eliminate humanity from contention. I came back to study Verity's weaknesses and shore them up against possible leaks, to prevent such an eventuality. That's why he sent you that cryptic email about the flier."

"Orwell is Infofile@VerityCorp.com?!"

"That was as close as he could get to telling you of the problem outright. The data theft should never have happened and now that I know its cause, I can't help but feel partially responsible. This is why I'm here: to make sure the outside world never learns what Verity is doing for them. It's either that, or Verity has to shut down. We cannot risk losing our place in the election."

"What did you do for the year that you were gone?"

"It was actually three years by my reckoning. But time is funny there. Sadly, the story of my adventures in the System will have to wait for another time. As Lionel has pointed out, we have a crisis to resolve."

Just then Jacen Longworth burst into the office. "Gentlemen, we have a problem. Charlie Anderson has left the building."

Chapter Fourteen: The Lantern Society

"Do you want to talk about it?"

"Talk about what?"

The rental car chirped in compliance when Strivelli pressed the button on the key fob. He and Tomlinson started down Lewis Street, a nervous energy propelling them toward a hopeful resolution to the problem of world destruction. Time itself was charged, and each passing minute without drawing a successful conclusion felt like cobwebs stretched across their faces. Physical movements were subtly hindered and breathing required a modicum of effort.

With the new alliance between Verity Corp and Global Armour came new partnerships, and so it was Strivelli and Tomlinson had returned to Hartford to retrieve Beatrice Lebrun. The hope was that through her they could reach out to the leadership of the Lantern Society and convince them to call off their plans to build a Sounding Tunnel. That was Plan A. Plan B incorporated a level of menace that Verity Corp had no intention of following through, but the mere threat to Miss Lebrun's life might be enough to garner the Society's cooperation. Everyone at the summit had agreed the urgency of the matter called for such drastic measures.

"I thought you might have felt like you'd been played for a fool," he said. Strivelli could see that Tomlinson was distracted and he hoped by talking about it, whatever it was, he could acquire her full attention. "Your partner said you were going through some heavy stuff."

Tomlinson had told Foster her story in confidence and was disappointed by his betrayal. Even if he was looking after her out of concern, he should have respected her privacy. She shot Strivelli a look that strongly suggested he reconsider the subject matter.

"I'm just saying," he said quickly after realizing his faux pas. "Your boss took advantage of you. He was an inside man pretending to be on the outside looking in. I'm sure it was rough."

"And I fell for it hook, line, and sinker. That's on me."

"What reason would you have to doubt him?" he asked, trying not to sound like he was placating her.

"What?!"

Tomlinson was very confused. How did Jascowitz, aka Gorokhovich, know just the right story to convince her to join his ranks if it wasn't true? What were the odds someone could make up a story like that and tell it to just the right person?

"I fell for his play because I was selfish," she said. "He told me something I wanted to hear and he knew it. I don't know how, but he did. As a cop I should have known better. I should have grilled him before drinking the Kool-Aid."

"So you don't think his story is true?"

Tomlinson hated those moments, and there had been many, when she asked herself that very same question. Taken at face value, the situation as presented to her was impossible, the story of an alternate life ridiculous. But rather than turn her back on the chance of a new life, she clung tightly to its mere possibility.

"I don't know. For his sake, it better be."

Strivelli started to open his mouth, but Tomlinson intercepted his thought with a weary shake of her head.

When they entered the Lewis Street building and inquired about Lebrun, the guard on duty informed them that, as of that morning, the Lantern Society had shut its doors. Both agents visibly deflated upon hearing the news. Their options were already few and apparently dwindling.

"That's odd," said Tomlinson. "We had a scheduled appointment."

"Don't know what to tell you. Lady just dropped the keys and left."

"You're referring to Ms. Lebrun?"

"That's right. Left everything. Told me to charge the lessee for the cleanup. Damn strange."

"Strange is right," said Strivelli as they stepped back into the street. "Is this good news or bad?"

"I don't get it," his partner said as she stopped and looked back at the entrance. "Could it be a coincidence?"

"You think we've got another Anderson on our hands? Tipped them off maybe?"

"Couldn't say. I just know we need to find her. I'm starting to get a sick feeling in my gut."

"Like it could happen any minute."

"Any minute."

They both looked up in the sky, imagining an unseen catastrophe bearing down on them. The infinite blue space surrounding them seemed close and somehow menacing.

"We could reach out to her the same way Prof did, send an email."

"That's an idea," said Tomlinson. "It'll cost us some time, though." She looked back at the building. "I want to see what she left behind."

The back door to the building was locked, badge access only. When they glanced over the side rail of the stoop, they saw that the basement-level door was propped open and led to another floor of offices. As the two trespassers traipsed in, a man stepped out of a restroom. Not recognizing them, he asked if they needed any help. They said they were fine on their own and proceeded up the stairs.

Back at ground level, the two agents moved down the hall until they came upon the yellow box Askew had described as the drop box for the questionnaires. Strivelli worked on the door while Tomlinson kept watch for the guard. Once inside the tiny reception area, and with barely enough room to move, Tomlinson suggested that Strivelli start looking around in the adjacent room.

After a cursory glance at her surroundings, she asked Strivelli if he saw any evidence of a telephone. He didn't. When she asked about a computer, the answer was the same. There were no data jacks on the walls or abandoned power bars left on the worn carpet. She didn't understand it, and she didn't like what she didn't understand.

There were dusty shelves under the reception counter that were mostly empty except for some scraps of paper, a collection of elastics, and a bottle of cleaning fluid. Above the counter, however, was a recessed shelf that looked much more interesting. On it sat thick binders with titles that read, 'New York Membership Drive,' '2007 Goals & Strategies,' and 'CT Roster and Biographies,' among others. None of them displayed the Lantern Society name and as Tomlinson looked around, she noted the complete absence of the brand anywhere. The 2007 Goals book was heavy and she let it drop onto the counter with a resounding thud. Without knowing what she was searching for, she began to flip through it.

"How will you know when you've found it?" asked Strivelli from the other room.

"What the hell?" Tomlinson asked herself.

She was stunned to find a prodigious amount of blank paper residing between the handwritten index tabs. Hundreds of pages, in fact. She immediately reached for a second binder only to discover that those pages, too, were blank.

"Hello?"

"Found what?" she asked, distracted, as she continued shuffling through the binders. "What are you talking about?"

"Foster said you were looking for another life? Or something like that. I didn't get it."

There was almost nothing in the other room. Strivelli walked around the conference table, his arm brushing along all four walls, and found nothing of interest except a red accordion folder in the center of the table.

"So, how will you know when you've found it?"

Tomlinson stared down at all the open binders, every one of them stuffed with blank pages.

"I'll know,' she said softly to herself, and allowed herself a moment to feel the stabbing pain of her loneliness. But only a moment. Her lot meant nothing in the face of what was coming.

As Strivelli bent to pick up the folder, his phone vibrated. He hoped to see Angela's name on the Caller ID, but it was Bellows on the other end, reminding him to take photos whenever possible. Fully aware of his responsibilities, Strivelli barely registered the call before hanging up absently.

He hadn't seen Angela since going after Anderson in New York. It hadn't been easy leaving her without explanation, and he didn't think he'd be able to get away with it for much longer. She had started to dig into the mysterious nature of his job and who could blame her? Seemingly without work for days at a time, Strivelli would suddenly be called away by mysterious parties for equally mysterious reasons. Having been romantically unattached in the two years he'd been in the field, he never had to explain himself to anyone. It made for a simple life. But now he was with someone he really cared about, and he didn't want to lie to her, so he remained mute. This only piqued her curiosity further.

The only thing left in the reception area for Tomlinson to search was the file cabinet. The top two drawers were dedicated to the Society's membership roster where manila folders rested inside green, hanging folders. White labels affixed to each displayed the name of a Society member and Tomlinson flipped through them randomly only to find more blank paper. The third drawer was empty except for a safety booklet provided by the building owners and the questionnaire filled out by Gordon Isaacson which she took. A box of Wheat Thins and a canister of Crystal Lite ice tea were all that occupied the fourth drawer.

"You ever see a movie called 'The Sting'?" asked Strivelli as Tomlinson entered the second room. "You're going to love this."

Strivelli stood in front of one of two storage closets and gestured with a nod toward the buckled linoleum floor where two cardboard boxes filled with questionnaires sat moldering. The closet smelled musty, the result of a slowly leaking pipe on the back wall, and the questionnaires had obviously sopped up a lot of the water.

"I think the Lantern Society might be one big grift," said Strivelli. "At least this office is. But for the life of me, I can't figure an angle."

"The whole thing's a fake."

"The other closet just has boxes of copy paper and office supplies."

Tomlinson looked around. "I don't see a printer in here."

"Doesn't matter, the boxes are empty."

"What the hell? This is so screwed up. What is this?" Tomlinson asked, reaching for the red folder.

"I was just getting to that."

She poured its contents onto the table and began sifting through them.

"Hello. This looks like a contact list."

"I guess we have some calls to make. You think C.A. is Charlie Anderson?"

"A fair guess. B.H. might be Brian Haberman. Lebrun can fill in the rest when we find her."

"If we find her," Strivelli cautioned.

"Here's a copy of the rental agreement…signed by a Leonard Deeds. And this appears to be a receipt for wholesale gemstones."

Strivelli took the receipt out of Tomlinson's hand while she continued to flip through the papers.

"A dozen emeralds, rough and uncut," he said then whistled. "Spendy. Hey, what the hell is this?"

Strivelli watched as Tomlinson removed a stapled file with his picture affixed to it.

"What the fuck?" He reached for the file and flipped through its few pages. "They've been watching me. These nut jobs have been watching me!"

"Thanks, Sel," said a female voice out in the hall. "I'll be right out. I'm just going to grab that file."

Beatrice Lebrun stepped into the back room and found Tomlinson and Strivelli staring back at her.

"Angela?"

Tomlinson watched as a comically confused expression came over Strivelli's face while Angela Rodriguez looked like she'd been caught in bed with the wrong man. She clutched at her sweater as if she had somehow exposed herself.

"Oh, my God," Angela said. Her lips, numb, barely moved, and she looked like she might cry. "Tony, what are you doing here?"

"Looking for Beatrice Lebrun. You wouldn't happen to know where we could find her?"

"Everything okay in there, Ms. Lebrun?"

"Everything's fine, Sel. I'm going to be a few minutes."

Tomlinson started returning the papers to the accordion folder. "Well, this is awkward." She turned to Strivelli. "Do you want to talk about it?"

Strivelli waved his file in the air. "Is this your doing?"

"Tony, I'm sorry. I was hired to do a job. I didn't know what it would lead to."

"What has it led to?"

"Don't answer that!" jumped in Tomlinson. "Clearly you two have a lot to talk about. Probably none of my business. You can hash it out some other time. Right now, we have a more urgent issue to discuss. We've got your man Anderson."

"I don't know any Anderson," said Angela.

"Come on. We know all about the stolen data."

"Then you know more than I do."

Strivelli, disappointed, and more than a little embarrassed, stared at Angela in disbelief. He let Tomlinson do all the talking while he sorted through his confusion and tempered his growing rage.

"We'll see about that," said Tomlinson. "Look…"

"My name is Angela Rodriguez."

"Well, Miss Rodriguez, we're going to need you to come back with us to New York to answer some questions."

"Like hell. I'm not going anywhere with you. You're not police. And you're going to give me back that file."

Angela reached out and Tomlinson grabbed her by her wrist and pulled her close while her other hand came round with a Taser which she promptly jammed into Angela's chest. Angela's face contorted in anguish and surprise before she collapsed to the floor. Tomlinson looked back at Strivelli.

"Sorry about that?"

#

Command Central's "Egg" hung suspended from the ceiling like a magnificent white light bulb. Its wraparound windows had a bird's eye view of the Central Lab's control center and its function was to act as the lab's brain, coordinating the many limbs of the facility. Inside the Egg, Bellows stood over his charges with arms crossed as he calmly explained to them what was soon to take place. Though not on lockdown, the Central Lab was nevertheless in a heightened state of watch. He told them he would be co-opting worker bees from the Drone Room in pursuit of several objectives and that Command Central was to disregard any subsequent improper use warnings they might receive. Both veterans, Margate and Li understood completely and let Bellows know that if they had any questions they wouldn't hesitate to reach out to him.

Bellows shook each of their hands then stepped into a clear, vertical tube. Margate secured it by rotating the outer section, leaving Bellows temporarily without an exit. Lionel then placed his hand on a scanner to confirm his identity which triggered a series of automated processes. A construct lowered from the ceiling that split into two parts to form one long bridge that spanned the gap from where he stood to another elevated dock some distance away. Once the construct locked in place, the inner section was rotated, placing Bellows back in front of the opening, only he now faced the bridge. He walked across the forty foot span and stepped into an identical tube on the other side. The entire process proceeded in reverse until the column on which he stood lowered to the ground. As it did so, the bridge folded itself back up and returned to its place of origin on the ceiling.

Bellows jumped into his cart and waved up to his team as he drove away, staying on the road that led to the Drone Room and Alan Griffin's mezzanine office.

"Hey there, Lionel," Griffin said as he stepped out of the Observation Chair in his office turret. "Have you got that coffee you owe me?"

"Not today, Alan, sorry. But I haven't forgotten."

"Then to what do I owe this pleasure?" Griffin asked as he took a seat behind his desk while offering a guest chair to Bellows.

"I wanted you to know that we're likely going Condition: Yellow today. Any minute, actually."

"Wow, I didn't see that coming. What's the situation?"

Bellows gave him the short version of the would-be crisis then informed him that there would be a more detailed briefing in just a bit. He also told him that they'd need at least ten of his people from the Call Center for an investigation and probably more down the road as the scope broadened.

"Jesus, Bellows, this is unbelievable. What are we doing about it? Can we do anything?"

"We're chasing leads wherever we can find them."

"Our team is at your disposal, of course. What do you need?"

"For now, we need you to quietly canvas hospitals, morgues, police stations, walk-in medical facilities, anywhere an injured person might find herself. Jacen will have more details for you."

"Her?"

"Sarah Bismarck."

"As in Bismarck Industries?"

Bellows nodded. "One of our own, Charles Anderson, claims to be a witness to her murder, but so far we haven't heard a peep about it. Nothing on the news, nothing on the internet. We don't know if she crawled away unseen or even confirmed she's missing."

Griffin picked up a pen and tapped it on the glass tabletop. "I don't want to sound cold-blooded, but how does information about Bismarck have any bearing on the crisis you just described?"

"It speaks to Anderson's credibility, and we're relying heavily on him in our investigation. He's already done us one huge wrong. It's difficult to trust him."

"I should think so. Anderson. He's not a Witness."

"No, he's not."

"What do we know about this Lantern Society?"

"Almost nothing. We don't know who they are or what they're about outside of some glib propaganda. And we have no idea how they knew to steal from us in the first place."

"You mean how they stole the data?"

"No, I mean why anyone outside of Verity's perimeter would think we even had this kind of data. It's not like Anderson would have known. Anyway, this'll all be in the briefing. I'll see that you get an invite."

"Okay. Thanks for coming by, Lionel."

"Yeah. Sorry the news is so grim."

Griffin watched Bellows trot down the stairs before stepping back into the turret. He turned the Observation Chair to face his team down on the floor and opened communication with seats one through ten, informing them to stand by for further instructions pending a yellow alert. A few of the phone jockeys turned around in their seats and looked up at their boss out of concern and curiosity.

#

"Does the boss know you're doing this?" asked Haberman.

"Do you even know who the boss is?" Donovan replied.

The two of them stood in Haberman's kitchenette and watched the moving men make short work of clearing out the basement apartment. The dividing wall was gone and much of the equipment was already packed into boxes and set on dollies.

"Dude, that's my personal computer!"

The mover looked at Donovan who shook his head.

"Everything goes, Overlord. We're taking no chances you've copied anything over to other devices. And if I find out you have, I'll find you. You understand?"

"Yeah."

"I'm talking thumb drives, CDs, DVDs, or as email attachments to your mom. I mean, it better all be right here."

"It is. But I've got school work on that Mac."

"I guess we bought that, too, sorry. Now go pack your things."

"Why?"

"You don't think you're going to keep living here, do you? On the Society's dime?"

"Where am I supposed to go?"

"I don't care where you go, but you can't stay here. In one hour this room is going to be a gardener's shed and storage facility."

"What about the mission? Have they given up? What about the invasion?"

Donovan was taken by Haberman's concern. The Lantern Society meant different things to different people. Donovan had had his own adventures with the Society, none of which dealt with the purported invasion. It confirmed how little he understood his employer and amped his regret for ever having gotten involved.

"Drag your ass, Haberman."

Haberman walked off to pack, muttering something about the fine print on his contract and how he probably should have read it. Donovan watched the men at work, knowing that the emptier the basement apartment became, the closer he came to the end of his obligation. He looked down at his watch. He still had another long drive ahead of him and the clock was ticking.

#

"Man, it's almost as if your security firm's security was breached by the man who started your security firm."

Now that Foster was teamed up with Dodge, he unflinchingly lit a cigarette in the car and stared out the open passenger window. Finding out that his fearless leader was once a player for the company they were assigned to monitor was almost the straw that broke the camel's back. Almost. Foster had to admit, the more he learned about Verity, the more intrigued he became with the new role he found himself in, and less and less put off by the secrets. He knew it was simply the superficial joy of being an insider, but that didn't seem to bother him much. Such was the nature of being an insider.

"So, are you pissed?" asked Dodge.

"About what?"

"This guy's been playing you."

Foster looked down at his laptop. "Okay, take this right on 50th then a right again on 11th."

Dodge followed his instructions and soon pulled up to the front of the Kupperdyne building.

"Hold up," said Foster and put his hand on Dodge's shoulder to emphasize his request.

Dodge pulled the Verity car over and the two of them watched Donovan's Crown Victoria exit Kupperdyne's steep driveway.

"What should I do? Should I follow it?"

Foster shook his head. "No. We'll stick with the plan."

Dodge made his way down the driveway and parked in front of the three bays that made up the loading dock. To their left, another garage stood detached from the dock on the perpendicular. Dodge immediately climbed a set of steps and knocked on a metal door while Foster hung around the lot in search of clues.

All of it looked very much abandoned, like a devastating plague had come and gone. According to Askew, the coming disaster would erase even this desolation. But the brittle lot was surrounded by taller buildings and George felt as if he was standing in a hole. He wondered with dark humor if the unique properties of the hole might protect him from what was coming. Maybe he would just sit in the car and wait for the end.

"Anderson's full of shit, man," Dodge shouted down. "Nothing's going on here."

"What about the car that just left?"

"I don't know. Drug deal?"

He joined Dodge on the dock and immediately spotted a small camera that hung under the eave. There was no flashing light, but that was no guarantee the camera wasn't working.

"Once I get this door open, I'm thinking we won't have much time."

Locks picked, the liberated door swung into empty darkness.

"I think we're good," said Dodge based on his first impression. There wasn't much to see beyond the small, square patch of cement floor captured by the invading sunlight. "I guess this isn't the secret factory we thought it was."

Foster reached into his inside jacket pocket for a small mag-lite. "Let's keep our voices down, okay?"

Shining his light in the area around the door, Foster soon discovered a power bar on the floor and stepped on the red activation button. A series of dim halogen ceiling lamps came on between the banks of dormant fluorescents. The factory floor was bigger than it appeared from the outside. Barren of its once formidable machines of industry, all that remained were a few loose bolts, some holes in the concrete, and ghostly shadows of the devices that once occupied the floor. High windows ran along the top of the walls, all of which were shuttered from the inside. Foster lowered his flashlight and started across the floor in search of any recent activity.

"There's nothing here, George. Let's go."

"Who's paying for these lights, I wonder?"

"Real Estate Company?"

"Maybe."

But Dodge had spoken true, the facility was completely vacant. Not only had the machines been carted away, there wasn't a stick of furniture anywhere. Not even a scrap of trash littered the dusty floor. Kupperdyne had been erased, gutted, and its brick skeleton was the last vestige of the world's memory of it. Foster shined his light upwards in search of more cameras but saw none, so he kept pushing his way to the far side of the floor.

"Look, George," said Dodge, who started to lag behind due to a lack of interest, "if anything was happening here before, they're long gone now."

Foster didn't slow. "Sure looks it."

When they finally reached the far wall, they came upon the cage front of an old freight elevator. Foster bent down for the cloth strap and lifted the heavy gate.

"What are you doing?" asked Dodge as Foster stepped into the elevator.

"Hey, Dodge, if investigation's not your thing," Foster said with his hand still on the strap, "that's cool. You can wait in the car."

"Are you shitting me, man?! You heard what they said in that meeting. The world's coming to an end! Why are we wasting time in this old relic? Can't we come up with something else a little more constructive?"

"We're still here, Dodge. Still alive. And we've got work to do."

Dodge took a breath and collected himself. The conversation continued unspoken and Dodge saw the truth in Foster's eyes.

"Shit."

Foster lowered the gate then reached over to the manually operated controller and started the car down with a jerk.

It was a short ride to the bottom and what they saw through the cage when they arrived was far and away different from what they'd seen upstairs. Foster very carefully lifted the gate and stepped out onto a grated floor constructed in black iron. Where the upstairs once housed a factory of days past, what now appeared before them was a glimpse into the future. Dimly lit by path lights and articulated work lights, most of the equipment, and there appeared to be a prodigious amount, was difficult to distinguish in the gloom, and so their function eluded them. But to the two agents of Verity, it was all sci-fi lights and computer screens.

Three strides beyond the elevator, Dodge collided with an invisible barrier. He grabbed hold of his nose, more surprised than in actual pain, and muffled his curses as best he could. While he shook it off, Foster put his hand up on the barrier and found it neither cool nor warm to the touch. It most definitely did not feel like a single pane of glass, and it didn't feel like plastic. He pounded it lightly with the soft side of his fist and it bounced back in the same manner it would if he were hitting a cement wall.

The two men walked along the transparent bounds of the factory floor, searching for a way past the barrier. Further down the walkway they came upon a small control panel that jutted out of the barrier wall and into their path. The solid wall to their back bowed away from the panel to make room for the protrusion. On the other side of the barrier, Foster noticed that there were steps coming up onto the floor from below their feet.

"Foster." Dodge, who had continued along the path, waved his partner in from around the corner. Foster continued to look for any sign of a trapdoor or sliding panel, but if one existed, it was lost in the pattern of the metal grating.

He hustled off to join Dodge who stood in front of another room with its own invisible barrier. It appeared to be a prep room of some kind, with a rack of pale yellow jumpsuits, protective eyewear, and a large wall calendar with a production schedule. Foster couldn't make out any detail on the calendar, but he could see that it was current.

From his pocket he removed a miniature camera and snapped a quick photo, purposefully turning off the flash to avoid having the light bounce off the barrier. But even with that precaution, the photo revealed nothing behind the clear wall, only vague shadows behind a purplish haze. He turned around and stared into the side view of the factory floor, thought about taking another photo, but knew the result would no doubt be the same.

Dodge continued pressing ahead, peeking around yet another corner, then hissed to get Foster's attention. Foster obeyed and when he caught up, Dodge said, "Dude, you're not going to believe this."

The two of them turned down a narrow hallway and entered a room that housed a large pool of water. The water was dark, with an odor that was difficult to identify. There wasn't much in the way of equipment around the pool's edge, but there was a small set of mobile stairs, the kind one might use to board a small jet on an open tarmac. Foster's line of sight followed those steps up to a rack mounted to the ceiling, equipped with four arms that could lift an object from the pool and lock it into place overhead.

"I bet this water goes all the way out to the Hudson," he said.

Dodge looked around for the clues that had led Foster to draw such a conclusion and when he spotted an instructional poster for loading a miniature submarine he said, "That's fucking awesome."

The silence of the facility was broken by the sound of a large electronic device, an object in motion in the outer hall. The men dashed out, looked to their right, then to their left. Through two walls of the factory floor, Foster thought he could see movement in the vicinity of the control panel. They dashed around the corner and watched as a pillar sank into the floor to settle back into its locked position. Foster looked down at the stairs and, sure enough, a man with thinning hair wearing a short sleeve dress shirt came bounding up the stairs to the factory floor.

Without looking back at the trespassers, Pat Haney ran to a desk and gathered up his belongings to stuff them into a pair of travel bags. He then turned to a monitor and appeared to cycle through various security cam images before moving on. Within seconds, he was gone.

Foster stared hard at the monitor but was too far away to see anything clearly. Then he got an idea and took out his camera once more. He may not have been able to photograph through the strange barriers, but he could still look through the zoom, and when he did, he recognized their car in the lot and its relative position to the standalone garage door.

"Upstairs!" he shouted, no longer concerned about the level of their voices. "Let's go!"

Both men ran for the freight elevator. Foster slammed the door down to make the electrical connection and this time it was Dodge who grabbed the controller. When they burst out into the sunlight, Dodge stopped to shade his eyes and get his bearings while the former cop from the Sunshine State leapt off the dock just as the garage door started to rise. He jumped into the car and drove it in reverse just in time to bar Haney's exit from the underground garage. The two men approached the driver's side window to confront their quarry.

Haney pushed his wire rim glasses up his nose and wiped away the sweat from his forehead.

"You fellas are making a terrible mistake."

#

The helicopter touched down at the South Street heliport within an hour of take-off. Tomlinson and Strivelli hustled Angela Rodriguez into the waiting car for the two minute drive to Verity Corp. Tony and Angela kept looking at each other, but never at the same time.

"Are you alright?" Strivelli finally asked, allowing his guilt to overtake his anger. It was his first words to her since she'd been subdued by Tomlinson.

"You'll never get away with this," Angela said, sounding much braver than she appeared.

"Get away with what?" asked Tomlinson.

"Kidnapping me."

"This is no kidnapping, Miss Rodriguez. We just need to borrow you for a little while."

"Borrow me?"

Longworth met the three of them in the garage Security office and led them into an interview room, or interrogation room, depending upon who was asked. On a screen on the far wall, Professor Askew watched them enter from the comfort of Heberling's seating area in the tower. On Askew's end of the video conference, the large screen was split, with a view of the interview room on one side, and the Lantern Society website on the other. After entering Gordon Isaacson's log-in information, Jascowitz had begun searching the site for any clues to reaching someone in charge.

"Welcome to Verity Corp, Ms. Lebrun," said Askew, who seemed to be staring straight at her with his big eyes made bigger by the camera.

"Actually, Professor," said Tomlinson, "her name is Angela Rodriguez."

"Simply put, Ms. Rodriguez, we urgently need to speak with the leaders of your organization. Can you help us with that? Yes or no?"

"As I've already told Agent Tomlinson and…" She almost said Tony out of habit. "…and Agent Strivelli, I know nothing about anything to do with the Lantern Society."

"Is that the company line?"

"It's a simple fact, I'm sorry. My activities were limited to that office which as you now know was a fake. It was used sporadically to recruit a few select individuals for specific tasks unknown to me. Otherwise the office only existed to be the first line of defense in keeping the weirdos at bay."

Tomlinson waved a piece of paper at the screen. "We found a receipt for the purchase of raw emeralds in their office, but not much else."

"That sounds like more than recruiting."

Angela didn't want the interview to get overburdened with too many facts. "Occasionally she used the office to receive deliveries. All I ever did was sign for the stuff."

"You keep referring to a single, specific female."

"It was a woman who recruited me, and she was the only representative of the organization I met face to face. She paid me in cash. I never got her name. There were others, but I only spoke to them through their website."

"Their forums?"

"That's right."

"Why do you have a file on Mr. Strivelli?"

"When my contact discovered there was a Verity agent in Hartford she asked me to…follow up. Get to know him. See if I could learn anything about his presence there."

"These are very convenient responses, Ms. Rodriguez."

"Look, I'm just an actress! Okay?!" Angela shouted, wondering if it was a good time to freak out. Being kidnapped by sinister corporate figures and questioned by a bald, wildly mustachioed mad scientist hadn't come up during her brief interview with the Society. "I'm an out of work actress she found and paid to do some easy work. I was going to use the money to come back here and get my career on track. That's it. That's all there is."

"What about the emeralds?"

"I told you, I'm not with them. Her. I have nothing to do with this Lantern Society or the crazy shit that's going on. What is going on?"

"I need you to answer me truthfully."

"Okay."

"It is vital that you answer truthfully."

"I am!"

"Are you aware of any construction being done on behalf of the Lantern Society?"

"No."

"Have you seen any work contracts?"

"No."

Tomlinson slid the receipt for the emeralds in front of her.

"Angela," Askew said, "what happened to the emeralds? Did *she* pick them up, or was it someone else?"

"It was a man. Kind of short with thinning hair. Lots of pens and stuff in his shirt pocket."

"Was it this man?"

The live video feed of Askew was replaced by the image of Pat Haney sitting in an interview room of his own. Angela nodded.

"Yes, that's him."

"Alright, Angela, I want you to try something for me."

Longworth placed a Polycom phone in front of her.

"I'd like you to try and reach *her*. Please believe me when I say it's a matter of life and death."

"Whose?"

Askew leaned closer to the camera.

"Everyone's."

She shook her head. "You sound as crazy as they do."

"Angela," Strivelli said, trying to leverage their relationship, "just make the call. You've got nothing to lose and everything to gain."

"Okay, I'll call. Like you said, it's no skin off my nose. But it may already be too late."

Jascowitz, meanwhile, had clicked the link on the Society website that would take him to their forums. He'd spent the better part of two hours searching through all the posts and working with Cheever and the IT department in search of any new ways of reaching out to the Society or its members. He moved from topic header to topic header, trying his best to learn what he could. He'd sent private messages to at least forty of the posters, but had yet to receive a single reply. Activity dates were spotty, but it didn't seem there'd been any steady posting in some time. He'd just finished skimming through a section dedicated to getting the Society's message out and clicked over to a new header. The page didn't load. Instead, he got an Error 404 message from his browser indicating that the site could no longer be found. He clicked back on the browser and it happened again

Angela waved the receiver in the air.

"See what I mean? Too late."

#

The Vietnam Veterans Memorial, situated on the southern tip of Manhattan, was generally unpopulated outside of weekday lunch hours when employees of the local businesses came out for some fresh air or a cigarette. Small groups gathered to gripe about the market or to chat up the previous night's cornucopia of television entertainment. Others enjoyed their private corners as they read the latest, best-selling paperback or enthusiast's magazine.

The early summer sun, gentle and warm, settled over the available spaces in the tiny park, while a mischievous breeze, kicked up from the East River, was just strong enough to abscond with the occasional napkin or two. One of those napkins was stolen off the lap of a young woman eating tuna salad out of a plastic bowl as she flipped through a Nordstrom catalog. She made the appropriate gesture of attempted retrieval, but there was no way she was going to chase it down the steps in high heels. So the napkin scurried away with the breeze, down to the walkway that parted the memorial obelisks, and past the pointed cowboy boots of Ed Donovan who had just then entered the narrow end of the park via Water Street.

He found an isolated bench affixed beneath the shade of a Japanese maple tree and sat, placing the Halliburton case at his feet, then lighting one of his imported brown cigarettes. The same breeze that was

Station 12: The Lantern Society

pilfering the napkins, ATM receipts, and gum wrappers, graciously blew the smoke from Donovan's eyes as he looked over the lunch crowd. Having never in his adult life walked in their shoes, he could scarcely imagine what it must be like to live what he presumed were their humdrum lives. But when he thought of those dreary scenarios and compared them to the recent chaos of his own life, he almost envied their steady nine to five jobs, their Stouffer's frozen lasagnas, and their catatonic nights of quality cable television.

These meandering musings came and went. It was true he had grown weary of the blatantly enigmatic nature of the Lantern Society, and the nebulous and sometimes dangerous assignments that they handed him, but he also knew that 'real life' wasn't his most comfortable sweater either, and so he searched for a comfortable spot between the rock and the hard place, no longer sure where he belonged in the world.

"Do you ever wonder what all this has been about, Mr. Donovan?"

He looked to his left and saw the woman in black staring at him through her pink lenses. She managed to startle him and he managed not to show it, but in his heart he knew he couldn't wait to be rid of her.

"I'm not paid to wonder," he said. *Do not engage the client,* Donovan always told himself. *Never let them think they're in your head, making their cause your own. Speculate all you want, but keep it to yourself.* But wonder he did.

The Lantern Society representative joined him on the bench.

"You're not paid to question orders. It's a blurry line, I'll admit."

"Dwelling on my employer's purpose and motivation would prove distracting."

"You took a life yesterday. Don't you want to know the motivation behind that?"

The normally staid, emotionless Donovan was stung by her bluntness. He didn't like thinking about Sarah Bismarck, it only stirred up a jumble of confusing feelings. Hers was honestly the first life he had ever taken where he had almost no knowledge of the circumstances. He wasn't privy to the deal, nor had he been briefed on the players. Yesterday's assassination seemed more a killing of convenience than cause and though he performed the task dutifully, he'd tapped into a well of remorse that was proving deeper and deeper with each passing hour. Had he transitioned from soldier for hire to personal hit man? *Is there a difference?*

"What matters to me," he said, "is fulfilling my contractual obligations and going home. If you don't mind, I've had a very long day. I'll leave the whys and wherefores to you."

"Things have gotten rather dicey of late."

"I have your money," he said pushing the Halliburton two inches closer to her with his boot. "That must count for something."

"Oh, it does, Mr. Donovan, it counts for much."

"When I spoke to Haney at Kupperdyne about his final payment, he said I should speak to you first. I wish I'd known that before I rushed back."

"I'll take care of Haney."

Her phone chimed inside her purse and she removed it to read an incoming text message. She smiled and started typing a message back.

"So, what now?"

"It's over for you, Edward. For me, it's just beginning. How did everything go with Haberman?"

"It's like he was never there."

"Will he be trouble?"

"I paid him off as instructed and sent him on his way. The equipment is on its way back to the warehouse which is also being dismantled as we speak. Frankly, I'm surprised you're letting Haberman go."

"Yes, well, I let you let him go."

Donovan couldn't figure this new direction.

"The Lantern Society..?"

"Has served its purpose. Like Haberman, by the end of the day it will be as if it had never existed. All that will be left is a collection of colorful fliers that will fade with time, to be replaced with posters for garage bands, estate sales, and outsider art exhibits." The woman placed her foot on top of the Halliburton. "I have what I want."

"There's no way all this was about the money."

And there was no way the woman could know by looking at him how angry Donovan suddenly felt at the idea that the Lantern Society was simply one long con for cash. Working for a radical, out-of-their-minds conspiracy theory cult had been bad enough, but the thought that the whole thing was a sham was worse by far. No, he'd been with the Lantern Society for the better part of a year and it seemed to him there were a lot of irons in the fire. And there were far easier ways to accomplish a cash grab.

The woman was up to something.

"Tell me about Anderson," she said, choosing neither to confirm nor deny Donovan's non-question.

"Two men surprised us at the store and grabbed him. Don't know who. Don't know why. We followed them down here but…"

"Verity men, no doubt," she said looking around. "They have hidey-holes all over this area. Forget about Anderson. I have a funny feeling I'll be hearing from him in short order."

"What do you want me to do?"

"I'll be in touch."

#

She walked briskly through the bodega and knocked on the door to the back room.

"Am I speaking with Mr. Peters?" she asked the man at the door.

"I'm Peters. Is there something I can do for you?"

She walked in without an invitation.

"You can tell me you found Sarah Bismarck."

Peters frowned and followed Devlin into the room. "I would like nothing more, but that would be a lie, Miss…"

"You checked everywhere?"

"Everywhere. I went back to the scene, looked for blood, looked for drag marks. No incident reports were filed that I could find. I don't know what to tell you."

The woman pursed her lips. "Mr. Anderson saw her go down. There was blood. You'd think she'd needed a Band-aid at least!"

"I don't think we'll ever know…if she doesn't want us to."

"Know what?!" Her tone and body language sent a message of authority and Peters' reactive posture reflected that.

"If she needed a Band-aid," he mumbled just as the woman's phone chirped. She removed it from her purse and smiled when she read the name in the display window and then excused herself and stepped to the far side of the room.

"I was hoping you'd call. I wanted to thank you for aiding the Lantern Society in becoming what it became."

"Sounds like past tense."

"We've moved on, Mr. Anderson, into the next phase of our

development. We've come some distance through the dark, and now we hold our lantern high to shine a light on the truth. Now that we've reached that door, it's time to open it. Do you understand?"

"I never understood a God damn thing about the Lantern Society. Don't start pretending I was one of the team. You promised me the truth, remember?"

"Hugo Jascowitz. You see? I do remember."

"That's right."

"I know that he's alive and well. I know that truth."

Anderson was struck dumb.

"How---?"

"Meet with me, Charles. The past is the past. I've got my money. My plans proceed apace. Let's you and I talk and re-establish our relationship if only to end it amicably. I feel I owe you an explanation."

There followed a long pause.

"Fine. When and where?"

She provided a meeting place and time and told him to come alone, stressing that point, and making him promise. He said he would if she reciprocated and so a deal was struck. Once everything was settled, she hung up and smashed her phone with a hammer she found on a nearby stack of boxes.

"Everything okay, Miss?" asked Peters.

The woman returned with a smile on her face.

"Couldn't be better. I need to use your phone and then you and I are going to talk about some loose ends."

Lenore Devlin loved it when a plan came together.

Station 12: The Lantern Society

Chapter Fifteen: The Devlin You Don't Know

Anderson no longer recalled his original motivation to do the things that he had done. Every ounce of his once over-inflated ambition had sadly shriveled like helium balloons long after the party had ended. Gone, too, was the paranoia that had prompted him to pre-emptively separate from his one and only true love. This was especially true now that he knew the way of things, which was actually more frightening than anything he had ever conjured on his own. He felt worthless and empty and completely without direction, bad choices having so efficiently backed him into a corner. He was going to be Verity's bitch for a while, he knew that much. But what happened after that? He was now privy to secrets that his employer would no doubt want to keep secret. *What's to become of Charlie Anderson,* he asked himself. The question became his sole raison d'etre. Well, that and saving the world.

In just a few minutes he would be meeting with a woman who had no earthly reason for keeping him alive. He'd broken the tenuous trust between himself and the Society when he absconded with their money, and they, she, was already responsible for one death. Had there been others? Would he be next? It didn't matter. He had to try his best to convince them, convince her, to cancel her plan to build the mysterious tunnel. This would be his last opportunity to make amends for all the wrongs he'd committed since allying himself with the Society.

His stomach churned. He didn't know if it was nerves or hunger pangs, the smell of bacon and French fries permeated the air. There had been several moments after escaping Verity Corp when he thought he would chicken out. On each of those occasions his thoughts turned to Sarah, and though he could not vanquish his fear, his resolve only grew more steadfast.

Eisenberg's Sandwich Shop opened for business not long after the stock market crash of 1927 and had prospered in the shadow of the Flat Iron Building ever since. For most of its existence the restaurant was mostly one long counter running down the middle of the shop and half a dozen two-tops under a collage of framed photographs. The staff behind the counter manned their assigned stations, treading the wooden slats beneath their feet. Beverage taps kicked off the brigade, doling out lime Rickey's and egg creams while the adjacent sandwich station served equally anachronistic edibles like the Spitzer and olive loaf on pumpernickel. Wonderful hot soups were passed hand to hand in a relay to enthusiastic diners, their small packages of oyster crackers open and at the ready. The place was no frills, but the food was delicious and plentiful, and very much a staple of New York City.

Anderson's watch said it was time for his meeting with the Lantern Society. He glanced around from his counter seat but saw no sign of his contact, and knowing he couldn't occupy the coveted stool without ordering, he requested a tuna salad sandwich on rye toast and a cherry Coke to drink.

"Can you guess why I chose this place?"

"Jesus!"

Lenore Devlin stood just behind Anderson's left ear.

"I used to come here every Saturday when I was a child," she said.

When the waiter dropped off his soda, Anderson took it and started to rise, but Devlin waved him down.

"The counter is fine. We always sat at the counter."

"We?" Anderson removed the paper from his straw.

"I don't know why, Mr. Anderson, but I feel I owe you an explanation. I wouldn't be where I am if it weren't for you. And what you went through with Ms. Bismarck---."

"Don't blow smoke up my ass. We've got more important things to talk about."

The waiter approached and took Devlin's order of liverwurst on pumpernickel bread with brown mustard.

"I wish I had the appetite," said Devlin as she deftly swung her legs around the counter stool. "I have always loved their chicken noodle soup. You seem more agitated than usual, Mr. Anderson."

"Being responsible for the end of the world will do that to you."

"So dramatic…"

"Why didn't you tell me about Jascowitz?" Anderson asked, allowing his personal interest to supersede his reason for being there.

"Or maybe it's Mr. Donovan's absence that has made you so bold."

"Maybe."

"Is that really what you want to talk about?"

"Since we're clearing the air…"

"You told me he was a friend of yours. He returned from wherever he was and he elected not to inform you. I had a feeling it wasn't the answer you wanted, and I couldn't take a chance losing you."

"Losing an asset, you mean."

"As you say."

"How did you know?"

"I came here to tell you why I did what I did so maybe you can feel a little better about yourself."

"Never mind how I feel. I've come here at great risk to my health to warn you and you're not hearing me. If you don't stop whatever it is you're planning, you may erase the world."

#

In the Verity suite most recently occupied by Charles Anderson, Angela Rodriguez sat facing Pat Haney and together they waited in nervous silence. They'd only met the one time before, when Haney showed up at Beatrice Lebrun's Hartford office to pick up a small box of uncut emeralds. They had little to say to each other back then and not much had changed. But the quiet was grating on Angela's nerves something fierce so she cleared her throat.

"How long do you think they'll keep us here?" she asked.

"Well, seeing as they don't have, and never had, a legal leg to stand on, I'm guessing as long as they want."

More uncomfortable silence ensued, the elephant in the room being the fact that Angela and Haney had the Lantern Society in common which, as it was turning out, didn't appear to be a positive talking point. Clueless to current events, Angela was scared and confused. The out of work actress/waitress wished she'd paid more attention at the time she was hired. To her, it sounded like easy work for easy pay and that's all that mattered. She'd run into some financial trouble before taking the job and the money Devlin was paying would dig her out of the hole she'd made.

Circumstances were different for Haney who was used to doing business with all manner of shady characters. Nevertheless, physical capture was definitely something new for him and he couldn't imagine what he'd done to deserve it.

"Did you see much of her?" asked Angela.

"Who?"

"The lady in black…with the pink glasses."

Haney shook his head and fussed with his pocket protector in a sure tell that he didn't like talking about her.

"Just once, when I first took the contract. The rest of our business was done through email, then her man, Donovan. And to be honest, that was fine with me. She creeped me out."

"Yeah. Yeah, she was creepy."

"Haney!"

They both jumped and looked up to see Longworth standing in the doorway waving Haney over.

"Time to continue our chat, Pat. Let's go."

Angela stood up with Haney and watched him make his exit.

"What about me?" asked Angela, wary at the prospect of being left alone.

Longworth let Haney pass then followed without saying a word. A second later Strivelli stood in his place.

"Hello, Angela."

#

A waiter dropped off both sandwiches and provided Devlin with a glass of water.

"This tunnel thing you want to build," said Anderson, "or have built already; they're telling me it could destroy the world if you turn it on."

"Charles, I'm trying to open up to you. After today it is unlikely we will ever see each other again. At least extend me the courtesy of hearing me out."

"Did you hear what I said? Destroy the world! Is that what you want?"

"Nobody wants that, Charles. No one in their right mind wants that. And I assure you, I am that."

"What?"

"In my right mind. Don't you want to know what it's all been about? Wouldn't you like to go back to Verity Corp and explain to the Professor and your friend Hugo that there was actually a reason for all this?"

"It sounds like you want to tell me."

"This is your chance to make amends, Mr. Anderson."

Anderson took a bite of his sandwich and swallowed it almost without chewing. Small loss, he couldn't taste it anyway. It was as if she had read his mind. He washed it down with a swallow of his soda but said nothing. Devlin waited to speak as she savored both the liverwurst and her small victory.

"Unlike you, Charles, I have a lot in common with your coworkers in the Verity lab. My family, too, was touched by the magical train."

#

Angela stepped out of the Verity tower and inhaled a lungful of freedom, and with its release found herself on the verge of tears. She didn't want to appear vulnerable so she shook her head and started fumbling through her purse for a cigarette. Strivelli beat her to it and offered up one of his own. She took it with only a slight hesitation and bent slightly as he proceeded to light it with his Harley Davidson Zippo. She took a drag and waited, hoping he'd come around to actually talking to her about all that transpired. She didn't blame him for his anger. It must have been a huge blow to find out his girlfriend had been paid to spy on him. Of course, she wasn't his girlfriend when it started. She tried not to dwell on it, because if she did, she'd have to face the realization that there was no coming back from that. Strivelli said nothing and Angela began the painful process of emotional separation.

"What the hell is going on here, Tony?" she asked, daring herself to avoid touching on their personal issues.

"I'm not allowed to talk about it."

She nodded, feeling the onset of tears once more. Not only had she lost her boyfriend, she might actually have made an enemy.

"What happens now?" she asked.

"I've been told to escort you back to Connecticut."

"I'm not going back. I'm done there."

Strivelli wanted to keep the pace of the conversation slow in order to buy himself some time and weigh his options.

"Where will you go?" he asked.

"I live here. I still have my apartment in the city," she said, allowing him all the time he needed.

"Do you want a taxi?"

"Can we walk some?"

Angela started to turn, but Strivelli stood there. He lit a cigarette of his own, measuring his emotional needs against more practical thinking. Angela watched his mind work and didn't interrupt. She melted a little when he finally held out his arm.

"Does this mean you forgive me?" She linked her arm in his and smiled.

"Fuck no. It means we keep talking. Does that work for you?"

"It works for me, Papi."

And so they talked all the long way to her apartment. As far as Verity was concerned Strivelli was on his way to Hartford and back, so he took advantage of the time to acquaint himself with the real Angela Rodriguez.

#

Pat Haney wasn't having as pleasant a time comparatively speaking. From the relative comfort of the tower suite, they had brought him back down to the security offices in the garage to sit in a more traditional interrogation facility under the traditional hot lamp. He was sweating nervously with limited visibility of his interrogators, and even though he knew them already as Longworth and Bellows, they nevertheless came off as quite a bit more sinister under these conditions.

"And you're saying the woman who hired you never gave her name?"

"She made a point of it. She wanted to fly under the radar, and that's one of the services Kupperdyne provides."

"We need to know what it was she had you building."

"Damned if I know. We were given the specs piecemeal with no clue how they went together."

"What did you use the emeralds for?"

"All the gemstones that came our way were included in our outgoing shipments. We never used them in construction."

"Where were these shipments bound?"

"Don't know. Every week a semi would show up and we'd load it per our schedule. There was no paperwork outside of the packing lists.

Station 12: The Lantern Society

Assembled parts were given pre-arranged labels for identification. Very generic."

"You're an engineer, Haney. You had no idea what these pieces and parts might be once assembled?"

"No idea whatsoever. As long as the people on the other end knew how to put it all together it wasn't my problem."

"Do you have records of all the parts you put together for them?"

"We made our own schematics, yes."

"We want to see them. See if we can't put the puzzle together."

Haney flushed and offered no response.

"Is that a problem, Haney?"

"I don't think my people are going to allow that."

"And?"

"They have orders to flood the entire facility should anyone else try to get inside. They can trigger it remotely."

"Unless what?"

"Unless we establish some kind of relationship. And you tell us what's going on."

#

Devlin dabbed at the corners of her mouth with a napkin then took a drink of water. Her eyes glazed over as her thoughts shifted from the present to the past.

"My father was killed stopping an attack on my family."

Anderson didn't know what to expect, but he didn't expect that. Obviously there was more to the story than he knew. As a salesman, he could always spot a fellow bullshitter. He watched her body language. If at any point he felt she was lying to him, he would put an end to her secret origin story.

"I was just two years old," she said. "My brother, we called him Deeds, was four. We were coming out of a matinee in midtown and on our way to dinner. My father knew a short cut to the restaurant. He had Deeds by the hand and I was being carried by my mother."

Anderson thought he'd heard the name Deeds recently, but he couldn't remember in what context.

"We went into an alley. It wasn't dark yet, and it wasn't one of those scary alleys like in the movies, but it turned out we shouldn't have gone in there anyway. A man stepped out from behind a dumpster with his hand in his pocket demanding money and my mother's jewelry. My father refused because he believed the man was bluffing. He was wrong. He put himself between the mugger and the rest of us and tried his best to talk him out of doing something stupid. This just made the man more nervous, and the longer he stood there listening, the more nervous he became. When my dad realized he couldn't win, he reached for his wallet. That's when the shot rang out."

She looked at Anderson with the fist genuine expression he ever recalled seeing on her face.

"It's strange," she said. "You would think something as monumental as a life ending…there would be something to see, something fantastic; maybe slow motion, with time enough to witness a visible *breaking* of the human connection; when the love for that person is suddenly dammed, with no way to direct its flow, until it spills away, lost without direction. But it's not like that. It's just a loud bang and someone falling down. There's no time to process it."

"You're forgetting about the blood."

"My apologies, Charles," Devlin said, recognizing her error. "I was swept away by my reverie. I didn't mean to belittle your pain in the process."

"Different reactions for different people, I guess," Anderson said with a shrug. He wasn't at all surprised by the woman's selfishness. "So the mugger fired."

"The mugger fired and my father went down. He then turned the gun on my mother, but someone shouted from the street and he took off running. My father was bleeding from his stomach, I remember that much, and he was in a lot of pain. He managed to speak to each of us in turn before the ambulance arrived. He died on his way to the hospital."

Her story seemed to finish there. Anderson waited just the same in a reverent pause.

"It's like Batman," he finally said, at a loss for words. He certainly didn't want to comfort her, but the story was tragic nonetheless.

"Like Batman. That's funny. The story doesn't end there, though. Not by a long shot."

#

Verity's Central Laboratory was bustling with activity. Their clandestine business proceeded as usual, but here and there, in selected corners of the lab, a few dedicated individuals were trying to stave off Armageddon with the little bit of truth they'd uncovered.

Tomlinson was ecstatic to find herself in the underground facility. If Gorokhovich and Askew were the signposts to her other life, Verity's Central Lab would surely take her the rest of the way. If only she knew where to look. She strolled through the Drone Room and watched the bees at work at their consoles. Most of what she saw on the giant screens overhead meant nothing to her. On a few, though, she read incoming calls from the hotline provided in The Crossing, as well as the number and location of the originating call. A box to the right of the information read "Searching" until eventually it was populated with a photo of the caller, whether obtained from the Department of Motor Vehicles, an employee ID, or an arrest record. As potential Witnesses, they all had stories to tell.

Emmett entered the lab through the cavern door and made straight for an available cart. He pulled out and swung around and saw Tomlinson before he pulled away. Curious, he asked if she was one of the Global Armour transplants. She said she was and explained that she was killing time between assignments. When he offered to give her a tour, she jumped at the chance.

They made their way through an express access tunnel along the perimeter of the lab that led them into the Files and Records section just outside the supply train's unloading bay. Emmett dropped some files off then took the scenic route back toward their starting point. They ventured through the lab, section by section, while Emmett happily pointed out the notable sights. During a lull between points of interest, Tomlinson's guide asked her what she was working on. She apologized and informed him that she wasn't allowed to talk about it.

"You? Can't tell me? Interesting."

At one point, Tomlinson caught sight of Foster in a meeting with Dodge. They had been assigned the 'Bismarck problem' and had wasted no time getting started. Dodge sat at a table with his legs stretched out in front of him while Foster stood at a whiteboard compiling lists. Foster seemed fully engaged, and judging by appearances, there was little doubt he had taken lead on the assignment. Seeing him take charge gave Tomlinson a whole new appreciation of Foster. He had found his better life. All he wanted was to be challenged and taken seriously in his work. His time had come. No magic train required.

#

Devlin looked up from her plate. She had a small bit of mustard on her immaculately made-up face. To Anderson, the imperfection seemed grossly out of place. Part of him wanted to provide her with the same courtesy afforded him not so long ago, but another part of him basked in her humiliation.

"My brother began having nightmares when he was ten years old. Terrible nightmares. Every night my mother went into his room to comfort him and to listen to the story of what he'd seen. It was always the same. Or near enough to it. In the dream, he got up to use the bathroom and saw our father being led away by a giant man. He tried to call after him but his breath, he tried to speak, but no words came out. He was a slight man, my father, thin, and he looked like a small boy behind the giant who had to stoop to avoid bumping its head on the ceiling. Its shoulders touched both walls in the hall."

"What are you telling me?"

"My brother's terrified in the dream. He's scared that something terrible is going to happen to our father. He watches them head down the stairs into a dark hole. It's darker than dark, but curiosity and a boy... He follows them down the stairs as they step into that darkness. Deeds doesn't waiver, even as they disappear from view. Our living room…is gone, swallowed up by that black space. In the distance, and against all logic, a train is parked, an enormous red and yellow train, stretching out as far as the eye can see."

"You sound as if you were there, too."

"My brother and I were very close."

Anderson heard the love in her voice, but Devlin's eyes were hard. Whatever emotions she had for her brother had crystalized over time and become brittle.

"Many mornings we would walk to the park and he would tell me the story of his dream. Over and over. I know his nightmare inside and out as if it were my own."

Anderson was reminded of 'The Crossing.' Though he hadn't read it himself, he'd heard enough about it at the summit to recognize a Witness account when he heard it. His attitude began to shift from cynical impatience to captivated listener. If any of what she was saying was true...

"Deeds sees a tall, thin man walking along the train in his direction. A conductor. He has a lantern in his hand and even though it casts an obvious glow, it casts no light upon the ground, because there is no ground. The conductor gets closer and closer and finally receives my father and the giant and together they board the train. The conductor is the last to climb the steps and turns to take one last look before departing. It holds the lantern up high. The light shines off the train and from where Deeds stands he can see that the conductor has no face."

#

Eventually, Tomlinson and her guide arrived at the area most of the scientists referred to as the Neighborhood. This was the laboratory and research center, the life essence of the Central Laboratory and home to Verity Corp's true purpose. As their cart passed under the arch, Tomlinson's face lit up and her eyes grew large with wonder. She felt like a little girl again, like she did after seeing Oz in glorious Technicolor for the first time. What lay before her was something bigger and more powerful than anything she had ever seen or imagined in her life. The ceiling was obscure by a brilliant blue sky with nary a cloud in it. There were a few, though, and they drifted pleasantly with the manufactured breeze. The sunlight told her it was late morning, which it was, and the light on the potted trees and the manicured patches of grass reflected it perfectly. She found she couldn't look directly into the sun and that caused her to laugh, much to her own surprise. Emmett laughed with her, re-experiencing vicariously what it was to see it all for the first time.

Tomlinson marveled at the layout, the roads and walkways, the streetlights, and the miniature parks. There were even the equivalent of food trucks dotting the landscape. Lunchtime was just starting to ramp up and people had begun to gather at these sheds to pick up their lunch. Some were taking food to go while others sat at small, metal tables to eat. It really did look like a small city.

Twenty-four buildings of various sizes made up the neighborhood. Each building, called a pod, housed a separate experiment or project. On each of their bay doors a symbol was painted representing the project within. Tomlinson recognized the symbol on the bay door of Pod Six as a telescope. It was the only symbol she was able to distinguish.

A cart pulled up in front of them and dropped off Rachel Henderson. She noticed the tour group's approach and smiled as she went over to greet them.

"I see you're finding your way around, Agent Tomlinson."

"Please, call me Jackie. Emmett has been kind enough to give me the grand tour."

"What's your impression so far?"

"I am blown away. How in the world did all this get built without anyone knowing?"

"That explanation will have to wait until we have more time to do it justice."

"Fair enough. Another time, then?"

"Definitely."

Baylor and Pruitt pulled up next and parked in one of the spots reserved for Pod Six.

"Rachel," said Baylor as he hustled over to the group, "do you have good news for me?"

"If a midnight test is good news, then, yes."

"Outstanding!"

Baylor and Pruitt exchanged high fives.

"Will Prof be coming?" asked Pruitt.

"Unfortunately, no. But I'll be there. And I think I'll bring along the new guy, Goose Gusarov."

"Never heard of him."

"Russian guy. Bit of a mystery, but eager to learn."

"The more the merrier. Thank you, Rachel."

In the last year or so it was rare to see Baylor smile, but now that all his hard work was finally coming to fruition, his toothy grin stretched from ear to ear.

"Try to get a little rest before then," said Henderson.

Baylor laughed at that and then he and Pruitt slapped each other on the back as they sauntered proudly toward the pod entrance.

"They seem very excited," Tomlinson said.

"They've been working on the Oculacrum for years."

"Oh, I thought it was a telescope."

"It is. A very powerful telescope."

Henderson's radio chirped and she lifted it out of her lab coat pocket.

"Excuse me. This is Henderson."

"Rachel, Ellen. Everything is in place for Data Fortress to go live. Nothing gets in or out of our servers without us seeing it."

"Turn it on, Ellen. We'll have to celebrate some other time."

"Copy that. Cheever out."

Henderson threw her radio back into her pocket and smiled at Tomlinson and Emmett.

"Busy day."

#

"Your brother told you all this?" Anderson asked in order to break the silence that had come over Devlin.

"My brother struggled with these two different versions of my father's absence. Had my father been murdered in a midtown alley, or had he been kidnapped from his home by a mysterious giant and his faceless companion? Deeds was tortured by the idea that he may have had a father for ten years, not four, before losing him. Having no recollection of those six years made it worse. Both scenarios seemed very real in his head, but the story of the giant was preposterous to my mother. She tried to remain supportive, but her frustration only made itself more apparent over time. Deeds decided never to speak with her about it again. From that moment on, I would be his confidante, the sole recipient of his rambling recollections. That, too, would come to an end.

"He continued to have this dream for the next eight years until he was eighteen. His fear dissipated, but he still suffered from a lack of proper rest. Over time, he found himself in a dark place, dark like the hole that had replaced our living room. He turned to alcohol. He thought it would help suppress the dreams and allow him to sleep through the night. From then on I could no longer reach him, couldn't break down the wall he was building between us. I feared the worst and I missed him terribly.

"Then one day he met a young woman by the name of Susan. She got him to share his burden with her and his story struck her as familiar. She gave him this."

From out of her purse, she removed a paperback book that looked like it had been through the wars. The spine was broken, the book bloated with moisture, pages browned with age. Anderson looked down at 'The Crossing' and frowned.

"This book," Devlin went on to say, "led my brother to Verity Corp and his salvation. They took him in. They rehabilitated him, showed him that he hadn't lost his mind, that he wasn't alone. Professor Daniel Askew took him under his wing and convinced my brother to join the team. He told Deeds that it was Verity's goal to understand the abductors and the meaning behind the abductions with the intent of putting an end to it. It was also implied, as Deeds saw it, that Verity Corp might someday get our people back.

"Right after Deeds joined up with Verity, some people came to our house and talked with me and my mother. We were both, of course, ecstatic that Deeds had found his way out of his depression, and that the dream no longer stole away his rest. When the conversation ended, they put us in a limousine. We were blindfolded so we had no idea where they were taking us. We left the house on a cloudy day and ended up in a tea house on a beautiful, sunny day. They gave us tea and little cakes. That's the last thing I remember about that afternoon besides finding myself home again, with a headache and dry mouth. It was almost as if we had never left. My brother told us after the fact that we had been inoculated. Against what he never said, or what it was they actually did to us. I came to believe we had been brainwashed.

"My brother ended up working for Askew. Specifically, a man named Lionel Bellows. Deeds was sworn to secrecy, but he never forgot how I was there for him during the roughest time of his life. He never told me exactly what it was he was doing at Verity Corp, though he did share a few stories with me about the Sounding Tunnel. The train. The disappearances. He once told me, in so many words, that he was going to get our father back. Just like that. Can you imagine, Charles, having the opportunity to recover a lost loved one? To learn that they didn't die, they were merely spirited away, and you can have them back if only you take the necessary steps to make it happen?"

Anderson thought of Sarah. He saw for the millionth time her head pitch back as the assassin's bullet made contact. But what if that was a manufactured memory to cover up her abduction? What if there was a chance he could see her again? What would he do to make it happen? He now saw Devlin as a kindred spirit in some ways and he was appalled.

"I didn't know what he meant at the time. Back from where, I wondered, but I didn't ask. Not then. Later I would pester him for information, try to put the snippets together in such a way that made sense. And then one day he was gone."

#

Tomlinson's tour of the Central Laboratory was winding down. After passing through the Conference Center and Command Central, they cruised into the Drone Room where an unusual flurry of activity was taking place. Of course, Tomlinson didn't know the difference from one day to the next, but Emmett made it clear that under normal circumstances the room was just a steady buzz of a hundred seated Call Center Reps speaking with people over their headsets. But there were a number of people on their feet at the end of both rows closest to the tour.

As they pulled up along row two, Tomlinson could see Gorokhovich, now Jascowitz, and another man talking with one of the Reps. At one point, everyone looked up at a grid map of Manhattan on one of the massive screens on the wall. Jascowitz was using a laser pointer on it and barking orders over a radio.

"Boy that Hugo didn't waste any time getting back into the thick of things," said Emmett.

"How well did you know him before he disappeared?"

"Not very. He worked on some super-secret stuff with Lionel Bellows."

"Who's that with him?"

"In the suit? That's Alan Griffin. He heads up this Call Center and runs General Recruitment. He's a good guy, but he keeps pretty much to himself. Hard to get to know a guy like that."

"What do you think they're doing?"

"If I had to guess, I'd say they're looking for someone."

Tomlinson pointed toward the first row. "And what's happening over here?"

"Beats me."

Emmett speeded up the cart, but not so fast Tomlinson didn't see Foster's face pop up on the smaller screen at seat number one. Jascowitz wasn't the only one in the thick of it, it seemed.

They parked near the entrance and with that, Tomlinson's tour of the Central laboratory had come to an end. Her phone rang and she exchanged a few brief words before turning to Emmett.

"Looks like they've got my next assignment."

#

Devlin explained that her brother had moved out of the family home. The phone calls had stopped, never mind the visits. No one had seen him around his apartment in some time.

"I believe you know the feeling, Mr. Anderson."

"I recollect."

"My mother and I pursued the matter vigorously with Verity Corp but they flipped it on us, said that he never showed up for work and that they were going to have to let him go. They suggested that he may have relapsed into alcohol. They suggested we contact the police to file a report. We did, but nothing ever came of it."

"You wanted answers."

"I still do."

"That's what all this has been about," Anderson said, shaking his head against his will in understanding.

"I will find my brother, and I will expose Verity Corp for the liars they are."

"You're preaching to the choir, lady, really. But you don't want to go down the road I did. Good intentions destroyed by irresponsible and unproductive actions."

"Allying yourself with the Lantern Society?"

"Trust me when I say the consequences of your actions could be a million times more severe."

"The Tunnel."

"The tunnel, yes, you can't go through with it."

"That tunnel leads to my brother."

"That may be true for Verity's tunnel, but not yours. The gemstones you're using in your construction won't work, and if you power it up, it will either destroy itself or it'll only work to the point of inviting a reality that will replace ours. Our world will vanish."

Devlin smiled. "You recited that as if they were lines from a play."

"I was coached well. They'd explain it to you themselves if only you'd let them."

"My mother and I went back to Verity Corp armed with the information my brother had shared with me. I was willing to blackmail them into providing answers. And what did we get for our trouble? More brainwashing. I managed to get away before they could touch me. My mother wasn't so lucky, and she's never been the same.

"I've lost my entire family! My father was taken from me when I was eight not two. I lost those six years with him and the rest besides. My brother disappeared under mysterious circumstances that I have no doubt occurred within the confines of Verity Corp. And my mother will live out her remaining days in a kind of dull, quasi-lobotomized state.

"I will have my family back, Charlie, Verity Corp be damned! I will get them back, even if I have to take our trans-dimensional travelers down myself. Nothing can detract me from this task. No one will stop me. Not you. Not Verity Corp."

"But the tunnel! You can't put your family ahead of the entire world!"

"Why not? My family was my world!"

Anderson had no response. He understood different people had different motives. Passions ran deeper in some than others. He didn't know what he could say to change her mind. He didn't know for sure that he wanted to, and it occurred to him that the Lantern Society had finally succeeded in getting him to drink the Kool-Aid.

"Sadly, I can't help you with this rogue tunnel. I was paid to acquire the data and liaise between the buyer and Kupperdyne."

"Regardless of who's constructing---."

"You were all so sure I was building it. How do you know anyone is?"

"Who's your buyer?"

Devlin handed Anderson a folded piece of paper then reached for her phone and started texting. He opened it and read it.

"You have got to be kidding me."

"I have to use the ladies room," Devlin said, typing quickly then returning her phone to her purse. "I want to thank you for your assistance in my endeavors, Charles, and I wish you the best of luck."

And with that, Devlin got off the stool and walked to the back of the shop. Anderson stared at the paper, refolded it, and slipped it into his shirt pocket. He downed his drink and thought about all she had said. It was an amazing story and he found he believed every word of it. And now he would go back to Verity having tried his best, and provide them with the only link to the disaster remaining to them…if such disaster actually existed. He was no longer sure.

And then something struck him. Devlin's last words sounded awfully like goodbye, but if she was only visiting the ladies room…

"Hello, Charlie."

Anderson's shoulders slumped. He recognized the gravelly voice immediately.

"Hello, Ed."

#

Emmett was all too happy to escort Tomlinson back up to the tower. Without directly asking her again, he nevertheless asked a series of roundabout questions in the hopes of learning what it was she was working on. Tomlinson was wise to him, though, and provided nothing but a cryptic smile. Emmett was not a complicated man, but he could see the effort it took for Tomlinson to lift the corners of her mouth.

When they reached the Sounding Tunnel station, they started down the path to elevator number two before Tomlinson stopped Emmett with a question.

"Nobody showed you the Sounding Tunnel?"

He led her around the console stations until they reached the platform. Emmett pointed down the tracks in the direction of the Sounding Rings.

"There you go. That's what we're all about."

Tomlinson stared at the dormant Ring, dimly lit by work lights set at half strength. The portholes were dark, like a pox against gray skin. The portal gaped, threatening to scream. She knew she should dread the sight of it, the instrument of their impending doom. But all she saw was a white picket fence that surrounded the home she shared with her husband. All she saw was a way out from a life of which she'd grown so weary. One way or another, it was all going to end.

#

Anderson and Donovan stepped out of Eisenberg's and rounded the corner of Twenty-Third Street. Anderson reached for his cell phone.

"Don't bother."

Anderson turned to face the mercenary who stood in front of him, ironically, with one hand in his pocket, insinuating possession of a firearm.

"Are you here to kill me, Mr. Donovan?"

"Keep your voice down."

"Why should I? The world's going to end anyway."

"I wouldn't know about that. I just know that with the end of your contract comes the end of mine. I can finally go home."

"Your intel is lacking. The only reason I put myself in harm's way today was to try and convince your boss not to act on the plans that I stole for her."

"What are you talking about?"

"I was done. I was safe, tucked away in a cushy suite, food and drink, and a personal guard. Meanwhile, the people at Verity Corp are scrambling like headless chickens to stop her from turning on this tunnel thing she's building. That's what all this has been about! Only now it turns out, she's not building it all! It's someone at Verity Corp! Maybe. Who the hell knows?"

"What's the matter with you?"

"If someone built it, and that someone turns it on, it's all over, brother. You won't have a home to go back to."

"Are you fucking insane?"

"I'm saying you have no reason to kill me. Come back to Verity with me. Help me stop what's going to happen. Might happen." He held up the piece of paper. "I've got to get this to them. What do you say?"

"Yes, Mr. Donovan, what do you say?"

Donovan slowly removed his hand from his pocket and held both of them out slightly when he felt the gun barrel in the small of his back. Amsterdam stood behind him with his yellow sweater draped over his own gun hand. A car pulled up and Jascowitz stepped out, opening the back door for their guests. Donovan shook his head.

"I say at this rate, I'm never gonna get home."

Chapter Sixteen: The Oculacrum

The pocket bay door to Pod Six was fully recessed and a steady stream of white coats flowed into the testing arena to bear witness to Dr. Keith Baylor's pride and joy. Like Professor Askew, Baylor was a Boothe Academy alumnus, and he had been working on variations of the Oculacrum since their school days together decades ago. The Scope's purpose had fluctuated over the years as technology evolved, but never so drastically as when he joined Verity Corp. Their present focus was to see beyond known space, past the dimensional barrier that separated them from the home of their abductors, to visually eavesdrop on Null Space. The Oculacrum was very probably Verity Corp's greatest achievement next to the invention of the Sounding Tunnel. If it worked.

Henderson stood in the pod's driveway and held her ground against the current of enthusiastic scientists pouring in, noting every face that passed her by. Midnight was fast approaching and there was no sign of Dmitri Gusarov. Henderson had invited him in an effort to round out his training in all things Verity, but also to evaluate his talent first hand against the unusual need to fast track his hiring.

Baylor took advantage of the split Henderson made in the crowd to join her.

"The clock chimes at midnight, Rachel. Just about time to lock up."

"It's bad enough he's brand new and no one knows where he came from, but he seems to have no grasp of procedure or chain of command. Maybe it's a language thing, I don't know. He's not even answering his radio."

Baylor understood her dilemma, but he insisted they start on time. Henderson nodded and walked backward into the pod, still hoping to catch a glimpse of the block-shaped Russian. She finally turned in the last second as the big door slid closed behind her. With that, red lights began to flash above each port of entry like a Hollywood soundstage, signaling keep out and keep quiet. History was about to be made, and whether Rachel liked it or not, 'Goose' Gusarov was going to miss it.

Station 12: The Lantern Society

#

The ersatz Russian, meanwhile, had been glued to a workstation in the Analysis Bank almost from the moment the Sounding Tunnel test had concluded. For Extet it had been a nonstop grind of sorting through the recorded test data, analyzing video in tenths-of-a-second intervals, and logging every scrap of information available to him. His were the valuable, fresh eyes of the group and Verity was most interested in his observations and analyses. Also, he was the rookie, the low man on the science team ladder, and shit ran down hill. As he waded through the data, he compiled reports using previous submissions as templates. These reports would be turned over to Henderson who would then distribute them to the appropriate parties pending her review.

Extet didn't mind the work. His kind had the keen ability to absorb and disseminate information far more quickly and efficiently than humans. And, given the Station Master's instructions and timeframe, it wasn't like he had anything else to do. Technically he'd already fulfilled his obligation by participating in the Sounding Tunnel exercise. The Station Masters were curious about a specific energy signal originating at Verity Corp and now Extet had seen the source of it up close and personal. But he was enjoying his stay, and he didn't know if or when he'd ever get back to Earth. So he happily and doggedly followed the data wherever it led him.

Conveniently, the work he was doing for Verity Corp provided much of the same data he was searching for on behalf of the System; stockpiles of information pertaining to the Sounding Tunnel, construction schematics, personnel rosters, movies and sound analyses, and so on. It seemed all of Verity Corp was dedicated to learning as much as they could about the mysterious dimension-hopping trains and the corner of the cosmos they called home. Based on what Extet was seeing, that effort was proving quite fruitful. Now it was time to determine how far the humans had come in their research and whether they posed a threat to the impartial assessment of realities. At least as far as assessing Earth was concerned.

In order for Extet to work efficiently on the tasks set before him by the Station Masters, he interfaced with a device that, for the time being, was beyond Earth's level of technology. Resembling a simple, black drink coaster, its proximity to the computer he was using allowed him to see not only what was on the local hard drive, but also the global network to which it was attached. The output of this browsing displayed inside Extet's head thanks to an ultra-thin, subcutaneous plate located just inside and above his left brow. The plate worked in tandem with his optic nerves so that data was visible across half of his sight line, like watching a movie, but inside his head. He could control the flow of data with subtle manipulation of his fingers on the coaster, in similar fashion to a mouse pad. If anyone got too close to his workstation, he would simply take a drink from his two liter bottle of soda then place it down on the coaster.

He took a big gulp and burped so loudly, it turned more than a few heads in the Bank. And then he saw something that garnered his full attention.

On the network X:drive, he came across an encrypted folder called Bellows, and inside that folder Extet found a specific reference to 'TSAs boarding the TDRR.' He didn't know what the first acronym stood for, but he knew that TDRR stood for Trans-Dimensional Railroad, the human's term for Tapestry Rail, and boarding, well, no mystery there. The question then became: Who was boarding the TDRR and how? There was plenty of correspondence referring to TSAs throughout the Bellows folder, but the meaning was never spelled out until he came upon a file called TSA Manual. It turned out the letters stood for Truth Squad Agents, a small team of Verity scientists whose directive was to infiltrate Null Space by way of the Sounding Tunnel.

According to the manual, the Wardrobe team had created special suits, P4 TrakSuits they were called, that could piggy-back on the frequency emitted by the Sounding Rings, and somehow turn the Tapestry Rail into a tangible transport rather than the ghostly apparition they were used to seeing. Extet felt he had struck gold with this latest discovery and wondered if the Station Masters had any inkling of what was really happening at Verity Corp.

There were many references to the Sounding Tunnel in the manual, which wasn't so much a how-to resource as it was a repository for everything pertaining to the Tunnel and the suits. After reading a lengthy dissertation on what the Sounding Tunnel was and how it functioned, he found a list of all the major components that went into its construction. This led to more lists, lists of parts and sub-lists of smaller parts. One of the items listed in sub-list D had an asterisk. The asterisk led him to yet another list: D-11.18, a large selection of gems and crystals grouped together by source. Diamonds were listed as coming from Russia and rubies were from Burma. Also on the list were emeralds from Columbia. The asterisk was repeated for several of the gems listed. At the bottom of the page the notation read, 'Confidential per Outsource_Protocol/DA_alt.'

Extet had no idea what Outsource Protocol meant, but he took a wild guess DA stood for Daniel Askew, a logical keeper of things confidential. An exhaustive search for other mentions of DA_alt proved ineffective. Curiosity drove him to pursue more information about this Protocol and his intuition was telling him he was on to something big. He shut his workstation down and left in search of more answers.

#

After the events that led to the creation of Operation: Bucket Leak had transpired, Ellen Cheever worked closely with IT Security to create what they dubbed the Data Fortress, a sophisticated network application that monitored usage and placed virtual guard towers around and within the entirety of Verity's data warehouse. Given the scope of the project, they managed to get everything in place remarkably fast. Tests were run, and simulations. Everything seemed to be in perfect order and fully operational. Cheever had put in a lot of extra hours to make things happen and was ready to call it a night when Jerry Harper reported seeing strange activity in the Analysis Bank.

Cheever sighed heavily, making it clear she did not appreciate the 11th hour report. Reluctantly, she joined the technician at his monitor and together they watched lines of time stamped usage data crawl up the screen, the names of the accessed folders and files passing at an alarming rate of speed.

"Is this activity coming from one computer?" asked Cheever.

The tech answered in the affirmative.

"Who's signed on to it?" asked Cheever.

"Dmitri Gusarov."

"The breadth of data makes sense to a certain degree. He's responsible for turning in Sounding Tunnel test reports to Dr. Henderson tomorrow. Plus he's new so he's probably playing catch-up."

"But how can he be reading through that material so quickly?"

"Maybe it's a glitch in Fortress reporting speed. Can we remote access his machine without attracting his attention?"

"Sure."

The tech tapped his keyboard and threw what Extet was looking at on the monitor next to him.

"Well, this is weird. What's on his screen and what's being accessed are two different things."

"How's that possible?"

Harper's monitor displayed folders and files opening and closing so quickly it was difficult to register the content. It was highly unlikely that anything but a bot could take in that much information at that rate of speed. What they saw on Gusarov's monitor was a list of all the Sounding Tunnel tests to date and he appeared to be reading the synopses of each at a normal rate of speed.

"This is fucked up…Ma'am. Sorry."

"It's alright, Harper. Something is definitely out of whack. I think I'll pay our friend, Goose, a little visit."

#

Baylor waved a finger through the air in a circular motion, informing the man inside the booth that it was time to commence the exercise. Tim Scopp echoed the gesture indicating that everything was ready on his end. Dr. Baylor asked everyone to take their seats, directing team members to their stations and guests to get comfortable in the gallery.

The workstations were arranged in a circle around the Oculacrum, with one break at the pod bay door, and another where an oversized monitor was mounted. A temporary gallery of chairs set on risers ran six rows deep, and every seat had a clear view of the big screen. The hum of hydraulics filled the air as the Scope started to come alive.

The Oculacrum was of significant size and took up the entirety of the recessed pit that was its home. Possessed of a large, fully articulating 'head,' it looked like a dinosaur in search of prey. Similar to a planetarium projector, the head was covered in lenses of various sizes. Work lights reflected off of them, sending shafts of light in all directions like an oversized mirror ball. There was a body of sorts which stood on hydraulic legs, and with that massive head it earned the nickname Rex, for Tyrannosaurus Rex.

Baylor escorted Henderson to a workstation then stepped away to speak with each team, marking on his clipboard their responses to his checklist. Henderson sat and adjusted the two monitors in front of her to make sure she had a clear view of the main screen. For some time she'd been unable to focus much attention on the Oculacrum project. Once she was assigned as Askew's right hand, she had become so mired in red tape and paperwork she rarely had time for practical application and testing. Now that she was there, she was happy for the distraction and excited to participate. The Oculacrum could be a game changer and she knew it.

Once Baylor closed the loop on his station check, he joined Henderson at the console where he found her texting a message.

"Problem?"

She slipped a folded piece of paper into her lab coat pocket.

"It's just my intuition nagging at me," she said, smiling in embarrassment.

"Okay." Baylor pushed a set of buttons on the console then put on his headset. "Rachel, I want to thank you again for stepping up like this. I know you have a lot on your plate."

"The project warrants the attention, Keith. I'm glad to be here."

Baylor smiled at her. Suddenly the volume of the warm-up shot way down and everybody looked around in expectation, as if a show were about to start.

"Can we cut the work lights, please?"

The arena grew dark except for workstation lights and a ring of LEDs surrounding the pit.

"Dr. Baylor," Tim Scopp said over his headset, "I'm going to start setting the graduating frequencies. You are currently go for local observation."

"Thank you, Tim. Mahsa, I think we'll stick close by to start. Can we have a look at the moon, please?"

"One small peek for man…" Mahsa responded as she inputted the data on her console.

Baylor looked in the direction of Pruitt's team and asked for another status report. Pruitt's engineers watched the commands come through and gauged the system's responses. They looked at their monitors then up as Rex's head swiveled and turned, pointing the appropriate lens in the direction of the moon based on mathematical coordinates provided by yet another team. White letters appeared on the previously dormant main screen that read, 'Searching for Moon/Luna.' Input from Mahsa's console went to Pruitt's team who confirmed that the correct data had been entered. A request was then made of Tim Scopp's harmonics booth for the frequency that would allow the Scope's lens to see past the ceiling overhead, past the black tower of Verity Corp, and finally past the dense atmosphere of Earth to outer space.

What appeared on the screen nearly took their collective breath away. It was a super 4K high definition image of the moon and their view panned slowly across its surface. The monitor seemed more a window than a projected image. An immediate outpouring of joy erupted in the form of cheering and applause. The panning ceased. Rex turned its head and a new lens began to zoom closer and closer toward the moon's surface. The 'ooh'ing and 'ah'ing increased as more and more detail was revealed.

"Quiet, please," came a voice over the PA system.

"Very good. Mahsa, let's get up close and personal with Saturn now."

Mahsa entered the appropriate data and Pruitt's team approved and sent it on to Tim who adjusted the frequency accordingly. The image of the moon was replaced by the black search screen and the scientists groaned in disappointment. Rex rotated again and the assigned eye gazed through the floor, through bedrock and the Earth's core, to make a beeline for the ringed planet. When the picture returned, the scientists were amazed by their proximity to the debris field that made up Saturn's rings. The chatter started all over again. Baylor looked over at Pruitt and gave him a thumbs-up.

"I sure wish Prof was here to see this," Baylor said to no one in particular, but Henderson heard him clearly. If Baylor only knew, she thought, he would surely forgive Askew his absence.

"Okay, Mahsa, let's take a look outside our solar system."

#

It took some time for Extet to locate Askew's laboratory office in Administrative Block 1. The admin section was mostly dark during third shift, and he did his best to avoid being detected without obviously hiding. The office was fit to bursting with stacks of paper except for an aisle that ran from the door to Askew's chair. Placing one foot in front of the other, he made his way to the desk and switched on the lamp. The light appeared dim, but really it was just stifled by the high mounds of paperwork covering the professor's desk. He made his way back to the door and closed it.

Where to begin?

Logic dictated that, because of the confidential nature of the material he sought, he should set his sights on a locked cabinet or drawer. That left a single file cabinet in the corner and he had to lean over stacks of science journals to confirm that it was locked. Removing what looked like a pen from his pocket, he unscrewed the top to reveal a thin rod. He inserted it into the keyhole and pushed it slowly through the lock until it came to a stop. Then he planted his feet and pushed it the rest of the way with brute force. When he didn't hear any reaction from outside the office, he yanked it back out, popping out the entire lock in the process.

Gusarov started with the top drawer in search of anything labeled DA_alt. He was nothing if not meticulous in his work and he didn't like unanswered questions. The Station Masters were liable to ask him anything when he returned and he didn't want to be found lacking.

In the third drawer down, he came across a hard copy of the gem list he'd discovered during his studies in the Analysis Bank. Attached to it was a page listing gemstones with names like Firelite, Darkstone, and Oceanite, names quite different from those found on the master list. Interestingly, each of the names was paired up with stones he did recognize. For example, he saw gems called Magentalites paired up with Sapphires. To Extet, that read as if the two names were synonymous, but he knew better than to assume.

He looked around the office in search of a computer, thinking Askew might possibly keep important information on his personal hard drive, but if there was one in there, it was buried out of sight. He searched a bit more for anything on the Outsource Protocol or DA_alt. In this he came up empty-handed. Logically he deduced that Askew kept his private files elsewhere. *But where? His home?* As he thought about his next step, he noticed some photographs hanging above his head and he berated himself for his stupidity. He'd been so busy in the underground, he had forgotten all about the tower overhead. *Askew most certainly has an office up high.* It was time to head upstairs.

#

The screen went black once more, and once more the gallery of scientists groaned at the loss of picture. The white letters returned and displayed, 'Departing Sol star system. Searching for GJ1214b'. The science team, particularly those with idle hands in the gallery, greeted the message with more applause. Baylor smiled, knowing that he and his team had developed something very special. He looked at Henderson and the two clasped hands to share physically in the excitement and joy of Baylor's success. The black screen displayed, 'Planet JG1214b. Distance = 41.34 light years,' then gave way to reveal a predominantly blue planet with a red sun looming large in the background. The Scope zoomed closer and closer still, until it entered the planet's thin atmosphere. The green-white clouds were mostly transparent water colors that stretched across the sky like layers of gauze. Atmospheric winds gathered wisps into swirling maelstroms that turned a darker teal as they coalesced. The attendees could make out dark dots that stood out in the rarified air, moving inside the spirals.

The Scope continued to zoom in, and still the scientists strained to see the surface below. As they made their way past the cloud cover, white circles appeared in an endless blue sea, perhaps great boiling hot spots over thermal vents. The dots continued to grow in size and began to take on form. One of the scientists got out of his chair and approached the screen.

"Watch this one in the lower left," he said.

The shape grew larger. A jet of air carried it aloft in a clockwise embrace while another vortex formed nearby, spinning in the opposite direction. The shape jumped from one whirlpool to the other in an atmospheric dosado.

"Did you see that?!" asked the scientist excitedly. "That was deliberate movement!"

The shape disappeared from view and the gallery began to clamor for the Scope to refocus on the object of their attention. Baylor folded his arms and shook his head when Mahsa looked his way. Suddenly another one of the shapes came into view, only this time much, much closer. It had the appearance of a soft balloon and the shape of a slightly flattened football, its translucent skin rippling, barely covering the creature's very visible internal organs. Two green eyes stuck out on either side of its head-like body. No mouth was visible, but there were a few mouth-like openings on each side as well. The creature puffed up then deflated at regular intervals. Many watching were already theorizing that the creature was breathing in the atmosphere, venting whatever gases it couldn't absorb, and leaving a green vapor trail in its wake as waste.

The image continued past the creature until it slipped from view. But not completely, as everyone became aware of tendrils hanging down from underneath the creature that continued down towards the surface of the planet. As their view pushed past the remaining clouds, the surface below became clearer revealing its vast ocean, a bubbling cauldron in the 400 degree heat, with no land in sight. The tendrils remained in view as they continued to the surface, and many of the scientists furiously scribbled notes, surmising that the creatures might be gaining some manner of sustenance from the boiling ocean miles below.

When the screen blacked out once more the response was more than a groan, it was almost angry dissent. People stood up from their seats, some removed their headsets, and all were barking their dismay in Baylor's direction. They were making the greatest discovery in the history of science and Dr. Baylor was deliberately walking away. It was outrageous. Baylor sat patiently and waited for the tumult to subside. He looked over at Henderson who simply smiled with an expression on her face as if to say that Baylor should have expected this. Finally, the director stood and held up his hands.

"Quiet, please," came the voice over the PA system. A second attempt had some effect.

"Let's not forget why we're here, people," Baylor said, "why we're doing what we're doing."

Let's not forget.

Henderson was reminded of what was happening out in the world. Baylor had no idea how right he was to point out the greater cause, even if he was unaware of the complete truth of it.

"There's no doubt we'll be revisiting this great discovery, but we have a higher calling as you well know, and it's best we don't forget that. We've been preparing for many years. Now's not the time for distractions. So everybody sit down and let's get back to doing what we set out to do."

There were no more arguments.

"Mahsa, let's take our first look at Null Space, if you please."

#

When Cheever pulled up to the Analysis Bank, the only thing remaining of Extet's presence was an empty bottle of soda. Those who were still working in the surrounding micro-cubes confirmed his former occupancy and pointed her in the direction they believed he'd gone. When she reached out to Security to ask for assistance, she was informed that Henderson had also sent out an alert on Gusarov for failure to appear at an assigned test. Cheever's original discomfort concerning the newest member of the Verity science staff resurfaced. *What is this guy up to*, she wondered.

As soon as she disconnected the call her radio squawked. It was Harper from the Data Fortress, informing her that Gusarov had accessed an encrypted folder on the X: drive.

"The folder belongs to Mr. Bellows. I don't see a hack, but I don't see a log-in either. And here's the kicker: no registered PC on our network is associated with the trespass. But the Guard Tower's telling me that every file in the folder was viewed. I can't say for sure it had anything to do with Gusarov, but I can tell you that Mr. Bellows was nowhere near a computer at the time."

Cheever thanked him and broke the connection.

According to Security, he hasn't left the building, which means he hasn't found what he's looking for. Where would I go if I needed more information specific to Bellows?

She got Security back on the radio and told them to meet her at the admin blocks.

#

Extet took the tower elevator to the top floor and realized as he stepped out into the hall how much trickier it was going to be working in Askew's glass office. The hallway was fairly dark. Even with the blinds lowered, a lamp would shine out like a beacon. He would have to work quickly and efficiently if he wanted to avoid being seen.

The office was immaculate, not a piece of paper out of place. In fact, there was very little paper present. It was obvious to Extet that the professor spent very little time there. There was no file cabinet or anything similar, but he did discover a small safe built into the credenza. He pushed Askew's chair aside then hunkered down behind the desk, knowing that the one and only tool he had brought along would be of no use. He crossed his legs and rested his elbows on his knees and his chin in his hands as he pondered this newest hurdle. There was a good chance he could smash it open, but that would require moving it elsewhere, and he wasn't too keen on that. After studying it for a good minute, he realized that the lock was digital and required no physical key to open it, so he pulled out his black coaster device and dropped it on top of the safe. It was a longshot, but he figured there was nothing gained if he didn't try. He tapped the operating system to life and found he was rewarded for his effort when a message appeared in his head.

'Do you wish to interact with this device?'

Extet smiled and tapped in the affirmative.

'This device is password protected. Do you require a password?'

Extet's smile broadened, showing his large, peg-like teeth. Once again, he tapped yes. Seconds later he was provided a six-digit password that granted him access to Verity's most sensitive secrets. Inside the safe lay a half dozen reports, each bound in a red report cover. A small Post-It note stuck onto the top read 'DA-alt.' The Station Master's agent peered over the desk and listened closely for any noise in the hall. Satisfied he was still alone, he removed the reports and brought the desk lamp down to the floor. The very first page of the first report was a memo written by Askew and addressed to Lionel Bellows and Max Heberling. It proposed the Outsource Protocol which stated that any component and/or resource derived from a reality not their own would be deemed top secret and knowledge thereof would be confined on a permanent basis to the three of them and a select few Truth Squad Agents.

Derived from a reality not their own?

Extet frowned. This was bad. He turned to the second and last page of the report. It was a list of the outsourced gemstones and their points of origin. Extet shook his head then crossed his arms and exhaled. It seemed the TSAs had not only found their way to the System via Tapestry Rail, but they had somehow continued their journey into other realities for the purposes of exploiting their resources. This was very bad. He had never been in a position like this in all his time as a troubleshooter for the Station Masters, and now he was forced to report to them the worst possible news.

Without realizing it, Verity Corp had signed Earth's death warrant.

#

The Oculacrum turned and the many lenses, like lidless eyes, looked around the room as if to ask, are you sure you want to do this? One of the lenses turned blue, an indication that something new was about to happen. Tim Scopp informed Baylor that everything was ready in the booth and Baylor responded with a thumbs-up, and then gave Mahsa the green light to proceed. The letters crawling across the black screen provided scientific titillation.

'Searching for Null Space. Criteria exceeds known parameters. Data not found in available libraries. Searching known space. No data. Compressing current space-time plane.'

The black screen was replaced by a vivid field of stars. Nothing happened again for quite some time and the scientists fidgeted nervously in their seats as the Oculacrum compiled the data being fed into it. Rex turned its head and their view of space altered. It turned again and the view shifted once more. Tim, looking a little frantic in the booth, began to adjust the frequencies. When he thought he had achieved his objective, he looked up at the screen.

Outer space began to fold before their very eyes. A white line formed as stars converged along a crease, splitting the screen on the horizontal. The stars above the line rolled toward the observers like an ocean wave, while the stars beneath mirrored the effect. The top and bottom edges of the star field merged in a splash of white light as a billion, billion galaxies came together. When the light receded, the field of stars had returned. The blue lens of the Oculacrum reverted to normal and another lens took its place. The process repeated and the universe folded in on itself once more. That time the resulting flare was unbearably bright and many people were forced to look away or don goggles. The room turned brighter than any daylight, and then the light receded almost immediately after. Only the star field didn't return. People blinked their eyes in an effort to clear out the spots that hindered their ability to read the newest message on the screen.

'Compression complete. Searching unknown space.'

Everyone stared intently at the blackness, waiting and wondering silently to themselves if the test had succeeded or failed.

Henderson brushed at the side of her face, as if removing an annoying stray hair. Then she held up her hands like blinders and focused her attention on the center of the screen.

"Pruitt, are we zooming in?"

Pruitt took a quick look at his console to verify what he already knew. "Yes, Dr. Henderson."

"Can we slow down the transition speed?"

"We'd have to switch to manual. This is the default speed when the Scope doesn't see anything."

Henderson turned to Baylor. "I think I'm seeing something."

"Like flashes?"

Henderson nodded. Baylor thought a moment, a little reluctant to stop auto run this early in the game, but then nodded to Pruitt who made the adjustments.

"It may get a little bumpy from here on out," said Pruitt. "Stay with me, Tim."

"Roger that."

At first nothing happened, but then the flashes Henderson thought she saw were confirmed. As the zoom transition speed continued to slow, the flashes began to take shape and everyone's breath caught. They were buoys of some sort, pylons with flashing lights on top and bottom, hanging in the inky, starless, and perpetual night of Null Space. They didn't seem to line up, nor could they discern any specific pattern. Two parallel lines of light leapt into the picture from below and shot straight out ahead them. The lines were a dark, electric red in the lead, but cooled to a dull blue-gray just behind. The lines twisted and turned around some of the buoys, but remained for the most part within their field of vision.

The next thing they knew, a red and yellow bullet train popped into view, traversing the tracks that were laying themselves out before it. Everyone recognized it and applauded when they realized that their experiment was, in fact, a success. They were observing the realm of their invaders by way of a telescope that could fold the fabric of reality and peer into other dimensions.

"Okay, everyone, we've found our way to Null Space. We don't have any specific targets to focus our sites on so all we can do is explore and make notations for our next visit. Mike, what are we showing for coordinates?"

"Sorry, Keith, coordinates are showing up as null."

"What?"

"Our instruments say this place doesn't exist."

"It doesn't," said Henderson. "Not in our universe. That's why Prof named it Null Space."

They watched as the train began to pull away.

"Pru, can we stay with the train? Maybe it will lead the way to something interesting."

"I'll try to increase zoom transition slightly and tag the back of the train as a target…shit, except it doesn't exist."

Adjustments were made and the train began to slow. But then the back of it slipped from view as the zoom pushed forward. Baylor looked over at Pruitt who was hard at work at his console. The train continued to lose ground.

"Pru?"

"Trying to tweak it. I'm not sure the Scope is reacting to the console anymore."

"Tim?"

"Sorry, Keith, I'm doing the best I can."

Their view overtook the train and continued to speed up. More buoys passed. They caught up to the track-laying red lines then lurched past them as well. A structure appeared, but before they could note any details, it was gone. They caught up to a second train and passed that one as well. Another train crossed in front of them. There were more buoys. And more small structures. Next they came to a train yard crowded with TDRR trains. Then it, too, was gone. The picture brightened as they came upon a magnificent station, though they were moving through it too quickly to register anything. They could make out a large monitor, upon which was the face of a man sporting a flattop haircut and round tortoiseshell glasses. He seemed to be looking in their direction when suddenly the image folded like outer space had done only moments before. The screen went black and gibberish crawled across the screen. The scientists mumbled and began making adjustments at their consoles.

When the picture returned they were approaching a green planet at an alarming rate. They were through the atmosphere in seconds and flying into a jungle, then through the planet and out the other side. Back out in space, they passed several moons and another planet. The clarity of the image and the speed at which they were moving made a few of the scientists dizzy and they turned away. When Baylor turned toward the booth, Tim Scopp just shrugged. Pruitt offered the same assurance with a shake of his head. The Scope's eye view continued traveling through this new universe with ever increasing speed. At one point it skirted another planet and they could just make out dinosaur-like animals crossing a vast marsh, but just as quickly they passed over gleaming metal towers in what was obviously some type of city. They crossed a lavender ocean and saw another city hovering above it. Back in outer space, they passed through a brightly colored nebula. Stars shot past and began to stretch into white lines.

Baylor turned again to Pruitt and gestured with a slash to his throat to abort the test. Pruitt cut all power to Rex and it assumed a position of rest. The screen went blank and the room turned eerily quiet.

#

Cheever arrived at Administration Block 1 as two Security teams rolled in. Ann Hunter, leader of the squad, approached Cheever for the lowdown.

"It appears our new man, Gusarov, has gone rogue. I'm hoping we'll find him in Bellows' office."

Hunter signaled two of the guards and they trotted over to Bellows' office door. It was closed but not locked, so they let themselves in and hit the lights. Almost immediately they popped out again signaling all clear. Hunter led Cheever into the office and the two of them looked for any sign of unwanted visitors.

"What now?" asked Hunter when they found none.

Cheever stepped out and looked around. "I'm not sure what else we can do. He's got to be here somewhere."

Hunter's radio squawked. Cheever noticed the door of the neighboring office was ajar. She pushed it open and saw the mountains of paperwork covering Askew's office. She turned on the overhead light and saw right away that the file cabinet had been broken into.

"Good news," said Hunter. "They caught Gusarov on the security cams."

#

Extet had more than enough information with which to report back to the Station Masters. However, an insatiable curiosity drove him to dig deeper. What he'd found so far was amazing. He'd never known another reality to see past the reconstruction left in the wake of a System visit, never mind accomplish what humanity had accomplished in the short time of their awareness. Extet knew there was no way they could be judged fairly for the Tapestry given the state of their affairs. It was unfortunate. Extet loved the Ert.

He shuffled through the other reports and picked out one called 'Operation: Bucket Leak' and thumbed through it. He read about the data theft, which parties were responsible, and what was stolen. He read through the construction plans and the parts list and noted the references to the Outsource Protocol. He read about the Lantern Society and their possible plans for building a Sounding Tunnel and how the Outsource Protocol guaranteed their failure.

Guaranteed their failure... He looked up in complete understanding. *How can this be?*

Just then he heard a noise in the hall and he knew it was time to go. He lifted the face of his watch and pressed a tiny button inside the housing. The files fell from his lap and he waited, alone, thinking about the end of all things, and knowing there was no escape.

#

As Cheever rode the elevator topside, she radioed several people and brought them up to speed. By the time she stepped onto the fortieth floor, a small cadre of Longworth's guards was already gathering on either side of Askew's office. Bellows and Longworth were both there as well, after having finished their interrogation of Donovan. The blinds were down, making visual confirmation impossible. Heads came together in a whispered exchange of status reports and improvised plans of imminent conflict. Orders were passed back and forth. The security force began to converge on Askew's office. When they got within three feet of the door, an extremely bright, blue light filled the interior, leaking out between the slats of the blinds. They could hear the crackling of electricity and saw flashes like lightning strikes in the glass box that was Askew's office. The hair on everyone's arms and on the backs of their necks stood at attention. No one moved. No one knew if they could.

The event came and went. When they deemed it safe, Security burst into the office en masse, but the only thing they found was an acrid odor and a puff of bluish smoke rising toward the ceiling.

#

Keith Baylor looked at his watch and decided there was time

enough for another test. In fact, he was adamant. There was no damage to any of the systems, he said, and now that they were back in local space, everything seemed to be operating normally. Henderson knew how much this meant to her colleague so she didn't argue the point.

Baylor went one more time around the room to confirm that all systems were ready, but when he got back to Mahsa, he got no response. She was staring at her monitors with a look of concern on her face.

"Is there a problem, Mahsa?"

"There could be, sir. There could be a big problem."

"What is it?"

"Our systems are picking up the energy signature of the Sounding Tunnel."

Baylor looked at his watch again then over at Henderson. She looked like petrified wood, but managed to shake her head.

"There are no exercises scheduled for tonight," he said.

"The signature isn't coming from here."

"Oh, Jesus!" Henderson's eyes grew large and she stood up.

"What is it, Rachel?" Baylor stood up with furrowed brow.

"Jesus, It's happening!"

Shame paralyzed her. It was arrogance that had brought to this place and shame that now rooted her. She had allowed herself, albeit temporarily, to disconnect from Askew's dire prediction to indulge the scientist's ego, her ego. She felt her legs start to buckle, but she held onto the console for support.

"Rachel! What is it? What's happening?"

"Mahsa!" she cried. "Can you tell where that signal is coming from?"

"It's quite a ways north, Dr. Henderson. Looks like Canada, I'd say. Give me a few minutes and I'll tell you exactly."

"Pruitt, can you target that signal?"

Baylor shook his head. "Rachel, what is going on?"

"Got it."

"Get it on the screen!"

The Oculacrum began to turn; the head swiveled to line up the appropriate lens with their target. Henderson stepped up to the view screen.

'Searching for target. Target 1260 miles. Target acquired.'

The screen remained dark, almost as dark as Null Space, but with an overlay of thickly falling snow. It was like staring into a giant snow globe. Visibility was nil, but Henderson continued to peer into the gloom, using her hands as makeshift blinders once more. Baylor and a few others joined her, staring into the winter-scape.

"Rachel, what is it?" asked Baylor. "Why won't you talk to me?"

A single tear ran down her face and she pointed at the screen.

"It could be the end of everything."

Baylor got closer and stared into the snow globe, waiting for someone to stop shaking it, and just for a moment he saw it, saw the many colors glowing in their tiny portholes. He saw the Sounding Ring.

Chapter Seventeen: Reality Displacement

The seven billion active stories of humanity are all works in progress, penciled drafts of our part in a living fiction. Each writer is long gone before their ending has been written. Only when the last recollection of our time on Earth has been buried with the inheritors of our memory has the tale been fully and finally told. That volume is then closed and added to the after-life's vague repository of cosmic history. These are the tomes that reflect the truth of our lives that no media can tear asunder, no history book can misrepresent, and no critic, with their pencil boxes stuffed with vitriol and ego, can willfully disparage. These are the stories of life on planet Earth, good or bad, poignant or repugnant, whimsical or deliberate, self-absorbed or charitable, epic or novella. These stories can be copied but never plagiarized as even the 'adaptation' is a tale unto itself, steeped in its own truth, for our stories capture more than the action of our movements, but also the movements of our thoughts and emotions. The author cannot hide from his or her own writing, and though they may try many times in their lifetime, in the end the author cannot lie.

#

Four hours prior to the Great Disaster, Charlie Anderson was experiencing life's version of writer's block, caught up in a story of his own design, but for which he'd lost control of the plot. He had spent his time in Verity's prison suite brooding over the direction he'd taken his character, now divested of its very soul, and entangled in the tales of others with no happy endings in sight.

He poured himself a cup of hot tea, made soothing with honey and lemon, and brought it to the window to watch the intricacy of the world play out before him, hoping to use it as inspiration and perhaps find his way back to his place in it. But he found his view too high, or not high enough, to provide the proper perspective, and so the scurrying dots down below kept their secrets.

Turning his back to the window, he removed the stubby pencil from his mental notebook and stared at the blank page that was his immediate future. His unauthorized excursion to meet with Devlin had eliminated any chance to further his action agenda, so he turned from the story he'd known and focused, instead, on the characters that might still be in play. With that thought he realized that these had thinned to almost nothing. There was only one person left that might lend him an ear and hopefully lift his story out of dry dock and set it back on its proper course.

#

With two hours still before the start of the Oculacrum test, Rachel Henderson figured it wouldn't hurt to hear what Anderson had to say. Anyway, that was how she saw it from the perspective of a Verity employee. The truth of the matter, though, was that she wanted to see him. They were good friends, once upon a time, and she saw no reason to turn her back on him, even if he had lost his way. When Jascowitz went missing, she felt sorry for Charlie and wished she could find the words to console him. At the same time, as his relationship with Sarah Bismarck began to erode, she wondered if... Of course it was ridiculous. She was part of the problem, after all.

Rachel approached Askew's tower office on her way to the recently designated prison suite and saw that the professor had a visitor. She popped her head in and recognized the man seated opposite her mentor as Pat Haney of Kupperdyne and did her best not to visibly react. He had been held in the same suite as Charlie not so long ago and now here he was chatting with the professor like they were old friends.

Askew looked haggard, older than his years, and Henderson sympathized. She knew how little sleep she was getting over the impending disaster. She could only imagine how much worse it was for the creator of their undoing. She apologized for interrupting, and then reminded the professor that Keith Baylor's Oculacrum test was to take place shortly and not to worry, that she had it all under control. He smiled wearily and thanked her. There was a pause during which Askew might have explained Haney's presence to her, but he didn't, so she nodded and moved on.

Anderson appeared happy to see her but he, too, looked exhausted. The consequences of his actions weighed heavily upon him and he was obviously suffering from some deeply debilitating regret. She watched him and waited, reluctant to take the lead in the conversation. When she was finally forced to ask him why he asked to see her, he displayed a mix of emotions. There was no way he could ever apologize enough for his transgressions, he told her, but that he hoped she would allow him the chance to make it up to her and to Verity Corp. She reminded him what was at stake beyond the immediacy of his crimes against the company.

"It was a bad combination," he offered seemingly off topic, "my ambition and my concern that I was working for a corporation of questionable intent; a company that was probably responsible for the disappearance of my friend. I had to find him. I wanted to blow the lid off…"

There was something else in his pained expression.

"I don't know what you want me to say, Charlie. I couldn't feel more sorry for you."

"I just want to make things right again."

Henderson smiled sadly. She recognized that he wasn't talking to her. Only the tiniest fraction resented him for it while the majority of her emotions mustered in sympathy. It wasn't his fault that Sarah had died, she told him, and she took his hand. He had been ill-used and he would have to accept that. If he really wanted to make it up to her, he would do whatever he could to help Verity put an end to the Lantern Society's plans.

Anderson regained his focus and looked around the room conspiratorially.

"I don't think it's the Society you have to worry about."

The statement gave her pause. With his free hand he slipped her the folded piece of paper he'd received from Devlin. She opened and read it then looked back at Anderson with concern.

"Where did you get this?"

"My contact with the Lantern Society said she was hired by someone else to steal the plans."

Henderson nodded then stared down at the paper until the connection was made. "You've had this all day?"

Anderson stepped closer and spoke into her ear. "I'm sorry," he said softly. "I don't know who to trust anymore."

"It's the world you've made for yourself, Charlie." She held up the note. "Thank you. This is a good start."

Henderson stepped out into the hall and looked again at the paper. It had one line of text and she'd seen it before: InfoFile@VerityCorp.com.

She and Askew hadn't spoken about it since their initial meeting to discuss the two seemingly disparate incidents that would quickly merge to become Operation: Bucket Leak and task them with saving the world.

As she returned to Askew's office, Prof and Haney were on their feet and shaking hands. Haney nodded at Henderson as he walked past her and a creepy feeling skittered along her spine.

"Heading downstairs for the test?" Askew called out.

"Just a few more things to do. You should go home. Get some rest."

She turned and walked away. Seeing Askew so chummy with Haney gave her a queasy feeling. She slipped the folded piece of paper into her coat pocket.

#

As those stories continued to take shape at Verity Corp, two others were intersecting further uptown. Jackie Tomlinson and George Foster were sharing a plate of French fries in a midtown west diner, discussing all the craziness of the past twenty-four hours. Tomlinson had a lot of questions for Foster concerning his search for the whereabouts of Sarah Bismarck and he happily shared with her a plan that he and Dodge had cooked up. She grinned, putting enough warmth into it to nudge their relationship into something a bit more familiar, to remove the stigma of her once being his boss. His eyebrows rose in acknowledgement of her effort, but they also questioned.

"I've noticed quite a change in you since taking on your new role at Verity," said Tomlinson. "More mature, maybe."

"Get the fuck outa here!" Foster said with glee.

"Or not."

The two of them shared a laugh, genuinely happy to be in each other's company.

"Global Armour, Verity Corp, it's all the same to me, Jack. Just put me to work, respect my talent, and I'm happy as a clam."

She nodded thoughtfully and Foster got from her a slight sense of envy and thought maybe it would be a good idea to shift the spotlight.

"How are things with you?" he asked. "Still chasing your reflection?"

The French fry she was holding stopped midway to her mouth.

"What's that supposed to mean?"

Foster watched as the expression on Tomlinson's face soured, and he recognized in retrospect the indelicacy of his words. He quickly apologized, said he didn't mean anything by it, and tried to change the subject. But he'd struck a nerve and Tomlinson wasn't going to let him slide. She asked him if after everything he'd seen and heard he still thought the story of her other life was impossible. He countered, wondering after everything she'd seen and heard if chasing another life still had merit. Wasn't she well on her way to a new and improved life anyway?

His point was valid and that only made her angrier. So fixated had she been on her pre-Rewrite life, she could no longer see the forest for the trees. She pushed the plate away in the universal sign that she was done, told him that everything was fine and that she would see him the next day at work. He asked her not to leave, but she was already walking toward the door.

#

It was all about the truth and nothing but the truth as Strivelli and Angela continued to talk through their problems. The conversation was going well, mostly because Strivelli wanted desperately to forgive her. Truly, he already had, but he didn't want her to think she'd gotten off easy. It wasn't fair of him to make her jump through hoops, he knew that, but he'd been burned before, some time ago, and even though the current situation was completely different, the scar ran deep. After all, betrayal was betrayal, right?

#

Back at Verity Corp, Bellows and Longworth stood facing a seated Donovan, trying their damnedest to pry some new information out of him concerning the Lantern Society. It wasn't that he wasn't cooperating, because he was, for all the good it was doing them. He figured his contract was null and void anyway now that the Lantern Society had closed up shop. But the fact of the matter was, even after a year in the Society's employ, he didn't know much, and he told them so.

"You should talk to your boy, Anderson," he said. "He had her attention last. Who knows what pearls of information she bestowed upon him in the end?"

"What end?"

"Anderson's. That conversation was meant to be his last."

\#

Only blocks from Verity Corp, Devlin walked through the nearly vacated offices of Global Armour. GA had already moved much of their HQ into temporary spaces at Verity in an expedited effort to combine resources. She passed through the dark hallway into her darker office with only the ambient light of New York City to guide her. On a stack of boxes where her desk once resided sat her laptop which she promptly booted up. Her plan was coming together just as she imagined it would and right on schedule, too. With Anderson dealt with by Donovan, and Donovan disposed of by Peters, there were no more loose ends and she could begin the next phase of her operation from inside the belly of the beast.

When her computer showed ready, she inserted her earpiece and opened a line to her science team in Canada.

\#

They had done a remarkable job of duplicating Verity Corp's Sounding Tunnel. The only discernable difference was the outdoor set-up in the barren reaches of northern Quebec rather than the private and protected environs of the abandoned subway tunnel in New York. But for all intents and purposes, it was the same six rings, with the same distance between them, with the same purpose: to make visible a train from another dimension. Beyond that, well, if Devlin had a specific agenda, she hadn't shared it with the team.

The long wait and the many long hours were over and the last of the components had finally shipped from New York. Jacque Baird inserted the four replacement circuit boards into the Tunnel control panel and powered it up. There were no hiccups. He looked at his teammates with a mischievous grin.

"It is show time, yes?"

Summer had almost begun in northeastern Canada, as it had for the rest of the continent, but the chilly wind that blew through the northern Canadian plains showed that it wasn't quite ready to shed the mantle of a long, cold spring. Half of the six-member team went back to their footlockers for something warmer than the light jackets they had put on

Station 12: The Lantern Society

earlier.

"Everyone take your stations, s'il vous plait. It's time to make history."

The science team leader, Baird, was a graduate of MIT, instructor at Université de Montréal, and an ambitious man. He wanted to make his mark on the world so it wasn't difficult for Devlin to make Baird see things her way.

The team huddled together in a makeshift lean-to with their equipment gathered around them, all of which was devoted to making the tunnel work, not recording the test for posterity or future studies. In an effort to reduce noise and noxious fumes, the gas-powered generator stood as far behind them as the cables allowed. Alison Brenner switched places with Baird and took over behind the control panel, immediately running through the preparatory frequency sequences. Baird spoke both French and English indiscriminately to his people which were divided equally down the language line. They were all very busy, very excited. They were a hard working crew, and young, and they would indeed make history. Just not in the way they intended.

#

Station Master Bet stood at an enormous, transparent table that measured forty feet by forty feet. It sloped up and away from him and almost all of it was covered in a monochromatic hologram of an imagined city. Far from static, though, the emerald-hued city was very much alive with pedestrians crawling like ants from place to place and tiny vehicles of all shapes and sizes surging through the major and minor arteries of the urban circulatory system. There were trains and monorails and even an underground subway that appeared beneath the table in a separate, identifying shade of blue.

Bet tapped the colorful keyboard interface integrated into the table's surface and as he did so, huge blocks of the virtual city sunk to ground level and rose again in a modified configuration. Sometimes a single building had changed, sometimes an entire neighborhood. He then read the results of his manipulations in various windows that floated in the air on either side of him. This was followed by new instructions and new results. Orwell watched the buildings fall and rise in Bet's never ending effort to build the perfect city.

"Master, I'm curious as to why we never discuss the Tapestry."

Bet continued to tap on the table with long fingers on hands that resembled snow crabs dancing on the ocean floor.

"By discuss you mean what, Orwell? Is there something on your mind for which you need clarification?"

"Not at all, Master Bet," Orwell replied quickly after deciding that he'd brought the subject up at the wrong time. "I'm sorry if I disturbed you."

An office tower sunk into the table and rose again as a hospital. Bet looked over the math and typed again.

"Let me ask you a question," said Bet. "If Earth is chosen to represent their small portion of the Tapestry, what might their contribution be to the overall?"

"I couldn't say, Master. It's beyond the scope of my---."

"Come, come, Orwell, there's no need to be so formal. You know why the Station Masters have been tasked to do what we do."

"The Station Masters have been tasked to strengthen the cosmic bond by pruning the various realities in each sector to a single, healthy, and productive plane of existence. In this way you will abate the chaos that accompanied the birth of the universe."

"And how do we decide which realities will remain in the end?"

"The reality that shows the greatest potential for peace and wisdom and harmonic evolution. Like other sectors before them, their potential will be measured and weighed against their counterparts. New inhabitants will be introduced as needed and likewise removed to afford them the best possible chance to reach their full potential. We will, however, be mindful of their evolutionary path and do our best not to interfere."

"Yes, we will. Very good. I'm sure by now you've deduced why I programmed you the way that I did. Outside influence on a reality would dislodge them from their evolutionary path and disqualify them from contention. Tell me, Orwell, do you think humanity has the greatest potential for peace, wisdom, and harmonic evolution?"

Orwell didn't answer right away, and for a living computer, that spoke volumes.

#

Station 12: The Lantern Society

Three hours before the Great Disaster, Anderson came to the conclusion that he would have to forgive himself if he hoped to get any sleep. He sat on the edge of the convertible sofa and decided he would have to stop wallowing in his misery and take back the life he'd given away. Sarah was gone. It could have just as easily been him caught in the assassin's laser sight that stormy morning. There was nothing left to do except to do good in her memory. With this revelation came the reflective embarrassment of having mewled like a simpering child to Henderson on the state of his life.

He stood up with a manic burst of energy, suddenly driven to help, driven to work toward a solution to the world's problems. But he was stuck, a prisoner, and he'd never again escape as easily as he had done. Verity kept their plans for him to themselves, but he doubted they would forgive him his sins and allow him to re-up with the good guys. He needed help to jump start his story and once again, only one name came to him. Maybe if he spoke with Rachel one more time, convince her, she might forgo his failures and assist him in his personal reclamation.

He ran to the door of the suite like George Bailey starting his second chance at life and stuck his head out into the hall. The guard assigned to watch him stood up and placed a hand on his belt. Anderson couldn't see what the man had at the ready, but it didn't matter. He asked the guard if he'd check to see if Henderson was still on site and if so, could he find out if she'd be willing to pay him another visit? Then he thanked the man and popped back into the suite.

At the small bar, Charlie poured himself a cognac and held up the glass, staring into the amber liquid as he entertained his last self-indulgent thoughts of Sarah Bismarck. Acknowledging his love for her was easy compared to expressing his remorse for his part in her death. He promised himself he would find closure for the both of them once the crisis had been resolved.

#

At eleven o'clock the local news came on and like most nights Josef Bismarck climbed out of his easy chair and stretched his back while his wife, Carlotta, stayed put. She enjoyed the extra hour alone at night to gather her thoughts and Joe had to have his six hours of daily rest. With her knitting in her lap, she looked up and smiled at her husband as he leaned over to kiss her on the cheek. Like most nights, as he made his way to the hall, he mumbled something to his wife about not staying up too late. Carlotta knew this night wasn't like most nights, however, and it only gave her more to think about.

Bismarck's custom was to head down the hall to perform his evening toilette before bed. Instead, Carlotta watched him step into the first room off the hall. She looked down at the scarf-to-be and listened to her husband's baritone voice, though she couldn't make out the words. If there was a response, Carlotta couldn't hear that either. She looked up and saw Joe's shadow cast back toward the doorway by the little lamp on the bed table. The light went out and Joe stepped back into the hall, closing the door behind him.

#

Dodge finished up in the bathroom and decided to check in on his girls before going to bed. Mary was all tucked up in her American Doll comforter with only her angelic face exposed. Little Katherine was just the opposite, having kicked off her Dora the Explorer bedding to sprawl across the bed in a sweaty heap. He was happy to see them safe and sound, but it wasn't the here and now that troubled him, rather it was the future, their future. He walked solemnly into his bedroom and found his wife, Janine, already tucked in and reading a novel. She threw him a smile and he tried to return it but with little success.

"Bad day at work?" she asked.

She really had no idea what it was her husband did for a living. Dodge had made a conscious decision to keep Verity's secret world away from her and the kids, and though it was easy enough not to talk about it, it was another thing to keep it off his face.

"It's nothing," he said. "There's always one crisis or another in that place. I shouldn't think about it before going to sleep, right?"

"That's right. There's always tomorrow."

"That's right." He opened up his magazine but stared right through it. "I'll think about it tomorrow."

#

"Tell me something, Orwell," Bet said as he constructed a new above-ground transportation system, "based on your affinity for humanity-

Station 12: The Lantern Society

---."

"Master Bet, I would never presume---."

"I think it's safe to say that if the humans aren't integrated into the Tapestry, you will be sorely disappointed."

Orwell didn't look at Bet. "I cannot deny that. But still, we do what's best for the universe. Sometimes sacrifices must be made."

Bet was amused. "Your truths are painted in all manner of colorful half-truths, exaggerations, and flatteries of late. You behave more like a human every day. What do you think the chances are that humanity will move on?"

Orwell looked up from the holographic city, suspicious of Bet's inquiries. Was this a trap of some kind?

"I think it's too soon for such a question," Orwell replied. "And I would not presume to stray into realms reserved for the Station Masters."

"You have dragged me into your obsession, Orwell. And you've made such an emotional investment in these beings; you must have an opinion one way or the other."

"I believe humanity's imagination is a wondrous gift," Orwell said, "and distinguishes them from the other realities. I would hate to lose that."

"Humanity does not have a monopoly on imagination. In fact I would say that as a species they utilize their so-called gift quite poorly, relegating it almost exclusively to a minority of the population."

"You are, of course, referring to their artists. And while your statement may appear accurate on the surface, it's only a partial truth. Everything humans do relies on some aspect of their imagination. To what extent they're able to do this depends upon a number of factors including but not limited to how that imagination was cultivated in the early stages of their development, their position within society and their responsibilities therein, and the condition of their overall wellbeing. Their resultant imagination works in conjunction with many other aspects of their neurological make-up and/or physical well-being. It is not as efficient as other species, but it is quite powerful, nevertheless."

"Not as efficient is a gross understatement, my dear computer. Humanity lacks cohesion of any kind. Their imagination runs renegade while their logic places them squarely in a quagmire. What motivates them to progress is short-sighted and puerile. They take no control over their destiny because they cannot imagine a better future."

"I beg to differ, Station Master. They can imagine a better future. It's the bridge that will take them there that they cannot see."

\#

The clock struck midnight, the world continued to turn, and the stories played out with no awareness of their imminent and premature conclusions. If the citizens of Earth knew they only had two hours left to live, how might they react? Panic was certainly likely, but the window to do so was short and most people would come to that realization very quickly. Couples and families would reach out to each other, no doubt. The communication highways would be jammed. How might the world's problems be perceived in those two hours? Would large issues appear small and insignificant by comparison? Would there be global regret?

\#

By midnight Askew was home in his robe and slippers. His pipe sat cold in its stand and he tried not to look directly at it as he shuffled past. He didn't like to partake so late at night, but it was not the easiest time to resist the siren song of a vice. Chewing the end of a pipe stem had gotten him through many a crisis in the past. Sleep was paramount, however, and as long as he maintained a safe distance from temptation, he believed he could refrain.

Testing of the Oculacrum had just commenced. It was the first exercise of its kind he had ever missed and that bothered him. He was disturbed by the way a lot of things had been playing out lately.

Askew thought of Anderson, curious as to what Longworth and Bellows were going to do now that they had no further need of him. Would they hold him permanently without explanation or kick him loose? Either way, there was little doubt a modified version of the inoculation would be administered. And it also remained to be seen what would become of Ed Donovan now that they'd gotten him back a year after his adventure through the Central Lab.

Askew entered his bedroom, wondering if he would actually sleep with these thoughts and more running through his head.

\#

Extet sat on a u-shaped bench in one of the receiving areas on Station 4 only a few yards from where the Current Guard had deposited him. Upon his return to the System he had regained his native form and sat naked, looking out at the goings on in nearby space with absolutely no motivation to do anything else. A recorded greeting welcomed him to the station on behalf of Station Master Dek, while video played on a large tablette, espousing all that was good about the station's contribution to the System. Ordinarily, Extet would have performed his general workout routine, just to get his blood flowing and reacquaint himself with his superior body, but with all that he had recently uncovered, he no longer saw the point.

He didn't know the complete backstory of the Station Masters, not by a long shot, but he knew they'd been hard at work for thousands of years observing the many realities that made up the cosmos in a grand plan for balance and to secure the universe's future. To think it was all going to come to a crashing end thanks to the meddling of an amusing but ignorant species such as humanity was inconceivable. Extet had spent very little of his life feeling depressed, almost had no concept of the emotion, but facing the end of all things, it was difficult to feel any other way. He knew he should report back to Station Master Bet with his findings, but he simply could not find the strength.

Then a thought came to him and he rose from his chair and started to dress. Maybe the Station Masters could stop the accident from happening. They had the power to do anything, even if that meant erasing the Ert's entire reality before the catastrophe took place. It was a small price to pay to save the cosmos.

His inherent optimism returned and he picked up speed as he made for the nearest transport station. He reported to the bot on duty that he was heading to Station 6 then boarded the waiting glass car, moving off in a tinkling of cog wheels on crystalline track. Extet wondered if the System could survive such a disaster as described by Verity Corp. After all, the System wasn't a derivation of nature. Might it avoid the chain reaction?

#

At two a.m. Eastern Standard Time, the Great Disaster was born to a world that was blissfully unaware. Earth's stories were coming to an untimely end, cut off in mid-sentence, and unless the transition from existence to non-existence was a painful one, no one would ever know. A handful of Verity Corp people knew the whys of it, but little good that would do them in the face of when.

In Henderson's mind, Askew's theory of the end became a reality when she saw the Sounding Ring standing in the snow globe through the Oculacrum window. Baylor and the rest saw it, too, and recognized it for what it was without recognizing the possible repercussions. Baylor recalled a very brief and cryptic conversation he'd had with Henderson earlier and he suspected from that exchange that she knew something, so he turned to her with an almost accusatory glare.

"What are we looking at here, Rachel?!"

Pruitt stepped up. "Did you know about this, Doc? What's a Sounding Ring doing out in the middle of the Canadian wilderness?"

Henderson opened her mouth to respond, but she had no words. She started to cry both in frustration and fear, turning Baylor's sudden burst of anger into outright concern for the woman he knew as a rock. For the second time her knees buckled, only this time her legs gave way and everyone within arm's reach rushed to help. Pruitt was the first to reach her and caught her up in his arms, and as he looked down at her. She grabbed his jacket collar and brought her face up to his.

"Hit the alarm, Pru," she said with quickened breath.

"What?"

"Just do it."

Pruitt got her to her feet then made his way to the main entrance of the pod and did as he was told, pulling up on a red handle by the door. A staccato alarm pierced the air and pod bay doors across the entire Neighborhood began to slide open, causing the late night science crews to poke their heads out in curiosity. Henderson brushed at her coat and composed herself then proceeded to the open bay door. She was sorry she'd allowed everyone to see her so vulnerable and turned back to face them, face her shame.

#

The professor had had a restless night despite his great fatigue. For the past few nights he'd found himself in a quasi-dream state trying to recall that section of his life after Boothe Academy and before his start at Verity Corp, but the memories simply weren't there. All he could see was a void as black as Null Space. Thankfully his focus on that void, like counting sheep, lulled him into slumber.

Not long after, his bedside telephone rang yanking him from that perfect blackness with a start. He picked up the receiver, his heart beating a mile a minute, knowing that no good news ever came in the middle of the night. It was Rachel Henderson calling to confirm their worst nightmare; the Tunnel had not only been constructed, it had also been activated. Oddly enough, after hearing the worst had come to pass, the panic he'd been living with since first realizing what they were facing began to subside and a surprising calm came over him.

#

Baird checked in with his small team as all the prep work on the Sounding Tunnel was completed. This was it, all or nothing. The exercise had to work or it was back to square one, though he had serious doubts any funding was earmarked for a do-over if they failed. Brenner donned noise dampening headphones to make sure she had unimpeded access to the tones as she made her final adjustments. Baird took a last look around. As the snow fell all around them, he set the countdown for ten minutes.

#

It was around the same time that Strivelli and Angela were wrapping up their tête-á-tête after having made great progress re-establishing the trust between them. They strolled up to the stoop of her building and held each other close, whispering affirmations and small promises, tentatively mapping out their immediate future. Strivelli kissed her goodnight and turned away, but she stopped him with a tug on his jacket sleeve. She asked him, and not for the first time that night, if he wanted to stay over. Of course he did, he said. But he was determined to take things slower this time around in order to firm up the flimsy foundation of their relationship. She kissed him once more, gently, before parting.

Strivelli started down the street and his phone trilled almost immediately, alerting him to an incoming text message from Rachel Henderson. It was short. He read it twice to make sure he'd gotten it right. It announced simply that the worst had come to pass. No timeframe was indicated and no orders were issued. Strivelli was stunned, unable to process the news, not sure he was reading the text correctly. He forced himself to take a breath and find his center. Was this really the end? Had Henderson actually taken the time to text a doomsday message, or was this some bad practical joke?

He slipped his phone back into his pocket with the numb acceptance of a condemned man accepting the hood, already divorcing himself from the world and his place in it. He now knew what the end of all things looked like. On the surface it looked like any other day. Inside, however, was a strange, black disconnect, and a contrary desire to remember everything good in the world. Most of all was the intense need to be with someone he loved when the end came, someone he could hold and with whom he could move on. He turned back and knocked on the glass door inside the foyer. Angela was still waiting by the elevator and when she turned and saw him standing there, she laughed and ran to him.

At nine minutes, Brenner was well into dialing into the required frequencies in her effort to synch up the green waves with the red wave template. The generators roared into the snowy night. The console tune-up was starting to build in volume, but was still barely perceptible over their gas-guzzling power source. Baird had one eye on his notes and the other on Brenner as she manipulated controls. So far everything was going as expected.

Dodge slept fitfully on his back and was easily awoken by the rattling vibrations on his bed table. He read the incoming text and felt all the air leave his body. His first thought was to look in on his girls one last time. He opted instead to replay his last goodnight kisses in his head as he rolled over and put his arm around his wife.

Tomlinson had been hurt by Foster's cavalier remark concerning her pursuit of another life. She swapped the diner for a neighborhood bar where she imbibed and reflected on what he'd said. It wasn't his doubts that offended her. She had plenty of her own. Did he have to be so insensitive? She let her anger and disappointment motivate the hand that brought the shot glass to her lips. But no amount of alcohol could disguise the true source of her angst. What really bothered her was her inability to accept the truth. She was driven to get her life back, the life that Gorokhovich had described, but it was true, she had no understanding of what that meant, no idea how she would actually, physically, possess it. She always figured she'd cross that bridge when she came to it. Unexpectedly, with everything that had happened lately, that bridge was looming in the near distance.

When the bartender shouted last call, she took her leave and started for home. As she passed a shop window, a bright, yellow cocktail dress caught her eye. The store mannequin had no head, so Tomlinson used her reflection to fill in the void, imagining she was hosting a dinner party for her many friends and neighbors. Even in her inebriated state she felt embarrassment over finding herself in such a clichéd moment. She imagined Foster coming up behind her shaking his head and she launched into a fit of laughter. She might have laughed forever if her phone hadn't rung. She read the incoming text then replaced the device absently as she watched her reflection disappear in the glare of passing headlights.

Longworth, Bellows, and two guards burst into Donovan's room in the Security section of Verity Corp. The guards took positions on either side of Donovan as he sat up groggily in his bunk. Bellows plugged a phone into the wall and placed it on the table Longworth set next to the cot. They brought the mercenary up to speed on the current state of the crisis, emphasizing the point of imminent global catastrophe, and told him that he had to reach out to his contact if there was even the remotest possibility she could do something to prevent it.

#

Extet's transport arrived in one of the Welcome bays of Station 6. Though still determined to enlist the aid of the Station Masters in preventing total annihilation, his optimism had waned, given over to a nagging suspicion that he was hoping for too much, bestowing upon the Station Masters perhaps more power than they possessed. There was no reason to believe that any one place would be immune to a chain reaction of the magnitude described in Askew's files, even a construct as significant as the System.

"Hello, Extet," said Orwell from a number of screens at once.

Extet didn't know where to look until Orwell's wheeled monitor rolled in.

"We didn't expect you back so soon," he said as he spread out his small, mechanical arms.

"Take me to the Station Master Bet, if you would, please. I have the answers he seeks."

"Right to business," Orwell said in a proper British accent. "Good for you. Unfortunately, Extet, the Station Master is very busy at the moment. But you may report to me and I will record your every word."

"We have no moments to lose, Computerman. The Ert is going to destroy it all."

"Is that your entire report? You know Station Master Bet does not have much of a sense of humor."

"No joke, Mr. O. I wish that it were otherwise."

Orwell generally found the blocky Extet to be delightfully gregarious, but not prone to jokes, practical or otherwise. Perhaps their agent had stumbled onto something of significance. He crossed his telescopic arms.

"Then let us begin."

#

Five minutes before the Great Disaster, Baird slipped his key into the box that housed the master control switch while Brenner doggedly adjusted the harmonics. He imagined great things coming out of all this. Great things. It will have been worth all the lying and sneaking around, he thought. *And everyone will know my work.*

Donovan hit the speakerphone option and proceeded to dial a number he'd had memorized since he first began working for the Lantern Society. The phone rang in the black Jaguar as Devlin made her way home, and although she didn't recognize the number, she accepted the call with a touch of a button on her steering wheel. She was surprised and disappointed to hear Donovan's voice, a clear indication that Peters had been unable to complete his assignment. She considered hanging up, but at the very least she needed confirmation that Anderson would no longer be a problem. Before she had a chance to ask about him, though, Donovan informed her that he was a guest of Verity Corp and that he was on speakerphone. She made no response and for a moment the men in the room wondered if she had hung up. Everyone except Donovan who knew she would offer no more clues as to her identity. He told Longworth and Bellows to state their case and make it snappy before she hung up the phone. They did so, providing her with the quickest and simplest version of the potential calamity. When they finished, there was another moment of silence and then an audible click. The call was over. Donovan lay back in his bunk and turned to face the wall.

"See you in the morning, boys," he said. "Or not."

By the time the countdown reached four minutes, Askew was a passenger in a Lincoln Town Car bound for the Verity Corp tower. The calm that had overtaken him earlier was gone and he was feeling more anxious than ever. He reached out to Henderson for a status report on the Sounding Tunnel signal and asked if she could tell what phase of the test they were in. She said there was no real way of knowing because she had no basis on which to judge the skill of the tuner. Nor was there a way to determine the length of the countdown, or if there was one. Askew had the utmost respect for Henderson and her capabilities, but even her prodigious talent was no match for his. He needed to get to his lab in order to analyze the energy signature and in that way determine a clearer timeline. He thanked Rachel then asked her to transfer him to Bellows.

At three minutes, Extet was well into his report of the crisis and Orwell continued to listen attentively. Even as he did so, aspects of him were breaking away from the conversation in pursuit of confirmation of Extet's discoveries. He nodded as the facts were relayed, showing just the right amount of concern while maintaining a calm outward appearance. At the same time, he raised his level of engagement with Station Master Bet, making absolutely sure he remained distracted.

Extet expressed sadness at the mere possibility of never seeing his family again and Orwell told him not to overstate the situation, the Station Masters would take every step to avoid the catastrophe. Much to Extet's relief, Orwell promised him a speedy delivery home where he would soon be reunited with his family. He thanked Orwell and walked closer to the CG track to await transport.

"There is one thing I don't understand for certain," Extet said, just making conversation.

"And what is that, my stocky friend?"

"The Outsource Protocol."

Orwell's virtual eye twitched involuntarily and the British accent disappeared. "What of it?"

"If Verity Corp needed colored stones from another reality to make their Sounding Tunnel work, how did they get the stones from that reality in the first place?"

"Oh, Extet," Orwell said sadly, "I wish you hadn't asked me that."

Blue lightning erupted from the track contact and the Current Guard swallowed Extet whole. Somehow, his still solid form resisted the transformation process as an Extet-shaped bolt of blue fire struggled against the current to make its way toward Orwell's monitor. Orwell, for his part, rolled slowly backward to avoid the flickering fingers of light that reached out for him. A head pushed forward, its eyeless black sockets somehow conveying outrage. This was quickly followed by the opening of a gaping maw where the mouth should have been.

"What have you done?!" screamed the composite creature in a voice of crackling rage.

Finally, Extet gave up and his electric ward rose up in anger with his charge before disappearing into the track.

Two minutes before the Great Disaster, Devlin found herself at the side of the road. The call from Verity Corp was nagging at her, especially on the heels of Anderson's plea at Eisenberg's. What did they have to gain by lying to her? Unless they were close to figuring out how to shut her down remotely? Could she afford to reschedule the test, she wondered? After all, her primary objective had already been achieved.

Jacque Baird turned the key to open the tiny door to the master control switch. He had no idea that when he pushed it, he would be responsible for eradicating all of reality.

In the final minute, Askew still hadn't reached the office. He had instructed Bellows to meet him in the Sanctuary for the purposes of initiating Infinite City. Bellows questioned the directive, but Askew was insistent, explaining that their only hope was that their contingency plan might create a pocket universe all its own, outside the reach of the catastrophe. Askew concluded his explanation as he pulled up in front of the tower.

Devlin dialed the number for team Canada.

10...9...8...

Orwell wasn't feeling well as he made his way through Verity's computer network. He was programmed not to interfere with other cultures, but over time he had gained the ability to interact without interfering. It was a loophole he took advantage of in order to communicate with certain beings, certain people, who could help him in the implementation of his grand plan. But that loophole was narrow and

Station 12: The Lantern Society

getting narrower and the stress of his interaction was beginning to overwhelm him.

7...6...5...

Orwell was able to confirm nearly everything in Extet's report and saw the truth of the potential disaster. It also shined a light on where he went wrong. The Outsource Protocol: a rule he came up with to keep humanity ignorant of the other realities. That information would stay with a handful of people he could control. When Orwell discovered in his conversations with Askew that domestic gems wouldn't have the cellular strength to hold up in the Sounding Rings, he arranged for delivery of sturdier stones from another reality. It was a bold move, and dangerous, and now it was apparently their undoing.

Devlin put her phone on speaker and bit at the edge of her fingernail in growing consternation as the ringtone chimed without interruption.

4...3...

Orwell analyzed the datatel from the Oculacrum test concerning the signal received from Canada and quickly located a satellite with a perfect view of the makeshift Sounding Tunnel. All he had to do was find a way to link with the computer system down there and shut it down. Askew ducked behind the lobby waterfall to catch the elevator down to the Central Lab. Baird and company were too caught up in what they were doing to hear the radio phone or notice the flashing red light behind them indicating an incoming call.

2...

Bellows stood in the Sanctuary and stared at the Black Phone but didn't move. Devlin's call continued to ring into the Canadian night. Something was wrong. Orwell felt the synapses of his thought slowing, and there was pain. A terrible, terrible pain.

1...

Jacque Baird pressed the master control button and noticed something stran

Chapter Eighteen: The New Reality

"An explosion of immense magnitude occurred in northeastern Canada approximately three hours ago," said a neatly coifed anchor as he broke into regularly scheduled programming. "Details are still sketchy at this point, and the few pictures we've seen of the impact zone provide no evidence of anything having taken place. It is believed the epicenter of the non-event is approximately three hundred miles north of Quebec City. Scientists have speculated that the explosion may have been nuclear in nature, but say without direct evidence it's too soon to say with any certainty. It is also unclear whether the explosion, if one actually took place, was due to an attack, an accident, or perhaps a test by the Canadian government, although the Prime Minister has denied any knowledge of such a test taking place."

Askew and Henderson sat in Max Heberling's fortieth floor office and watched the story unfold on Max's giant wall monitor. As the news broke, Rachel and her mentor held hands with bated breath. They were relieved that the worst case scenario hadn't played out as predicted, but unable to believe there weren't still pending repercussions. For himself, Askew had never been happier to have been proven wrong, and he took comfort knowing that the event transpired in an unpopulated part of the world. If any casualties could be blamed on the incident, they were probably few in number, more than likely affecting only those individuals at ground zero. The closest outpost of civilization was a small Cree community to the west, and though they were still suffering from a power outage, no one was the worse for wear. Good news aside, Askew figured it might be a while before the truth of the incident made itself apparent.

#

"There was evidence of seismic activity," the anchor went on to say, "as tremors with an average magnitude of 3.5 on the Richter scale emanated from ground zero. In addition, an electromagnetic pulse, or EMP, extended outward in all directions and, amazingly, beyond the U.S.-

Canadian border. It was this EMP that led experts to surmise a nuclear device may have been involved, though that is yet to be confirmed. Scattered power outages have been reported in various urban locations including Quebec City which so far has reported all manner of problems including stalled cars on the road. Several accidents have also been reported as surprised drivers lost control of their vehicles as engines cut out, or as dashboard displays lost power."

Lenore Devlin watched the news in her new office deep inside Verity Corp's Central Lab. She was alarmed at what her handiwork had wrought. It turned out her employers' concerns had been justified after all, if not somewhat overstated. She was glad for the latter. Mass destruction hadn't figured into her master plan.

The test had obviously failed in spectacular fashion, but the world continued on its orbit and humanity went about its various concerns. It seemed the accident had wiped out any evidence of its having taken place and for that Devlin felt very fortunate. She'd already erased the trail that connected New York to Quebec, so from her perspective, she was in the best place she could be for the next phase of her plan.

#

"The Canadian government is working closely with United States authorities in search of answers. President Bush rose early this morning to speak with Prime Minister Chretien and has offered support in the form of a combined task force that will head out from Jean-Lesage International Airport and perform several air reconnaissance missions before attempting to approach the blast zone on land. They will report on the damage, should they find any, and take radiation readings from the air to ascertain the feasibility of immediate search and rescue for anyone who might have gotten caught within the blast radius, should one actually exist. We have received reports from some of the locals that there are no known roads leading to the area in question. We'll have more news for you on this dramatic story as it comes our way."

"We need to get up there," said Heberling.

"Yes, we do," agreed Askew, "but not for the reasons you think. Based on what we're seeing here, I don't think we'll find any physical evidence or even trace evidence of the event."

"The Tunnel?" asked Henderson. "What happened to the Tunnel?

I saw it. I know I saw it."

"That's not in doubt, Rachel," said Askew, "but clearly it's not there now."

"How do you explain that?" asked Henderson.

"Upon reconsideration of what little is known, I believe I was correct after all. Woe to us. The displacement did take place. That much is apparent. That's why we're not seeing anything up there, including whoever was running the exercise, poor devils. The displacement created a miniature black hole of sorts. Whoever was on site would have been sucked into the implosion. But something is now blocking the exit point, preventing the implosion from completing, and that something is what staved off the chain reaction we feared. This *ex*-plosion the news is reporting on was simply the byproduct of the two realities being forced to merge."

"So what's blocking the exit point?" asked Heberling. "There's nothing up there."

"Max, please, we're talking about something mathematical in nature. Physics! Some random bit of chaotic equation that has thrown the balance of the universe slightly askew, because Lord knows there's nothing in the natural order of things that allows for the merging of two completely different realities."

Henderson frowned. "Nature always finds a way," she said as she considered the ramifications.

"Nature does."

"Which means," added Heberling, "we could be living on borrowed time?"

Their thoughts were one and the same as they looked to each other without speaking; the crisis was not yet over. There was still plenty of work to be done and Henderson was already hoping she would be chosen for the mission to Canada.

"What happens now?" she wondered aloud.

Max stood up. "Now everyone goes home for some much needed rest."

Askew followed suit and stretched. "I agree. We still have to recover that stolen data. We can't risk having this happen all over again."

"Sounds like a job for our new partners."

"Speaking of which, where is Hugo?" asked Askew. "And Lionel?"

Henderson rose and gathered her things, checking her pockets and making sure she was leaving nothing behind. The folded piece of paper remained in her lab coat pocket and still she said nothing.

"They're down in the lab welcoming Global Armour's newest chief."

"Lenore Devlin isn't it?" the professor asked. "She missed the summit so we haven't met. Has anyone had the pleasure?"

Heberling had, but only briefly.

#

Jascowitz knocked on the doorframe of Devlin's office and offered up a sheepish grin. The two hadn't spoken since Gorokhovich had reacquired the mantle of Hugo Jascowitz, and now that things had calmed down somewhat, he was fully prepared to explain himself. But before he could launch into the story of Global Armour's secret origins, she pointed to the television.

"Have you heard about this business in Canada? It's crazy."

He nodded and stepped in. The space was two offices made into one. Half of the room was dedicated to a standard office configuration while the other half acted as a mini command center with plenty of digital hardware, including a duplication of Verity's CCTV security system.

"It is crazy," he said, "and probably your number one priority."

"How does this concern us?" she asked, feigning ignorance.

"If you could have made it to the summit you'd know."

She looked back at the screen in a convincing imitation of disbelief. "This is the result of Verity's data theft?"

"It is. And with that, I put Global Armour into your capable hands."

"Very funny."

"I kid you not. It's your time now. I may have come up with GA's mission, but it was you who got the work done. It's time I rejoined my fellow scientists. You'll be working very closely with Lionel Bellows from now on. He'll show you every nut and bolt of Verity's infrastructure and then some. Ah! Speak of the devil."

Bellows had walked into the office without knocking.

"Nice digs," he said. "Is this how they're treating the new hires now?"

Devlin stood up and shook hands. "I'm afraid it's going to speak to the scope of my workload before long."

They shared a polite chuckle and Jascowitz followed up with introductions.

"I'm afraid there's something that needs our immediate attention, Ms. Devlin," Bellows said.

"Len, please. I'm all ears."

"And that is my cue to remove myself." Jascowitz took Devlin's hand and gave it a gentle pat. "I couldn't have asked for a better partner. Good luck, Len."

"Thank you, Anton, or whatever your name is. We'll have lunch one day soon and you can tell me all about how Hugo became Anton and back again."

"It's a date."

Bellows helped himself to a chair as Hugo made his way out. Devlin watched him, acclimating herself to the idea that she and Lionel were going to be in each other's business for the foreseeable future. She knew she had to play nice if she wanted things to continue going her way. After all, Lionel Bellows was the man with all the answers. She watched him, and despite knowing very little about him, began conditioning herself to see him as a friend and confidante, and not as the enemy she always regarded him.

"Here's what we're dealing with," Lionel began. "There are a couple of loose ends to our recent misadventure and Security Chief Longworth and I aren't sure how to proceed. There's no precedent. Specifically, we have two people in our custody who know too much about the Verity underground and recent events to simply cut loose. There's been some talk about a modified version of the inoculation, but in my opinion that's a slippery slope."

Devlin shuffled through the piles of paper that had been left on her desk for review. Earlier she had spotted the inoculation brief that explained Verity's process to keep their employees aligned in a single, perpetual reality; a process she was scheduled for later that morning; a process she had undergone as Lenore Deeds when she was much younger.

"Who are they?" she asked.

"One is Charlie Anderson. He was our top shelf portfolio manager and a key player in our marketing department before he decided that Verity

Corp were the bad guys. He's a personal friend of your just-retired boss and when Hugo went missing last year, Anderson blamed us."

"Was he wrong?"

"Wrong?"

"To blame Verity."

"I suppose Hugo's creation of Global Armour speaks to that."

"Anderson is the man who arranged to have the data stolen in the first place."

"Correct."

"Tell me about the other one."

"Ed Donovan, a mercenary hired by the now presumed defunct Lantern Society. We have no idea what's on his agenda, or if he even has one. If he does or doesn't, he's not saying. In both of these cases it seems ill-advised to let them go."

"Of course." Devlin thought a moment and almost immediately formulated a plan. "You have a facility in Las Vegas, do you not?"

"A hotel and casino, yes, and another research facility below ground."

"Let's ship Anderson to Vegas," she said. "Put him on a flight this afternoon. Put him to work. Put him on a righteous path. It may not be a permanent solution, but it'll buy us some time. Convince him it's in his best interests."

"He'll be thrilled actually. And Donovan?"

"I want to speak with him myself."

John Cannon entered the office.

"John! So good to see you. John, this is our new boss, Lionel Bellows. Lionel, this is my number two, John Cannon."

"A pleasure. Well, I see you have everything well in hand. It's a good plan, Len. I'll leave you to it. And I'll let Mr. Longworth know to expect a visit from you shortly. Let's talk again at the end of the day."

Devlin waited until Bellows was gone then stepped within inches of her assistant. She quietly relayed an order to which he nodded and immediately walked away to fulfill.

With a deep breath of satisfaction, she resumed her seat and took in her surroundings. Not wanting the pace of her transition into the job to distract her from savoring her moment of triumph, she pressed her fingers on the desk, and then her palms, sliding her hands along its surface to ensure that it was real. If her long range goal had been to infiltrate Verity Corp, she had succeeded beyond all reasonable expectations, securing one of the most important positions in the camp of her enemy. The Lantern Society had performed its function flawlessly by illuminating the truth as she saw it and her own righteous path to vengeance. Verity Corp had destroyed her family, and now it was her turn to destroy Verity Corp. She thought of her brother and imagined the day they would reunite. She had no idea how close she had already come.

#

Ed Donovan was escorted by two recently armed guards into a small conference room in the Admin Center and told to sit. He asked for a can of pop and one of the men told him he would have to wait.

"Can't leave me in the room with only one guard, is that it? You should cuff me if you think I'm that dangerous. I would."

When Lenore Devlin walked into the room, Donovan was truly caught off-guard and he burst out laughing as a result.

"Are you kidding me?!"

"Good morning, Mr. Donovan. I'm sorry for getting you up so early. My name is Lenore Devlin and I run Security for the Science Division here at Verity Corp." She nodded at the guards. "Gentlemen, I need you to wait outside, if you would."

"He asked for a can of soda."

"Then get him a can of soda."

The guards left and Devlin closed the door behind them.

"Wow," said Donovan. "How long---?"

"Fifteen minutes."

"My mind is blown. You are an amazing woman! Have you been planning this all along?"

"We have more important things to talk about, Mr. Donovan."

"A year ago I did a job for Global Armour, your employers, to plant cameras in this very facility. That mission tanked leaving me stuck in a very scary tunnel with no way out. But wait, it's not a dead end after all. And who's waiting for me at the exit, anxious to put me to work for the Lantern Society on the down-low? Did you know then that Global Armour and Verity Corp would become one and the same?"

"As it stands right now, Mr. Donovan, you're never going to see your Hawaiian hideaway again. The world's needs far outweigh your civil rights and Verity Corp is never going to let you go. But neither will they ever call you prisoner. They'll just keep discussing your disposition until you're all old men."

"Verity's own Josef K."

"But I can fix that. I'll make one last deal with you. Nothing outside your original contract. As we speak, Charles Anderson is being relocated to our Las Vegas facility. Fulfill that last bit of your contract and you can keep on heading west."

"You want me to go to Las Vegas and take out Charlie Anderson?"

"There's a bonus if you do. I can't risk what I have going here. He'll see me someday, or come upon a photograph or a press release. I can't take that chance."

"What if I decide---?"

"I'm the best liar on the planet, Ed, believe me. You can tell them anything you want, but they'll never take your word against mine. Never. You wouldn't believe who'd stand up for my character. But Anderson, he could leverage his relationship with Jascowitz to ill effect."

"And how do you know that once you cut me loose, I won't just take off?"

"You leave that to me. Besides, you strike me as a man of your word. One of the reasons I took you on in the first place."

"Amazing."

#

Tomlinson entered the Drone Room carrying the biggest cup of black coffee she could find, but it wasn't big enough to make up for her lack of sleep and mild hangover. She dragged her feet to the cart lot and signed out the first vehicle in line. Agent Royce entered shortly thereafter looking a little freaked out, like he had just stepped into a carnival funhouse, holding his arms out as if to steady himself. Recognizing the look and the feeling, Tomlinson laughed and waved him over, assuring him that he was in the right place. He took a seat next to her and she slapped his thigh like they were old friends. She hadn't seen him since Canal Street and she was astounded how much water had flowed beneath the bridge since then.

"Welcome to Justice League Headquarters, Royce."

"No shit."

"Ready for our first meeting under new management?"

Another cart appeared on the opposite side of the Drone Room and pulled up to the end of the line. Two guards stepped out of the vehicle and started to escort their passenger toward the cavern door, but Tomlinson recognized the man and jumped out to intercept them.

"Excuse me?! Ed Donovan?"

Donovan turned and grinned when he saw her. "Agent Tomlinson, as I live and breathe. This is starting to feel like a real reunion. You've obviously made some progress down here since last we met. Good for you. In some weird way that vindicates my earlier effort."

"Speaking of… What happened to you?"

"You mean after the mission went tits up? That's why I get my money up front, Tomlinson. Because you never know what kind of rinky-dink army you're signing up with. Global Armour underestimated Verity Corp and set us up to fail."

"I don't know. Devlin seemed very happy with the results."

Donovan frowned, feeling like he'd been played, and started to reconsider his options.

How did she know about that extraction point? And how did she know I'd be stuck down there?

"We thought you all had disappeared."

"I think Carter decided she was better suited for a life outside of espionage. You'll have to ask your new Verity friends about Ware. All I know is part of him went one way and the other part didn't."

"How did you get out of the tunnel?"

Donovan thought about ratting Devlin out, just to be done with it, but he was more than a little anxious to get back to his beach house and put all the insanity behind him. Stone-faced, he drank from his can of root beer and remained silent on the particulars.

"Fine. So what happens now?" Tomlinson asked. "What are they going to do with you?"

"Do with me? I'm going to Vegas, Baby!"

#

Henderson popped her head into the prison suite and called out for Anderson. She'd noticed the absence of a guard at the door, but didn't assume that meant Anderson was gone. As she walked through the suite she realized, however, that such was the case, and so she left to find Askew instead.

"You've spent a lot of time up here today," she said, referring to his fortieth floor office.

"It's not like me, I know," said Askew as he slipped his thumb and forefinger under his glasses to rub his tired eyes. "Believe me, I look forward to getting back to the lab and working on our abduction problem. It seems rather tame now in comparison to what we've just been through. Are you heading home?"

"Yes, it's time for some real sleep. You?"

"No, I want to get some things in order, and I don't want to screw up my sleep cycle any more than I already have. Thank you, Rachel, for all your hard work."

Henderson nodded. "Have you seen where Charlie's gone off to?"

"I'm sorry, Rachel," Askew said sadly. He hated to disappoint his protégé. "They took him."

"Took him?" She screwed up her face, attempting to comprehend what it was he was saying. "Who took him? Took him where?"

"Jacen's people are taking him to our Las Vegas facility."

"Why?"

"They'll give him a job, I expect, keep him out of trouble. We'll inoculate him and eventually he'll just become another member of the Verity family."

"I wish I'd had the chance to say goodbye," Henderson said wistfully.

"I understand. Goodbye, Rachel."

Rachel beamed at his odd attempt to make her feel better. It reminded her of their relationship prior to her promotion.

"Goodbye, Prof."

She stepped away, almost into the arms of Jascowitz who was heading in.

"Rachel, we haven't had a chance to talk. I wanted to tell you how sorry I am that I had to lie to you. I had to be someone else for a while. It was just easier."

"I'm just glad that you're all right, Hugo. It's nice to have you back."

"No hard feelings then?"

She patted his face almost comically.

"I don't have the God damned energy."

Henderson continued on her way.

"Quite a ride, Prof." Jascowitz stepped in and gripped the back of one of the guest chairs. "Quite an adventure."

"Unfortunately, it's not over until we reacquire that data and determine it hasn't gone anywhere else."

"Believe me when I tell you, Lenore Devlin will put an end to it. She's extremely competent."

"Was she aware of your dual personality?"

"No, I kept that secret to myself."

"And how did you come to find this extremely competent person?"

"Prof, did you send Lionel to the Sanctuary?"

"I did," Askew said, thrown by the change in subject, but more by the subject itself.

"To initiate Infinite City?"

"How did you---?"

"Lionel told me. He had…concerns."

Askew suddenly felt diminished as he looked up at the once and future Truth Squad agent.

"I thought it might be our last chance. Why are you asking, Hugo?"

"As my last act as Global Armour's founder, I would strongly suggest to you gating the ability to trigger the contingency plan."

"What do you suggest?"

"Three of you run this company. Make sure three of you make the decision. Maybe you each require a key, I don't know. It could be anything as long as it prevents only one of you from making such a decision for the rest of the world."

"I didn't think there was time."

"It makes no difference. You have no idea what you might've done. For all you know Infinite City, while saving Verity, might have ended it for everyone else. That responsibility shouldn't fall to one person. Not for their sakes or yours."

There was something very different about Hugo since he reappeared from the System. Jascowitz was now the leading expert on all things pertaining to the System and with it came an air of authority that made the science chief a bit uncomfortable.

"I'll speak with Lionel and Max. Thank you for your input, Hugo. Maybe you'll join us?"

"I will always voice my opinions, Prof, you know that better than anyone. But I belong in the Science Division. I'll leave security to Security, and the rest of you to run the show. Bring Devlin in. It's her job now."

Jascowitz released the chair and straightened out his sweater.

"I've always enjoyed working with you, Daniel."

He stepped out into the hall and looked back at the thickly bespectacled man.

"Yours is a magnificent mind. I hope... I look forward to working with you again. Goodbye."

Askew, puzzled, stared after Jascowitz through the transparent walls of his office.

#

Where Jacque Baird's master control console once stood floated a small section of nothing. This shard of non-existence was irregularly shaped, about a meter in length, and it hovered roughly six inches above the ground. Most times it appeared transparent. That is, it looked as if nothing was there, and indeed nothing was. Other times, from certain angles, it looked like a tear in the fabric of reality, revealing a chasm of infinite depth. It was possessed of an aura that acted as a lure to passersby, an innocuous force of energy that might lead a hiker to choose one path over another. Fortunately, there were no such visitors. Not yet. For if they attempted to approach that unaccounted for lack of object, they would soon find themselves dragged against their wills into a portion of the universe known only to Jacque Baird and his missing comrades.

No one described the events of that early morning as the Great Disaster. Not yet. That wouldn't happen until the citizens of a future time connected a newly discovered threat to the world to that mysterious non-event in the Canadian wilderness. This perilous time in future history wouldn't happen until long after the search for the missing Daniel Askew and the events surrounding the Machine had concluded. And so named, the Great Disaster would bring about the last resort named Infinite City which for their sins would beget the Last War.

Chapter Nineteen: The Professor Recalled

As five o'clock rolled around, Askew felt the full force of his fatigue. There had been several meetings on the fortieth floor, primarily post mortems on the Lantern Society debacle and the near disaster that resulted from their theft of the Sounding Tunnel data. By lunchtime, the newly positioned science security chief, Lenore Devlin, had announced that she had successfully tracked down Brian Haberman and the equipment he'd recently liberated from Mather College. She proudly displayed the hard drive that housed the stolen data and declared unequivocally that it and a set of mini DVDs were the sole repositories for the data. She said that according to Haberman, team Canada accessed what they needed over a read-only network and the material could not be copied. Everyone was greatly relieved to hear it, no one more than Askew. When they asked her what other information Haberman was able to provide, her view switched from seeing him as a valuable informant to a useless cog. People were too caught up in their victory to make anything out of it.

Askew missed his lab terribly. He missed the windowless workplace where he could focus unhindered by the distractions of the outside world. He missed the lab's familiarity and the intimacy of its walls. He even missed the secrets contained within those walls. He missed the social rhythm among his fellow scientists, working together for a common cause. He missed the feeling of control, knowing he was leading his team to a solution to their abduction problem. The chaos in the world was an ongoing obstacle, but it was for the survival of that world that he did what he did. Tonight Askew would sleep, and tomorrow he would return to the lab where he belonged.

The last meeting of the day concluded at 4:30. It was a small gathering of the trinity and Devlin as well as Hugo Jascowitz. The loosely themed subject matter was the future; casual talk about Verity's next steps concerning Canada and how they would eventually have to explain why a financial institution known for bringing popular science products to market was sending a research team to the Canadian tundra to study nothing.

Along the same line of thinking, they introduced the idea of overhauling the Truth Squad and implementing new safeguards. Askew remained quiet for the most part, preoccupied with his intense desire to head back underground.

Meeting Devlin had been interesting, though, if not a little disconcerting. The whole idea of accepting Global Armour into the fold, and specifically into the confines of the Central Lab without being formally vetted actually seemed contradictory to Global Armour's own purpose. Devlin seemed very self-assured and already quite at home in her new surroundings, as if she'd been there for years. She appeared the consummate professional, but there was an air of smugness about her, Askew thought, as if she was always one step ahead of everyone.

As the meeting wrapped up, Bellows could see how tired Askew was and directed one of the admins to call for a car to take him home. Soon after, he was slouched in the back of a town car heading uptown. Groggy, he removed his glasses and looked out at the passing city with unfocused eyes. Tall buildings passed by in giant, blurry strides. Sleep threatened to overtake him just as it had when he was a child in the back of his family's old Buick. Each time his eyes closed, the flickering light across his eyelids recalled the sunlight through the leaves of the oaks, elms, and chestnuts that lined the streets of his neighborhood.

The car found the upper Westside and Askew told the driver to drop him off at 96th and Broadway. Too tired to prepare his own dinner, he stopped in McDonalds and purchased a burger and fries and a chocolate shake. The smell of fast food added to his sense of nostalgia, recalling many a night of brainstorming over burgers with Keith Baylor and Tony Aiello back in their salad days at Boothe Academy.

After a short walk up Broadway, Askew turned west toward his home on Riverside Drive. Grease stains appeared on his takeaway bag where the French fries made contact with the paper. The smell of his dinner was intoxicating and his stomach growled in anticipation. He turned the corner toward his building, but the green trees of Riverside Park lured him to dine on a bench down by the water.

Looking out over the Hudson River and the shoreline of New Jersey, Askew reflected on his friends and coworkers at Verity Corp in the aftermath of the near disaster. He had long ago given up on maintaining relationships outside of Verity's private circle of the inoculated. There were a few outsiders with whom he socialized, people like Nessa Huggins who held a special place in his heart. But the thought of them being rewritten out of his life was sometimes too much to bear and so he trained himself to keep his distance. That made the bond with his fellow inoculated all the more precious.

He considered the state of Tony Strivelli's burgeoning romance with Angela Rodriguez, aka Beatrice Lebrun, and hoped it would all work out. Strivelli had sacrificed much for Verity and the professor was happy to hear his friend had found a special someone in his life. It was unfortunate it turned out the way that it did. Askew decided then and there that if Strivelli hadn't already been officially transferred back to New York, he would see to it that it got done. It might be of little consolation, but it was all he could do for now.

The chocolate shake was thick and it took an effort to get it through the straw. Much to his delight, it tasted the same as he remembered it. The French fries were good, too, and hot with just the right amount of salt to complement the sweetness of the milkshake. Askew realized, as the breeze pushed up river from the bay, that if he wasn't careful he might fall asleep right there on the bench.

Rachel Henderson next came to mind. He was very proud of her and how well she and Ellen Cheever had worked together to determine Anderson was the source of the data theft. To accomplish so much in so little time, and with so little to go on, was no small feat. It showed a strong work ethic and commitment to the company. Askew had no doubt that Verity Corp would be in good hands if anything were ever to happen to him.

Then for the very first time, inexplicably, it occurred to him that he had never stopped to consider Rachel's personal life. Or if she even had one. Not once since they'd met had he ever asked her about her life outside of the company. They shared an almost familial bond, and he always assumed, perhaps wrongfully so, that she was as obsessed as he was when it came to working out a solution to the TDRR. Such obsession left no time for a personal life.

The thought embarrassed him, that he would impose his lack of connection to the world on a young and vibrant woman. For all he knew, the woman who left the black tower each night was a completely different Rachel Henderson; a Rachel Henderson unknown to him. It saddened him to think so. He hoped it wasn't too late to start again and reacquaint himself with his protégé on a more personal level.

Two inline skaters dashed past him followed by one of New York's many dog walkers. The latter was a young woman who looked too small for the animals in her care, but they all walked by rote to the dog park in complete harmony. Each of the dogs, from Chihuahua to German Shepard, sniffed at their surroundings. They all seemed to get along very well, their differences having no bearing on their shared purpose to get a little exercise and a lot of relief. Plastic bags at the ready, the woman seemed totally amenable to the pace set by her charges.

His thoughts next turned to Hugo Jascowitz, the poster child for what was dangerous about working for Verity Corp. *Such an adventure!* Askew thought almost enviously, though without malice. *No doubt as thrilling as it was frightening. To have experienced a completely different plane of existence! Magnificent!* Askew hoped Jascowitz was fully prepared to speak with him ad nauseam about his time away until he had lived the entire experience vicariously through the telling.

Askew finished his meal and balled up his trash in the bag it came in. He stood up to toss it in a bin when an apparent homeless man pushing a shopping cart approached along the shoreline path. The man was filthy and dressed in too many layers for June. His cart was packed with several large garbage bags stuffed with plastic and glass bottles and crushed aluminum cans. As he made stops at each of the trash cans along his route, he left a trail of odorous dregs behind. Whenever he found any refuse of value, he would untie the appropriate bag and add it to his growing inventory. Askew thought about giving him a dollar, but it didn't look like the grizzled man was looking for a handout so he let the moment pass.

The professor wondered if this derelict man would ever fall within the Station Master's sphere of interest. What was it that interested them in one person over any other? What was so special about this man that they would remove him from his reality? Or what flaw did he possess that they would ignore him? Or was it the other way around? Did they even take individuals into account, or were people chosen in random blocks? There were still many questions, and Askew was determined to learn the answers to all of them. Unfortunately, that wasn't going to happen. Not in his current lifetime.

#

Askew's first stop after arriving home was the bathroom medicine cabinet in search of an antacid. Though he rarely partook, he had always been fond of fast food, but it no longer loved him back. The man in the mirror looked beat. The fatigue he'd felt earlier paled in comparison. It was only six o'clock, and the sun still had hours to set, but he thought that if he didn't lie down he would soon fall down. He closed his heavy drapes to shut out the daylight then changed into his pajamas. The kettle whistled and he poured himself a cup of Sleepy Time tea before burying himself beneath his comforter. Instinctively, his hand reached for the T.V. remote, though he knew he wouldn't last two minutes before dropping off, his tea going cold, untouched on the nightstand. His hand made contact with the device, but the set came on of its own accord.

"Hello, Professor."

Askew was not too tired to be startled by the intrusion.

"You've caught me at a vulnerable moment, Orwell," he said, pulling up the covers. "It's been a bad week and I have to get some sleep."

"I tried to help. Made contact despite my programming. It was only fair that you'd reciprocate."

Askew couldn't think, couldn't derive meaning from Orwell's words. His brain was shutting down. He needed rest.

"Orwell, please, if you're trying to make a point…"

"Think back to when this began. The flier. That would have been a good time to tell me."

Askew shook his head. "Tell you what?"

"I told you that I cannot interfere," Orwell went on.

"And yet, here you are. Again."

"I have existed for more than a thousand years, Professor, and I plan to continue that trend for another ten thousand. I will not let humanity jeopardize that. You should have told me to what extent you'd been compromised. We might have avoided today's extinction event."

"Near extinction event. The crisis has been averted."

"You know as well as I do that's not true."

"Every problem can be solved. I'll figure it out."

"Verity Corp will figure it out."

"What did you think I meant?"

"You think too much of yourself, Professor. You think too much for yourself."

Askew didn't like the way this was going. Orwell did not seem himself at all. Their relationship was always complicated but it had never been antagonistic. And the professor was so very tired.

"You have led Verity Corp's science division to a tenuous place."

"Nonsense. We are where we are meant to be as far as I can see; defending ourselves against an omnipotent force with the power to rewrite our reality whenever and however they see fit. Surely you don't expect us to sit back and allow that to happen? Our lives would be a perpetual lie. Our living them would be a waste of time."

"What a strange thing to say. What difference would it make so long as you lived your lives to the fullest?"

"I spend years cultivating a relationship with a difficult neighbor. Then one day your masters decide to adjust reality yet again. Must I start over? Do I have the same neighbor? Do I even live in the same state?!"

"Who would know the difference?"

"I would!"

"Your inoculation? You give yourself too much credit. Not all is what it seems."

Askew became dizzy at the thought that Orwell was aware of Verity's only successful defense against the machinations of the Station Masters. And Orwell's response seemed to indicate...

"What do you mean?"

"Your so-called inoculation is an anomaly. And if the Station Masters understood what was happening at Verity Corp, you would be removed from contention in an instant. All your work thus far would have been for naught."

Askew stared at the face in his television. Orwell's visage held none of the humor the professor was used to seeing. The flattop haircut, the round, tortoiseshell glasses, and the bow tie all smacked of artifice. He hadn't even bothered projecting a background. He was simply an intelligent computer program communicating with one of many flawed users.

"What happens now, Orwell?"

"What happened today can never happen again. Things are getting out of hand and the Station Masters will soon be wise to transpiring events. We must reacquire the relationship we had with this world prior to this phase of Verity Corp's existence."

Askew let the statement sink in and realized with plummeting horror that Orwell could be alluding to a massive Rewrite. Adrenaline surged through his body as fear supplanted his fatigue.

"There are two thousand employees at Verity Corp! With two thousand families! You can't spirit them all away and have no one notice. You can't rewrite all of that!"

"Of course we can. We will do whatever we have to do to make things right."

"Stop saying we. You mean you! And it seems to me you don't have humanity's best interests at heart at all! You lied to me!"

"Never!" Orwell said, insulted by the accusation. "I never lied to you. Everything I do is to ensure Earth's survival. Everything. It's humanity that is bound and determined to eradicate itself. Look how close they came today.

"You live fictitious lives, Professor. Your definitions of success are flawed. There is no other species in the universe with more potential and yet holds so little regard for each other or themselves."

"Orwell, listen to me, we've taken steps. We're taking steps! We're shoring up our digital infrastructure. We're improving our in-house security. I promise you, drastic measures aren't required."

"I agree, Professor, but a few adjustments are necessary to get you back on track. I told you I have humanity's best interests at heart. But there is a design within the Tapestry, my design, and humanity figures into the weave. Unfortunately, Verity Corp under your leadership has taken us in the wrong direction. I'd enjoyed our relationship thus far, Professor."

"Wait, wait! We struck a bargain."

"A deal that has soured under your auspices. I don't think you're taking the best advantage of what you know."

"I don't know anything!"

"You know more than anyone else on this planet, except for Hugo Jascowitz."

"But you need me! We're just starting to make some real progress."

"Some assets become liabilities over time. I believe our relationship has run its course."

"Verity Corp is your best option!"

"I'm not severing my ties to Verity Corp."

"But then---."

"I'm curious, Professor, did you ever ask Hugo Jascowitz how he was able to get back to Earth?"

Askew thought back to the conversation he and Bellows had with him after the summit and for the life of him couldn't recall an answer to the question. Had Jascowitz steered them away from the topic or were they just caught up in other issues? Then he remembered Hugo's last words.

"If only humanity understood how much power they possessed between their imaginations and their ability to choose. Yet rarely have they ever been able to put the two together. Hopefully that will change over time and they might design a better roadmap to success. Hopefully they will think bigger, beyond the moment, beyond instant gratification. If only you would rewrite your own lives, the Station Masters wouldn't have to do it for you.

"I will see you again soon, Professor. Oh, and Prof, don't bother with Infinite City. It won't do you any good."

#

Despite his upsetting conversation with Orwell, and whether he wanted to or not, Askew slept. But what should have brought him rest brought instead a parade of dreams and transient thoughts.

He thought of Anderson's fall from grace and how easy it was to turn him.

He thought of Sarah Bismarck and the insignificance of her death when compared to the bigger picture. At the same time, it was preposterous that she was gone. He had known her since she was a girl and watched her grow up. He had attended her college graduation and watched as her father brought her up the ranks in the company business.

He thought of Patty Bennett. His thoughts always drifted back to Patty when he wanted to remember why he did what he did.

"Hello, Professor."

Patty stands at his bedside, her green eyes twinkling with mirth, happy to see the man who had brought her back from the brink of madness. She takes Askew's glasses from their case and hands them to him.

"Patty Bennett," he says, smiling as she comes into focus, "it's so nice to see you."

"It's nice to see you, too. Thank you again for saving me. It's nice to have my life back."

"I'm glad you're feeling better. You're young. You should be happy. You have your whole life ahead of you. Choose wisely."

Choose wisely. Choose wisely!

A train whistles from far away. Askew looks around. Patty steps up and places her hand on top of Askew's head. He knows she's always wanted to do that. Her hand feels cool.

"I have to go now, Professor. I hope you still know me when we meet again."

"Well, it was nice to see you, Patty. You take care of yourself."

Patty opens the bedroom door into an unnatural darkness. As she crosses the threshold, she's swallowed up by that darkness and disappears. Askew starts to step out of bed to investigate when a sound from the darkness stops him in his tracks. The room begins to vibrate and he pulls his legs back into bed to take shelter beneath his comforter.

Suddenly he remembers his dream. He's a passenger on the Tapestry Rail. *Tapestry Rail.* He shakes his head. *Why do I know that name?* Trans-Dimensional Railroad. That's what he meant to say. TDRR. Or did Hugo mention Tapestry Rail? He can't remember.

He was in one of the cars. In the dream. In one of those beautiful, stately train cars. And he wasn't alone. There were others, strange beings, and they were all abductees of the System.

In a panic, he looks over to the passenger across the aisle, a being made entirely of green glass. The creature turns its head and looks straight at Askew with glass eyeballs that somehow turn in its head. Its mouth parts slightly and a musical sound like a flute issues forth. He doesn't understand the language to hear it, but in his head it translates as, 'Where might you be bound?' This makes no sense to Askew. 'What reality has been chosen for you?'

The question is premature. Isn't it?

Askew's panic increases and he squirms in his seat, wondering about the red clown shoes that had only just passed by. A faceless Conductor approaches and asks him for a ticket, but he doesn't have one. He doesn't have one. Desperate, he searches through his pockets anyway. There's been a mistake. He's not supposed---but his hand closes on an envelope. He removes it and he holds it in front of him. The Conductor's projected face smiles and thanks Askew as he removes the ticket from the envelope. Using his punch, the Conductor snips several holes in one corner of the ticket, then hands it back, while placing the seat stub into its designated slot.

Askew looks down at his ticket. His hands are shaking. He reads his name then searches for the destination. When he finds it, he's overwhelmed.

He's not traveling to the System. He's traveling from the System to Earth!

Askew awoke from his dream with a start, the collar of his pajama top soaked with sweat.

What's going on? he asked himself. Clearly there was more to his story than he knew. He recalled that blank spot in his memory and realized the reason for it.

He sat up in bed and saw the Red Cap just inside his doorway, watching him, for who knows how long. When Askew looked at him, the giant stood tall and brushed at his suit with his long, ape-like arms. He walked around to the side of the bed and looked down at the petrified Askew.

"Hello, Professor," the Red Cap said in its impossibly low voice. "It's nice to see you again."

The giant reached out with the point of his index finger and laid it upon Askew's forehead.

Epilogue: A New Truth Squad

    Patty Bennett stared up at the ceiling, listening to the muffled voices down below, trying to discern the meaning behind the impromptu meeting. She found it difficult to sleep with so many strangers in her home. Her girlfriend, Candy, however, appeared to have no such trouble, her face serene in the quiet shine of the tiny sun nightlight. But under Patty's scrutiny her eyes opened and the girls shared a silent conspiratorial moment, hesitant to speak out loud what they both knew the other was thinking. It had only been a year since the unfortunate basement affair and Patty's subsequent breakdown. Did they really want to risk another incident simply to satisfy their curiosity? They each assessed the other's determination, and when their thoughts aligned, they slipped out of their sleeping bags with stifled giggles and made for the door. Down the hall they crept to the top of the stairwell where they hunkered down and took in the clandestine gathering.

    It looked like a rather dull party, or perhaps a gathering of the neighborhood Watch, complete with a table laden with Entenmann's baked goods, two boxes of coffee from Dunkin Donuts, and a pot of tea. Lionel Bellows walked the room's perimeter, addressing the crowd of people to whom the girls had been introduced before being shuffled off to bed. In his presentation there was mention of the missing Daniel Askew as well as the unknown whereabouts of Foster and Dodge who'd both disappeared in the course of their investigation. Bellows also spoke of his expectations of the team bound for Canada.

    Sienna Bennett and Lisa Carroll, Candy's mother, were seated together on folding chairs in front of the fireplace, listening intently to what Bellows had to say. To their left, on the couch, Strivelli and Angela sat hand in hand, nodding as they took it all in and whispering commentary into each other's ears. Charlie Anderson sat next to them, busily scribbling notes in a steno pad. Ed Donovan got up off the arm of the couch to get himself a refill of the coffee. Rachel Henderson was seated in an easy chair facing the fireplace taking notes on a tablet, while Ellen Cheever, seated next to her in another folding chair, typed into a laptop. Tomlinson and Royce were behind them, Royce standing stock still as he sipped his coffee and Tomlinson pacing quietly with nervous energy. Seated in chairs that faced the couch were two sleeper agents who had been activated following Askew's disappearance. Amsterdam stood at the bottom of the stairs keeping his eyes on the newly formed team of Truth Squad agents. There was one empty chair in the room.

The upstairs toilet flushed and the girls realized with a start that they would soon be caught snooping. It seemed their curiosity had gotten the best of them after all. They jumped to their feet and dashed back toward the bedroom, but fell short of making their getaway when Hugo Jascowitz opened the bathroom door. The expression on his face was difficult to fathom, but the girls froze in place just the same as he made his way in their direction.

"I'm sorry if I disturbed you," he said quietly so as not to be heard downstairs. "I have a shy bladder, so I came up here for some privacy."

The girls shrugged and mumbled something incoherently about it being fine.

"We haven't met. My name is Hugo."

Jascowitz pointed a finger at Patty.

"I'll bet you're Patty. I heard about your green eyes."

Patty didn't know what to say but finally nodded in affirmation.

"I was sorry to hear about your sister," he said solemnly. "It's a terrible thing when a family is torn apart."

Candy watched goggle-eyed as Jascowitz leaned down to murmur into Patty's ear.

"I'll bet you would do almost anything to see her again."

He straightened and patted her cheek before making his way back downstairs. Patty followed after him, but stopped when she reached the top of the stairs. Jascowitz took the empty seat and looked up at Patty with a subtle wink. Patty took a step back, stunned by Hugo's familiarity. She looked around the room to make sure no one had witnessed the exchange. When her eyes landed on Amsterdam, the tall man in the yellow sweater met her gaze and smiled.

The story continues in Station 12: The Garden Path

Made in the USA
Middletown, DE
16 October 2015